MADYLAN
OF
MANHATTAN

MADYLAN OF MANHATTAN

Amazing Adventures

(Short Stories)

Charles T. Mitchell

Madylan of Manhattan: Amazing Adventures

Copyright © 2022, Charles T. Mitchell

www.charlestmitchell.com

ISBN: 978-1-7334881-4-3
Library of Congress Control Number: 2022918469

Washington, D.C.
Published in the United States of America

**

DEDICATED TO

Madylan Paik Hong

For All Little Ones, Old and Young

CONTENTS

PROLOGUE

"Uncle, can you tell us a story?" Madylan, grandniece and goddaughter to the older visitors in the room, asked over her shoulder as she looked out at the cold and rainy, late evening sky hanging over her family's Carnegie Hill apartment, nestled in a quiet corner of Manhattan's Upper East Side.

The young girl, just entering her tenth decade, had had a busy day, in spite of the rain, running all over Manhattan with her aunt and uncle, who had come up for the long weekend from their home in Northern Virginia, just outside of Washington. As she looked back to her aunt and uncle, she playfully spun around one of the day's treasures, a small plush animal, one of many plush toys the two doting godparents had bought for her on similar outings over the years.

"What kind of story?" the uncle asked, looking up from his phone where he had been sorting through the photos of the weekend's various activities.

"Any kind. Funny. Silly. Even scary, when you-know-who is taking his bath. He's still too young for scary," Madylan replied, cocking her head to listen for her little brother.

"Well, I guess we could come up with one or two," the uncle answered, putting his phone down.

"But, you know, I don't mind ghost stories," Madylan added in a whisper.

The talk of ghost stories caused the aunt, who had been fighting off an urge to take a quick nap, to suddenly sit up and join the quiet discussion.

"No, he's not telling any ghost stories, dear. I'll never get to sleep if he does," the aunt declared from the couch where she had been trying her hand at Madylan's origami book before sleep had battled for her attention. "And nothing too scary, either."

"Yes, sir, ma'am!" the uncle quipped, with a mock salute, causing Madylan to giggle.

"Maybe you can also tell Greyson one, when he's older?" Madylan asked, always thinking of her little brother, even when she was exasperated with his antics.

"Oh, I have a spoof that I call 'Clueless Blue' that I used to make up for your now older cousins out in California. Your cousins used to laugh and laugh at those," the uncle replied, smiling at the memory of the often sophomoric and childish tales he used to tell his nephews when they were stuck on the California freeways.

"You'll have to do that for the bother-brother," Madylan suggested.

"When he's older, dear," the aunt interjected, eyeing the uncle. "Your uncle's sense of humor can be a little less than polite, when it's all boys."

Madylan smiled, winking at her aunt. She then gave her uncle the 'are you going to start' look that she was so good at.

The uncle quickly picked up on his goddaughter's hint and put on what he hoped was a thoughtful and storytelling sort of face.

"So, let's start when you were a little younger and you used to love to go on walks with me," the uncle replied, lowering his voice to avoid alerting the little brother, who was getting ready for a bath and then bed. "Since you were easily bored at fancy dinners or even brunch, I'd take you on walks around the neighborhood to see what we could see. Sometimes we'd sit on a bench and watch the world go by and you'd ask questions about cars, people, the buildings, and just about anything. You probably don't remember, but one time we met Alex oppa and his friends at a place downtown that was called 'Bar Dumpling,' years ago. You had just begun to spell things, so, when we were returning from a walk, to rejoin the group at the restaurant, you, maybe five-years-old then, were spelling, at the top of your voice as we strolled down Ninth Avenue, 'B-A-R, Bar!' causing all manner of people to turn and wonder if they should call the police."

"I remember those walks. And, sometimes, we had doughnuts," Madylan giggled.

The uncle nodded and let his mind wander along the years, selecting small events that Madylan might remember, which he could then stretch out into a story. His face then let her and the sleepy aunt know that more ideas had come to him.

"Then we could spin a pizza tale, maybe one where you tell the story to your little brother and his birthday friends one afternoon. After that, maybe a story about Easter, when you guys visit, down in Virginia…or, maybe a 'Madylan Day' yarn, which might be pretty silly," the uncle suggested.

"What's a yarn? Oh, right. I know. A tall tale," Madylan offered, answering her own question.

The uncle then let his eyes scan the photos arrayed on the shelves to the left of the white marble fireplace, smiling at the ideas forming in his mind.

"Then we could take a trip, somewhere we've all been, but maybe not together. Like Florida, or up in Maine, Ogunquit or Kennebunkport, or somewhere we all like. We all like the ocean, which has many, many mysteries. Finally, even though our ancestors came from very different places, we can try our hand at looking back at history. Not so much history that it makes you roll your eyes, but a backdrop to show where we have a lot in common with those who worked and strived so we could be here today in your parents' lovely home," the uncle said.

"Okay. Where to go…? Maine is always nice. And, maybe something about Korea? Where my grandparents come from?" Madylan replied, climbing into the cushy chair opposite her uncle.

The uncle nodded at his niece's comments while she continued.

"Let's all get comfortable. But, not too comfortable, Auntie. You sometimes fall asleep at Uncle's stories. I'm sure I'll stay awake," Madylan giggled, her eyes giving her aunt a twinkle, causing both to grin the same mischievous, blood kin grin that they had both shared since the little girl had been a baby.

"Right. Gang up on me," the uncle playfully muttered, then settled back to spin a tale or three, tucked in the cheerful living room of the tranquil apartment overlooking the misty streets of Manhattan.

1

UNDER THE NEW YORK CITY SIDEWALKS

Outside of the bustling island of Manhattan, the vast bulk of New York City is spread out among the other boroughs. The Bronx is to the north. Staten Island is to the southwest. Brooklyn is to the east and southeast. Finally, Queens, largest of the boroughs, is due east and hosts quickly evolving Long Island City. Nestled up against the East River on the west and bounded by Astoria to the north, Brooklyn to the south and Sunnyside to the east, Long Island City is a collection of fast growing high rises, old school neighborhoods, art galleries, expanding restaurants, and cozy park spaces, to include inspiring river walks. While it's fast becoming a mini-Manhattan, there are still neighborly areas that harken back to simpler and less hectic times. The following tale is from those less hectic and more serene times, when one was more likely to see young children playing along the streets than see frantic twenty-something's stepping into rideshares, chasing down taxis, or running to the subway.

One particular morning, a number of years ago, a choice was made to eat Sunday brunch close to home, via a short walk, instead of driving to one of the family's favorite places, quaint mainstay Café Henri of Vernon Square, or to another favorite, Sweet Chick, in Williamsburg, a large neighborhood in Brooklyn. The alternative brunch place, its name lost to time, was one of those local spots that popped up from time to time, thrived for a few years, and then succumbed to the inevitable churn of restaurants opening and closing in a competitive world. But, while it lasted, it had been a favorite morning spot of young families, to include the family of one young Madylan, a child of around four and a half precocious years that particular morning.

Young Madylan was in high spirits during the short walk to the restaurant, because her doting aunt and uncle, in town for one of their far too infrequent visits, were joining her and her mother for an amazing breakfast before they drove back to Virginia.

After the French toast and bacon had been consumed, the little niece had begun to get antsy, as any small child would when constrained to the polite etiquette of eating out. Once the uncle had noticed the signs of the child's restlessness, he made the suggestion for a walk, to the nodding smiles of both the mother and the aunt, and, of course, of the little child.

In a credit to her upbringing and to her own innate grace, Madylan never pushed to go for a walk, but would only drop hints about what might be down the street, especially if the street happened to hold a doughnut shop, a pet store window, toy store, or some other amazing place for a young child.

As the two stepped out of the brunch spot and turned to walk down the sidewalk, Madylan's little hand gripped her uncle's as usual. She then scolded him, with polite concern, about his skin's dryness.

"Scratchy! So scratchy," young Madylan admonished her uncle. "You should use lotion. At least three times. Three times a day."

The uncle grinned, realizing he had forgotten to slather his dry hands that morning, but then assured his niece and goddaughter he'd remedy the problem once they got back to the apartment.

After just a few yards, the two had to sidestep a gaping hole in the sidewalk, created by one of the omnipresent cellar doors one sees embedded in the sidewalks all over the city. In fact, the morning bustle of businesses preparing for the day was reinforced by a string of those rectangular, metal holes, most of which were opened up, all the way down Jackson Avenue and beyond.

Always ready for new ideas for conversations with the goddaughter he only saw every few months, the uncle decided to pause at the gaping maw of the first cellar door, and to quiz little Madylan.

Since the time young Madylan had been able to talk, the uncle had used their little outings to impart some new idea or experience to his young niece. Often they would find a snack, sit on a bench, and he'd tell her about the type of birds hopping about or flying overhead. Even in New York there were more than pigeons, and Madylan was a quick learner. He would also make a game of counting cars of a certain color, with a score given to the most and least popular colors. So, when he saw the open cellar doors along the sidewalk, he quickly thought up something unique to pique little Madylan's insatiable curiosity.

Paused in front of the restaurant they had just left, the uncle held Madylan's hand a little more tightly as she leaned over the first dark, well worn, metal steps leading into the semi-dark subbasement of the café.

"What do you think they do down there?" the uncle asked, pointing into the shadowy cellar below.

For a moment, Madylan was silent. Then, she scrunched up her nose, looked back at the front of the café, and then answered, slowly, with a question in her voice.

"Where they make…the food we just ate?" Madylan offered, sniffing the air like a miniature bloodhound.

"Yes, probably. And where they store a lot of it for making later. A kitchen just might be down there at the back," the uncle replied.

At that moment, a worker, clad in the universal white garb of the food service industry, appeared at the bottom of the steps. He smiled up at Madylan, causing her to return the smile and give the man a little, parting wave.

"I wonder if they like living underground?" Madylan said, smiling, imbued with confidence as she headed for the next sidewalk pit, pulling her uncle along.

Stopping to peer over the more polished metal of the second sidewalk cellar door, Madylan stood straighter and stared at the shiny opening and the brightly lighted room beneath. Looking up at the storefront, her face showed recognition and she pointed at the windows as she spoke.

"I think they make clothes down there…? No, wait, they wash the clothes down there?" the little sleuth suggested.

"Yes, probably, because it's a drycleaners, their big machines are probably down there," the uncle answered.

"Do you think…do you think, Uncle, that they make and clean the clothes for the café's underground people?" Madylan asked, a visible thought seeming to form behind her eyes. "Maybe the basements and cellars are connected. Why, there could be a whole town under our feet, with people running about. Yes?"

The uncle nodded at his niece's intense stare and questioning look, and decided to expand his examples beyond their shores.

"It's possible, I suppose, dear. In fact…one of the places your aunt and I want to take you one day is in London. Just north of Kensington Palace, where some of the royal family lives, is a wondrous little shopping area called 'Notting Hill,'" the uncle replied, being careful to weigh how much detail to pass on to his small niece. "There are shops along Portobello Road, which you would love. And street stalls selling anything you can imagine, to include yummy foods. Years ago, I was looking for lady who had always been at a corner stall, but had to move inside when most of the buildings became condos, and the new owners did not want stalls on their sidewalks. I asked one of the older guys if he knew her and, he did not, but an even older man, who looked ancient, but was still quite spry, said he did, and he took me down a set of stairs into a basement. We then walked nearly the entire block through a series of basement corridors, and even through one under construction, until we came to the right stairs and then popped up in what is called the Admiral shops. A few feet later, there she was. So, yes, I suppose these shops could be connected, too."

"What did the lady sell?" Madylan asked, looking down the street for the next cellar door.

"Well, old toys, mostly, but she also had a few of the old, handmade marbles. Like the ones I showed you at our house," the uncle replied. "We even showed you how to play marbles last year. Do you remember?"

"Yes. They were all manner of colored glass. I was very little. Do you think the cleaners and the café people play marbles with each other? After work, of course," Madylan asked.

Grinning at her own comments, Madylan didn't wait for an answer, but hurried her uncle along to the third opening, which was closed at that time of day. However, that did not deter her.

Looking at the front of the building for clues, Madylan turned to her uncle, her eyes asking him to tell her what kind of business is was, given that she had only begun to read and was not certain what the array of various signage might say.

"It's a bank, Madylan. You know what they do in a bank, right?" the uncle asked.

Madylan nodded and then stared hard at the closed portal to the bank's basement. The double metal doors were shinier and less marred than the heavily used previous two.

Finally, a small sound of triumph burst from her little lungs.

"A bank! That's where they make the money!" Madylan declared, then added an important bit of information. "I have a bank. But, it's a piggy bank, so it doesn't make money. It just takes money. From Grandpa, Dad, Mom, and you and Auntie. Through a skinny hole in his back."

Smiling, the uncle had to humor her youthful confusion over the monetary system.

"Yes, maybe. Maybe they make it down there, or maybe just store it before giving it to the people doing business at the bank," the uncle replied. "Maybe this is where the café puts the money we spend on breakfast?"

"Maybe this is where my money was stored after I paid for breakfast at the Henri last time, Uncle?" Madylan mused, her eyes running over the bank's façade as she reminded her uncle of a wonderful morning where just the two of them had gone out for breakfast while her mother and her aunt had gone shopping.

"Could be. Could be," the uncle replied, keeping his chuckle low over the memory of her play money and his niece's shock when the waitress, playing along, had actually kept the play money after using the credit card the uncle had slipped to the waitress. "Yes, since they kept your money, which was a good lesson in commerce, I think, it might be right here."

Madylan thought for a moment and then added an entirely new angle.

"And, do you think there are underground bank robbers? I saw the news about bank robbers last week. Maybe they live in the abandoned building over there?" Madylan rattled off, quickly creating her own image of her imaginary, underground town. "And then they dig a tunnel to the money making machines under the bank. Steal it. Then wiggle back to the other building. So, when the cleaners and the restaurant people come to get their money to buy things, it's all gone because of the robbers? That sounds right, yes?"

"Well, maybe, but the police and guards are good about keeping the robbers away, so maybe there are no robbers in that vacant building," the uncle replied.

"Is there a police house nearby?" Madylan asked, looking up and down the street. "The police might wander over from their basement. Patrol. That's it. They probably patrol the underground city."

"Hmm. There are always a lot of police cars at the courthouse, near your apartment. Maybe they stay there?" the uncle replied, looking down the street at the next businesses.

Nodding at her uncle's answer and grinning at her success in figuring out the basement activities, Madylan squinted against the glare from the buildings down the avenue, looking for the next challenge.

"Wait! Doughnuts!" the little girl suddenly shouted with excitement.

About half a block on, one of the ubiquitous doughnut chains stood close to the corner, its orange and brown façade beckoning the youth.

"What's that place before it, though?" the uncle asked as his niece pulled him along.

"Oh, that's the sushi place. Where I get avocado rolls," Madylan answered as she passed the sidewalk door, which was only half open, as if preparing to fully open, or just before closing.

Pausing in front of the sushi place, the youthful sleuth peered over the open side and spoke.

"Maybe that's where they keep the fish and the avocados?"

"Maybe. Could also be where they prepare some of the dishes. Do you go here a lot?"

"Pretty often, I think," Madylan replied, then added a question. "Do you think they grow the seaweed and the rice down there?"

"Well, that's a very good question, one that I think needs some 'health' food energy to help us think about it," the uncle responded, winking, and guided the little sleuth over to the doughnut shop.

"Yes! But, only one. And, we should get some for my Dad. He loves doughnuts, he does," Madylan cooed as they stepped into the cozy shop, with sugar, baked goods, and coffee assailing all their senses.

After they had eyeballed all the choices, little Madylan chose a glazed with colorful sprinkles and the uncle went with the chocolate cake. She then pointed to a couple for her Dad and waved off suggestions for her mom. The uncle added an Old-fashioned for the auntie, just in case.

Taking the purchases outside, the uncle guided his niece back to a metal bench that was near the sushi place. She climbed up without help, being that she was at that age where independence was becoming more and more important to her. The uncle sat beside her and, using wipes that her mother had loaned him, cleaned off her little hands before she took the doughnut.

Munching away, the uncle took the bench break to add a little to his niece's knowledge about sushi places.

"So, do you really think they grow the seaweed in the basement, under the sidewalk?" the uncle asked between bites. "And the rice?"

For a moment, Madylan quietly chewed her small bite of doughnut, then swallowed and answered.

"Well, Uncle, it is called 'sea' weed, so I know it grows in the sea. Like in the ocean where we see it during the summer. Except, it's slippery and slimy, so they must cook it to make it crunchy for the avocado rolls and, oh yes, the California rolls Auntie loves," Madylan replied, swinging her legs as she spoke. "And, I didn't see or smell or hear the sea in the basement, so I don't think there is any sea...wait. Maybe they grow it in an aquarium? I've seen seaweed in aquariums. That's it! They have a huge...super huge aquarium down there under the building to grow the seaweed in."

Grinning up at her uncle with a look of sheer triumph at breaking the puzzle of the underground seaweed, Madylan rocked back and forth on the bench, attracting the attention of a young couple walking by. The woman of the couple initially smiled and then briefly allowed a frown to pass her face when she noticed that the little girl's companion did not look at all like the little girl. The woman even slowed her pace, but then resumed her stride after hearing the little girl call the older man 'uncle,' thereby apparently allaying the woman's fears that the man might had kidnapped the little girl to sit on a bench and eat doughnuts.

"Yes, they also might squish out all the water and dry the seaweed to make it crunchy," the uncle added, watching the couple hurry away before asking a second question. "And, do you think they grow the rice there?"

Taking another small bite, Madylan let her shoulders and head lean forward, her gaze staring off into the distance, telling the uncle that she was deep in thought about rice growing. After a minute, she finished her little bite and answered, but slowly, as if thinking about the question while she formed an answer.

"Well, rice probably grows on a rice farm. And, we learned about how farm plants need lots of sun to grow. Just like Mom's plants and my garden at your and Auntie's house in Virginia. So, if plants need sun and rice comes from plants, because rice is not an animal, then rice plants need sun, right?" Madylan reasoned.

"Yes, exactly. Rice needs sun. Lots of sun, to grow," the uncle replied.

"Have you ever seen a rice farm, Uncle? They must be huge, because rice is everywhere. Like wheat for bread. Just like the Red Hen made, yes? Even Rice Krispies?" Madylan asked, looking up at her all-knowing, to her, uncle.

"Well, yes. When I was stationed at my first Air Force posting, years and years ago, long before I met Auntie, I saw rice paddies, what they call rice farms. In Korea, where your grandparents are from," the uncle replied, wiping a bit of sugar off his niece's chin with a napkin. "It's quite an amazing thing to see, looking out from a hill or a mountainside at the miles and miles of rice paddies. They look like huge tic-tac-toe boards, all linked together."

"Does all rice come from Korea?" Madylan asked.

"All rice? No, only a little that we get here. Nearly everywhere it can be grown has rice farms. Even in South Carolina, where I'm from, there are old rice farms, near the coast, where it's flat. And hot. Has to be pretty hot to grow a lot of rice," the uncle replied.

"Where do the avocados come from? For the avocado rolls?" Madylan then asked, after swallowing the last bite of her doughnut.

"Probably California, where your auntie was born, and maybe Mexico, which is far south of us," the uncle answered as he wiped the bits of sugar off her fingers with a fresh wipe.

"There's a lot of sun in California and Mexico, yes? It's always sunny and hot when we visit Grandpa and Grandma in Los Angeles," Madylan stated, then continued. "So, any rice or avocado farms under the building would have to have a lot of sunlight?"

Staring at the building, Madylan then pointed straight up in the air.

"The roof!" Madylan suddenly declared. "They grow them on the roof! That way, they can send them down on the elevator when they make the sushi in the basement."

"The elevator?" the uncle asked, marveling at his little niece's imagination.

"Silly, the stairs would take too long. Of course, the elevator. Duh!" Madylan giggled in response to her uncle's apparently silly question.

"Why do you think they grow it on the rooftop?" the uncle asked, dropping the used wipes and napkins in a bin next to the bench.

"Well. If you look around, there are a lot of trees on rooftops. And flowers. All over the city. So, why not rice and avocado trees?" Madylan proposed, her head cocked to the right as she looked up to the top of the building.

"They could take the dirt up there, on the elevator. And, since it's the roof, they would get rain," Madylan added, swinging the bag with her Dad's and Auntie's doughnuts side to side.

"I have heard of urban gardening," the uncle replied.

"Turban gardening! A garden on your head?" Madylan exclaimed, chuckling at the odd concept.

"No, dear, not a turban. 'Urban.' It means the city. Another word for describing city related things," the uncle replied, trying to not let himself chuckle at his niece's confusion.

Nodding, Madylan then lost interest in the dictionary lesson and pointed down the street as she switched subjects.

"Okay, that's the sushi place. Where to next?" Madylan asked, watching a young couple approach with a small, mixed breed white and brown puppy.

"Oh, so cute!" Madylan exclaimed, as the passing young couple gave her adoring looks and then, like the young woman earlier, gave the uncle brief, puzzled looks, given that the little girl and the old guy didn't look a lot like each other, but continued on their way, the puppy oblivious to Madylan's cooing.

"Well, we are close to the end of the block. Maybe we should go back?" the uncle suggested, looking at his watch.

Hopping off the bench, little Madylan looked back toward the café and then turned to look down the street to the next block, beyond the overhead subway tracks, at a collection of graffiti-covered walls.

"Well, we could go one more block, but that's just one big building down there, full of graffiti. Maybe such a huge building has a huge underground, too. Maybe it's the underground lair of some evil queen from a fairy story? Might be too scary. Or, we could cross the street under the train tracks, and hold our ears if a train comes because they are so loud. There's a pizza place over there where we order take out. And a bodega with kimchi that Mom likes. And the owner has a live fish tank in the back for all manner of fish. Maybe even for feeding mermaids? If you have a friend that's a mermaid, that is. We don't. But, there are a lot more stores over there, so it might take a long time. Or, yes, we could walk back to the restaurant and see if Mom and Auntie are talked out yet. But, since they never get to see each other, they are probably going to talk a really long time. But, they may be on coffee and dessert, so we probably don't want to miss dessert? Right, Uncle?" little Madylan rattled off with sensible logic far beyond her years.

"Why, yes. I think missing dessert would be tragic, even after those doughnuts. But, they were tiny doughnuts. Right?" the uncle replied, grinning at his little joke and then at his niece's eye roll at the silly comment.

The uncle then took up his little niece's hand and the two retraced their steps, glancing into the open sidewalk stairwells as they passed each one.

"Oh, we missed this one," Madylan suddenly said, stopping at an old, tarnished green-black, open sidewalk cellar door. "I don't think it was open before."

Peering in, Madylan seemed to be straining to hear, so her uncle leaned over as well.

Singing. Distant singing.

Puzzled, the uncle looked back to the façade of the building above the sidewalk door.

A closed, boarded up grocery. Closed a long time, from the disheveled appearance beyond the windows in the interior, and there were no notices proclaiming a new business was coming.

"Maybe someone is opening a new place?" the uncle offered, in spite of the abandoned look, while the singing increased in volume, almost as if the group singing was moving from the back of the basement toward the sidewalk stairs.

"What are they singing, Uncle?" Madylan asked, turning her inquisitive face up, with her left eyebrow cocked as she did when she expected her uncle to have an answer to any question.

"Not sure, dear. Maybe Italian? Hard to say, it's so muffled," the uncle replied, catching only brief syllables here and there of the singing.

"Wait, if this building doesn't have a business and it's not an apartment building, then…then the only singing from the basement can be from…oh, Uncle, I think I know!" Madylan suddenly blurted out, but then lowered her voice to a near whisper.

"What do you think?" the uncle asked, lowering his voice as well.

"Ghosts, Uncle. Ghosts of old New York?" Madylan replied, her eyes wide, but then she changed her assessment. "No, it's daytime, so not ghosts. Maybe elves? Or goblins? What else lives underground? Pirates? Oh, they're in caves."

The uncle, suddenly concerned that his little niece might be frightened at the thought of cellar ghosts or goblins floating about beneath their feet, down the metal stairs, moved to pull her away from the opening and the now eerie singing. However, Madylan protested, shaking her head and calming her uncle's fears.

"Uncle, don't worry, they wouldn't be bad goblins or even ghosts if they are singing, would they?" Madylan asked, patting her uncle's hand to calm any fears he might have. "Besides, they could be regular people. Just people who live underground. Like…what else lives underground, but are not rats or mice? Something nice…?"

The uncle, holding back a small chuckle at his niece's concern for his well-being, changed his face to one of feigned nervous concern, playing along with his young niece's comforting logic.

"Well, lots of critters live underground. The chipmunks in our back garden burrow underground. Rabbits dig burrows as well. Lots of animals live underground," the uncle replied, avoiding the creepier animals that dwelled in the darkness.

"Bunnies? Like the Easter Bunny? Does she live underground during the year? No matter. Yes, so probably not goblins or ghosts. Maybe farmers are down there taking care of all the underground farm animals?" Madylan suggested, her voice becoming less strained. "Farmers sing, right? Like Old MacDonald?"

"Yes, there are a lot of songs about farms and farmers. And, the only pirates I ever heard singing were at Disney. And they were happy pirates, not mean. Not sure about singing goblins. Elves? I think they sing in the fairy circles. Like in Europe," the uncle added, drawing out the niece's idea, but avoiding any scary elements.

"Silly, that's only in stories. And, the pirates were only in the

Caribbean. We've seen their castles on vacation," Madylan replied, her tone quite matter-of-fact, then added another thought.

"And, all they sing about are ships and gold. And the building would have to be flying a Jolly Roger flag for it to be a pirate building. But, a building can't float to be a pirate ship," Madylan added, firm in her rationale.

The uncle slowly nodded and made a mental note to show his niece, much later in life, the old Monty Python sketch of business pirates and their office building pirate ship.

"What do we do?" Madylan then whispered, her eyes growing a bit wider and her little hand squeezing her uncle's with a tighter grip. "Whoever is singing…they might not like us listening at this basement door."

Madylan then crouched low and quietly stepped back from the opening, her eyes never leaving the door. At the same time, she pulled at her uncle's hand to emphasize that it might be time to go.

"I think we should let the goblins or ghosts or underground farmers alone. You are probably right, that they might not like strangers listening to their song," the uncle replied, leaning down to whisper in Madylan's ear. "We probably should move on."

Madylan nodded, mumbled something too soft for the uncle to hear, and then moved even farther away from the sidewalk opening.

As they walked away, with Madylan glancing back to check that no pirate farmers or goblin ghosts floated up out of the cellar, the uncle strained to try to catch any of the words of the song, but had no luck.

Arriving at the café, the two companions noticed that the doors of the café's sidewalk cellar stairwell had closed, cutting off their earlier view into the restaurant's basement.

Once inside, the two saw that Mom and Auntie were chatting away, but both then paused when Madylan appeared.

"So, what great adventure did you two go on for so long?" Auntie asked, helping Madylan into a chair.

"Well, Auntie, we saw many wonderful things," Madylan began, then lowered her voice before explaining.

"We walked on top of bakers and bankers, Auntie. And cafés and laundries. And heard goblins and elves and ghosts singing. And farmers with bunnies and chipmunks. But not pirate ghosts," Madylan said, her voice taking on a conspiratorial tone. "We had new clothes made and cleaned by the mole people of New York City, we did. Uncle, I remembered that moles live underground. And they made us avocado rolls from the rice and avocado trees growing on the rooftops. With seaweed from a huge aquarium, bigger than a building! Well, they looked like doughnuts, but it was sushi. Doughnut sushi."

Madylan then giggled a bit at her little joke, repeating her punch line.

"Doughnut sushi!"

"Really? Doughnut sushi. Wasn't it too sweet?" Auntie replied, her eyes narrowing at Uncle, wondering what outlandish tales he had been telling. "And, mole people?"

"That's a new one for me," Uncle replied, holding up his hands in genuine surprise at his niece's new twist on the cellars under the sidewalks.

"Well, moles live in the ground. And, all those sidewalk metal doors lead to stairs that go into the cellars in the ground. So, there are mole people down there who do the work for the businesses up top. Right, Uncle?" Madylan finished. "They can't be real moles, or they wouldn't have the hands to do all the different jobs. So, they are mole people."

"What? Of course. We even saw a group of bakery mole people. Well, at least a bunch of cook mole people right under this very restaurant. Right, Madylan?" the uncle replied.

Suddenly, the thought of sitting in a café that had mole people underneath making all the food seemed to make Madylan a little less comfortable. She stopped her giggling and even leaned over the table to look to the back of the little restaurant, no doubt thinking she might see mole people peeking out from the door leading to the kitchen. Sitting back, she spoke up.

"Well, maybe the people here are regular people, right, Mom? We come here a lot and we've never seen any true mole people. Have we…?" Madylan asked quietly as she snuggled up against Auntie.

"No, honey, I don't think there are any mole people under us," her mother answered. "What was that about those goblins or ghosts, though? Were you scared?"

"Scared? Never! But, I had to calm down Uncle when we discovered the singing goblins and elves, or just regular mole people. We decided they weren't ghosts since it's daylight. Just down the street. In that old, abandoned building. The one near the cleaners.

There's nothing in that building, but there was singing in the underground. Why, it was so loud it felt like it tickled our feet. Right, Uncle? I don't think Uncle was really scared, just surprised. That's all," Madylan related, using a number of hand gestures in her excitement.

"Ghosts and goblins? Mole people? Really, Uncle...?" Auntie asked, looking daggers at her husband for possibly giving their little niece nightmares later.

"What? No. She determined, with zero input from me, that the singing we heard was coming from some mysterious creatures under the sidewalks, but, oh, not from pirates. She said pirates only sing about ships and gold," the uncle answered, realizing it didn't matter what he said, the aunt would place any future nightmares squarely in his lap.

"Yes, Auntie. Uncle didn't think they were ghosts or goblins or fairytale creatures. I had to explain to him," Madylan answered, coming to the defense of her uncle. "And, as we were leaving, I told them in a whisper not to bother us, because my brave uncle would send them packing."

"Send them packing? Where on earth do you get these phrases?" Auntie asked the smiling Madylan.

"A Western," Madylan replied.

"Well, what else did you see?" the mom asked.

"Doughnuts!" Madylan quipped, holding up the small bag. "These are for Dad. And Uncle got one for you, Auntie. None for Mom."

"Sounds like you had quite the adventure," the mom replied.

At that moment, the waitress came by with the check and Uncle took it. He looked it over and then placed a credit card on the tray, without mentioning possible dessert in deference to Madylan's mother's silence on the subject.

"It was only a small adventure, Mom," Madylan answered. "We thought about going to the next block over, but there was only one old building full of graffiti. I think it's a warehouse since I never see people coming out of it. And, the graffiti is done by sneaky artists at night, so I don't think I'll ever see them, either. The paintings are interesting. But I can't read, not yet, the big words spread all over. It might have a palace underground, though, since it's so big."

"Then we sat on a bench. The one near the doughnut place. And watched people go by. We didn't see many, and only one dog came by with its owners," Madylan continued as the group gathered up their things to depart the café. "Bench talks, Uncle calls them. It's fun."

"Bench talks?" the mom asked.

"That's what we call it when we sit and watch the world, wondering about the people, the cars, the buildings, what's underneath the sidewalks, and on the rooftops," Madylan answered as she hopped down the few steps at the front of the café.

"There are amazing and, I think, sometimes, magical things under the sidewalks. I'm glad I was able to help Uncle learn what was under there. In those basements. Did you have sidewalks when you were little?" Madylan asked as she skipped along, holding the right hand of her Mom and the left hand of her favorite auntie.

"Yes, I think we did. Not so many with those magical doors in them, though," the mom replied.

As the little group passed through Court House Square, Madylan looked up at the imposing building and, after identifying the sparrows and the crows hopping about the fountain, she asked her mother to remind her what the building was.

"It's the courthouse, dear. Where they have judges, lawyers, and trials," the mom answered.

"For bad people?" Madylan asked.

"Well, the trials are held, with judges and juries, to find out if the people were bad, or innocent," her mother replied.

"Is that where they have…where the jail is?" Madylan whispered, lest the inmates hear her.

"I don't think so, dear," her mother answered.

For a moment Madylan walked along quietly past the fountain and then spoke.

"It must be where the bank robber pirates are kept before the judges see them, then," Madylan declared. "It's a good thing we have courthouses, or the pirates would be running crazy in the streets."

After Madylan's last comment, the auntie looked back at the uncle and gave him a small frown, certain that he had planted such thoughts in the small child's mind. The uncle's shaking head did little to dissuade the auntie, so he was careful not to make a comment.

As the little troop headed to the apartment building, one of many that had been converted from an old factory years before, Madylan turned to look back at her uncle.

"Uncle, I think we need to cross the street next time and see what's over there, under the sidewalks. That flower shop probably grows flowers on the roof, too. And the huge high-rise probably has more apartments underground. Wait! Maybe that's where the mole people in the other buildings live at night? Under those huge high-rises? Maybe?" Madylan suggested, pulling her mother and her auntie closer.

The uncle lagged behind, but nodded to his niece's comments.

"Better hurry up, Uncle. The pirates in the courthouse might be looking for gold," Madylan quipped and then began swinging from the hands of her mother and auntie.

As the small group turned the corner and left the street full of normal and mysterious sidewalk cellar doors behind them, and where they were well beyond the cold reach of the pirates holding the old courthouse, little Madylan looked back at her uncle with a goofy face. He had just taken a picture of his three favorite ladies walking hand in hand. She then turned back and began pulling her mom and aunt toward the waiting doorman up the block.

"Wait!" Madylan suddenly called out, causing the adults to all halt in their tracks.

Holding her finger to her lips, Madylan pointed at a small, metal square embedded in the sidewalk, close to the front wall of her family's apartment building, not far from the entrance. She then motioned for the group to cautiously walk around the small, one-foot square plate. Once the group was a few feet beyond the plate, the little girl let out a long breath, as if she had been holding it.

"Whew, that was close!" Madylan declared.

"Why, what was that, dear?" the aunt asked, looking back at the square and then at the uncle.

"Well, if the little cellar door, which is quite little and not big like the others, is in front of our house, our apartment building, then what do you think they make down there?" Madylan asked as they neared the entrance.

"Well, maybe apartments for the building?" the uncle suggested.

"No silly. The apartments are already there for parents to buy. No, that's where they make the families to go in the apartments," Madylan replied, waving her head at the building, since her hands were occupied.

"Oh?" the uncle answered. "And, who makes the families?"

"Well, God of course, silly. Who else can make families? Oh, and puppies. And kittens," Madylan replied, her matter of fact tone causing all the adults to smile at her reasoning.

Just as the little sleuth stepped away from the metal plate, she stopped, dropped her mom and aunt's hands, slapped the top of her forehead, and turned back.

"Silly me, for a change!" Madylan exclaimed, rolling her head from side to side. "Not families! I know what's in the basement of our building. Elves!"

"Elves?" the aunt and mother asked at the same time, while the uncle simply nodded.

"Of course! What's in our basement? A pool! And a playroom! And the storage room with all the bicycles and my old trike," Madylan replied.

"Yes, dear, but...elves?" the aunt asked, looking sideways at the uncle.

"Well, every time we go to the pool or the playroom, we have so much fun that it's a mess when we leave. But, when we go back, they are both spotless! Who cleans it up? Elves! And, my old trike had a loose wheel, but when we went down to check on it, Dad discovered that the wheel was fine. Elves!" Madylan answered, using her fingers to count off the various elfin activities. "And, when my first bike arrived at our door in a box and then we went down to the storage rooms to build it, Dad and I found the bike already built! Elves!"

Madylan stood, dropping her hands to her hips, looking up at the adults, who all seemed a little skeptical of her logic. She then stared at her uncle, who was always her ally, regardless of the outlandish ideas she might have, and gave him an expectant look.

"Well, you can't argue with her rationale of cause and effect, based on the vast amount of evidence as she sees it, can you?" the uncle finally stated, slowly nodding. "And, the small stature of the little people would explain the small size of this, uh, door. So...elves it must be. But, if there are elves in the basement, then the families must be made...where?"

Madylan didn't hesitate to answer, as if she had been anticipating that very question when the issue of elves arose.

"Heaven, uncle, is where families are made," Madylan declared, then turned, grabbed her mom and aunt's hands again, and led the group to the entrance.

Arriving at the steps to her building, little Madylan dropped her mom and aunt's hands, and then turned to wink at her uncle as she spoke.

"Uncle, Mom, I think we need to take the train into the city next time. The stores under the sidewalks in Manhattan must be even more amazing, since so much of the city shares its underground with...well, with amazing things," Madylan declared, her uncle nodding in response, with her mother looking a little puzzled, while her aunt was still frowning at the uncle.

"Well, Manhattan is a lot bigger than Long Island City, Madylan. It might take years to look under all the sidewalks there," her mother replied, hiding her smile at her daughter's decision to vastly expand her underground universe.

"Yes, but we're going to move there one day, anyway, so I might as well learn about it, yes?" Madylan replied. "I don't want to move there and be surprised by all the underground people and animals and stores. Do I?"

Nodding at the logic of her daughter, the mother simply smiled in response and pointed the chatty little girl up the steps.

Grinning widely, young Madylan then led her little family into her home sanctuary and, looking back to the street once more, she let her mind run all the way back to the bench near the sushi place, then spoke one last time, or so she thought, as the little group prepared to disappear into the building.

"You know, Mom, Uncle certainly learns a lot of new things when we have our bench talks during our walks. He asks me so, so many questions about everything, that I sometimes think he might need to go back to school one day," Madylan giggled, causing her uncle to make his own silly face at his cherished little niece's sharp wit.

"School? What? Who needs school when I have you, Madylan, to teach me so many things? Even things that are hidden underground?" the uncle replied in mock surprise.

Madylan beamed at her uncle and then paused, but just briefly, to stare at something across the street. She then turned back to the steps as she again spoke.

"Next time, Uncle, we must look into the turtle people living under the road, just there," Madylan said in hushed tones.

"Turtle people?" the uncle replied, looking back across the street where he spied a construction fence around a large, open manhole, with only the tops of the workers' heads visible above the street. "Oh, I see. Yes, we must."

"Dear, those are just workers in hardhats fixing the road," the aunt replied, rolling her eyes at what she saw as the uncle's silly encouragement of wild thoughts.

"Yes, Auntie. But, have you ever seen workers wear turtle shell hardhats…?" Madylan replied with a sly smile at her aunt and uncle's astonished faces as the large, double doors slowly swung shut on the imaginative young girl's morning adventure under the New York City sidewalks.

2

THE (NOT VERY) EVIL PRINCESS
OF THE UPPER EAST SIDE

"Brawh, hah, hah, haaaaah! The game is afoot!"

The high-pitched, cackling voice of one (not very) evil princess echoed off the walls of her high castle fortress, not far from the vast woodlands of the king's, no, the queen's park bordering Manhattan's Upper East Side. According to the young girl behind the cackling voice, some of the common folk called the place Central Park, but the princess and those she allowed into her confidence knew the lands were secretly part of the vast holdings of the wicked queen of the western boulevards, stolen years before from the rightful heirs, one of whom was herself, the princess of the Upper East Side, a domain shared with her child-prince little brother.

Leaping from her throne, which looked a lot like a grey, cushy, swivel chair in her family's large, otherwise white-themed living room, the princess bounded for the door, where she regally nodded to her weekend entourage, consisting of one lady in waiting, in the form of her visiting aunt, and one yeoman warrior, her visiting uncle. The aunt and uncle were in town for only a few days, so the princess didn't want to hesitate and lose even a moment's adventure with them.

"Fly! We must fly from this warm, full of new treats, high castle and venture forth into the hostile land to claim our birthright!" the young girl called from the doorway, waving her aunt and uncle to follow.

"Honey, don't forget to wear your warmer boots. Are you guys sure you want to take her out?" the princess's mother asked from her study, craning her neck to see.

"Yay, verily, kind mother mine, my royal feet are shod in cushy warmth. Now, we are off to the royal wars!" the youth answered with a sweeping bow.

"Also, M——, sorry, your highness, did you remember your certificate?" the uncle asked, referring to the special day pass that he had created for his niece's birthday each year since the girl's little brother had been born, a special pass that promised her very own day (and any multiples) where she could do whatever she wanted to do, just her, with her aunt and uncle.

"Safely stashed in my royal cross body, good yeoman knight," the little niece princess replied, patting the side of her small purse.

"Knight? Did I get a promotion?" the uncle laughed, donning the well worn and widely traveled, formerly blue, but now quite faded and loved hat his niece had given him her first year at her school.

"Well, let's see how the day goes. Maybe," quipped the niece princess, winking at her lady-in-waiting aunt.

With that, the youthful heir to the great gilded pigeon throne (since there were no peacocks nearby) of East Central Park flung open the door and dashed to the elevator, with her two attendants following closely behind, the aunt carrying the girl's jacket in case the early fall weather changed.

At the elevator, the young lady pressed the down button and declared their magic carpet was arriving post haste.

"Our floating carriage, no, flying carpet box is on its way. I can hear the wings of the griffins flapping as they lift...the lift!"

After the elevator car arrived, the young lady held the door for her two attendants, using a twirling flourish of her left arm to stay the brass doors, while welcoming her two companions into the car with her right hand.

"Welcome to my flying carpet carriage, my noble attendants. Welcome!"

As the car rattled a bit on the way down, the young lady assured the two, from out of town and unaccustomed to fickle New York elevators, that the noises were simply echoes of little animals.

"You know all those hamsters and alligators that escape as pets?

In New York? Well, they use the elevator tunnels…tunnels or towers? Whatever. They use them to sneak around the buildings to steal food from the rats and pigeons."

With her two attendants smiling at their goddaughter's vivid imagination, the young lady again held the door upon arrival at the lobby and then followed her two companions into the art deco expanse.

"Be careful," the youth whispered as they crossed the lobby. "There be pirates waiting just outside the…oh no! Did you see that? A pirate on his mystery bicycle ship, carrying away the loot and booty taken from the good souls of our hallowed streets and avenues! Pray, let's be most careful, kind servants…uh, attendants."

Grabbing the hand of her aunt, the young lady spoke briefly to the doorman, nodded at a young woman entering with a well-groomed little pooch, and, after pausing to look out the double glass doors before exiting, stepped into the world of mid-morning, Upper East Side Manhattan, or, in her current state, a fantasy land of endless possibilities.

"Do we commander…?"

"Commandeer," the uncle gently corrected.

"Do we commandeer a horseless carriage to carry us to the far reaches of the kingdom? Wait, why is it called a kingdom and not a queen-dom? Doesn't seem fair, does it?"

Turning to walk up the hill to the corner, the two attendants took up positions on either side of the youth.

"Keep a sharp eye, dear chivalrous uncle…yeoman. Many a usurper to my crown, well, my tiara, lurk in the dark corners of the bodegas and the coffee shops. Oh, did you want to get an espresso, Uncle?"

Smiling, the uncle replied that his obsession with New York boutique espresso bars could be delayed. The girl smiled and hurried the little group to the closest corner. Once there, she scanned the rushing traffic for a taxi.

"Hither comes a lighted carriage, its noble steeds all ready for their exulted…."

"Exalted," the uncle gently corrected.

"Exalted passengers of royal blood!"

Waving down the taxi, with her uncle just behind her holding out his hand as well, the three piled in, with the youngster in the middle, where the uncle fished around for a seatbelt for the youth to wear.

"Did you decide where you'd rather eat, dear?" the aunt asked once the uncle had closed the taxi door.

Whispering, while she made cautious eyes toward the driver, the young princess answered.

"Our royal fare must be fit for such a royal personage as the royal me? Let me think…this one's easy. Sarabeth's?"

"That's a great choice, dear…I mean, dark princess. Since we are going downtown after, let's go to the one on Central Park South. It's at 59th Street, driver," the aunt replied.

As the car traveled the two miles in light traffic from the high 80's to Central Park South, the little princess whispered instructions to her retainers, her attendants.

"First, we eat. A banquet fit for a queen to be, of course. Then, we investigate the stories of vast riches in the land of rocky fellas, maybe acquiring samples of said riches. After that, I think we should see if our great ships are still…? No, wait. We should check that the royal menagerie is intact, and that the animals have not escaped into the city. You know, those escaped hamsters and alligators might have given our royal animals ideas, right?"

"Yes, I suppose they might have, if they can all understand each other," the uncle offered, then added a question. "Oh, and where might your menagerie reside, wise and formidable queen of the East Side?"

"Princess. Of the 'Upper' East Side. One of my best friends is the princess of the 'Lower' East Side. Wait, is Tribeca on the east or the west?"

"Hmm, the west, I think," the uncle replied.

"Okay, then she's the princess of the Lower West Side."

Thinking for a moment, the youth continued.

"After we secure the animals, I think we then go to the land of rocky fellas and seek out the riches. After that, we can go where the clocks all gather after dark, when the humans have all gone to bed, and the clocks all conspire to speed up the alarm clocks so we have to go to school even earlier on Monday. Why? Why do the clocks have such vengeful feelings against us kids…against us royal princesses, and even the smelly brother-bother-prince? What have we ever done to them? Why, I even wind the great, hallowed clock of Northern Virginia when I float down to visit you in your grand manor. And visit my royal garden."

The uncle had to listen closely and then, after thinking for a long minute about the mouthful his niece had just uttered, he answered.

"That's a good question. I wonder why the clocks conspire so. And, is that why they call it Times Square? Maybe they should call it Times Sneaky Square?" the uncle offered, to the rolling eyes of his niece.

"Okay, I think that's enough planning, little princess," the aunt suggested. "Let's see where we are after that, before we decide if we want to eat dinner out, or do pickup to take home, or even meet your mom and little brother somewhere fun for dinner, and order something for your dad for when he gets home later. Okay?"

"Yay, verily, sweet lady of the far south, I hear you," the youth replied and fell into reflective silence for the remainder of the taxi ride.

At the popular restaurant, the three were able to score an outside table without a wait, the efficient maître d' sweeping them into a table with such grace that the young girl thanked him in her normal voice, not her evil princess persona. She also smiled when her uncle ordered his first espresso of the day when the attentive waiter appeared moments later.

Throughout the brunch, the young girl mostly hid her princess side and acted like any happy child out with her godparents who doted on her. She was especially happy when her uncle reminded her and her auntie that the uncle and her big cousin Alex had frequented the old Mickey Mantle restaurant that had been at the same South Central Park location for decades.

French toast, bacon, a bit of scrabbled egg to appease the uncle, fizzy water with orange juice, and half of a chocolate croissant were enough to give the growing princess energy to tackle all the secret missions she had planned.

The niece was so satisfied with her feast that she drew a small sheet of paper from her purse and, in what seemed like a few blinks of an eye, constructed a small, origami bird that she asked her aunt to present to the maître d'. She then created a second one for their waiter, which she asked her uncle to present to him.

After being a little embarrassed by the two men's effusive thanks for the paper animals, the niece brought out her princess persona, once the men had gone back to their positions. She pointed across the street at the park.

"Wait! What do we spy across this wide river of mechanical carriages? They are but the brave, silent soldiers of the horse-drawn carriages of the Great Parklands, standing vigil against incursions by our dastardly foe, the troubling Queen of the West," the well-fed niece princess declared.

Glancing in the direction of the child's gestures, the two attendants watched as the Central Park horse carriages began their morning rounds. No evil queens in sight, but a number of tourists were hiring the carriages, which then clomped away toward the park gates.

"Ah, the pirates from…from New Jersey…no, the Caribbean. The pirates have stolen our brave spies and are taking them to the evil queen's headquarters, near the zoo…too near our menagerie."

"Wouldn't the evil queen of the west have her headquarters somewhere on, oh, maybe the west side?" the uncle asked, gently nudging the young princess to straighten out incongruities in her tale.

"Well, it's a mobile HQ, just like you see in the shows," the girl replied, winking at her aunt, given that the two of them routinely conspired to throw off her uncle, especially when he was being too literal.

Nodding, the uncle waved over their waiter and asked for the check. Turning back, he saw the girl and the aunt whispering to each other. The only thing he could hear was a vague reference to soup dumplings. Maybe later for lunch?

"Let's go," the aunt suggested, taking her niece's hand.

The three then maneuvered around a group of large, earpiece wearing, security operatives who seemed to be waiting for the arrival of their charge, their dominating presence silencing even the chatty little princess.

Once the group had reached the corner crosswalk, the little lady spoke up, but in a very soft voice, while her eyes darted back to the group of security people and several large, black cars.

"See, the evil queen is so bold she sends her security…her henchmen to take control of the entire block. Or, at least the half-block around Sarabeth's. It's our good fortune that we slipped away unnoticed before those earwig soldiers realized that I, the queen's arch enemy, the evil princess of the Upper East Side, was within mere inches of their steely grasp."

With dramatic flair, the little lady then pulled her aunt and uncle across the street and easily found the quickest route to the zoo, her royal menagerie.

After a few minutes' walk, the three passed the quaint gatehouses on either side of the zoo's open gates. The little girl let go of her aunt's hand and began to skip from one 'hiding place' to another as the three walked toward the zoo's…the menagerie's main entrance. She'd stop suddenly, dead still, and crane her neck in an exaggerated attempt to see around real and imaginary corners. The two adults with her, not wanting to alarm passerby, continued to walk normally, if a little slow, to stay abreast of their niece. For, a child acting out inside the walls of that famed Central Park institution was not at all unusual. But, if the aunt and uncle were to do the same, a few eyebrows would no doubt be raised and such antics might possibly draw an inquiry from one of the security guards.

When the little group arrived at the ticket windows, just a few yards inside the gate to the right, the little princess continued on, waving off buying tickets.

"Honey, don't you want to go in to see the animals?" the aunt called, recalling fondly the last time the three had visited the zoo when the girl had been much younger, around five years old.

"Do you remember when we were here with her last?" the uncle asked, seeming to read his wife's mind. "When that snow leopard came out of its den to look at her through the glass?"

"Yes. And her comment was so on point for her. 'Do you think the leopard came out to see me because I'm so pretty?' Priceless," the aunt replied, a hint of nostalgia in her voice. "And now look at her. Growing up."

The object of their collective admiration had just arrived at the corner of the gift shop, where she paused, scrunched up beside one of the large, ornamental plants at the shop's entrance, no doubt hiding from the evil queen's henchmen, who appeared to be disguised as ordinary deliverymen unloading boxes from one of the ubiquitous brown transit vans.

Playing along with their niece, the two didn't stop at the bush, but slowed their pace and began calling out to her, as if they could not see her a few feet away.

"I'm right here!" the little princess whispered. "Hiding from the robbers of worldly goods in the great, dark caravans from the west."

Acting surprised, the two attendants hurried over to shield their niece from the workers, and she then darted toward the door of the gift shop.

"We must inspect the menagerie, before the evil queen's henchmen and henchwomen make off with everything," the girl called over her shoulder to her aunt and uncle. "That is, well, is it okay to go in the gift shop? That's where the menagerie lives, you know."

Both adults nodded and the uncle opened the heavy door for his niece. He then let her and the aunt go in before he followed.

Once inside the shop, the young lady only showed her normal, youthful self, not the character of the princess that had just been her entire world a few minutes before. Puzzled, the uncle commented on the change to the aunt, letting his voice carry just enough so that their niece would hear, causing the little one to comment.

"Uncle, we have to be normal. Very normal, while inside here. We don't want to raise any suspicion or extra questions from the staff, who might be zombie clones of the normal, nice staff, but working, as the zombies, for the evil queen."

Nodding, while holding back a smile, the uncle glanced around at the three staff members and concluded they were excellent clones, who all looked just like regular gift shop clerks.

"Look," the niece called from a rack of plush animals. "Look. It's just like that sea turtle you sent from Florida, from that aquarium, last year."

"Mote Aquarium?" the uncle offered.

"Yes, I think that's it," the girl replied as she returned the plush toy to the rack.

Moving to another set of various animals, the little princess in the child suddenly returned as she spoke up.

"All's well, my faithful attendants. All in the menagerie appear safe and undisturbed," the niece princess commented in a lyrical, almost singing voice.

Looking at the way his niece was lingering over a small seal, soft and furry brown, with tickling whiskers, the uncle and the aunt nodded in agreement.

"I think you might need to take one of the menagerie with you," the aunt suggested, to the continued nods of the uncle. "That way, the seal can keep an ear to the animal network, jungle drums, so to speak, and let you know if the evil queen's henchmen come around."

"Well, I don't really need this…," the girl in the princess began, remembering her dad's admonition to not take advantage of her aunt and uncle's generosity.

"It's educational," the uncle replied, mimicking a comment from the girl's father about how educational toys were okay, as a counter to the aunt and uncle spoiling the girl. "And, the money goes to support the princess's living menagerie in the park."

Smiling, the niece carried the small seal over to the register, waved off suggestions of other things that her aunt and uncle offered, but then she remembered her little brother.

"Wait, yes, let's get him this turtle. He loves things that swim around in the bathtub. He saw the turtle king of the boathouse lake last month," the girl commented, holding up a bright green, plastic turtle.

"Turtle king?" the aunt lady-in-waiting asked.

"Oh, yes. The turtle king of Central Park…the Royal Woodlands, is why the queen of the west hasn't tried to invade the east side," the princess niece replied. "Through the park, that is."

"How's that?" the uncle yeoman asked, pulling out a credit card at the register.

"Well, he's neuter…," the princess began.

"Neutral," the uncle gently corrected.

"Yes, neutral, like a Swiss prince keeping the peace," the princess replied. "The Grand Turtle King of the boathouse lake, a monster of a snapping turtle, is very powerful and only rises to the top of the lake to take tributes from all his subjects, who throw bread and small treats to him and his turtle armies. He's far too powerful for the western queen. Besides, he loves the child-prince brother of mine. Always appears when we visit or have brunch at the boathouse. So, he favors the east side and, with his bird allies and squirrel spies, he prevents the evil queen of the west from invading through the park…woodlands."

Nodding, the uncle yeoman paid, smiling at the wild complexity of his goddaughter's vivid imagination.

After the purchases were made, the three exited the shop by the same door and, just as before, the princess used the cover of the doorways, trees, and statuary alcoves to make her way back to the zoo's gates.

Along the way, the princess side of the girl seemed to be whispering to the bronze statues that stood here and there on the way to the gates. Seeing her uncle's puzzled expression after she had bowed to the dancing goat statue with ducklings at its hind feet, the girl whispered so that only her two attendants could hear.

"Spies…shhh! These and others keep a lookout and send out the live animals to travel the city and watch for the evil queen's henchmen…hench-people? Everything thinks this is just a hunk of metal, but she and her friend, the bear across the way, are far more than that. Yes. Spies…shhh!"

The aunt and uncle both nodded, looking at the dancing goat a little differently as their niece darted toward the gates.

Once the niece reconfirmed that she did not want to visit the animals, the small group passed back through the gates, and walked back down the path to 59th Street to find a taxi to the next destination. If they had had more time in the city, the aunt and uncle would have suggested walking to Rockefeller Center, but, since they only had one day to spend with their niece, taxis were the order of the day.

After hailing a cab, climbing in, and giving the driver the destination, the three spent the next few minutes watching the Fifth Avenue storefronts fly by as they headed south. Exiting the cab near St Patrick's and Saks, the three made a beeline for one of the 'treasure houses' that the youth had mentioned during the ride.

The Lego Store.

"Many treasure houses dwell here, in the lanes and alleys of the rocky fellas, my dear attendants. We may, just may, need to carry samples away to test them that they are still strong," the young child side of the princess rationalized as her wide eyes took in the various magnificent displays at the front of the busy store.

"Yes. Maybe a whole bucket of samples?" the aunt asked, smiling at the sight of the colorful wall bin displays of various bricks and the like, something she and the uncle knew that their niece loved.

"The buckets!" the niece uttered in excitement, shedding her princess persona for one of a gleeful child in a favorite store as she ran over to the collection of various sized buckets.

Without hesitation, the niece, her princess persona on hold, extracted a medium bucket, as she always did, and, handing the lid to her uncle, she started scanning the wall for the building bricks and other items she needed.

For the next several minutes, the little girl in the princess fully took over and she had a grand time taking samples from nearly all the most colorful bins. After she had taken the final handful of small, clear discs, to serve as lights or centerpiece decorations, she asked her uncle to try to fit the lid onto her bucket. After a few vigorous shakes to settle the bricks, the uncle finally was able to seal the container and tuck it under his arm as his niece turned to the more serious work of building people.

Stepping over to the always crowded Lego people manufacturing station, the uncle placed himself squarely behind his niece, blocking the bigger, more aggressive kids and some ill-mannered parents from muscling his niece out of the way. Her aunt stood at the girl's side, helping to find specific pieces in the people bins.

"I think we need to make a witch, or a sorcerer, to help protect the east side from the west side evil queen," the now princess said over the din to her aunt, while glancing back to grin at her uncle running interference for her.

After a number of minutes rummaging through the various bins, the niece princess, with help from her aunt and with a few well-selected pieces found by her uncle, was able to build both a witch and a sorcerer without too much trouble.

Once the little princess was satisfied, she placed the figures in the little plastic holders, then realized she needed three figures to complete the set, so created a small princess as well, but one that only looked vaguely like her.

"This princess is to fool the evil queen, you see," the princess explained on the way to the cashier. "Her spies will see me with the little princess and, since she's so small, will try to steal her, instead of me, when she is not protected by the witch and the sorcerer."

Nodding, both the aunt and the uncle smiled as they accepted the curious logic of their little niece while they stood in the cashier line.

"Oh, wait. I forgot. Need to get something for Gr—, I mean the bother-brother child-prince," the big sister in the niece princess suddenly exclaimed.

"Maybe one of those motorcycles over there, dear? I know he has the green one. Maybe the black one?" the aunt suggested, to which the big sister nodded, rushed over, grabbed one of the black, stunt motorcycles, and brought it over to the register, where the uncle paid for all the items.

Once outside, the (not very) evil princess turned down an offer to visit the American Girl shop, explaining that she had gotten everything she had needed from there over the summer, to include several stuffed animals from her aunt and uncle to add to her vast collection. The group then decided to head over to the skating rink, which they didn't know was open or not, and maybe go down into the food court area.

As they approached the rink, they saw that tents were set up for dining, so it was too early in the season for ice-skating. Turning to the outdoor elevator on 50th, the three stepped aboard and descended.

The young girl pressed her face against the glass and spoke in a very happy, wistful voice.

"Remember when I was little? And we took this for the first time and it was magical because it was an elevator into the ground? Into the ground! Can you believe it? And we saw the dirt and the roots through the glass? That's all gone now. They put shiny sides up now, so no more underground. Looks just like a building now," the niece said, somewhat pensively. "But, I remember the magic like it was just yesterday."

Once in the food court under the plaza, the three sought out a suitable place for an evil princess to have a snack.

After settling on French fries, milkshakes, and chocolate cookies, in that order, the three found a clean table in the concourse and sat, people watching, as they inhaled the treats.

"Any west side evil queen henchmen down here below the plaza?" the uncle asked, taking only a small bite from one of the aunt's cookies.

Looking up and down the concourse, then turning to look out over the tents outside, the young princess leaned over to her uncle and whispered her answer in a solid imitation of a crime show star's conspiratorial voice.

"I think her henchmen are afraid of the underground. They will use the subway to move around, but run to the exits to get out as soon as they can. Whenever you're in the subway, look for the riders who dash to the exits. Those are the brood of the evil queen. Yes, yes, yes…," the niece princess replied.

"Brood? So they are all the queen's children?" the aunt asked, feigning confusion.

"What? Oh, right. Not brood, but bunch. The queen's bunch. Although, she does have spoiled brats…excuse me, spoiled little ones who boss the brood…the bunch around, she does," the niece princess answered, her voice so low it was hard to hear.

Once all the treats had vanished, the uncle suggested he put the various treasures in the backpack that he always carried on visiting days, often with additional treats hidden in the various pockets. The little princess agreed and helped stuff the seal, inside its own bag, and the Lego bucket and motorcycle into the pack, holding onto the Lego witch, sorcerer, and princess to distract the evil queen's henchmen. She secured the three miniatures in her small purse.

After the little group ascended from the concourse via the more conventional escalators, they made a beeline for the FAO Schwartz store on the corner.

Years before, when she had been quite young, the aunt and uncle had taken their niece to the original store on Fifth Avenue, where they reminded her that she had managed to consume nearly an entire chocolate milkshake on her own. Sadly, the new store did not have an old-fashioned soda fountain and candy store, but did have an endless supply of fascinating toys.

After running the gauntlet of tourists and locals, with many, many kids on overdrive, the three made it to the second floor collection of various dolls and other toys, to include odd little twisty creatures, which seemed to be the only thing in the store that appealed to the little niece.

After convincing her uncle that she didn't need an entire set of the little twisty creatures and that the lavender cat-looking one was enough, the three checked out and then waded through the bustling humanity to the large revolving door, exiting into the cool of the afternoon.

"Here, honey, please wear your jacket," the aunt said to the niece. "I think your uncle wants to walk for a bit, maybe get a snack of…what was it that you were craving yesterday?"

Leaning over to whisper to his niece, the uncle uttered words that were magic to the child's ears.

"Soup…dumplings!" the uncle whispered.

"Soup dumplings! Oh, I think I agree…yes, yes, I agree with Uncle that we need to check on those soup dumplings. Yes!" the niece replied with gusto and danced a few yards down the sidewalk, then ran back to take her aunt's hand.

"Well, it does mean we have to cross over into…into the west side, over on Eighth Avenue, at 49th. Do you think it's safe? With the evil queen's men probably everywhere over there?" the uncle asked, a small grin spreading from his lips to his eyes.

For a moment, the niece princess was struck silent, trying to rationalize why the three should chance capture by the evil queen for the sake of soup dumplings. After about a hundred feet of silence, as the three approached Sixth Avenue, she offered her reasoning.

"Well, since she's the queen of the 'Upper' West Side, I think her henchmen will not be as many. Yes, she's probably chasing small children in the park, looking for new recruits and not paying attention to the restaurants. Besides, she hasn't many henchmen below Lincoln Center, because everyone knows all those musicians, opera singers, and others are too creative and clever for the evil queen to gain too much power over them. And, we all know what happens to evil queens in those plays and operas, right…? So, no, the soup dumplings should be safe. But, we have our decoys, so we can use them to fool any henchmen that get close," the niece princess said in rapid succession. "Yes, I think we should go soon and watch for any spies."

As the three made their way across the wide Avenue of the Americas, the little niece princess pointed out the various food carts scattered about. Taking a deep breath as they passed one of the pretzel carts, the little princess rattled off her perception of the cart's loyalties.

"According to my 'spies,' these carts are loyal to the east side princesses, until Times Square, where all the loyalties…are suspect, given that all the clocks and therefore all the plans of anyone working there could be altered without their knowing, because all the clocks conspire to move time around when they are working in the square, so we three have to be careful and not look any of the cart bosses in the eye. But, if you do look them in the eye and the eyes look like glass, then they are probably henchmen…temporary henchmen of the evil queen, but they don't know they are. So, they are zombie cart bosses of the trickery laced Times Square," the princess offered, pausing to take a long breath after her wild explanation, before finishing. "So, my loyal attendants, be careful not to let any of the cart people with the glassy, zombie eyes sell you anything."

As the little group passed through Times Square, the uncle used a harsh face, hidden from his niece, to scare off any and all street cartoon characters who might have thought of approaching his niece. In addition, the well-traveled uncle kept an eye out for other, less savory characters that might mistake the three as easy targets for pickpocketing or panhandling.

"Wait. How does the evil queen turn these okay guys into zombie henchmen?" the uncle asked as they crossed Broadway and headed down 49th to Eighth Avenue. "And, do all the clocks in the city gather in Times Square?"

"Only the boss clocks. Like the big ones on top of buildings and on those poles some places. Oh, she tricks them with smells," the niece replied as a blast of deeply delicious bakery aromas almost forced a detour into Junior's on the corner. "Since there are so many smells in Times Square, she can fool them into thinking they are making food with one smell, when they are really conjuring up evil witch's brew for her unsuspecting victims…tourists victims, since most people who actually live here aren't fooled by smells."

Nodding at the disconnected rationale of his niece, the uncle hurried the little group along so that they were no longer tempted by being so close to Junior's. However, he filed away a suggestion for later to visit the Junior's on Shubert Alley, one of his family's favorite spots after a show.

Arriving at the little dumpling shop on the corner of Eighth Avenue and 49th, the three were lucky and did not have to wait for one of the few tables in the small, bustling place. Both the aunt and the uncle breathed a sigh of relief. The last time they had brought their famished niece to the cozy place, Covid had prevented any seating, and the weather was rainy and cold. Fortunately, the place next door, aptly named after the nearby Times Square, had allowed them to take a table inside to feed the starving little girl. They also bought a second lunch from the place and tipped everyone in sight.

"We have to be careful, here," the niece princess whispered as the three were led to one of the shared tables. "These customers are not evil queen henchmen, but secret spies for the princesses of the Midtown East Side. We usually go to the one on 55th and Lex, where the spies know me."

"Wait, there is more than one evil princess of the East Side?" the aunt asked, winking at the uncle.

"Why, auntie, yes. There's me, of course, of the Upper, then there's Lulu of the cat people and her faithful auntie princess Luna, then my BFF of the Midtown East Side, and my other BFF of the Lower East Side…wait, she's on the west side. So it must be my other BFF, well, almost BFF, who is the evil princess of the Lower East Side," the niece replied, her eyes following the trays of steaming noodles and dumplings being delivered to other customers.

"So, are there many princesses of the west side as well?" the uncle, quite confused already, asked while signaling to their waitress that they were ready.

"Well, she's very selfish, so only the brats…sorry, the spoiled ones are allowed to be princesses, but only between Columbia and the Lincoln Center. I already told you she doesn't move around too much below Lincoln Center or Columbus Circle. Well, she just can't grab any power at Columbia or above. The students there are too smart for her," the niece princess replied, her eyes continuing to follow the yummy dishes moving around the small restaurant like a waiters' ballet. "Oh, and the law gang of the great Fordham knights, where Alex went to undergrad, also scares the evil queen. Right? We all know what happens to evil queens if they get dragged into court."

Smiling at the curious rationale of their little niece, the aunt and the uncle finished ordering several types of soup dumplings and a dish of noodles. The aunt was happy to move on to other topics, but the uncle, who tended to carry silliness a little too far, asked a question on a point that had been puzzling him.

"Little princess…," the uncle began, but was politely silenced by his niece.

"Shush, please, Uncle…I mean yeoman knight. Don't use my royal title. Use my code name. Just like you taught me and my friend to use on those walkie-talkies ages ago," the niece whispered.

"Oh. Okay. Uh, what is today's code name?" the uncle asked, with the aunt echoing.

"Code name…? Bobara—, of course," the niece replied, using the name of one of the star characters of her monthly Facetime video show she performed for the aunt and uncle.

"Yes, sir, ma'am! Bobara—,," the uncle answered, snapping a short salute to his niece before he finally asked his question.

"If the queen of the west…western avenues, I think you call

her…," the uncle began.

"Boulevards," the niece princess corrected.

"Boulevards. If she is the 'evil' queen and is so dastardly, why are you and the other princesses of the eastern side also 'evil' princesses? Did she convert you all from being good princesses or nice princesses?" the uncle asked, thinking his logic was sound.

Her eyes still following the various dishes around the small dining area, the young niece thought for a moment, then slowly laid out her logic.

"Well, we are only 'evil' to those who are 'evil,' like the evil queen," the niece princess replied, letting out a little sigh of exasperation at her uncle's apparently simple way of thinking. "If we were always good and nice to evil queens, then the evil queen of the west would be too strong for us and we'd never win any of the great sorcerer wars, would we? So, we are only evil to those who are evil, but not to each other, because that would be silly since we are all friends and know that we are good fairy princesses and only are forced to use evil to help the poor people of the east from being overrun by the very, very evil queen of the western avenues…boulevards…you've got me saying it, uncle…keeping her and her henchmen from turning the poor east side people into the queen's zombies."

Fortunately, for the confused looking uncle and the chuckling aunt, their order arrived and everyone's attention was riveted on the steaming, mouth-watering aromas and then the amazingly delicious flavors.

In silence, the uncle served the delicate dumplings first to the aunt and then the niece, then to himself, showing the niece how to grasp the tip of the dumpling and gently rock it, so the wrapping did not stick to the paper at the bottom of the steam tray and tear, losing the precious soup. After the niece had one of the steaming morsels on her large spoon, she took her drink straw and, puncturing the side of the dumpling, she commenced drinking the soup through the straw, to the delight of her two surprised attendants.

After a few minutes of no talking as the three gorged on dumplings and noodles, the niece princess continued, her voice dripping with conspiracy.

"You know, I don't think the evil queen likes soup dumplings. I think all the steam and the amazing flavors and all these happy people…spies, that is, would be too positive and happy for such an evil, unhappy, nobody loves her evil queen. Don't you think so?" the niece princess mused between dumplings.

"Yes, dear," the aunt replied, after helping her niece switch to noodles. "This is definitely one of your uncle's happiest places. He's been known to come here twice in one day!"

"Only because I was going to see a show. And it was cold," the uncle offered in his defense.

"Which soup dumplings do you think are the best?" the uncle asked of the niece princess, trying to change the subject from his New York obsession with the rarities that were good soup dumplings.

"All of them!" the niece chirped as she finished off the last of her six dumplings, while her aunt and uncle marveled that such a tiny stomach could handle so many, and then start on the noodles.

"You see those music videos? On that screen?" the niece princess asked, then cautioned her uncle when he turned to look. "Don't look! It's a brainwashing video that the evil queen sneaks into…into shows and programs to lure those who don't have strong minds."

"Lure them where, dear?" the aunt asked, finishing off her own noodles.

"Where? Her lair? Her lair for luring? Oh, just where does that queen lure her victims?" the niece princess asked herself, her brow briefly furrowed in thought, but then she answered. "Why, what's the biggest, scariest place on the west side?"

"One of those huge apartment buildings along Central Park West? The ones that look like Batman villain headquarters?" the uncle suggested as he motioned to their waiter for the check. "But, not the one across from Strawberry Fields. I don't think anything evil could exist there."

"No, the evil queen never, ever goes to Strawberry Fields, uncle. She knows she would be drawn into the…the mosaic, the Imagine place, and would be instantly melted into…well, would be changed into a good queen, she would. Hey, maybe we should try to lure her there? We could set up a decoy. Little brothers are great decoys, didn't you know? And, she'd think he was a new henchman, but lost. So. She'd want to nab him, since he's a princess's little-bother-brother. Yes, and then she'd sneak up on him and, just as she's ready to pounce…herself, because she wouldn't trust her henchmen to do it right because evil queens never fully trust their silly henchmen…we'd pull him away and she'd fall into the mosaic and melt into…well, turn into, a good queen of the Upper West Side."

Having trouble following all the twists in their niece's logic, the two attendants simply nodded and worked on finishing their respective dishes.

Once the niece had finished, long before her aunt and uncle, she busied herself with first looking over her three Lego figures and then slipping out another small sheet of paper. While the two attendants completed their dishes and then called, again, for the check, the niece princess had already completed another origami, an owl. She perched it on the napkin-holder against the wall, where she left it for their very helpful waitress.

After the check had been paid, the aunt then helped the little niece princess on with her coat and the three departed, thanking their waitress before they waded through the crowd gathered around the door waiting for open tables.

"Did you want to go to the park?" the aunt asked as they stood in the cooling air of mid afternoon. "To…?"

"No…no thank you," the niece replied. "I was just telling you how we could trick the evil queen into becoming good. And, I was telling you where her lair is. Maybe on your next visit we can try to lure her to the good side…to the nice light. But, where do you think her lair is, that we'd have to in…filter…?"

"Infiltrate?" the aunt suggested.

"Yes, infiltrate?" the niece asked, her wide eyes looking expectantly at her aunt and uncle.

At the silent stares of her two attendants, the niece princess discreetly rolled her eyes. Discreetly, for she knew it was impolite to roll one's eyes at her relatives. Then, using her lecturing voice, she quietly informed her aunt and uncle on the whereabouts of the evil queen's lair.

"The Museum of Natural History, of course. Where else has caverns and caverns of dark, spooky places in the basement? Creepy exhibits of all manner of frightening things to small children? Of course a queen…the evil queen of the west side would have her secret lair somewhere in there. No doubt a lot of those exhibits are not really wax and reconstructed bones like Alex oppa said, but victims of some dastard…dastardly? Yes, dastardly evil queen's henchmen converting process. That's it. All the good is extracted by some henchmen process and is left to the museum to use for the exhibits."

"Smart queen," the uncle answered. "No one would ever think to look for her there. But, that place is huge. It would take days to find her? How would you try to find her?"

"We could use the decoy princess that I made just now and set her in the big lobby in the basement. When the…the steamy fog…just like what we saw in that kitchen in the back…rolls in and engulfs the decoy, we can see where the fog comes from and be ready for a trap," the niece princess replied.

"What kind of trap?" the aunt asked, absently, as she was looking for a taxi.

"The mosaic. We get her to follow us. Once she wants the decoy, we'll grab up the decoy princess and run…no, walk quickly so the henchmen spies won't know who we are…maybe divert their attention with doughnuts, because everyone knows that henchmen love doughnuts, and go over to the park to spring the trap," the niece princess answered, triumph in her voice.

"Sounds like a sound plan, oh, great, evil (not very, I think) princess of the Upper East Side," the uncle replied, who then looked at his phone map while mumbling a thought under his breath. "Are they teaching Machiavelli in grade school now…?"

"Ships? You said something earlier about checking on your ships?" the aunt asked, fussing with her niece's coat to cover the uncle's comment.

"Ships? Oh, yes. The grand fleet. Some days the royal admirals moor them in the East River and we can commander…commandeer one of the fast ships to carry us to the far shore to visit the lands farther east in Long Island City, where my castle used to be. Oh, Uncle, remember when we went to Café Henri when I was little and had French toast and my friends were there? When I was little?" the little girl in the niece princess chirped, recalling the long ago fun morning when she had treated her uncle to brunch.

"Yes, I remember that well. And your two friend's moms who wondered who the strange man was with their daughters' bestie," the uncle chuckled, vividly recalling the iron grip of one of the mothers, whom he learned later had been ready to tackle him, if his niece's mother had not responded to them with a positive identification.

"But, other days they are at the great Clinton Fort, refuge of sailors being chased by giant pirates hiding by the giant lady guardian of the harbor," the niece princess continued. "Today, though, I think they might all be down by the modern aircraft carrier. But, that's on the west side, in the Hudson, so we have to wait until they move around the point and swim...float? Float up to the east side and we'll know they are not zombie sailors from the evil queen."

Nodding slowly and trying to not look too confused, the uncle conferred with the aunt and they concluded they could make one more major stop before they needed to move back closer to their niece's home so that she would not be too tired out for school the next day.

"Dear, we have time to do one more adventure before dinner, probably takeout to take back home so that you are not out too late. It is a school day tomorrow, right?" the aunt asked.

"Yessssss," the niece answered with a long, dramatic sigh. "And I have a little bit of homework, so I have to do that before I'm too tired."

"Okay, let's do something not too far away," the uncle suggested, looking at his map again.

For a couple of minutes, as the little group walked back toward Times Square, several ideas were considered, then discarded as too time consuming, or too late in the day.

The Ice Cream Museum, with all its interactive exhibits, tasty treats, and clever layout, to include the two-story tube slide that had almost broken the uncle's back (to hear him tell it) when he had followed his niece's lead, was deemed worthy, but too late in the day to spend enough time there.

The Children's Art Museum, where the niece had made a clay dragon a couple of visits before and had been awarded the only free, next visit ticket of the group she had been in, for her amazing red dragon, was another idea. Yet, once the aunt did the math on timing, it was too late to go that far south.

"Maybe make a stop at Ladurée down in Soho, where you had to walk the zigzag bricks? Not far from that amazing Italian place on Spring, by Thompson? Could take some treats back to her mom?" the uncle suggested. "Or maybe that ceramics painting shop?"

However, the aunt tapped her watch, which nipped that idea in the bud, and suggested a crepe cake from Lady M on the way back.

"Crepes…?" the uncle then mused, prompted by both the aunt's cake suggestion and from seeing sleepiness slowly creep into their niece's eyes, which then popped open at the mention of one of her favorite snacks.

"The place near my house?" the niece chimed in, perked up by the prospect of a favorite treat at the end of her special day.

"Yes, that way, we'll be just a few blocks from home at the end of the day's adventure," the aunt replied, looking around for signs of empty cabs.

"Yes!" the niece almost shouted. "And, it's a special, protected place, that the evil queen's henchmen cannot get into. If they step over the doorway there, the crepe machine will fling a hot crepe at them and scare them away."

"Sounds scary. What if the machine doesn't like us and throws one at us?" the uncle asked, flagging down a taxi.

"Silly uncle. How many times have you and auntie been there with me? Three, four times? More? Have you ever been thrown at by the crepe machine in any of those visits, uncle?" the niece asked in her matter-of-fact voice she used when the uncle was being a little too silly.

"Good point. I've only had Nutella flung at me when a ravenous little girl…I mean evil princess, eats her Nutella and strawberry crepe too fast," the uncle chuckled as he helped the aunt and then their niece into the cab.

After giving the address of the crepe place, on the corner of Lexington and 94th, the three settled in for the long ride back to the niece's neighborhood. Both the niece and the aunt seemed to doze a bit, while the uncle stared out the window at the life and energy of the city, something that he always marveled at, and hoped he would never lose his fascination with.

Seeing the marquee for the old Ambassador Theater, where 'Chicago' was still running, the uncle commented on taking his niece's cousin Alex to see it during one of their many theater trips to the city after 9/11. They had been happy to do their small part in helping return the city to its earlier vibrancy, as the mayor, Bloomberg at the time, had said. They had also taken in '42nd Street' as well during that trip in the dark days a few months after the towers had fallen. The aunt and uncle also reminded their niece that they longed for the day that they would have enough time and schedule flexibility to take her to a Broadway musical or to an opera at the Met.

After the cab had found its way onto Park Avenue, the journey sped by. The niece's mother replied to a text from the aunt that they didn't need to stop at Lady M, because the mother had already been there and had bought the aunt's favorite flavor and had also set up dinner delivery to the apartment later. The aunt then joined the niece in a long snooze during the cab ride. Eventually, the little group was let off near the crepe place.

Groggy from their snoozing, both the aunt and the niece seemed a little disoriented, but the niece quickly perked up when she recognized where she was.

"Okay, we're here," the niece said, her voice low. "But, let's pretend we're not going there and jump in at the last minute. That will fool any zombie spy cab drivers under...under the spell of the evil queen."

"In thrall, that would be a good term," the uncle offered.

"Thrall?" the niece princess asked, her faced scrunched up with a slight frown at the alien word.

"When someone is under the power of an overlord, like an evil queen," the aunt answered, frowning at the uncle for using such heavy terms.

"Yes, zombie cabbie spy thralls of the evil queen. They could be anywhere," the niece princess replied, then literally jumped the few steps leading up to the door of the crepe place and crouched, looking for those very zombie thralls.

Seeing none, the niece let the uncle open the door for her and her aunt and they all piled in, with the uncle feigning fear of getting hit in the face with a hot crepe.

"Uncle! You're with me, so the evil queen can't get to you to make you a zombie," the niece laughed, then looked surprised at her statement.

"Wait...," the niece said as she hopped over to the sturdy chairs in front of the crepe cooking area. "That's a scary thought. What if...oh, what if the evil queen was able to convert you and auntie to her evil ways? What if...oh, no, the thought is too terrible to think. I think I'll just focus on the crepes."

Once inside the warm and cozy corner place, the little niece princess transformed back into more of a happy child niece than a scheming, (not very) evil princess of Park Avenue. Maybe it was the soothing aroma of crepe batter toasting up on the large, round cooktops, or maybe it was the mouth-watering prospect of Nutella drizzled strawberries, but something had moved the princess in the little girl to the background and the chipper little girl had surfaced.

After ordering, the niece hopped up on one of the chairs that fronted the cooking station, where she peered through the glass barrier to watch the expert cook spread out two crepes on the two round cooktops. She then paid special attention to when he added the strawberries and the gooey, hazelnut chocolate, her eyes riveted to the one she had decided had the most of both ingredients, and should, by all that is right in the world, belong to her.

As the cook slipped the folded gems into the paper pockets, the uncle had also noted which had the most filling and commented to his wide-eyed niece.

"Since your aunt and I are sharing, maybe that one with the strawberries spilling out should be....ours...?" the uncle teased, knowing the niece's answer.

"Well, uncle, if you must...," the niece replied, her sweet disposition and her experience with her uncle's antics evident in the way she let the words hang in the air.

"Silly, of course we are not going to deprive you of the biggest crepe. That would just be wrong," the uncle replied, his bluff called by his own guilt and his niece's carefully tilted head showing off doleful eyes.

Humming one of her piano lessons, lost on the uncle, but recognized by her aunt, given her aunt's humming along, the niece watched the cook like a hawk, smiling at each step in the crepe creation dance. Once the magic was done, she hopped down from the chair, took her lemonade, and preceded her uncle to the corner table, just beyond the coffee bar opposite the crepe station and cashier, taking a seat next to her aunt. There she patiently waited for the server to deliver the piping hot treats, smiling as her uncle steered the crepe with the largest bulge to his niece.

With no preliminaries, the niece dug into her crepe, expertly slicing large, bite-sized portions, stabbing strawberries and swirling them about in the chocolate ooze. The young girl's smiling face warmed the hearts of the aunt and uncle, who were always saddened by the impending departure from their goddaughter, favorite grandniece, and generally adorable little girl who was quickly growing up in leaps and bounds since they only saw her and her little brother every few months, and less during the worse days of the pandemic.

As the aunt and uncle worked on their own crepe, with the uncle having his second espresso of the day, the niece's crepe quickly disappeared. While the adults still had about a third to go, the petite little girl had literally wolfed down her substantial snack, causing the aunt to comment.

"My, that's even faster than when we pick you up from school and come here. The last time, your uncle and I had almost finished by the time you had gobbled yours down that time," the aunt said in her always lovingly affectionate voice she used with her soul-mate niece.

Grinning, the niece gently placed her fork and knife on her nearly empty plate, which only held a smudge of chocolate to let anyone know what might have been there minutes earlier. She then cheerfully finished off her lemonade.

"Is that enough for you?" the uncle then asked, smiling. "Do you need another one, just in case you are still hungry?"

"Uncle, that one was huge!" the niece replied, grinning at her amazing feat of gourmand.

"Right, then, shall we head home?" the aunt suggested, gathering up her things and the niece's coat as the uncle finished the crepe.

After a long sigh, the niece nodded, her eyes showing some of the inevitable sadness of the eventual parting, but held off on any comments. She then pulled out a piece of paper and, with sugar induced speed, created a small origami turtle, leaving it on the napkin holder for the staff.

On the short walk to the apartment, the (not very) evil princess was still held in the background as the niece gripped both the hand of her aunt and her uncle's hand as the three walked the couple of blocks south. As they approached her cross street, the uncle brought up his inevitable question.

"Hmmm, do we need to go to the, you know, that store that has educational items?" the uncle asked.

"Uncle, you mean the t-o-y store?" the niece asked in an almost admonishing voice, as if the uncle were the child and not vice versa. "No, I think we have enough. And, something…tells…me…that there might be surprises somewhere, later."

Without answering, the uncle shot a glance at the aunt, who shook her head at his mock surprise that the little niece had figured out long ago that the uncle would sneak small toys, books, plush animals, or whatever the niece's interest of the moment might be, into her room before they departed, to be found later in the evening, or even on a later date.

"Oh, okay," the uncle replied as they passed a corner bodega, which then gave him an idea.

"You know, I wonder if the evil queen has any of the bodega owners on her payroll?" the uncle mused as they crossed the last street.

"The evil queen? She'd not dare try to turn our loyal, East Side shopkeepers to her dark ways!" the niece princess replied in her reborn princess voice, its tone one of regal indignation. "Even an evil queen is no match for the bodega guys, my Dad always says."

"But, we are almost back to the castle, with the happy family and the child-prince little brother, so I think the evil princess will retire until the next great adventure," the niece continued, her voice returning to the normal little girl voice, which also betrayed how tired she was.

"Okay, dear," the aunt replied, waving at the uncle to stop probing the niece on the princess elements.

However, the uncle, who was never one to shy away from encouraging childhood adventures, had to ask one more question, which he did without looking the aunt in the eye.

"Well, what might that adventure be, Oh, Great and (Not Very) Evil Princess of the Upper East Side?" the uncle asked in his best retainer voice, trying to avoid the nonverbal signals from the aunt.

The little niece took a couple of long minutes to answer, so the three were nearly at the green awning of her apartment building before she replied, her voice thoughtful and her mind briefly far away on some regal adventure just before she crossed her threshold back to the real world.

"Mayhap, dearest retainers, when your carriage next delivers you to within our castle walls, we can try...attempt, yes, attempt to trap...to confuse and trap the evil queen of the western boulevards in her own, deep, dark lair in the Museum of Scary and Supernatural History Basement Dungeons. Yes, that would be an adventure," the niece replied, putting the princess to sleep for a couple of months until her aunt and uncle returned.

Just as the little group stepped under the awning and the doorman opened the glass doors, the uncle saw a delivery bike careening down the sidewalk in a direct line to crash into the three, but more specifically, his niece. Stepping around the niece and the aunt, he blocked them from the oncoming bike, which he assumed would swerve once closer.

At the blink of an eye before the delivery bike would have crashed into the uncle, the driver swerved, said some unpleasant words under his breath, and then jumped across the curb to fly down the street. Oddly, the delivery bike driver had an elaborate radio headset on and was yelling into it as he drove away, with the uncle only hearing a short bit about failure to deliver.

Turning away, but watching the bike bounce down the street, the uncle managed to catch the name of the delivery service on the large yellow and red basket on the back of the bike.

'West Side Delivery—Special Requests Handled—Queenly Rates.'

"Did you two see that...? Why is a west side delivery...?" the uncle began, but then saw the aunt's eyes glaring at him, telling him in no uncertain terms to drop the evil princess comments.

"What's that, Uncle?" the young niece asked with an odd twinkle in her eye as she too had watched the angry delivery driver fly down the street.

"What? Oh, nothing dear. Nothing. I think I need another espresso, that's all," the uncle replied, giving his niece a quick wink while the aunt was stepping through the door.

With that, the niece princess capped off her day-long Manhattan adventure with her loyal and loving retainer attendants, her visiting aunt and uncle, and stepped grandly into her apartment building, back into the person of the young niece, the cheerful big sister, the caring daughter, and the cherished goddaughter. Bravely, she also put on a cheerful face and held back any tears at the impending departure of her dear aunt and uncle.

For, as any loyal retainer could tell you, such a regal, (not very) evil princess of the Upper East Side would never, never ever, let anyone see her cry.

3

THE GREAT MANHATTAN PIZZA SCARE

A cold, mid-winter wind blew hard against the windows of the eighth-floor apartment, whistling a series of high notes as it blew across one of the vents a few feet above the chilled panes of glass. The nannies had all gathered in the study in the back, their multiple accented voices chattering in hushed tones as they enjoyed a few minutes of down time while their half-dozen charges were engaged in birthday party play, overseen by the mother of the host and the host's own nanny. Helping the mother to entertain the four-year-olds was her daughter, older than her brother, the birthday boy, by a good five years. While their own beloved nanny rustled about in the kitchen, setting up for the as yet to be delivered birthday cake, both mother and daughter were bravely entertaining the young boys, first with a sort of pantomime, then with a series of simple games. Yet, as is the case with the very young, the boys' various attention spans seemed to get shorter and shorter with each passing minute. The daughter watched her mother's eyes wander to the corridor leading to the refuge of the nannies.

Fearing that her mother was on the verge of calling the nannies back in, which would cause the boys to become even fussier, the daughter decided to engage the small ones with a story, one that her uncle had told her during a visit a few months before. She signaled her mother to hold off on calling in the reinforcements of the nannies. Then, like a general overseeing the assembly of her troops, the big sister placed the children in a semicircle around one of the large, comfy living room chairs, not far from the windows. The big sister then called for the little ones to focus their wandering attention using that tired and true method with small humans of their age and socio-economic experience—simple bribery.

"The cake has been delayed, but should be here in less than ten minutes," the big sister said slowly, watching the pained expressions ripple across the faces of the little boys. "But, if you all listen quietly and are nice, the cake slices will be all the bigger for those who are good listeners, and more ice cream will fill the bowls of the quietest boys."

After a few chirps of discontent, accompanied by encouragement from the more mature in the group (two boys were at that magical four-and-a-half year mark), the boys all settled down and collectively put on their listening faces.

"Pizza! Who here loves pizza?" the big sister asked, almost rhetorically, given that any child born in Manhattan, or any of the New York City boroughs for that matter, had been weaned on pizza and would laugh at such a question.

All the little boys shouted their hearty endorsement of all things pizza, with a couple of the younger ones (by months) looking back to the dining room where they had just enjoyed pizza for birthday lunch. Too far uptown for Joe's or John's, the local pizza pie place's offering had been wolfed down without complaint.

"Well, listen closely as I tell you a tale of tragedy and woe, when the city of New York, and maybe the whole country, had no…dare I even say it? No pizza…!" the big sister exclaimed, her eyes fiery, with her hands thrown to the imagined sky in a gesture of surprise.

Looks of shock and disbelief erupted from the faces of the youths, with several voicing their own surprise.

"Never!"

"That…that would never happen…right?"

"No pizza? When? Where?"

"How could that…?"

One of the little ones, his eyes beginning to bulge as a prelude to a flood of tears (as he was well-known as a crier), caused the birthday boy to wrap an arm around the overly sensitive child, while whispering assurances that the story was from long ago.

"Yes, as my brother just said, this tale of pizza sorrow happened long ago, even before we had to wear masks. But, the woeful tale is told again, from time to time, to ensure we never forget. Never forget. In case…in the rare and unlikely case that…perish the thought, as my grandmother says…that such a horror might happen again."

The big sister's explanation for inadvertently scaring the little ones seemed to comfort them and even the floodgates child calmed down, allowing her little brother to let go of the boy's shoulder. She then leaned forward, her voice low and full of expectation.

"Now, sit back and I'll tell the tale, as it was told to me by my aged uncle, and his dad, or maybe his uncle or aunt before him, long ago, back, maybe even before the streets were paved. He called the strange tale 'The Great Manhattan Pizza Scare!'"

The big sister scanned the audience, looking each child directly in the eye when she spoke, just like her uncle had advised her not long ago when she had had to do a school presentation on origami. Her tactic worked, as each child felt she was speaking directly to him, she guessed, from the way each seemed to calm down and focus on her.

"Back in those days, the mayor of the city was much more important than today. He was almost like a prince, not quite a king, but more like a prince. He would often call for various days off when one group or other asked him, especially when some group or other made a big contribution to his campaign. A contribution is like money you give to help someone get elected. Anybody can do it, but some groups do it more often than others."

The little heads bobbed in agreement.

"One day, the pizza confederation, which is a very big group, asked for a 'best pizza' contest to help with sales and combat all the fast food chains that were coming into the city. The mayor, after waiting until the pizza guys had made an extra-supreme size contribution, agreed to the contest, which would be judged by a panel. A panel is a group of important people, made up of the mayor, his wife, or sometimes several distinguished guests from a few areas, like fashion, education, and such."

"Sports?" one of the boys, pale skinned with a shock of nearly white, blonde hair, suggested, his voice respectful of the host's big sister.

"Yes, and sports. A Yankees pitcher, I think. Or the Mets. Well, there was a lot of excitement and so many pizza places joined the contest. So many that the contest had to be held in stages, sort of like when ball teams compete to get to a pennant race or the World Series. Everyone in the city was cheering on their favorites. My uncle tells me that our family cheered on several, given that we love pizza from Joe's in the Village to John's on 44th, among several others."

The little heads continued to bob in agreement.

"For a few weeks, there were tasting contests all over town. Some were turned into big block parties, like in the Bronx or Queens. Others were more…were fancier affairs held in museums and art galleries by the big shots. My mom went to one at an art museum. But, when the big day of the final contest arrived, the entire contest had come down to just three pizza places. One from downtown, one from midtown and one from across the river, Brooklyn, I think."

A couple of the boys asked, meekly (they were only four, after all), if their favorites had made it into the final three.

"Maybe. Uncle didn't say which three were in the final taste test, but I'm sure at least one of our favorites was there. But, let me continue."

The big sister paused for a moment to pull her legs up into the chair, causing one of her two Siamese cats, young Lulu, to hop up and nestle into her lap after having lurked about the chair for a few minutes. Her other Siamese, Luna, was quite a bit more shy and had disappeared into the sanctuary of the back master bedroom when the rambunctious children had arrived around two hours earlier.

"So, all the press and news people were there. The TV stations. The radio. Even the Internet news. The contest set up a table outside City Hall, down near Ground Zero, with large, mobile pizza food trucks stationed nearby so that the pizzas would be piping hot when the tasting began."

"I've been to City Hall. My uncle works there," one of the boys, dark haired, with deep brown eyes, offered.

"Yes, City Hall," the big sister replied, nodding her recognition of the dark haired boy's comment. "Once they had set up the tables, the blind taste test would start."

"Our old dachshund is blind," called another boy, who was quite small, with unruly reddish blonde hair that he tried to smooth back with his left hand.

"Oh, that's sad. But, a blind test doesn't mean the tasters are blind. It means that they don't know…so are blind to…the makers…the pizza shops who are the last three contestants."

Once she saw the nods from the wild hair boy and the others, the big sister continued, lowering her voice so that the boys had to lean in to hear her better, another tactic her uncle had shown her to help focus an audience.

"Once everything was set up, Mayor…hmmm, I forgot his name…anyway, Mayor Somebody stood and made a long speech, since that's what mayors do. He then introduced the judges. A panel of five, so there would not be a tie."

"A tie? My Dad stopped wearing ties. He says they make him look old," the dark haired boy with the uncle at City Hall offered, with a grin.

"Yes, a different kind of tie. Not one you wear around your neck, but when a score is even between two teams," the big sister replied, a hint of impatience in her voice.

"So, Mayor Somebody read out the names and the businesses of the judges. Four of the judges were from New York. A ball team player. A designer. An actor, an old one. And a local borough chief, a woman. But, the fifth and last person was a stranger to most of the crowd. He was selected via a Broadway contest, I think Uncle called it a lottery, for out-of-towners, tourists, so that there could be an unbiased judge."

"What's…unbi…unbiased?" asked the birthday boy, rubbing his eyes as his sister's stories often made him sleepy, as did their uncle's stories when the uncle and auntie visited.

"It's when you don't already have a favorite pizza place, since you are not from here," the big sister replied, signaling her little brother to not rub his eyes.

"So, as the pizzas came out…from the trucks so they would be hot…the five judges each had all three slices, one after the other. Since the contest was held outside, and there was a threat of rain, the mayor decided to speed up the contest. So, each judge, in order, ate three slices, picking which one they thought was the best. Then the next judge would do the same, pick his…or her favorite…and then the next judge would go."

"What kind of pizza?" asked one of the oldest of the boys, his dark, wiry hair trimmed neatly over his deep brown eyes.

"Pepperoni, of course. But, Uncle said in other tellings of the story, it's plain cheese and, in others, veggie supreme," the young storyteller responded, then continued.

"Now, as each judge picked their favorite, a helper placed a score on a scoreboard on the stage. Each pizza joint had a letter, A, B, or C, and not their name or where they were from. The board showed the buildup to the winner. Remember, the mayor called for the contest, so he wanted a lot of suspense, and he got it."

The boys all nodded in agreement with the suspense, since they all were curious as to which pizza would win.

"The first judge, the baseball pitcher, went through his pizza slices quickly, folding each one, in order, into the typical and proper way to eat pizza slices. He wolfed them down, since we all know pitchers are always hungry. After downing a large Cherry Coke, he made a huge burp, and picked 'C.'"

The boys all laughed at the big sister saying the word 'burp,' since, in their circles, such words were normally frowned upon.

The mother, who had retreated to the kitchen to help their nanny, but was leaning out the kitchen door from time to time to keep an eye on the little ones, smiled at her daughter's ability to keep the little boys tuned into her story when she saw all the giggling faces and heard the chuckles.

After the laughter had died down, the big sister used the eye contact tactic again and continued, even leaning toward the boys who seemed a little less attentive, in order to ensure they listened.

"The next judge was the fashion designer. One that all of the big magazines follow around. She was a little fastidious, so used a paper plate to hold and fold her pizza, so that her hands stayed clean as she ate about a third of each slice, which she studied very closely before actually biting into it, as if looking at the colors and the texture, which is what design people do. A number of loud guests in the crowd called for her to eat the whole slices, but we all know designers and models barely eat enough food, to stay skinny. So, she just froze those loud men with her stare. Finally, she selected 'A' for her best."

The big sister paused, because a couple of the boys had decided to practice frosty stares, to the giggling delight of the others. Once that amusement had subsided, she cleared her throat like a teacher would do, and moved on to the next judge.

"After the designer, the next judge was the actor, who was old, so ate very slowly, almost too slowly. But, before he ate, he made all sorts of gestures and silent miming over the pizzas, each time one was given to him to taste. The crowd roared in laughter at his antics, that's why he was play-acting, and he smiled his huge, toothy smile each time. The old actor only folded the pizza into a loose fold, more of a valley, and only ate the tips of each entry, chewing so, so slowly, with more gestures and silent acting, that the scorekeeper almost dozed off. But, finally, after the last bite had been taken and the actor seemed to swoon, that's almost faint, after his final piece, he picked number 'C,' just like the pitcher had done."

"My mom is an actor. She would do the same thing," the smallest of the boys called out, using hand gestures to mimic his idea of what the actor judge had done.

The big sister nodded to the boy and then hushed the group, which was starting to let their minds wander, so she decided to speed up to the exciting part of the story.

"The next judge was the borough chief, who spent a lot of time getting ready to eat her slices, asking questions, and, as politicians do, making sure her name was mentioned a number of times. Then, she first set each slice carefully on a paper plate."

"Why paper plates and not real plates?" the brother asked.

"To make it feel more like a pizza place in the city," the big sister replied, then continued.

"The borough chief then lined her slices up in front of her, ensured the cameras could see her, then closed her eyes and one of her aides placed a dark blindfold over her eyes. Very dramatic, but there were rumors the borough chief was going to run for mayor, so she wanted as much publicity out of the contest as she could get. So, with the help of her aide, she slowly sampled each slice, using a napkin when she folded the pizza to bite it, allowing her hands to get a little messy, but not too messy. Uncle said it was just the right amount of messy for a politician. After taking strong bites from all three slices, the borough chief went back and had second bites from each one. Finally, after a short speech on how all the pizza deserved to win, and that she was saddened that she could only pick one slice, she picked 'A,', just as the designer judge had done."

"So, let's recap. How many votes have there been so far?" the big sister asked of the four-year-olds.

"Two?"

"Five?"

"Four?"

"Why are they voting? I thought they were judging?"

"I dunno."

After a number of similar comments floated around the little semicircle, the big sister sighed and enlightened the little ones.

"Four. Four votes so far. With 'A' getting two votes and the 'C' pizza getting two votes."

"Oh, so 'B' will get a vote from the tourist?" the little brother asked, rubbing his eyes. "That's the fair way to play, isn't it?"

Sighing a little more heavily, and sensing her audience was one silly comment away from losing all interest and breaking away to play until the cake came, the big sister decided to get to the major turning point quickly.

"It's a tie! Two to two! So, unless the tourist picks 'B,' which had no picks so far, either 'A' or 'C' will be the winner. So, the crowd was hushed. It was so, so quiet. Even…even the subways underground stopped running to hear the final judge speak. The pigeons, usually trying to beg a meal from people in the crowd, also quieted down and turned to face the stage to hear the fifth and last judge. Even the cars zooming around downtown all stopped and opened their windows so that they could hear what the final judge said. Why, even the airplanes and helicopters slowed down so that they could hear."

Watching the eyes of the little boys grow larger with anticipation, the big sister paused for effect and then continued.

"The final three slices were placed in front of the last judge, the tourist, the man from out of town. No one was sure what his business was. Some thought he was a banker. Others said he was a government man. Others claimed he was actually foreign, but had visited for years. Anyway, for a couple of minutes, nothing happened, as the tourist judge seemed to be asking for something. He first asked the scorekeeper, who was standing nearby so he could hear the tourist's final pizza choice. Everyone saw the scorekeeper suddenly and violently shake his head and step back from the tourist, a wild, scared look on the scorekeeper's face. Next, the tourist asked the helper ladies, who had been bringing the pizzas and then taking away the finished plates each time. One of the helper ladies seemed to nearly faint at whatever the tourist had asked her, and she had to be helped off the stage by the other helper lady who just kept shaking her head as she left. The other judges seemed confused, but sat quietly, looking from the tourist judge to the mayor. Yet, no one seemed to want to answer the tourist judge. Finally, the tourist called over to the mayor, and called out his fateful question, which was...?"

"What? What?" shouted the group of boys almost as one. "What did he say? What did the tourist say?"

"The tourist, seeming a bit flustered by everyone's reaction, called out in a loud, exasperated voice. A voice that was definitely not a New York voice, or anywhere nearby. He called out, 'Mayor, can I have...can I please have a knife and fork?' Yes, those were his shocking words! A knife...and...a...fork!"

Stunned silence blanketed the shocked boys, as stark disbelief formed on their little faces. Seeing their expected reactions, the big sister swept her hand across her brow in a dramatic gesture.

"Yes, just like you now, the crowd gasped, not believing what they had heard, and leaned back, as if to try to get away from the stage and the crazy tourist. The entire crowd of people then went silent, except for a couple of roustabouts who had helped set up the stage and were waiting in the wings to dismantle it. They were wise guys, so repeated the tourist's question for the mayor, saying, 'Yeah, your honor, you gonna give this guy a knife and fork?' To which the mayor stammered and then stood, his face blanched, wondering how to address such an egregious breach of New York pizza eating etiquette."

The group of little boys all leaned toward the big sister, each one looking almost frightened at what the mayor might say.

"For the longest time, the mayor just stood there, not knowing what to do. For, if he gave the tourist a knife and fork, which someone would have to run to one of the food trucks to find them, the mayor would be violating a sacred New York way of life, in front of a crowd of witnesses, who were also voters, during an election year. While the mayor wavered, the borough chief, who had initially gasped at the tourist's request, began to grin at the mayor's dilemma. She then secretly told one of her aides to go find the knife and fork and give them, not to the tourist, but to the mayor, so people would see the mayor give the upstart tourist the knife and fork."

The big sister then waved her hand across the room, as if scanning the crowd at City Hall.

"As the mayor huffed and puffed, not knowing what to do with the offensive knife and fork that had mysteriously appeared in his hands, the other judges shifted their seats away from the tourist. The designer looked like she would faint. The actor was carrying on a silent dialogue with the frightened scorekeeper, who was trying to hold down the pitcher, who seemed to want to hustle the tourist off the stage. Only the borough chief seemed to be enjoying the scene, but not too much, and mumbled some words about welcoming outside, alien ideas, but those in the crowd booed her into silence."

"Finally, after watching the mayor just stand there, the tourist reached over and took the knife and fork from the mayor's drooping hands. The tourist then turned to his first slice of pizza and, holding the fork like a devil's trident, he plunged the offending cutlery into the still steaming mound of luscious cheeses, tasty, spicy sauce, just right pepperonis, and delicately crisp New York City dough."

"Oh!" gasped the boys, turning their faces away from the big sister's gestures, where she was mimicking using a knife and fork on the pizza.

Cries of fright rose up among the younger boys, while the older boys, by a few months, bravely held back their own calls for pizza justice.

"Never!"

"How did they let him into the city?"

"Close the bridges and the tunnels! Stop the trains! Don't let the tourist in!"

"Silly, he's already here, using…using…those…those things on our beloved pizza!"

"Mommy!"

The big sister, fearing the ruckus would bring the nannies, paused her story and then hopped around the room to console the more frightened of the little boys. Once the murmuring had died down, she returned to her chair, took a deep, dramatic breath, and continued.

"Then, with one swift motion of the deadly knife, the tourist lopped off a chunk of the first pizza, ate it, and then did the same with the other two slices. As the tourist was cutting up each of his pizza slices, the people in the crowd, almost all New Yorkers born and bred, began to moan and exclaim in horror at what they were seeing."

"'No! The end is here! Run! Help us, Mayor Somebody! No fork madness!' were just a few of the things the angry crowd called out. Mothers were covering the eyes of their little ones, lest the babes of the city be scarred forever. Grown men, burly, strong men, all began to cry, as they, too, could not bring themselves to believe what they were seeing. All the priests and rabbis and ministers and holy men began praying, some calling out that it was the end of times, whatever that is. Even the police and firefighters, on standby for the event, were dumbstruck from the shock and simply stood about, trying to comfort one another. Some say that the lights on Broadway flickered at that moment!"

The wriggling of the boys was becoming more intense again, so the mother stepped out to find out what was going on, but the big sister waved her back, signaling that the story was almost over.

"Finally, above the moans and cries from the distraught crowd and the mumblings of the thoroughly discombobulated mayor, the tourist raised his hand to give his verdict on the best pizza. But, just as he was about to speak, a little old lady, standing near the front of the crowd, called out, 'Never let it be known that this New Yorker stood still for such an insult.' She then threw herself onto the stage, scrambled over to the tourist and ripped the knife and fork out of his hands, swept the disgraced pizza slices off the table and into the crowd, where nearby people jumped back, lest they be tainted by the disfigured and deformed slices from the tourist's senseless butchery. The old lady then pushed the tourist over to the mayor and shouted that the city 'must have its honor restored,' or something to that effect."

"The mayor, after flinching at the tough little old lady's demand, finally spoke. But, he was so flustered that, instead of saying something that would calm and console the crowd and save himself from the angry little lady, he made a mayoral decree instead."

"The mayor called out, 'In light of this…this savage assault on our very way of life…due to this unfortunate development, I declare this contest null and void. There will be no pizza in New York City until we have called another contest and picked a winner.'"

All around the living room, jaws were hanging open in disbelief when the little boys heard what the mayor had said.

"Now, what the mayor had meant to say was there would be 'no winning pizza' until a new contest, but he was so flustered by the tourist's actions, the borough chief's veiled attempt to get the mayor to hand over the offensive knife and fork, and by the angry mob, embodied by the fierce, little old lady, that he misspoke. Yet, as soon as he had said it, it was the law of the land, since he was the mayor, and all the newspapers, television, internet, and everybody, announced that there would be no pizza in New York, by mayoral decree, until some unknown future date."

"As soon as the words were out of the mayor's mouth, the people in the crowd, initially frozen in place at the stark news that there would be no pizza, began to run away, but not to home. Where do you think they were going?"

One of the quieter boys, another starkly blonde kid with piercing blue eyes, raised his hand as he spoke.

"I think, big sister, that they are all going to the pizza places to buy the last pizzas?" the boy offered.

"Exactly! The people in the crowd, and all the people they called or spoke to, and everyone who had seen the news, descended on all the pizza joints in the city, even the not very good ones, and bought all the pizzas that could be bought. Before sundown, that is."

"Why sundown?" the same boy asked.

"Well, everyone knows that mayoral decrees begin at sundown," the big sister answered.

"So, after sundown, all the pizza places were shuttered. Closed up. Any restaurant or bar that had pizza on the menu had to stop making them. All the grocery stores had to remove all the frozen pizzas from their freezers and remove all the pizza makings from their shelves. Even our WM grocer's down the street!"

The big sister let the boys mumble to themselves in disbelief before she continued.

"So, for many, many days after, the only way to get a pizza in New York was to drive over to New Jersey or, and I shudder to think about it, take the train up to get Connecticut pizza, whatever that is. In the city, young entrepreneurs set up secret pizza parlors in abandoned restaurants, but you had to know the secret code word to get in. Church ladies were secretly baking pizzas in the church basements and smuggling them to members. Why, even the firemen got in on it and were making secret pizzas in the firehouses and then driving their fire trucks around at night to deliver pizzas to the orphans and homeless. There were even stealthy pizza boats!"

Scanning the gaping jaws and wide eyes of her little brother's friends, the big sister raised her voice, almost as a call to arms.

"Can you imagine, truly imagine? Not having pizza for days, weeks, months and even, dare I say it? Years?" the big sister suddenly cried at the top of her lungs, both for effect and to give the boys a little jolt.

"Shuttered pizza joints. Pizza speak-easies hiding in dark alleys. Even deep dish Chicago pizza was smuggled in, horror of horrors. Rich people had pizza flown in, secretly, from Naples, Italy. Children cried themselves to sleep each night with no pizza. College students had only ramen to eat! Our dad had to sneak pizza in from New Jersey for us! Oh, the tragedy! Sheer tragedy! The tragedy of it all!"

"No! It can't happen!" the little boy who was the crier suddenly screamed, tears beginning to run down his face.

Concerned that the nannies would hear and come running, thereby making her mother mad, the big sister moved quickly to the end of the tale. She also did not want to really scare the little boys, since she had a big, kind heart, after all.

"Wait. No, no, it only lasted for a week, less than a week, until the mayor called another contest, retracted his decree and declared the best pizza in the city after a new panel of different judges, all true-blue New Yorkers this time, picked a pizza joint from the Village as the best."

The crying boy seemed to be bolstered by what he heard, so he wiped his eyes and smiled.

"So, the lesson here, my little ones, is to beware of those who might think lightly of our deep pizza traditions, in the city. And, to be on the lookout for those who bring strange and dangerous ideas to our dinner and lunch tables. New ideas and new foods are good, but some traditions should not be tampered with. Why, if we allowed such things as knives and forks for pizza, what's next? Forks for sushi? Forks for ice cream? Knives and forks for...no, not that...doughnuts? Bagels? Where, I ask you, good children of the city, would such fork madness ever stop? Where?"

The boys all seemed on the verge of a group shout, with the crying boy threatening his floodgates again, when the doorbell stopped them all short.

Ding, dong!

"Cake!"

The boys' collective cry for the finally arriving cake immediately distracted them from the creeping horrors of the great pizza scare tale and provided a needed safety valve for all the energy they had bottled up in nascent anger at the knife and fork tourist.

With the birthday boy leading, the boys all rose as one and, with quick nods to the big sister, coupled with mumbled thanks for the scary tale, they rushed to the door to mob the birthday boy's father who had arrived with the cake in a huge, flat box.

The big sister smiled at the little friends of her brother and silently thanked her uncle for the old story that had kept the boisterous little ones quiet until the cake had arrived. She then gently picked up the snoozing Lulu and placed her back into the chair before heading to the dining room to help with the cake.

"Honey, how did you keep them so quiet?" the mother asked as she brought the nannies in to also help with the cake and to keep their charges from getting too messy.

"Mom, remember when Uncle was here and we had pizza that time? Well, I told them that story Uncle told us after I was shocked by his using a knife and fork on the pizza that night."

"Yes, I remember you said something not very nice to your uncle, didn't you?" the mother half-joked and half-admonished her daughter.

"Yes. I said, 'Uncle, you can never, I mean never, ever, do that (use a knife and fork) in a public pizza place with me,'" the big sister replied, grinning from ear to ear at the sudden stares of the little boys who had overheard her.

'Her uncle was the tourist?' was then whispered by the surprised boys all around the room, while the nannies laid out the plates, napkins, and forks for the cake. While the big sister did not confirm the tourist in the story was her uncle, the boys, already shaken up by the wild tale, used her comment to jump to the conclusion, right or wrong, that the crazy tourist was, indeed, her uncle.

Fortunately, just before the boys could call out the big sister's and, by association, the birthday boy's uncle for being the fiend who nearly destroyed New York, the father called from the kitchen to get ready to sing, because he was bringing in the cake.

So, turning to the prospect of the cake, the boys, the big sister, the nannies, and the mom and dad all started singing 'Happy Birthday.'

The father then appeared with the cake, candles blazing.

All the boys stared at the flickering flames, mesmerized by the cheerfulness of the four thick, blue candles as the father placed the large sheet cake in front of the lucky birthday boy, who leaned in to blow out the candles. All his friends leaned forward as well, hoping to hear his wish. They finished the birthday song just as he blew out all the candles with one breath.

"...birthday to you!"

With the candles out, the singing boys, once they saw the cake, suddenly stopped singing, while the birthday boy leaned away from the cake in sudden surprise.

Silence.

Shocked, dead still, silence.

All around the table, the usually loud and restless bunch of four-year-olds, including the birthday boy, simply sat speechless, several with their mouths hanging open and a couple with their hands thrown up to their faces in shock.

Pizza!

The birthday cake was made to look like a giant pepperoni pizza!

Puzzled at the eerie silence of the normally loud little boys, the father shrugged and quickly placed slices on all the plates, slipping the last slice, a bit larger than the rest, onto his son's plate.

"Go ahead, boys, you can start now," the mother called from the side, wondering why none of the boys had started.

Slowly, one by one, each of the boys picked up their respective forks and, turning the forks over in their small hands, stared hard at the shiny metal things. They all then turned to stare at the birthday boy, to see what he would do.

The birthday boy, encouraged by his dad standing nearby, slowly lowered his fork to his large slice of pizza cake. All around him, the other boys' eyes grew wider and wider as they watched, with the crier adding sniffles to his horrified stare.

Then, with no warning, the young birthday boy, inspired by his big sister's sweeping tale, jerked his fork back from the cake, held the offensive instrument over his head, and then tossed it to the floor.

"No...fork...madness!" the birthday boy cried out in a loud, almost eerily adult voice.

On such a dramatic signal from the birthday boy, the revolt of the four-year-olds of the Upper East Side began, and the boys all tossed their forks under the table, to the horror of the nannies, who all then tried to retrieve the forks at the same time.

The boys then called out in unison.

"No knife and fork madness!"

"No fork madness!"

"No fork madness!"

All the shouting boys, to include the birthday boy, then picked up their slices of pizza-cake and gobbled the slices down as if they were slices of actual pizza. However, cake doesn't fold as well as pizza, so chunks of cake and icing were flying all about the room, causing the boys to break into robust laughter, followed by loud play, which included dodging attempts by the nannies to get them all to use their forks. Under the table, Lulu and even the shy Luna were gobbling up the many crumbs falling from the boys.

The parents, flabbergasted at the antics of the usually well-mannered children, to include their own son, turned to the big sister for an explanation, their searching eyes asking their daughter the silent question. The mother then voiced what both parents were wondering.

"Madylan, dear, have you done anything to cause Greyson and his friends to, you know...?" the mother asked, her voice low so as not to sound accusatory.

Madylan, the storytelling big sister, with her cheeks a little red, took a deep breath, smiled at her parents, winked at her little brother and their own beloved nanny, scanned his friends' gleeful faces, and only then offered her explanation.

"Well, we are, everyone, one and all, true blue New Yorkers...aren't we?"

With her parents still confused, Madylan, the new favorite storyteller of Carnegie Hill, ignored her fork, picked up her own slice of pizza-cake, carefully folded it using both hands, and then took a huge bite, giggling the whole time.

4

THE MERFOLK OF KENNEBUNK COVE, MAINE

"Hurry, it's going to get away!" the young girl called out to the small boy, her voice loud enough to escape the din of the surf and to grab the attention of the small boy, who was lingering over a tidal pool, common along the uneven, rock strewn beaches along most of Maine's southern coast.

The small boy reluctantly looked up and, casting his eyes up and down the broad, windswept Ogunquit Beach, he saw that his mother was not too far away up the beach and that his father was nearby as well, making repairs to the sandcastle the boy and his big sister had made earlier. It was not a grand sandcastle, and the grey sand of the Maine beach was gritty and wet, so did not hold complex shapes well, but it was still a castle to be proud of. The boy had stocked the castle with a variety of beach pebbles, shells, bits of washed up seaweed, and even a couple of small sand crabs for the half moat his dad had built with him.

"What is it?" the boy called back to his big sister who was frantically waving at him.

"You have to come see! Quick! It's going to swim away!" the big sister called as she stepped closer to the surf, a little rough for early July.

Kicking at the sand, the boy took a meandering path toward his sister, stopping to check any interesting bit that he might come upon. Using the toe of his water shoes, he'd gently kick at objects, study them for a moment, and then continue on. His progress was so slow, however, that, by the time he was close enough to his big sister to see what the fuss was all about, she was staring out to the ocean, watching a small dark shape, with glints of silver, wriggle its way back to deeper waters.

"Uh, what was it?" the boy asked, but was then distracted by a shell tumbling over and over in the retreating surf.

The big sister, somewhat cross with her little brother for taking so long to get to her for him to see the fantastic creature she had wanted him to see, just waved her hand and stepped out of the surf back to the wet sand.

"Too late. You missed it. It was quite amazing, though. I've only seen such a thing once or twice," the sister replied, her brow furrowed, indicating she was forming something else in her mind. "That is, when I was much younger."

"Well, what was it? Tell me!" the boy yelled, quickly frustrated with his evasive sister. "Did Dad see it, too? He'll tell me. Dad!"

The children's father, a fair ways back up the beach, looked up from his castle repair, hands streaked with grey sand, and waved back at the two.

"Silly, adults can't see them," the sister suddenly said, the seed of a thought finally sprouting in her head. "Only children can see them."

"See what? Why can't big people see them?" the boy asked, stepping closer to look out to sea just like his sister was doing.

The sister took a moment to look up and down the beach, to ensure no one was nearby. She then leaned over to whisper to her younger brother, who, understanding that he was about to hear something special and maybe secret, hunched his shoulders and leaned in as well, ready to hear the amazing thing.

"Merfolk, that's what was here," the big sister said in a quiet, whispered voice.

"Mer...? What?" the boy asked, his own usually loud, brash voice a hoarse whisper.

"Mermaids and mermen. Mer-people. Folk. Merfolk," the sister replied, lowering her voice even more as a couple of large golden retrievers jogged by with their humans in tow. "People who live with the fish, dolphins, and whales, in the sea."

"What? Really? I wanna see!" the boy cried out and stepped into the chilly surf, his eyes scanning the water for something that might look like what he had seen on TV or online.

Nothing. No fins broke through the choppy water. No sea songs lilted up from the water like in a cartoon he had seen.

"Not true," the boy then retorted, crossing his arms over his bare chest. "You're just saying that so you won't tell me what you really saw."

"Look, here's the thing," the sister replied, wrapping her arm around her little brother's sand covered shoulders. "Yes, they are magical creatures, I know. And, they are hard to see. But, the younger you are, the more likely you will see them. Remember the dragons you saw when we were driving to Virginia last Easter? In the clouds?"

"Yes! I saw dragons. Big, puffy, white and grey dragons!" the boy answered with gusto.

"So, if there are dragons, why not merfolk?" the sister asked in her matter-of-fact voice.

For a long moment, the little boy's face was a contortion of different emotions as he thought through what his big sister had just said. Eventually, he slowly began to nod his head in agreement, lowering it like a conspirator so that no one else could see.

"Remember how Uncle says that, as we get bigger, a lot of the magic of childhood falls away," the sister replied, putting both her arms over her little brother's broad shoulders. "You have to go to college. You have to get a job. So, you work all the time. Get married. Then have kids yourself. So, before all that grownup responsibility, Uncle said there is a brief, 'all too fleeting' he called it, time when the magic finds the children."

"Oh. I know...I know I have a magic dresser. Where trucks and toys and even Pokémon just appears. Out of thin air!" the boy replied in an excited voice.

"Yes, I used to have a magic pillow when I was little like you and many wonderful things would appear. Usually after a visit from Uncle and Auntie. One time Uncle came to visit New York for work by himself, but the magic still happened," the sister said, with a wistful air. "Now, I don't see as much magic as you, because I'm getting to be so old."

"Sorry. I wish you could have my magic," the boy answered, patting his sister's hand. "But, you saw the mer...the fish people, so you must have some magic?"

The sister smiled at her little brother, whom she sometimes called 'bother brother,' but knew he really loved her and she him.

"Yes, I suppose I did. You know, this summer, or maybe the next, might be the last one of magic for me," the sister then said, with a serene acceptance in her voice. "It's not a bad thing, but I do wish I could keep some of the magic, even when I'm old."

"You can always have my magic, because I will always be younger than you," the boy answered in that rational way toddlers often have, and then walked over to look at a tiny pile of white and tan shells that were caught in a small pool.

"Pirates," the boy said suddenly, looking up and pointing out to sea.

Turning, the big sister looked for a pirate ship, or any ship, since her little brother, at his age, thought all large, ocean going ships were pirate ships.

Just coming around the point of land north of the beach, a large sailboat slipped quietly along, its white sails bulging from the windy day. While the sailboat did not look like a pirate ship to the big sister, she jumped at the opportunity to tell her brother a story.

"Look. Do you see the pirate flag? Dark and waving crazily in the wind?" the sister asked, lowering her voice to sound even more conspiratorial than earlier.

"Yes!" the boy answered, straining to see the flag, or any flag so far away.

"That ship reminds me of a story Uncle told us the last time we were all up here together. You were very little, so you don't remember. But, I do. Would you like to hear it?" the sister asked as she led the boy away from the surf and back toward the sandcastle when she saw that their mother had joined their father's repair efforts.

"Yes, but hungry," the ever growing little brother replied.

"Okay. I can tell you at lunch," the sister offered as they reached the parents.

Once the castle repairs were complete, photos taken, and a small flag, fashioned from a sprig of driftwood, carefully placed on the tower, the father helped the little boy return the sand crabs to a large, rocky tidal pool, explaining to the boy that the castle moat would probably dry out, which would not be good for the little creatures.

After the mercy mission was complete, the little group of beachcombers headed back to the small village of Kennebunkport, which was where they had their basecamp for a weeklong escape from New York.

After parking at their hotel, one of several grand resorts that sprawled along the Kennebunk River to the sea, the family quickly cleaned up, changed, and took the five-minute resort shuttle into the center of the charming little village.

Dragging at her mother's arm so that the siren songs of all the amazing shops would not delay them, the big sister held her little brother's hand, while she herded her father in front of them, and led the group to one of their favorite foodie spots in all of New England, the village's famous clam shack, just beside the bridge. For old timers, it was the new bridge, since the old swing bridge had been replaced with a more modern and utilitarian bridge that could better handle the hordes of summer tourists.

While their father stood in the inevitably long line to turn in their orders, one clam roll (with bellies), one scallop roll, one shrimp role, and, for the boy, a hotdog, their mother found an open table near the back of the plaza, just beside the rocky embankment where the ducks liked to congregate at the river's edge. Once she had claimed the table, she opened up her work phone and, telling the two children to not leave the table, she lost herself in work emails and project details.

Given that the typical wait at the wildly popular shack was at least an hour, from the time of stepping in the line, making the order, and then getting the order, the big sister knew she had enough time to tell her story, paraphrased from the one her uncle had told them a year before. So, she asked her little brother to sit quietly and to try to not ask a lot of questions. Once she was certain she had his attention, or as much attention as someone so young could give, she began the tale, her voice low and melodic.

"You know, a long time ago, when Uncle first started coming here, with his older son from New Hampshire, he said that the bridge just over there was a real drawbridge, or, actually a swinging bridge, to let the tall sailboats from that little cove in the river get out to the sea," the sister began, swinging her legs under her as she spoke and using her hands to show her brother how a swing bridge worked. "They didn't even have cell phones back then, that's how long ago it was. But, the clam shack was always there, at least."

"Yes, just a few feet from here, on a cloudy and windy day...why, just like today...the drawbridge had been opened to let one of the tall sailing ships float down the river, past the village and even our hotel, to the sea. A sea full of all manner of surprises and, says Uncle, full of some of that magic we were talking about at the beach. Let's see if we can't bring the magic one more time. Yes, one…more…time…?"

The big sister's voice joined the other sounds of the bustling dock, of the cars and people along the main drag, and of the water below. Her words flowed like the lapping of the river against the pilings nearby, giving her tale a rhythmic pulse that caused the little boy, already tired from a long day of earnest beach play, to lean against the top of the picnic table. While he did not actually fall asleep, he did let his eyelids flutter a bit as his big sister's story unfolded all around him, his loving family, and the cheerful little village by the happy river on its way to the wondrous sea.

Smiling at her content little brother, the big sister began her tale.

Years and years ago, one early, overcast afternoon, the aged iron of the old swing bridge groaned as it opened, sounding like an old man trying to stand after sitting far too long on a hard, wooden bench. The counter-weights pulled the small section of road to one side, while traffic, people, dogs, cars, and bicycles, all waited on opposite sides of the opening.

Not too long after the bridge had opened, a large sailboat, more like a small ship in the eyes of the tourist crowd, slowly made its way through the narrow passage and into the lower part of the Kennebunk River. The boat's tall, central mast seemed to sway in the muted light, causing the onlookers to wonder if the craft might bang into the bridge, or into one of the restaurants overlooking the river. Fortunately, the mast did not bang into anything as the boat made its way through the town's collection of docks and colorful riverside buildings, thanks mainly to the boat using its power motor and not sails to move through the choppy water in the narrow part of the river.

As the boat passed well beyond the city docks and disappeared behind the buildings lining the river, a collective cheer was heard on both sides of the river when the bridge began to groan again as it slowly moved back into place.

Not far from the clam shack, where a thoughtful sister would tell her story years later, one young girl stood apart from the crowd. She was tall for her age, and thin, with jet black hair, pale skin, and deep, hazel-green eyes that flickered back and forth as she watched the crowd surge toward the bar blocking the road. Her clothes were as any other of her age might wear, except that her light, gold-colored scarf, worn even on a summer afternoon, seemed to shimmer from the dim, reflected light on the river, even though the girl was standing quite a ways back from the river's edge. In sensible trousers and wearing a light teal jacket over a white blouse, the girl blended in with the crowd of mostly day tourists, a few vacationers staying in town, and the rare townsfolk. In fact, she blended in so well that you would have had trouble picking her out of the crowd that day, which is exactly how she wanted it.

If anyone had noticed the girl, she would have been dismissed as a summer resident, having been seen around the village and the beaches, especially Gooch's Beach and even Goose Rocks, peddling her oversized bike, awkwardly, like kids who learned how to ride later in life. From the snatches of conversation overheard by the other summer kids, the girl was staying with an aunt who was a summer worker at one of the better resorts, all of which prided themselves on their guests' privacy, so little was known of the girl by the other kids exploring the village and environs each summer, and because the girl tended to wander about alone. When other kids had tried to make friends with her, she had always had an excuse to fade away into the background, so the more outgoing summer kids had dismissed her in favor of easier topics.

All the summer kids, that is, except one, a young boy who had crossed paths with the young girl several times and had tried to strike up at a conversation a few times, but had always failed. He would sigh to himself and say 'next summer' and move on to more important things like swimming, fishing, going out on his uncle's lobster boat, and listening to ghost stories at night in the park down by the old yacht club.

As the weathered bridge groaned and rattled back into place, the bridge keeper, an old, wizened man, with an even older helper, a severe, but kind little old lady, moved to lift the bar blocking the road. Once the bridge span had finally clicked into place, the little man and the wisp of a lady moved the blocking pole and then scurried, almost like the crabs one could see along the shore, to the other side and moved that pole as well.

Once the poles were lifted and the crowds were able to move across the bridge, the girl stepped away from the flow of people and stood near the bridge keeper's hut and watched those very people stream by. After the bunched up crowd had thinned out, the girl then stepped to the path and, looking around her carefully, walked over the bridge to the Kennebunkport side. As she crossed the short section of road spanning the river, the girl leaned over the railing and, oddly, appeared to wave at the water, which the girl was certain no one saw, as she knew no one paid much attention to a child's antics during summer vacations.

At least, that's what the girl had thought until she saw, standing on the far dock, just to the right of the old candy shop after the bridge, an old, old man who seemed to be watching the bridge and her crossing.

Pausing, pretending to look at the ducks waddling along the riverbank, the girl watched the old man out of the corner of her sharp eyes.

"Who are you? Maybe...maybe you are the one?" the girl said under her breath, her voice almost musical, as if she were a trained singer, except that she was far too young to have had much training.

Down in the water, as if the fish had heard the girl, several large splashes happened one after another, but no fish could be seen.

"Right, I must move on," the girl said to herself, nodding her thanks to the ripples in the water that had reminded her that time, like those ripples, would soon fade away.

Reaching the far side of the bridge, the girl turned and looked back, like she had been taught by...well, let's just say she had been taught to always 'check her six' by her very thorough teachers. Checking her six meant that she always made sure she not only looked where she was going, but also checked what was happening behind her, at her six, as on the face of a clock.

No one following, the girl decided, and then turned back to look for the old man.

Gone. Nowhere to be seen, but he had let me see him, the girl realized, so the old man must have wanted her to either follow him, or was letting her know that someone knew she was in town again, and looking for...well, looking for what she was looking for.

Turning back to the main drag, the girl headed up to that critical information source all youth know about, where all the news, rumors, and general current affairs are discussed by the children, as the parents chatter on, oblivious to their children's own chatter.

The local ice cream parlor.

("I want ice cream," the little brother interrupted.

"Shush, later," the big sister hushed him and continued.)

Yes, nearly any information on who was doing what, who had come into town and who had left, which boats were running and which were laid up for repairs, who had the best catch and who came in bust, could be had at those little news bureaus. Most importantly, since kids are kids, anything unusual or strange that might have happened recently would be ripe for discussion around the ice cream parlor stools or the seats outside.

Fortunately, for the girl seeking information on the week's happenings, the village had two major ice cream parlors. Remember, this was long before the chain stores would invade such quaint towns in later years.

Arriving at the first shop, Rocky's, near the large car park, the girl ordered a small cup of something called sea mist. She bought a cup because, even though she had tried over the previous summers, she had not yet mastered the art of licking a cone, although she was certainly well within the age range when most youths would have ordered a cone. She also looked old enough, in fact, to not raise any adult eyebrows at her wandering around alone in the village.

Sitting along the railing outside of the bustling shop, the girl kept her head down, shielding her eyes, which tended to attract undue attention from the adults, who always seemed to comment on them in passing. While she tasted her treat, shuddering from the intense cold she felt after taking a small bite, she listened closely to the chatter of the children, filtering out the babble and focusing on those tidbits that told her the newsworthy items of the day.

"Two boats lost rudders, just outside the jetty," a young boy was saying to a friend. "Yes, in two days. Two rudders. My friend's dad is mad because he just had his repaired. No. No one has even found them and they should have at least washed ashore with the tides."

The girl let that conversation fade into the background and leaned closer to a group of tween girls, close to her own age, and listened to their fast paced banter, which almost gave the girl a headache as it was always hard for her to understand the fast chattering girls.

"Old. Sooooo old, he was," one of the tweens said, rolling her eyes. "But, Mom said he was okay. Came out of nowhere, just beyond the old sail maker's house. She said Dad walked right into him. I didn't see it. Didn't faze the old guy. He just picked himself up with his long walking stick and waved off any help. Dad was worried about getting sued, I'm sure."

"What did he look like, the old man?" another of the tweens asked.

"Old. Nice clothes, but old. Odd hat, though. Looked like one you'd see in an old movie or something. Roundy. Oh, and he had an accent, so not from around here. Maybe Boston? Or English?" the first tween replied, and then turned the conversation to the boys they had met that week.

The girl then listened to several other chats, but none held any new information, so, she dropped her unfinished cup of ice cream into the bin and crossed the little village square to head to the second ice cream parlor, which was along one of the raised docks that extended into the river.

Stepping into line at the second shop, The Wobbly Dock, the girl almost passed out from being slammed by the strong aroma of coffee, the shop's main draw, in addition to serving ice cream. The coffee aroma was so strong that she immediately sat down at one of the few empty chairs and took a few deep breaths.

Coffee, especially the espresso the man in front of her had ordered, with its lethal amount of caffeine, was dangerous for her kind, the girl knew, but the need for information outweighed the dangers. Besides, she told herself, she was not going to drink any, no matter how delicious and amazing it smelled.

Steeling herself, the girl finally stood and ordered another small ice cream cup, simple vanilla, wrapped the cup in several napkins to protect her hands from the cold, and stepped to the little clutch of tables just outside the door to get away from the nearly intoxicating fragrance of coffee and the stranger's espresso.

Since the little place was full of the afternoon coffee crowd, which was mostly adults, only a few youths were there having ice cream. Sitting with her back to the largest group of kids, the girl listened carefully and, once she heard what they were talking about, she turned slightly so she could see the speaker.

A tall boy, close to her own age and vaguely familiar, was talking to a group of four or five boys and one girl, all about the same age as the speaker. He was tanned and brown haired with blond streaks, no doubt from a lot of sun. Probably from being on boats, the girl decided, watching the boy's movements out of the corner of her eye.

"I tell you, I saw it happen. As clear as day. We were no farther than thirty yards away. The few sailboats around us had to trim sails and use motors, it was that calm," the boy said. "Four times it rang. And loud. As if three-footers were bashing into it."

"Three-footers? Really?" one of the tallest boys scoffed, slouching, with body language signaling he did not believe anything the other boy was saying.

The girl's ears picked up and she let out a small gasp, attracting the attention of the sailing boy who had spoken first.

"Hey, hi. Did you hear them ring, too? When there's no wind nor surf, sister?" the boy asked, waving at the girl to get her attention.

Startled that the boy had noticed her, the girl's first reaction was to hide her face and flee, yet, she also needed to know more, so she forced herself to calm her voice as she replied.

"Once. Long ago. Someone said something about underwater currents causing it. But, it was pretty strange," the girl replied, trying to make her voice sound more like the kids who had been talking, while she tried to keep her hands from shaking at being talked to by the oddly familiar boy.

"Strange. Yes. See, I'm not crazy," the sailing boy called to his friends.

"When did…when was this?" the girl then asked, crossing her fingers as she'd seen kids do when stressed, and then dared to look the tall boy in the eyes.

"Two days ago, maybe around noon. I was going to go back out, but we had rudder…issues, so couldn't," the boy replied, his own eyes boring into the hypnotic eyes of the near-stranger, for he was a summer local and suddenly realized he had seen the girl before and had even tried to talked to her a few times.

"Rudder issues," the tall, slouching boy mimicked. "More like no rudder."

"How many. That is, how many times did you say the harbor buoy's bell rang?" the girl then asked, her heart skipping a beat as she waited for a confirmation that she had heard correctly.

"Why? What?" the boy answered, distracted by the girl's eyes to the point he had to shake his head and collect himself. "How many? Four times. And, even. I'd say a long breath between each peel. Now that I'm thinking about it, it made my skin crawl a little."

"Thank you," the girl replied in a quiet voice, turning her face away from the tall boy's piercing and far too inquisitive eyes.

Waving her nearly full cup as a goodbye, the girl then stepped off of her stool and, being careful to not look back, walked to the street side of the dock and turned down one of the colorful alleys lined with cheerful shops. Near the main art gallery, the girl found a bench, more of a half-log with legs, and sat, her hands trembling at the news.

("What's a harbor boy?" the little brother asked, stopping his sister's flow.

"Buoy. Booo—wee. It's those large swaying floats we see out in the water. They mark the channels and the dangerous rocks under the water," the sister replied.

"Auntie has a buoy bell in the garden," the little brother replied.

"Oh, yes. The one that looks like a lighthouse, with the lobster clapper. Yes, like that, but bigger," the sister answered. "Now, listen.")

"Four bells," the girl then said to herself, her melodic voice obviously stressed. "Four! They've halved my watch already! Not enough time. They said I'd have more time. Why now? I'm so close. Why now?"

"Why now what?" a newly familiar voice asked not far from her ear.

Looking up in a panic, the girl saw the smiling, oddly kind face of the sailing boy who had just spoken of the buoy bell. He was alone, but several of his friends were standing at the alley entrance, obviously trying to call him to join them.

The girl, nearly panic stricken at the appearance of the boy and by the fact that he had heard her mumblings, stammered and, thinking her cup was a drink instead of melted ice cream, put it to her lips to take a drink while she thought up a reply. Except, of course, it wasn't a drink, so the melted ice cream dribbled down her cheeks, with a large blob landing on the right front of her jacket, causing her to give a little yelp and leap up, bumping into the boy and smearing her spilled ice cream all over his own jacket.

The girl then mumbled apologies and tried to use her sleeve to wipe off the boy's jacket. The boy waved her off, chuckling kindly at her efforts. She then offered to clean it and even to give the boy her own jacket. As she moved to remove her jacket, the boy held up his hands in protest and, after a bit of back and forth, convinced the girl that the ice cream would rinse off easily from the waxed coating on his jacket. He also reached into his backpack, which the girl had not noticed, and took out a bottle of water, which he offered to the girl to rinse the ice cream off her own jacket. She did so and the boy then rinsed off his own, tossing the empty water bottle into a recycle bin a step or two away. The boy then brought the conversation back to why he had followed her.

"So, when you heard the bells, how many times did it ring? And, that calm day, when was it, if okay to talk about it?" the boy asked, his manner almost too formal, which surprised him, but he didn't want to scare the girl away, not after bumping into her again, but for the first time that summer.

The girl simply stared at the boy, wondering how to answer him without lying, since she never liked to lie and rarely did. Suddenly, her face brightened and she replied.

"Well, the number was different each time," the girl answered, happy she had not lied, but had not given the boy any information that might make him suspicious, or his friends, the two who had remained at the end of the alley after the others had moved on.

"Each time? How many times have you heard the bells during the calms?" the boy asked, a look of fleeting suspicion crossing his suntanned face.

Just as the girl was about to answer, with the truth, which she thought would shock the boy since she had heard the bells many, many times during calms over the years, the old man she had seen earlier abruptly appeared at the opposite end of the alley, near the small iron bridge that crossed from one dock to the next. The old man was beckoning to the girl, using his right hand, which held a long walking stick, while he held onto the iron railing with his left.

"Hey, do you know that old man? He's the one that Jess's dad knocked over, yesterday or the day before, I think. Odd bird. Wanders around town, turning up in out of the way places, mumbling to himself. Not sure he's safe. Let me walk over with you," the boy offered after the girl had stood and had stepped toward the small bridge.

The girl began to protest that it was okay, but the boy had gone ahead of her and was already talking to the old man.

"Yes, sir. There are several main ones, a couple of small ones. Statues? The park across from the yacht club has a large statue of a fisherman and his wife," the boy was saying when the girl caught up. "That's probably what you are looking for."

As the girl stepped onto the bridge, a loud ruckus erupted under the three in the water of the river below them. Unable to see what was going on because the planks of the bridge were too close together, the boy leaned out over the edge, but the old man pulled him back using the walking stick.

"No need, young man. The waterfowl are just stirring things up a bit. Right, my dear, my little seafarer?" the old man said, turning his question to the girl.

"Sir, you have the advantage," the girl replied, quite formally and with no hesitation, surprising the boy, but not the old man.

"I've waited a long time, little one, for your...for someone's arrival. When I heard the bells, I knew it was time to step out of the shadows," the old man answered.

Sweeping his arm wide, the old man pointed to a small alcove just beyond the little bridge, away from prying eyes, and hurried over to it, waving at the two youths to follow. Once the three were at the alcove, the old man offered one bench to the youths and then sat down with a thud on a second bench, which looked more like a tree stump repurposed as a stool. He removed his hat, an old, worn companion that might have been a bowler or possibly a homburg in its youth.

"Ah, these sea legs take longer to take to land the more the decades pass by," the old man wheezed, evidently out of breath. "Yes, dear. I have the advantage, though I will not speak your name. No, not that. Not now. Too long I've been alone and have no need to entertain your kin by calling them that way. And, long has it been since I've been called anything by others."

The old man shifted his weight and continued.

"So long these old bones have been nameless, that I scarce recall. Sam...no...Silas? No...Simon? Yes, let's use Simon, little one," the old man answered, his head swiveling back and forth like a bobbing old crow watching a tasty lizard running to and fro, as if waiting for someone he expected to show around one of the corners.

"You have it?" the girl asked without formality, now completely ignoring the boy, as she knew she had little time, now that the old man had shown himself.

For his part, the boy was content, for a while, to simply listen and observe the girl he had admired for a couple of summers and had finally broken the ice with, sort of. Besides, anything new in a coastal town where he had, over the years, seen and done everything there was to see and do during long summer vacations, was a welcome break. So, he sat quietly, trying to figure out what the two odd associates were talking about.

"I have only the signposts, little one. Only the signposts. For which you know the price, I think?" the old man asked, visibly wincing when he said the word 'price.'

("What's wincing?" the little brother interrupted again, brought out of his half-sleep by an unfamiliar word.

"Making a face when you don't like something, now listen," the big sister replied.)

Without speaking, the young girl reached into her jacket and withdrew a small but sturdy purse, dark red, nearly black, with a gold clasp. She held the purse for a moment and then, as the old man's eyes grew wider, with something akin to hunger, she opened the purse and withdrew a small, wrapped object. Carefully, as if the item would shatter, the girl pushed back the green cloth covering the object.

A pearl?

Yes, a large pearl, oblong, nearly an inch, with a small cap or metal cover on the thinner end.

A break in the clouds had opened up, throwing sunlight into the little alcove and across the docks, at least for a few minutes, which allowed the boy to see the curious object quite clearly.

The boy, shock showing on his face, stared at the largest pearl he had ever seen as his eyes nearly fell out of his head. He also let out a small exclamation, which caused the old man to lean closer to the girl and to look suspiciously at the boy. The boy had exclaimed, for he had realized that the pearl was a vessel of some sort, like a petite bottle of rare perfume. He rubbed the back of his head at the paradox of someone drilling into such a priceless gem to make a small bottle out of it.

The old man then stood, ensuring he was between the suspicious acting boy and the girl, extended both of his shaking, gnarled and sun-leathered hands to the girl as she passed the obviously precious, pearl-formed vessel to the old man.

"So long. Too long, I have waited," the old man gushed, his voice reverent as he took the obvious treasure in his hands. "And, within its tiny heart...?"

The girl nodded silently, her teeth set, her now fully green eyes flaming as the old man took the precious object and drew it to his thin chest.

"You have your blood price, old one. Your...elixir. Now, your part," the girl stated bluntly, her hand hovering over the top of the old man's walking stick, as if ready to snatch the treasure back again. "The...our heart, you have it?"

"My, but you have it, little one," the old man replied cryptically as he stood straighter, shook off his feigned feebleness and nimbly stepped back, away from the girl, leaving her to catch the falling walking stick.

Bowing low, but only briefly, the old man began backing toward the edge of the dock while quietly hissing out a confusing collection of odd warnings, like one heard in misty legends from the great seafaring days of old, chronicled by Robert Louis Stevenson and his contemporaries.

"Seek you wisdom from stern to stem," the old man called, his words foggy and seeming to come from far away as he continued. "Await the light of the thunder moon, a blink away. But two heartbeats past the king's trumpet blast, turn your cheek, young one, for your eyes to fill and make haste to the holy house nigh third bell's end and earthly heaven will answer your pleas. On your path, beware crows swimming in the sea, fear the tide that rises from the west, and cower as the crabs show their bellies to the gulls. Make haste. Beware and prevail, and if fate smiles on you and your...your kin, then your quest will be at end."

With those final strange words, the old man quickly turned and, taking a long leap, jumped over the dock railing to the riverbank below and, fading back into the shadows of the pilings under the houses and businesses, disappeared from view.

The old man's dramatic exit had surprised the boy, who had then leaned over the edge, but had caught only a glimpse of the strange old man before the fellow had vanished.

For a very long moment, the girl simply sat, her empty purse in one hand and the old man's walking stick in the other. Her eyes seemed to look far beyond the little alcove above the river. Her gaze was so intense that the boy thought the girl might have fallen into some kind of trance when he turned back.

"Hey! Miss? Are you okay?" the boy, returning to the silent girl's side, asked abruptly, passing his hand in front of her face.

Bam!

In the blink of an eye, the seeming wisp of a young girl had grabbed the boy's hand and had thrown him, full body, against the wall of the alcove. She then jammed the walking stick under his chin before she realized where she was and that she had just roughed up a local youth.

("Whoa! She's a ninja?" the little brother asked, now fully engrossed in the tale after completing his half-nap.

"No, silly, she's just really, really strong. All of her kind are very strong," the big sister replied, sighed, and continued, putting her finger to her lips to remind her brother to keep quiet.)

Quickly pulling the cane away from the boy's chin, the visibly shaken girl backed up to the little bridge and spoke a quick apology as she turned to run off.

"I'm so sorry. I didn't see...I didn't know it was you. Tired, very tired. Only have two days left. Maybe only one day," the girl mumbled, seemingly disoriented by her sudden burst of violence.

The boy, shaking off the girl's sudden surprise attack, but marveling at the strength of such a slim person, stepped over to the bridge.

"Sister, I don't know what you and the old pirate were talking about, but I think you could use some late lunch and maybe a rest in the shade," the boy suggested, offering his arm to the disoriented girl to show her he was not offended by her getting the best of him. "And, if that pearl was real, I want to know where you dive for them."

"Dive?" the girl repeated, then laughed, bringing a smile to the boy's concerned face.

After a bit of back and forth, where the girl said she was fine, but the boy, who was a bit wiser than his young years, refused to let the girl just wander off, the two set off together. But, the girl did not take the boy's arm. Quietly, then, the two walked back down the alley, where the boy saw that his friends had finally moved on.

As they turned to head up the alley, the boy caught a glimpse of someone on the bridge they had just left. He saw what he assumed was probably a returning lobsterman or other boatman as the dark man's trousers from the knee down were dripping wet, not an unusual site amongst seafaring folk, but odd for that time of day. Standing with the man was the tall, slouching boy from the coffee shop, a boy that the sailing boy had not known, but had immediately disliked. The sailing boy filed away the stranger's sullen face for later reference, nodded briefly to the slouching boy, and then guided the girl to the square. The girl had not seen the odd stranger, nor the slouching boy talking to him.

Once at the small, but main square, the boy looked up and down, trying to pick a place that was quiet and not too full of tourists, where the girl could eat and also rest, away from prying eyes. The Sea Squall, just across the street, he decided, was the best choice since it had seating out on the deck. Also, since his dad and the owner were friends, he knew the staff, so they could find a quiet corner and not be disturbed.

("What's a squall?" the little brother interrupted, yet again.

"A really, really big windstorm, like we saw last summer. With lots of crashing waves and such," the big sister replied, holding her finger to her lips and shaking her other hand at her brother to keep silent.)

When the boy suggested the restaurant, the girl tried to beg off, saying she did not want to spend a lot of time eating. So, the boy compromised and ordered sandwiches and fries from the take out window, not wanting to go inside alone and lose the girl in the crowds. Once they had their orders, the boy paid, waving off the girl's money, and suggested the park by the yacht club, since it had a few benches and tourists almost never wandered in there.

As the two walked through the crowds to the park, the boy

noticed that people seemed to flow around them, not even pausing, but slipping by the two quiet walkers as it they were rocks in the way of schools of docile fish. Only once did the two have to stop, when a large black dog accidently brushed the girl's leg and then let out a whelp of pain, cowering in a doorway, refusing to emerge at the coaxing of the owner.

At the park, the boy suggested they sit near the top of the small hill, a number of yards behind the prominent statue of the fisherman and his wife. The girl nodded, almost in her trance again and stepped gingerly into the park.

Walking by the path to the reading garden, a tribute to former First Lady Barbara Bush, the girl wandered over to the entrance wall and stood, her eyes closed, seeming to listen as the gentle wind tossed her dark hair about her pale face.

"What is this place?" the girl finally asked, her eyes opening and looking around at the flowers, the stones with the initials, and, in the back, the bronzes of hat, shoes, and book.

"It's the First Lady's garden, miss. Ganny's, the grandchildren call her," the boy replied, using a hushed and respectful voice.

"So, magic does still live on these shores," the girl said and then continued on with the boy to the bench at the top of the park.

("What's a first lady? Does she do magic?" the little brother asked, his eyes wide.

"She's the president's wife, but does a lot of things herself. I can't remember if her garden was in Uncle's story, but I like it, so it's in ours today," the big sister added, giving up trying to hush her brother as she continued.)

Once the two were seated amongst the shade trees and had sorted out sandwiches and bottles of water, the boy decided to get to the point immediately.

"What did the old man mean?" the boy asked. "Oh, I'm John. Sometimes Jack."

"John, Jack. Strong names. Trusting names," the girl replied, then, as if she were thinking about what name to use, gave her own, or, at least one that her new friend could use. "I'm Marin."

"Marin. Has a good ring to it," John replied. "You may not remember, but we've met a couple of times, over the last two or three summers. You always seemed to be in a hurry, so we never really had a chance to meet properly."

"Yes. That's it! I knew your face…John, but I didn't know why. Sorry. I have always been a bit shy and, yes, always in a hurry," Marin replied, then continued without skipping a beat. "You see, John, we've lost…I've lost something, something that has been lost for a very long time. The old man…wait, you called him 'that old pirate.' Why?"

"Why? Why, because he seemed like he had just stepped off of a seventeenth century square-rigged galley. Even walked like a man not used to being on land too long. Like he said, sea legs don't take to land too well," John answered, noticing Marin's smile at his last comment.

"Yes, he was…is what you might call an old pirate. One who, in his aged years, thinks the old days are gone forever. All his brotherhood has passed on, as far as we know. Which, I think, is why he was willing to help, for a price…a steep price. Well, help to a point. I still don't know where…how to find it," Marin replied. "Only that it is close. Very close."

Just then a couple of small children, chasing a small orange ball, scurried by, the girl pausing to beg their pardon at the interruption.

"Sweet, isn't she?" Marin stated after nodding to the retreating little girl and giving her a quick wink.

"Yes," John answered and then steered Marin back to the odd encounter on the dock.

"Well, as odd as he was, and as strange as his little speech was, he did say you had the answer. Sounded to me like the cane there," John offered, tilting his head at the walking stick leaning against the bench. "Is there anything written on it? From the bottom to the top?"

"Bottom to the top?" Marin repeated.

"Yes, since he said 'stern to stem' and not 'stem to stern,' my guess is there's lettering or something running from the base to the top. Let's have a look," John answered.

Picking up the cane, Marin looked up and down, but then just shook her head.

"Just some scratches. Nothing that looks remotely like writing, runic or otherwise," Marin replied, propping the cane up against the bench.

"Well, if he really is a pirate of the old school, he might use a few pirate tricks," John replied, only half believing he was seriously considering the old guy had been a modern-day pirate. "Let me see the walking stick."

("Pirates have swords, not sticks!" the little brother quipped, swinging his right arm as if he wielded a sabre.

"He's on land, silly. And old. So, needs a stick to help him walk," the sister replied.

"If…if he needs it to walk, why did he give it to the girl? Huh?" the brother asked, grinning.

"The story, silly. So the girl…well, just wait," the sister answered, controlling her momentary fluster and continuing.)

John carefully examined the cane, even to fiddling with the top handle, a worn brass cap that did not budge. Seeing nothing, he then held up his bottle of water over the cane. At Marin's nod, he slowly poured a little bit of the water over the end of the walking stick, turning it slightly. Slowly, as the water soaked into the aged wood, faint markings began to appear. As old as the cane was, he was surprised that the water managed to show anything.

"Some writing. Some symbols, like animals, I think. Words are faint. I can only see a couple. 'Follow the cove' and 'bells to end.' That's it. The water's gone now," John said as he poured water closer to the middle of the stick.

"A cat? 'Feeding the lock?' No, maybe, 'bleeding the locker?' Doesn't make a lot of sense, so we're missing a lot of it," John said, a little frustrated. "What we need is some oil. Something that can soak in for a few minutes and bring out the words."

Marin, having sat quietly watching her new associate study the cane, made a small, triumphant noise and spoke.

"You are a boatman? A fisherman? Like the statue?" Marin asked, her eyes boring into John to the point he looked away, almost embarrassed by the strange girl's intense stare.

"Well, I'm not a professional. I help out my uncle. He lives up here. We visit. Keep a small launch on the river, at his place. I know a little about the sea," John said, in true modesty.

"But, you do know this village?" Marin then asked, leaning close to John, so close that he leaned back into the bench.

"Well, yeah. We've been coming here since I was…before I could walk. Not always the entire summer. Sometimes we go to California, or to Europe," John replied.

"Will you help?" Marin asked, her eyes drawing John in to the point that he leaned toward her, the back of his mind wondering what it would be like to...

"What? Help? Me? How?" John suddenly babbled in reply, pulling himself away from the girl to stand and walk back and forth in front of the bench and the sitting Marin. "You've obviously got some sort of old mystery going on here. What, with the old man and that other guy on the bridge. I'm not sure I can be any...."

"Wait! What other man?" Marin asked, standing to block John's pacing.

"What other...oh, on the bridge. As we were leaving. Some sort of boatman. His trousers were damp and he had the air of the sea about him. Mean looking cuss, as my uncle would say. Dark clouds probably follow that guy around," John answered, wondering anew what sort of trouble the girl and her odd friends might bring. "That tall boy from the coffee shop, don't know him, he was talking to the dark guy."

"Did he follow?" Marin asked, her voice low as her eyes scanned the park and the lanes surrounding them.

"No. They just stood there. Where the old man jumped. I didn't think anything of it," John replied, wondering if it was time for him to say his goodbyes to the odd girl and get back to his friends.

"You're sure about the boy? The man wasn't alone?" Marin asked.

"Alone? No. That tall kid was there," John answered and then became a little put off by the strange girl's questions.

"What is this all about, anyway? Is there some danger to you? Others? Should we go see the sheriff? He's a good friend of my uncle. And a smart guy," John asked, trying to sound authoritative.

"Sheriff? No. No, nothing like that. No danger, really," Marin answered. "I was just surprised that someone else was there. Probably an associate of old Bellamy...oh, the old man."

"Bellamy? Is that the old guy's name? Simon Bellamy?" John asked, his mood a little more relaxed, as a long forgotten bit of information pulled at the back of his skull at the mention of the name.

"What? Oh, something like that. I'm not...he may use other names," Marin replied, almost telling a lie, but catching herself.

"I asked you if you'd help me," Marin repeated, sitting back down on the bench and resting her head in her hands, her breath coming sharply, alarming John and pushing him to decide.

"Well, sure I'll help. And, I have friends that can, too," John finally offered, worried that the strange girl was going to faint. "And, I think the first step is to find some oil. Vegetable, so it doesn't damage the old cane. And, you can translate that odd little speech the old guy made before he jumped off the dock."

Smiling up at John, the clever summer teen who seemed to know her, Marin nodded, and, gathering up her lunch things and the cane, she waited while John picked up his sandwich papers and water bottle. Once the two had dropped the papers and the fry holders in a waste bin at the edge of the park, John suggested they stop by a little eatery nearby where he knew the owners, to get a small cup of vegetable oil.

After a short walk, John acquired the vegetable oil from the small café, just at the bend of the main avenue running along the north edge of the river down to the series of hotels and then to the sea. He and Marin then stopped in at the small grocers on the square and bought a notebook to write down whatever they might discover written on the cane. They then walked down to the sloping park beside the old millpond below the white steeple church, passing the spooky old post office on the way, all the spookier because the clouds had again crowded out the little bit of sun that had broken through.

("The post office where we mailed those post cards to Auntie and Uncle?" the little brother asked, recalling how hard it had been for him to reach the mail slot.

"Yes, it's the same," the sister replied. "Uncle loves to send us those old post cards, so they'll be happy to get them from us for a change.")

At the millpond, the two found a perch on some out of the way rocks and placed the cane in some long grass.

"Okay, here goes," John said, but then Marin stopped him and held out her hand for the oil, which was in a coffee cup.

"I think I should pour it and you read. Your eyes are sharper than mine in this overcast weather," Marin suggested as John gave her the small cup of oil.

While Marin poured, John leaned in close to see any words that might arise. At first, very little could be seen. But, as she poured and slowly turned the walking stick as she did so, more words began to appear and, unlike with the water they had used earlier, the oil caused the words to remain for some time.

John was mumbling to himself as he struggled to read the old script. While it was clearly visible, the curves and curls of the old style lettering hindered his progress.

"I think we need to let the oil soak in a bit before we try to figure out the words," John finally said, a little frustrated.

Marin nodded.

"Why only two days?" John then asked, as the two waited for the oil to soak in to better reveal words on the cane.

"The bells...the bells you heard were a signal. That the...the others would take over the task if I failed, or they thought I was about to fail. They are...they are like the stranger you saw. Darker. Less accepting of...let's just say they are not as patient as I have been these past summers," Marin responded, twirling a lock of her jet black hair with her left hand. "I didn't hear them, not sure why, so missed that there were only days remaining. One loses track of time here in Kennebunkport. Maybe the charm? The generous and caring people? The lazy flow of the river to the sea? Not sure, but I missed the bells, so I've only two days left. Really, only one and a half as the moon of the high tide at the end of the week is the signal."

"Signal?" John asked, wondering why the girl's voice had grown darker and more distant.

"Yes, John. At the high tide moon hence, a blast from the king's trumpet will sound and the sea will unleash its unbridled wrath on this peaceful village and cove...and its charmed life will be no more," Marin replied in a voice suddenly laced with gloom as she looked out over the millpond to the village beyond.

"Okay, this is getting a little too weird, even for me," John answered, thinking he was probably ready to back away and let the strange girl spin her story with someone else.

"John, haven't you ever wondered how certain places seem to be charmed? Why the fires from the old days along this coast would hop a village or a farm, sparing everyone, yet destroying others, seemingly at random? The cyclones, the great winds, the snows that blind, can be mindless in their destruction. Yet, there are places that are rarely damaged. Those few places ride out such disasters as if wrapped in a cocoon of good fortune," Marin said, her usually level voice suddenly seething with passion.

John thought for a moment, began to nod, and then replied.

"Yes, the floods of the turn of the last century were the last here, that I've heard about. And I have relatives near Charleston, on the South Carolina coast, where hurricanes rarely hit. And those wildfires in California seem to hop over entire towns along the coast," John answered. "How does that apply to this cane?"

Marin stared at John for a long moment, her eyes seeming to bore straight into the boy's soul. He even looked away, briefly, a bit embarrassed by Marin's bold stare. The strange girl's eyes then signaled that she'd made a decision and she spoke, her voice seeming to swell from the depths of some distant ocean, capturing John's attention like an iron hook.

"Years ago, John, a deal was struck. Some say the deal was with your devil, but it was with a man, a pirate. Not sure if he was our pirate, but maybe his father, or grandfather. That deal was sealed...sealed with the blood of both sides. This cove village would remain protected as long as somewhere within its walls, well, what passes for walls these days, our heart...our missing heart, resided. We had to protect the village. For, by protecting the village from the vengeful elements driven by the sea, the moon, the stars, and even the sun, we had selfishly been protecting ourselves," Marin answered, picking up the cane to examine it.

"This simple stick, hewn from what looks like ash wood, handed down over the decades to land with us, carries both my own quest and the fate of this and nearby coastal villages. A rift has occurred amongst my...my people. Some demand revenge for the years and years of fear that the heart will be forever lost. So, now, we must find the heart, return it to its home. Heal the rift and protection will continue, for all of us," Marin finished, handing the stick to John.

"And, if you don't find this heart? What then?" John asked as he looked over the cane, finally seeing, much more clearly, the writing brought out by the oil.

("Rift? What's a rift? Is that some kind of raft?" the little brother asked, his face scrunched up in his heavy thinking scowl.

"It's a kind of break. When something that is whole is broken in two, or torn. Like when you get mad at someone and don't talk to them for a while. That's a rift between two people. Wars are fought over rifts between countries," the sister replied.

"Did the pirate make the rift?" the brother asked, his face still contorted.

"Yes! You are paying attention, aren't you?" the sister exclaimed, causing her little brother to beam at her rare praise as she continued.)

Marin simply lowered her head, unable to tell her new friend of the true extent of the vast devastation that would be visited upon the area if the less caring of her kind were to take over the search for the heart. She knew she had to succeed, and quickly. Shaking her head to clear it of such gloomy thoughts, she turned to John and smiled as she answered.

"That's not to happen, now is it? Not now, when I have a summer resident from a wee babe who is my guide?" Marin laughed, trying to make her voice more upbeat and positive.

John simply returned Marin's comments with a slow nod, wondering, yet again, if he should just hand the cane over to the strange girl and get back to enjoying the summer with his friends.

"Those are 's's', John," Marin said, interrupting John's thoughts of escape.

Marin then joined John in examining the walking cane and they both tried to decipher the odd script together.

After about fifteen minutes of staring at the cane, turning it slowly as John wrote while Marin read, since she was more familiar with the formal script, the two seemed to have exhausted the cane's contents. Wiping the remaining oil on some fresh grass, they turned to John's notebook to review what they had discovered.

Marin read the words aloud.

"From the wee mouth, fix the steeple's light, let your eye find the pointing hand, follow for twenty breaths along the river, turning to the crows' feast. Slide up the chin for a dozen blinks and scale the village's psalms halfway beyond the watery volcano's minute hand. Too far, and the porpoise's laugh spells doom. Backwards march the tides to the moon's reflection. Blink at the bells and fail. Wide eyes and triumph. Godspeed."

"Not much there, is there?" John commented after Marin had

read the cane's words aloud a couple of times. "What do you make of it?"

"More importantly, John, what do you make of it?" Marin countered. "You said yourself you've been coming here for years, so you know this village and the coast far better than I."

As his face took on a slow scowl, John scratched the back of his head while he stared at the page, forcing himself to think of landmarks that might match what the cane had contained.

"Well, some of it is apparent. Like the steeple. That's either the old church just there, or the older one farther up the road a bit. The pointing hand must be some landform or such. Maybe one of the islands around Cape Porpoise. The river is obviously the Kennebunk, so that helps to anchor the other places," John offered. "But, the chin? Crows' feast? Some of these are probably old references to places that might not be there any longer."

"Maybe some of your friends might know? Ones who might live here year round?" Marin suggested, tracing the words with her fingers.

"Well, there is Caleb. He's so local he bleeds Maine saltwater. He's also a math nut, so those distances might make more sense to him," John replied.

"Is he around?" Marin asked.

"Yes, he's always close by. It's a small village, after all," John replied and stood, extending his hand to help Marin up from the rocks. "Let's wander up to the shack and see if he's hanging around there. He's sweet on one of the girls that works the afternoon shift."

The two gathered up their things and wandered through the large parking lot, availing themselves of the public facilities, and then crossed the old swing bridge to the Kennebunk, or southern side, and found a spot to sit near the clam shack.

After only a few minutes, John's friend Caleb hailed them from the side of the small food prep building and, after some hand gestures, grabbed three of the fresh lemonades and joined John and the strange girl.

("Can I have lemonade now? I'm thirsty," the little brother whimpered in his best sad voice.

"Dad's almost at the window, so soon," the sister replied.)

"Well, what have you been up to buddy? Missed you at the square earlier. Your mates said you'd found a friend, so I guess they were right, miss...?" Caleb asked, in a rambling, comfortable way of talking, which immediately put people at ease.

"Marin, Caleb. Marin, this is Caleb, the math whiz and local historian I told you about. Caleb, this is Marin. She is a summer bird like I am, several times over, so almost a local," John replied, his face telling Caleb to be nice to the new girl.

"Delightful, young Marin. Cool name for such a delightful visitor to our fair seaside village," Caleb added, his eyes smiling at the girl and with a wink for John.

After a few more pleasantries, John got right to the point.

"We've got a bit of a puzzle here. Marin has...well, a family research project. Looking for old hints from things in the past. More later, but these scribbling's of mine are a big part of solving the puzzle. Was hoping you could give us some local color that might match some of this rambling text and a few symbols, mostly of animals," John said, with Marin nodding from time to time.

John then showed Caleb the page of words and symbols from the cane.

For a number of minutes, Caleb read over the few lines and then, taking a pen from his pocket, he used a separate page from the notebook to make out two lists, the words of what seemed like locations from the cane's words and then where he thought those places were in and around Kennebunkport. Once he seemed satisfied with his two lists, he put the notebook down and, looking hard at both John and the strange girl Marin, Caleb asked what he thought was a sensible question.

"So, it's pirate treasure you are after, is it?" Caleb asked, a twinkle in his eyes.

"What? What makes you think...?" John began, but stopped when he saw the triumph in his friend's laughing eyes.

"Really, John? Pirates? You? The sensible one of the summer gang? Where did you get this? From the library in the eighteenth century section?" Caleb asked.

Looking at Marin, John cocked his head at the cane, signaling that she should show it to Caleb. Marin then held the cane at an angle so that Caleb could see the words plainly visible since the oil had not yet worn off.

Letting out a low whistle, Caleb gingerly took the cane in his hands and, turning it slowly, he mumbled to himself as he read the still visible words. As he started to read a second time, he turned back to the page John and Marin had worked out and made minor corrections. Finally, he put the notebook and the cane down and took a hard look at his friend and new companion.

"Later eighteenth century, maybe earlier. From the carving near the top. And some of the words went out of style after our revolution. But, some in this last group of words are more recent. You can tell from the lack of wear and a different hand carved them," Caleb said, then continued. "Is it a family relic, Marin? It's not something you'd normally see outside of a museum."

"Family. Of a sort, yes. We've lost something and this stick is a key to its whereabouts, we think," Marin answered.

"Well, if you've lost something, this thing should certainly help. It's a map," Caleb declared, watching his friend's face. "Hmm, I see you are not surprised. The words form a verbal map. If you take out some of the nonsense words, a common practice among pirates and even modern day thieves. Throw in a few red herrings to queer the scent of the hounds, right?"

"How do you know which are nonsense words?" John asked.

"They're the ones purposely misspelled," Caleb replied. "For the writer, or writers, was or were obviously very educated, but failed to realize his education, or hers, would come through in the way he, or she, intentionally misspelled certain words. A less educated person would have misspelled a lot more words and would have spelled some of the harder words by simple phonetics, sounding them out. The author of this knew how to spell. He just wasn't very good at misspelling or misleading. However, my guess is that he was a rare bird among the thieving herd and that whoever else was supposed to be able to read this thing would not have been very educated and would have not suspected the misspellings to be the red herrings."

Grinning like a schoolteacher after a long lecture, Caleb waited patiently for the praise he knew his friend would convey.

"Marin, didn't I tell you he was a whiz at history and math and now ciphers? Who knew, Caleb? Are you sure you don't have pirate in your bloodline somewhere?" John asked, clapping his friend on his left shoulder.

Marin, who was looking at the page with fresh eyes after Caleb's pronouncement, smiled and looked up at both boys.

"Amazing. It does read like a map. Do you know the landmarks?" Marin asked, her eyes, more pure sea green than hazel green in the fading afternoon light, boring into John's friend.

"Well, I think we can cover most of them. There are two though, just there, near the bottom, that might call for a trip to the library to look at old maps," Caleb answered, trying to avoid the burning eyes of John's new friend.

"Porpoise beach?" John asked. "Isn't that just over by Cape Porpoise? And the other, the watery volcano. Isn't that just the old blowhole?"

"Not sure about either. No one calls a blowhole a volcano. And it's 'water born,' not watery. And, porpoise is used a lot around here, especially in the old days, when the first town was abandoned since the locals who had been here first, read first nations, ran them off a couple of times. So, no, not sure," Caleb replied.

"So, off to the library then?" Marin suggested. "Which way?"

"Give me a couple of minutes to say goodbye," Caleb called as he sprinted across the plaza to the shack to talk to his lady friend, giving John an opportunity to try to clarify a few things with Marin, away from his friend's very perceptive ears.

"Okay, Marin, we need to tell Caleb the details, but I don't really have any, other than what little you have said and what the old guy mumbled. Oh, we should write that down as well and see if any of his ramblings match up to the words from the cane," John said, then flipped to a new page in the book, mumbling to himself as he wrote.

After a minute or so, John then read his version of the old man's speech from the bridge, correcting his text where Marin had suggestions. Once the two had agreed on the final text, they were able to show it to a returning Caleb.

"Wait? This came out of the mouth of some old pirate? Where was I? Why can't I run into such throwbacks to the golden era of romance?" Caleb asked, jokingly, but with a wistful tone. "Seriously, John, miss, you two have got to clue me in on all that has happened."

"Right. Let's walk," John suggested, letting Caleb lead the way.

John picked up the three lemonades and tossed the two empty ones in the bin and held up the third.

"Marin, you haven't touched your lemonade," John commented.

"Oh, too much ice for me," Marin answered absently, looking

toward the river. "Never really developed a taste for ice like your…like most people,"

Tossing the last cup into the bin, John joined Marin, and the three set off from the plaza and crossed the bridge, walking against the tide of people heading to the clam shack to get a jump on the long lines that would form as soon as the sun started to go down.

As the three gained the other side and then passed the square, John brought Caleb up to date on the odd happenings of the previous couple of hours. From time to time, Marin would add a bit, but John did most of the talking. Oddly, Caleb had no questions, but would look back at the trailing Marin with veiled eyes. Once the group was in sight of the library, Caleb finally spoke.

"Well, fitting we're headed into an old bank, to decipher an old cane, to find some sort of something…the word 'treasure' has not been spoken, so I'll hold off on speculation…some sort of old pirate remnants," Caleb said in a jaunty, carefree fashion. "Our best bet is to use the few map books they have here. A couple of atlases and maybe a few of those old summer resort schemes, those had pretty detailed maps."

Once the three were in the library, both John and Marin deferred to Caleb and let the affable fellow follow his historical nose.

For about an hour, Caleb, after getting help from the reference librarian, dug into the village's past. The knowledgeable old librarian, a delightful older man who seemed to know everyone coming and going, save Marin and John, both of whom had never visited the library, was also able to help Caleb find the right era of maps in a much quicker time, saving the youths untold hours of research.

Using the annotated text from John's notebook, Caleb was able to draw out a crude map of the elements from the cane. The cane, of course, excited all the librarians and, once the three had finished and Caleb was certain of his information, one of the library volunteers commented that the cane would be a great addition to the local museum one day and gave Marin a small flyer on the museum.

Outside the library, John and Marin were bursting to ask the questions they had avoided inside the library since they had no idea who might have been sitting nearby. Before they could speak, Caleb made a suggestion.

"Let's walk back by the captains' houses and get over to…well, not back to the village, but over to the beach. I need to see something. Maybe with bikes? Mine's near the store. And I need some mosquito repellent," Caleb said, looking down at the notebook as he walked, then looking at the old historic homes where the wealthiest of the village had lived over the decades.

When they arrived at the corner of the village green park, where John and Marin had found the bench for a short lunch earlier, Caleb paused and, squatting, squinted at the far statue of the fisherman and his wife, while lining his eyes up with the stone corner marker rising about a foot out of the ground, giving Caleb an almost crab-like stance. After a minute in that position, he uttered a triumphant note and stood back up.

"Got it! The pointing hand. Not a land mass, as we thought, but the statue. Probably the direction the wife is looking," Caleb offered with some pride in his deduction.

"Wait. The hands aren't really pointing at anything and that statue hasn't been there all that long, how can it be...?" John began, but was cut off by his friend.

"It's in the newer line. The faces tell us to go toward the sea, not upriver. Without that clarification, you could look up and down the river for ages, trying to find the landmarks that fit," Caleb answered. "They don't need the hands to point, the sculptor's name is Handlen."

John nodded slowly and Marin then asked if the rest of the landmarks would be below the park, maybe along the river.

"Yep. Also, along the coast, maybe as far as Cleaves Cove or even Cape Porpoise, so we need transport. And, even though there is a mention of a village, there have been fishing camps at the mouth of the river since before Europeans landed here," Caleb replied, continuing on to Ocean Avenue.

Standing back from the sidewalk, where strolling tourists and a few locals were walking up into the main village, the three discussed the next steps, which involved Caleb retrieving his bike and Marin borrowing two bikes from the resort where her aunt worked. The three would then meet up there or down at Colony Beach, just at the end of the river, before it slipped between the two protective jetties into the sea.

As John had suspected, by the time the two had walked the five minutes to the riverside resort, known for its stunning setting and equally amazing weddings, there was no sign of a returning Caleb. So, knowing his friend, John suggested he and Marin continue on to the beach using the two bikes she had borrowed.

The bike ride to the beach was quiet, and the two only had to dodge a few tourists. As they passed the old Booth Tarkington author's studio, which stood over the slowly incoming tide, only Marin noticed the dark shapes coursing just under the water, trailing close behind her and her companion. She let her eyes scan the river as they progressed, but didn't see the shapes a second time.

At the turnoff to the small Colony Beach beside the river's mouth, the two found a spot to stash their bikes and lock them. They then strolled over to the raised jetty that extended into the surf. John continued to look back down the road for his friend, so chose a spot to sit where Caleb would see them without having to look too hard.

Sitting on the rocks of Colony Beach, at the mouth of the Kennebunk River, the strange girl, Marin, with the deep green, hypnotic eyes, which looked hazel-green when thicker clouds rolled by, musical voice, and ageless beauty, turned to John, the kindly boy of summer vacations and few troubles, on the threshold of his life, and quietly changed his life forever with her fantastic tale.

Whether John fully believed the tale he was about to hear was irrelevant, for, once heard, he would never be able to un-hear the young Marin's story of the tragedy of the merfolk of Kennebunk Cove.

("Oh! That's what you saw at the beach today? A mermaid? Huh?" the little brother suddenly asked, tapping his fingers on the table, indicating he was starting to get hungry.

"Well, I'm not sure yes and not sure no. It was something, though," the big sister replied and, looking for her dad, found that he was at the window.

"But, does she tell the boy that she's...that is, does he know she's...you know, one of them?" the little brother whispered, looking around at the other diners, no doubt wondering if one of them might be from some strange land.

"Well, we can say it because we're telling the story. The boy thinks it, but is afraid to say it, because...well, just because," the big sister answered and looked back to where their father was ordering. "Dad's right there, giving our order, so it won't be long now. Let me hurry, okay?")

Marin slipped her scarf off her shoulders and slowly wrapped her right hand, as if trying to use the distraction to help her shape the words she was about to speak. Finally, she stopped winding the scarf and spoke boldly to John, the young man she had pulled away from his carefree summer into her own, decades old story.

"Tears, John. That's what was in the pearl bottle given to the old pirate," Marin said, her voice mixing with the sound of the surf against the rocks. "Tears of my mother's issue, John. Final tears, as a matter of fact. Sacrificed for...my kin, to bribe that old pirate into revealing his secrets. Since the girls are the only ones who can...who regularly go ashore, my mother chose me before...well, before she moved on."

Marin turned to look far out to sea, giving John a start, but only briefly, as the strange girl's eyes seemed to join with and disappear into the shifting colors of the ocean beyond the cove.

"I've lost track of time, John. I...I can't remember how many years my mother has been gone," Marin continued. "Time for us is...it's not the same for you and yours. We measure time with the tides and the moons. With the passing of the comets and the rise of the fire mountains...volcanoes. Often, time seems compressed, like now, that I only have two days left. Other times, the years drag on into decades. That old pirate had mastered that as well, using what he had stolen over the years, to wander along this coast, south and even on the other side of the world from here. He has traveled far and wide. He was lost to us for, we thought, forever. But, one day, scribbled on a bit of blue-green sea glass down Newport way, one of my kin found the pirate's mark, telling us he was near and wanted a parlay. A negotiation, for what is rightfully ours. And, a promise that the old pirate would walk free, and with youth. Yes, the only thing his kind value more than gold, or pearls, or power...is more time to walk this land you cherish so."

Turning back to John, Marin waved her arm to cover the ocean, the cove, the beaches, and even the hotels running up the river.

"This is all only part of it, you know, John? There is more, even when you've moved on. I've always marveled how the pirates of your world always seemed surprised, after," Marin said, falling silent for a moment before resuming.

"Since it fell to me to find old Bellamy, a name we use to avoid confusion, I ventured into coastal towns from Newport to Bar Harbor, hitting upon Kennebunkport a few years back when reports of the old pirate surfaced. He had taken up as a roustabout for a lobster fleet. Even though he was old, he obviously knew the sea, so he became something of a trainer, an instructor," Marin said, looking at John strangely.

"That's him!" John suddenly burst out as an old memory surfaced. "When I was…well, younger, there was an old guy who used to come down to the river and would talk for a bit about the sea, boats, tying lines, even safety tips. Man! I knew the old guy seemed familiar!"

John then stood his full height and stared down in disbelief at Marin.

"You! You were the little girl with all the questions! That was you, right?" John stammered out, shocked that the Marin sitting before him was the same chatty little girl from several years before.

"Yes, John. Back then, I was able to conceal my true self from the old man, given that the younger we appear, the fewer differences we have from…well, from you. I have to admit I did not remember you until today, even though we have bumped into each other over these last few summers, as you said. I have been…let's just say my focus has been elsewhere," Marin replied, turning back to look out to sea.

For a few minutes, the two odd companions sat in silence, letting the afternoon sounds lull them into a false sense of peace. The gulls chattered on their way up river to accost the tourists for a final time before nightfall, while a few boats motored by with muffled sounds. Even the happy sounds of playing children across the river's mouth at the larger Gooch's Beach drifted across to where the two were sitting on the rocks. Finally, Marin continued her tale.

"We've been in turmoil for years, John. I won't tire you with what you already know about the damage to the seas, but know that eons of traditions have been upended. Whether by the thievery of pirates like the leech you met again today, or by the captains of industry looking for immortality of their name on a library once they've passed, it's all caused a great rift among what used to be the kindest, most gentle of folk," Marin said, unable to disguise the sadness in her voice.

"That rift came to a head when old Bellamy stole our heart…a literal heart of empire. It's been gone so long that we young ones think of it only as a legend. Yet, my mother had known the heart. It was at the center of all life for her mother and countless mothers before her. That's why she chose to shed the tears. Trade a few years for the life of the empire. Empire? Your word. We simply know it as life for us," Marin concluded, falling silent for a long moment, until John quietly spoke up.

"Tears, are rare in your...experience?" John asked, the hair on the back of his neck starting to stand up as he realized he was facing something beyond his understanding.

"Tears draw the life from us, John. We rarely shed them. When we do...well, unfortunate events occur, John. Terrible events," Marin replied. "Pain...tears of pain bring devastating storms, years of famine on land and currents of death in the sea. Anger, which is rare, brings the worst of all. Massive cyclones grow that sweep entire civilizations off the maps. Deadly fire mountains rage, then shift the very core of the planet. Yes, rare are these tears."

John gulped and then quietly asked a simple question.

"Are there no tears of happiness? Of joy?" John asked, his voice strong as he struggled with believing the bizarre tale.

"The rarest of all, John, are the tears of happiness. Those are what brings life, or gives an old pirate a few more suns to wander the land," Marin answered, then choked up.

"And, those are what your mother cried, Marin?" John asked.

Marin nodded, her chest heaving, but no tears coming.

"She was happy. Eternally happy, that her sacrifice would bring us back to the source, to the heart, and to seal the rift. She had seen too many of our kind move to the dark, like the one you saw today. Too many had given up and were simply moving about like wraiths, lost ghosts, ready to do harm to anyone," Marin said quietly.

"But, why would the tears cause your mother to...well, to move on?" John asked.

"Tears are life. Once shed, they can never be recalled. They are finite and, like life, once they are gone, so goes the life that shed them," Marin answered, her head lowering as she recalled the last days of her mother.

John remained silent for a few breaths, turning to look for his friend.

Far up the avenue, Caleb's lanky form finally appeared biking along, but he was not alone. From what John could tell, there were two other kids on bikes riding along with Caleb. Alarmed that new faces might spook the already overly sensitive girl, John decided to press his questions to both get a few answers before Caleb and the others arrived, and to ensure that Marin was still in a mood to talk.

"This heart you have lost, what exactly is it?" John asked, moving to a different stone so that Marin had to turn, cutting off her view of the approaching gaggle.

"Stones. Your jewel merchants call them aquamarine," Marin answered. "Yet, the heart is more than that. Embedded in the center, in the core of the largest of the seven stones, is a deeper green, that flashes red in the right light, that the old ones say talks to the keeper, the one who holds the heart for the people."

"How was it lost?" John asked, seeing his friend and the gang getting closer.

"How? How have countless treasures over the centuries been lost? Love? Infatuation? Misguided trust? All, John, all," Marin replied, then, her brow furrowed, plowed on.

"She was not much older than that mother there down by the water, there, with the two little children. Her young husband had been lost heroically battling the cyclones. A tragedy, but, after a long mourning, she had moved on for the sake of her family...and her child. Later, the man who came into her life was an apprentice. Lost in the Indies, abandoned by...well, I don't know the full tale. She nursed him back to health, I'm told. Fell in love. Trusted him. Then, one night, at the yearly meeting of the...those who govern, the young sailor saw the heart," Marin said, her eyes staring through John and back along the decades to that fateful day.

Just then a small gull, white with a black head, landed not three feet from the two, surprising John, since they had no food that the gull might want. Yet, the little gull hopped closer, its eyes locked on Marin.

"You see, John, for the likes of us, the heart is like...like the sea, the sky, the stars. It just is. We see no other value than its value to the group. That it keeps the storms and the tragedies to a minimum," Marin said, reaching out to stroke the gull when it walked over to her.

"Yet, for men...men like the old pirate from the dock, the heart was the kind of thing that tore at their minds. A thing to possess. A thing to call 'treasure,' and fight wars over, like the men of ancient times. Sadly, though all say the young sailor did love her, he had always intended on returning to...wherever he had come from,

England, we thought, until a few years ago. So, on that day when all eyes and ears were on the talks between those who govern, he threw away his trust and love for my mother and, taking the heart, escaped beyond…well, he got away without our knowing. Once we did know, he was well beyond the reach of the leaders. My mother, knowing the tragedies that would soon befall our kin and all those along the coasts, from the Leeward Islands, to the mouth of the St. Lawrence, she left me with my aunt, and then spent years hunting for the evil in men. Yes, all men. She knew that evil attracts evil and that, one day, word of the wretched deed would spread and, over time, word would make its way to her," Marin said.

"Then, as I said, a few years back, that word did reach her, near Newport. Walking along the old cliff walk, one of the watchers met her and let her know that the young man she had loved had passed. Raving mad, the watcher said, somewhere horrible that they throw away such people. Yet, in his madness, he had wanted to share his most shameful secret. That he had taken the heart, but wanted it returned to the rightful heirs. Sadly, the only ones who could hear his ravings also had minds as lost to this world as his. Save one," Marin continued.

"The old pirate?" John offered.

"Yes, the old pirate. Or, maybe his father or other relative," Marin answered. "But, probably the same, since the old man we met this morning knew of the pearl bottle and its contents. Yes, he must have been the one."

"How do you even know you can trust that old guy?" John asked as Caleb hailed them from the top of the beach. "For all we really know, the cane might even be a fake, a red herring to throw you off the trail."

Turning, Marin then saw Caleb and began to wave, but suddenly noticed the other two kids on bikes and dropped her hand. Glancing around, she looked like she was looking for a path to run away without passing Caleb, but then stopped herself and turned back.

"John, it's okay," Marin said when she saw John start down to send Caleb's companions away. "We need Caleb and he must have a reason for bringing the others."

"Are you sure you can trust the old buzzard?" John repeated, his jaw set, finally accepting that he was in for a long evening.

As the two climbed down the rocks, Marin answered John in

hushed tones.

"No, John, we don't know that we can trust him. Our only advantage is that he has probably never seen the actual heart, otherwise he'd never give it up. So, he may just want us to solve the puzzle for him and then he pounces," Marin said in a low voice so only John heard as they neared Caleb and the others.

Pausing, Marin briefly held John's arm and looked him straight in the eye.

"Yet, the man we see later as the old pirate will be a different man, John, so be wary of any new face that crosses our path before sundown tomorrow," Marin said, an ominous tone in her voice.

"Colleagues of the grand treas—, right, of the grand scavenger hunt, I bring reinforcements," Caleb called as John and Marin approached.

After introductions had been made all around, Marin mentally sorted out the newcomers. John knew them already.

Pete, sometimes called Striker due to his soccer playing, was the grocer's son and a local from way back. Caleb touted Pete's hands-on knowledge as more detailed than his own, so saw him as an invaluable addition to the team. Pete also knew the coast as an avid boater.

Jenna, or Jen, Marin wasn't too clear on the girl's true name as the boys used different ones each time they talked to her, was also a summer resident, but had extensive family in the village and all the way up to Goose Rocks. As an information source on what was happening anywhere in the county, she was priceless, according to Caleb. If she didn't already know something, she could make one call and find out anything.

Winking at John so that only John could see, Caleb then laid out his reasoning for expanding the group.

"Since Marin here is leaving in a couple of days," Caleb said, letting his eyes tell her he was adlibbing, "I thought we might be able to solve her family heirloom hunt puzzle quicker with some help."

"So, what's the next step?" John asked, given that Caleb had had plenty of additional time to think about the clues and talk to his little gang on the way to the beach.

"Map reading," Caleb replied, hopping off the bike and walking to one of the corners of the gravel covered car parking lot where a long, low wall provided handy seating.

Leaning on the wall, Caleb pulled a map out of his back pocket and unfolded it on the top of the wall.

"I know it's just one of those tourist maps from Pete's dad's store, but it will allow us to get a bird's eye view of what we need to check out, once we label the places the cane mentions. And, maybe that old guy's ramblings you wrote down will match up as well," Caleb stated, taking out a black pen to mark up the map.

In the waning afternoon light, with winds increasing, blowing the map and the papers, Caleb walked the little group through the landmarks outlined on the cane and from the old man's odd speech. Jenn and Pete added bits as well, with Pete giving insights into the coastal features more likely visible from a boat just off shore.

John spoke up as he looked down on the sketches arrayed around the map.

"Looks a lot like a man's head. In profile. Maybe one who's either wearing a scarf, or...?" John offered, but stopped himself from making additional comments.

"Well, the coast from just below us to above Walker's Point, Cleaves Cove that is, does have the rough shape of a profile. The Point's the nose, you see, just above the blowhole, or that stream as the mouth. The bit that juts out, just across from Bumpkin, that's the forehead or a shock of hair. The river's mouth is the scarf, or the...well, these are pirates, after all, right?" Pete added, sticking out his tongue to emphasize what often happened to pirates caught by the authorities.

"Gross, Pete," Jenna scolded, then added her own take. "My guess is the Point is the 'volcano' in the notes. Pete?"

Pete continued to stare at the papers and the map, and then looked over the notes again before replying.

"Yeah, right. Used to be part of its name way back," Pete replied. "The blowhole, though, where the mouth would be, just might be the king's horn or trumpet."

"When does it usually blow? Isn't it normally at the high tides?" John asked, his eyes tracing the outline of the shore on the map and the drawing.

"Right," Pete replied. "Around nine or ten o'clock this week for the second tide. First is earlier."

"But, what about all the nonsense lines from the old man?" John asked. "Does any of it make sense to you guys who've been here a long time?"

"Some of it," Pete answered. "The tide from the west could be the reverse surge from a storm, but no storms are around now and none predicted. But, I don't know who that might...."

"Wait!" Caleb shouted, squinting to see the drawing and the notes. "That's exactly the sort of thing that would uncover rocks usually fully covered by water, even at low tide. The backwards surge draws water out of the river and away from the coast, but only briefly."

"How briefly?" John asked.

"At most, maybe an hour. More likely for a lot less, before it rushes back with a vengeance," Pete answered. "Dangerous stuff. Best to not be anywhere on the water when it happens. But, I think we can write that off. There are no storms predicted any time soon."

Suddenly, immediately below the group, a loud commotion erupted in the river, just where the waters entered the two parallel jetties that protected the river's mouth from the sea. The noise, from what sounded like crashing waves and thrashing fish, was so loud it drowned out Marin's abrupt call to head over to the blowhole.

Once the racket had died down, John asked Marin to repeat her suggestion.

"We have to be at the blowhole at the high tide," Marin argued, walking over to where she and John had left their bikes.

Suddenly, from a few yards away, at the waterline of the small beach, a huge wave, looking like a bulge in the water, roared toward the group and then broke as it hit the sea jetty. Water crashed all over the bikes and hit Marin and the group.

"What the devil was that?" Pete yelled, jumping back, avoiding most of the salty water.

"Freak wave?" Caleb offered, shaking the water off of his jacket.

As the watery bulge receded back into the small cove, Marin turned to the group and spoke, her voice distant, almost as if she were talking from the bottom of a deep well.

"The old man, the leech of the pirate world, the one who should have had a black spot sentence decades ago, has finally opened the rift. He has torn the very fabric of our seas and the coastal life. A storm will come tonight. A terrible, life-taking storm of such immensity, your instruments will not even see it coming. We have to be at that cove when the bells ring tonight," Marin called to the group, almost singing the words.

("Black spot? What's a black spot?" the little brother asked, watching his dad walking over to the prep hut that held the lemonade machine.

"It's a pirate's curse," the sister said, her voice low, but not too low or mysterious to actually scare her little brother. "Any pirate who had betrayed...been bad to his other pirate friends, would be given a black spot, which meant that he...that no other pirates would ever play with him ever again."

"Ever?" the little brother gulped. "Does he lose his pirate ship? And his hat and sword?"

"Yes, he loses everything," the sister replied.

"I don't want a black spot. I want lemonade," the little brother answered as their father appeared with four of the cold, delicious drinks, and placed them on the table before he walked back to wait near the shack for their orders.

"Don't worry, no ice for you," the father called back to the big sister, who smiled at her little brother's puzzled gasp.

"Wait! You don't like ice...either," the little brother said, but was soon distracted by his lemonade.)

John was fast to recover and he stepped close to Marin. Taking off his own jacket, he wrapped it around her shoulders, which were bone cold to the touch. Briefly wondering why her own jacket was draped over her bike, he then stepped back and spoke.

"Guys, I think you've done enough. I'll take her to the cove by the high tide. You guys go home. Caleb, stop by my uncle's place and let him know I'll be doing some late evening fishing, which isn't a lie, is it?" John said, his eyes watching a thin line of darkness far out to sea, a line that had appeared after the freakish wave.

"What? Miss the adventure of the summer?" Caleb retorted. "Nope. We'll call your uncle from the old hotel."

"Wait! How do you know that the thing you are looking for will be near the old blowhole?" Jenna asked. "There are several, smaller blowholes along the coast going north. Couldn't it be one of them?"

"Maybe, but the one at the cove tracks with all the clues," John replied. "Still fuzzy on the odd comments by the crazy old pirate."

As if to answer John, a flock of jet-black crows suddenly descended on the beach, landing a few dozen yards away, near the far end of the small beach. There the crows waded into the water and began pecking at something the youths could not see.

"What the…?" Pete exclaimed. "I've never seen crows walk into the surf like seagulls."

"Just what I was looking for!" Caleb blurted out, waving one of the papers. "That line about the crows reminded me that some kids were talking about a gang of crows that fished. Down at the beach. I thought they were making up tales, but it was in the old man's speech. Funny it happening while we are here."

"Not funny, Caleb," John said, his eyes still watching the thickening dark line on the far horizon. "Part of the sequence he was warning us about."

After a minute or two, a huge flock of gulls flew over the crows, screeching at the interlopers and diving on them, trying to drive the crows off. After several attempts, the gulls were successful and the crows took off, but not into the air.

Oddly, the crows ran out of the surf and up the beach, cawing as they headed to the small stand of sea grass and bushes near the beach's entrance, disappearing into the brush.

Back at the waterline, the oddly receding tide had exposed dozens of crabs, which were not running away, as they had been turned on their backs, probably by the crows.

"Beware of crows that walk in the surf and crabs that show their bellies to the gulls," John said, his words wooden, with a hint of disbelief.

"What's that?" Pete asked, walking closer to the feasting gulls.

"No! Stay away from them!" Marin called to Pete. "They are not well."

Pete stopped and, picking up a small pebble, he tossed it at the closest group of gulls, none of which reacted to his intrusion. He then slowly backtracked, wondering what he and his friends were witnessing.

"The old pirate. He warned us about this," John called to Pete, who then hurried back to join his friends.

"What do you think it means?" Jenna asked.

"Omens," Caleb stated. "Harbingers of misfortune. Something has upset the balance. Why in the world would crows help gulls get a meal?"

"Where did he come from?" Jenna asked, tilting her head toward the far end of the jetty, which was being pounded by suddenly violent waves.

A lone figure, almost a shadow, stood facing the group. The figure was too far away to see his, or maybe her face, and the sea spray obscured the figure to the point that the shadow melted into the spray.

"Okay, this is starting to really creep me out," Pete said, after the sea spray subsided and no figure was to be seen on the jetty. "I've lived here forever and I've never heard or seen three weird things like that within a half hour."

"Three?" Caleb asked. "Oh, the freak wave."

Suddenly, the gulls, as one unit, stopped their frantic feasting, raised their collective heads and stared out to sea. Then, with a massive push, all the gulls took off as one flock and, turning over the small beach, flew with breakneck speed inland, disappearing over the tree line in the distance.

"Man! Have you ever seen birds fly that fast?" Pete exclaimed.

Marin, after watching the speeding birds, walked over to pick up a small bit of driftwood, bleached white from its ocean journey. She walked back and pointing up, spoke.

"Watch the stick. I think I know why our feathered friends are so frantic," Marin said, then tossed the small stick up into the air.

For the first twenty feet or so, the driftwood flew straight up, then, abruptly, the stick jerked away at ninety degrees and flew about a hundred feet in the same line as the birds, eventually tumbling into the river reeds on the opposite bank.

"Storm coming," Pete stated. "That kind of air speed will bring it quickly."

For a moment, no one spoke. Each of the youths mulled over the odd events and then each spoke up.

"I have to get my boat out of the river, and help Dad batten down the store," Pete said, getting on his bike. "If that wind holds, there's a huge blow coming. And, if I'm right, we might get a whopper of a reverse surge before the storm hits. Those can rip up boats into toothpicks. See you and, good luck, lady. I wouldn't want to be you on those rocks tonight. Better to wait until the storm passes. Jenna?"

"Yes, coming. I have to get back to the compound before the storm, or they'll be out looking for me," Jenna answered, and giving John and Marin a quick shoulder shrug as an apology, she hopped on her bike and followed Pete back to the village.

As the two brief companions rode away, the remaining group turned and watched as a number of boatmen rushed to the nearby docks lining the lower river. The boatmen began to lash the larger boats to multiple lines and anchors. Others were winching the smaller boats out of the water onto land and lashing them down. Far upriver, they could also see that massive groups of seabirds and others were flying inland, no doubt to safety.

"Caleb, you should go. Your mom will be freaking out if you don't show up before the storm," John said to his friend. "My folks are down in Portsmouth, so won't worry. And, Uncle is a cool guy. Just tell him I met someone and am taking a sunset stroll along the Ocean Avenue walk."

"No worries," Caleb replied. "They know I'm out exploring and won't worry. They know I never take chances. Besides, there are several friends' houses along Ocean where we can duck into if things get dicey."

During the departure of John and Caleb's friends, Marin had been scanning the far horizon, trying to gauge when the freak storm would hit the coast. At Caleb's comments, she turned back and beseeched the two friends to go home.

"John, Caleb, you both have been more than gallant and helpful. But, this is my…my problem, my fight, and I can't ask anyone to join me. While everything you say makes sense, there still might be danger out there. And, John, remember what I said about the old pirate? He could be watching us from any of those buildings there, or even from the road," Marin pleaded, her eyes wide. "Please don't risk it."

Both John and Caleb waved Marin down.

"Sorry. This is our town, if only for the summers for me. We can't let some crazy old pirate mess it up with his antics and selfishness. We will find the heart, restore it, and put everything back into balance," John declared, half-believing the strange girl's wild tale. "So, I guess you are stuck with us. Right, Caleb?"

"Heart? Is that what you're looking for? Some kind of heart?" Caleb asked, then added. "Right. Stuck with us, you are, young lady. What do we do now?"

"Well, let's find the other landmarks," John suggested, pointing to the few streetlights that had popped on. "And, maybe somewhere to eat a bite and wait for high tide?"

"The village is too far, I think," Caleb replied. "Maybe the church? It has a youth rec hall that stays open late on certain days. Today is one of them."

"Good idea. St. Anne's?" John asked as the three prepared to depart.

"Yep. And there's the restaurant at the inn, just up from the chapel. It's a little fancy, but I know the owners, so we could use one of the small lounges," Caleb answered as he turned his bike.

"Caleb, where's this church?" Marin asked, then added a comment. "John, remember old Bellamy said to rush to the church before three bells, after the trumpet sounded?"

John thought for a moment and then took the notes from Caleb. Tilting the notes to the light, he read over the old man's comments.

"Yeah. Right. Maybe the hiding place is near the cliffs by the church?" John replied. "It's not far from the blowhole. The little point there sticks out into the ocean. The chin in Caleb's profile drawing. If we don't have too many clouds tonight, the moonlight should help us see the cliffs."

"Guess we'll know in a couple of hours," Caleb added. "Recall Pete told us high tide is earlier tonight, around nine."

"And, three bells at that time of night is nine thirty," John replied. "That's when we need to be at the church."

"Yeah, but where, John? That's a big spread. Sunset will be approaching. How will she know where to look?" Caleb asked.

"I have a feeling we'll have help," Marin answered, pointing to a dark shadow walking hastily down the avenue, toward the bend in the road.

"Do you think that's him?" John asked. "That guy's got a lot younger step than the old pirate from today."

"My point exactly," Marin said. "Let's go."

"Wait. Marin, wouldn't it be better if you changed your look? To throw off this guy, whether he's the pirate or one of his goons or helpers? I mean, there are a lot of tourists around and we could find some clothes and maybe a hat to make you fade into the background noise of all the people?" Caleb asked, his eyes swinging between the nodding John and the doubtful looking Marin, who turned down the idea.

"Caleb, while it sounds like a good idea, I think it doesn't matter what I'm wearing," Marin responded, seeming to choose her words very carefully. "He's been tracking my movements for a long time, from what I learned earlier today, so he can probably spot me in a crowd just by the way I walk and hold my arms. Best we focus on locating the landmarks and worry about him when we have to."

So, with that, the three youths agreed to continue. They took their bikes and rode the few minutes to the seaside church. Oddly, they did not pass the dark stranger.

As they neared the gates of St. Anne's, Marin waved the group away from the church and continued to the inn just up the road. Once they had stopped in the inn's driveway, she turned to the puzzled boys.

"If he overheard us, and I think he did, he will be hiding somewhere around the church," Marin began. "We don't want to encounter him until the last minute. I think he kept some part of the puzzle from us, but he probably doesn't understand the map, the profile, so will wait for us to go to a place and then pounce."

"So, we need to lead him somewhere else, but give ourselves enough time to get to the actual spot, once the tide turns," John added.

"Before the reverse surge hits. Or, rather, right as it hits," Caleb offered. "But, we still don't have the exact spot. You can't be wandering around as the storm comes up, looking for some random cliff face."

"Not random, Caleb. You told us where to look," Marin replied, then waved her two companions to the inn, where they stashed their bikes beside the wide porch.

Caleb ran inside first, while Marin and John found a quiet bench on the grand porch and, smiling at several older couples out enjoying the evening air, they sat quietly and waited. After just a couple of minutes, Caleb reappeared and waved them into the inn. He then led the little group to a quiet, unoccupied lounge just off the main lobby.

"We can hang out here. My buddy will send some food in later, so we can avoid the dining room," Caleb told his companions as they settled into the comfortable chairs.

Caleb then spread the notes, his drawing, and the map out on a low table and cleared his throat in a grand gesture worthy of an Agatha Christie mystery.

"Ahem, now. How did I manage to tell you where this...your heart is, when I have no idea?" Caleb asked, waving his hand over the table with a flourish.

"Your profile, my clever detective," Marin replied and then asked her companions a question.

"If you were a repentant pirate, or simply a guilt ridden sailor and you wanted to protect something that would not be damaged by nature and would not be easily discovered by some shell seeking tourist, where would you hide the heart?" Marin asked, her eyes searching the youths' faces for hints of understanding.

"Well, most of the cliffs around here offer a lot of protection, and most are not easily accessible," Caleb replied.

"Right. But, this sailor would have had to have been able to reach the place. Not in a boat, as any boat would be smashed on the rocks before getting close enough. So, he had to get there from the land," John speculated.

Suddenly, the wide front door of the inn opened and the couples who had been sitting on the porch rushed in, with a loud wind blowing them about, as well as papers and various items around the lobby. One of the clerks rushed to help an older man close the door, just as a peel of lightening flashed across the large picture windows, followed by a deafening boom of thunder.

("I'm not 'fraid of thunder," declared the little brother, his jaw set. "Dad says it's just the sky making a loud burp."

"Right, of course Dad would tell you that. It also is a sign of a storm coming," the sister replied and then continued.)

"They're here," Marin said, her voice low.

"They? Don't you mean it? The storm?" John asked, stepping to the door of the lounge to watch the commotion in the lobby.

"They come with the storm, John. It conceals their movements," Marin replied, sinking farther into her chair.

Another loud crash of thunder, one that shook the inn to the foundations, causing the lights to flicker, was followed by the front door flying open again. Before the clerk could close it, three figures, men in dark traveling clothes, stepped into the room. Oddly, the high winds from earlier did not follow the three into the lobby, so the clerk closed the door easily and welcomed the three travelers.

"How are we this evening, gentlemen? Are you here for dinner?" the polite clerk asked, beaming at the new arrivals.

However, the three men simply nodded without replying and then walked straight to the side lounge where the three youths had sought refuge. Two of the men entered the room, while the third, who, to John, looked a lot like the man on the iron bridge earlier, closed the door behind them and then stood at the door, almost as a guard.

For a long breath, John and Caleb both considered challenging the boldness of the two men, but Marin intervened. She was standing between the two boys and the men, even though no one had seen her move.

"It is time, young one," the taller of the two men said, his voice deep and somehow soothing. "These two know?"

Both John and Caleb had seen their share of security types to know the second fellow was some sort of henchman to the taller man who had spoken. When the second man turned slightly, as if he were ready to silence the two youths, John realized the second man was the slouching boy from the coffee shop earlier in the day.

"Only a little. Nothing that will last," Marin replied, her voice strong and, to John's ear, almost regal.

With Marin's comment, the slouching man, no longer seen as a boy, relaxed and stepped back to the door to stand silently.

"Do you have the location?" the tall man asked, his eyes a similar green to Marin's but with what John would swear were glittering pupils.

"Yes. We are waiting for the signal," Marin replied.

For a long minute, the taller man held his words. Then, smiling, he replied.

"And, young one, you will not tell us, will you?" the tall man asked, his face telling her he knew the answer.

"No. But, we do need your help," Marin replied.

"Our help? After all these years? Your mother before you and now you? Our help? If she had sought our help those decades ago, this rift would have at least begun to heal and not fester and pull us apart as it has. Our help?" the tall man nearly wailed in reply, causing John's and Caleb's skin to crawl at the eerie sound.

"Bellamy is still about," Marin stated, watching the tall man's reaction carefully.

"Bellamy?" the tall man repeated, then, letting out a long, but silent sigh, he stepped to one of the chairs and sat down, his long, black coat draping over the sides.

"How are you sure?" the tall man asked.

"Because he wants the heart. He's never held it, but it holds his mind, counselor. He waits in the shadows for us. To find it. To practically give it to him," Marin answered.

"We are only three, this night, young one. And, we need a fourth wall...the bond is stronger with one of his own kind," the tall man replied, looking from John to Caleb and back.

"We have the fourth wall. This one here," Marin declared, resting her hand on Caleb's shoulder.

"He's just a boy," hissed the slouching man from the door. "The tides would pull him under."

"But, the tides will recede. Just before. Enough time to hold old Bellamy and enough time for me...for us, to get to the heart, before the water's return," Marin replied.

"You'll only have a few heartbeats, young one. Are you fast enough?" the tall man asked, his face showing his doubt.

"I've trained all my life for this moment. I will be fast enough," Marin answered, her eyes flashing her spirit.

Standing, the tall man walked over and conferred in whispers with the slouching man. They then called in the third man and the three whispered for another minute or so. The first man then turned back to Marin.

"Why do you think this one will stand with us?" the tall man asked, peering at Caleb with a doubtful eye.

"Because it's the right thing to do, sir," Caleb replied before Marin could answer. "I may not understand everything happening here, but I do know that something is majorly out of whack and she's the key to putting things back in balance. I don't want to see the village, my family, my friends put in danger. So, I'll be your fourth wall, whatever that is."

The tall man slowly nodded to Caleb and then turned to John.

"And, this one?" the tall man asked, leaning into John.

"He's the fisherman, counselor," Marin replied.

"Ah! That he is. That he is. And, the bait...you?" the tall man asked.

"Of course," Marin answered.

"You must at least tell us when? The cyclone riders are not going to wait forever. If you are...if you fail, they will unleash their havoc by midnight," the tall man added.

"In less than two hours time, at three bells and a few breaths," Marin answered.

"We will speak with them," the tall man answered and then pointed at Caleb. "You will go with us. A show of good faith, young one."

"Caleb, you don't have to, you know," Marin said, contradicting what she had just said to the tall man. "It's not a simple task."

Caleb, grinning from ear to ear, shook his head as he replied.

"Marin, most of what I know I've gotten from books. I'm not going to pass up the chance to both help the village and have a live experience with…with whatever we're going to do," Caleb answered.

Caleb then joined the three men and, pulling his coat closer, crossed the lobby and, to the shocked expressions of the few couples in the lobby, followed the three quiet, dark men out the door and into the raging storm.

"Tell me he will be okay," John said to Marin, resisting the urge to run after his friend and stop him, out of respect for his friend's wishes.

"They are counselors, even the guard who stood outside the door. They are far too strong to let old Bellamy break their square. One of his own kind simply makes the square even stronger and nearly impossible to break. So, they will hold the old pirate while we dash to the hiding spot before the waters return," Marin answered, wringing her hands behind her, knowing she was stretching the truth a bit.

"So, where is it then?" John asked, his tone a little blunt, revealing that frustration had finally gotten the best of the good-natured lad.

"Below the church. The old pirate is probably standing right above it and doesn't know. I'm sure he thinks it's the blowhole, with the other clues being red herrings," Marin answered, her voice so calm as to make John wonder if the storm really was happening outside.

("What's a red earring?" the little brother asked, slurping on his lemonade.

"Red herring. It's a fish. A little fish. It means to divert attention. A fake, like when you play at football with Dad and he showed you how to fake one way, but run the other," the sister explained, trying her best to make the idea easy for her brother.

"Oh. I know how to fake," the little brother said, using his sloshing lemonade like a football.

"Okay. Okay. Don't spill any more, Mom will notice," the sister said, causing their mother to look up from her phone, but only briefly.)

Just a few minutes after Caleb had left with the three strangers, his friend with the inn popped into the lounge with a tray of food, tea, and sodas. He asked about Caleb and John let him know that Caleb had gone out for a bit, but that they'd take him some of the food.

After eating a small amount, since neither John nor Marin were very hungry, the two noticed a lull in the high winds that had been battering the windows.

"They've gotten them to hold off," Marin said. "Now we do the dance macabre for the old pirate to watch."

(Suddenly, the big sister shot a glance at her little brother, realizing she had just mentioned a rather scary part of the story, when the girl mentions the old, medieval ritual of parading around to invite or scare off death, since death was everywhere in the old days, before doctors and nurses. Fortunately, the little brother was blowing loud bubbles in his fast disappearing lemonade, so had not heard the scary term. She let out a little sigh of relief, reminded herself to avoid scary terms, and continued.)

"Do what?" John asked, understanding the reference, but not what they were to do.

"We lure old Bellamy to the blowhole, by walking from the church, along the road, looking around and pausing, so it looks like we are lining up with landmarks from the cane and his own babble. Then, we stop at the blowhole and, if we can, try to hide somewhere, but let him think he's been clever and unseen to us," Marin answered as she put on her coat and John picked up his backpack.

"No, leave your pack. You need to be nimble on the rocks," Marin added as she considered leaving the cane, but then picked it up, no doubt thinking it might still have some purpose before the evening was over.

John nodded, but took out the mosquito repellent and a small flashlight and dropped both in his coat pocket.

After finding Caleb's friend and thanking him for the food, the two took a small plastic bag of snacks for Caleb and stepped out into the calm that had descended in the middle of the storm.

On the inn's wide porch, a number of guests and diners had gathered to watch the stunning scene along the horizon. A long line of storms was churning the ocean only a few miles off shore, but had seemed to have stopped and maybe even had receded a bit over the previous few minutes.

John fished around in his pocket and took out the repellent, offering it first to Marin, who shook her head.

"What's that?" Marin asked, peering at the small can.

"Mosquito repellent. They can be a bear at this time of evening, especially with the wind so calm suddenly," John replied as he sprayed his arms, legs, and the back of his head.

"Oh, they never bite us," Marin replied.

"Never?" John asked, dropping the spray back in his pocket.

"Something about our blood, I guess," Marin responded as the two passed their bikes and headed across the road to the sidewalk and ocean side.

("That's silly. 'Squitoes bite everybody," the little brother interrupted, waving imaginary bugs away from his face, and showing his bites from earlier in the day.

"Well, not everybody. Not her kind. They don't like the taste or something. It's one way you can tell, maybe, who they are," the big sister replied, winking at her little brother who smiled in return.

"The wind helps, too," the boy added, happy that a strong breeze was blowing and keeping the little bloodsuckers away.)

Turning right, John and Marin hurried the five to ten minute walk to the stone chapel by the sea. Once through the gates, they stopped at all the main points of interest, where other tourists were wandering about as well, in spite of the looming storm. Their hope was that the old pirate, if he were mixed in with one of the small groups, would see them and then start secretly following them.

After viewing the outside of the chapel and lingering by the rectory, John suggested the open seaside chapel, where the two spent a number of minutes reading over the notes and Caleb's map, using John's flashlight and the fading sunlight filtering from behind the tree line. While they were there, they pretended to study the papers, but actually watched the few groups that were there late, mesmerized by the storm holding on the horizon.

Nothing.

After nearly an hour of wandering about the grounds, going back over places that they had already been, John and Marin decided that the old pirate was not following them, nor was he sneaking about in the bushes.

"He's probably in Portsmouth by now, if that elixir actually works," John quipped, but was immediately sorry for his callous comment, given what Marin's had said about the sacrifice to give up those tears.

However, Marin was focused on watching the horizon and did not register John's remark. Instead, she pointed out to sea with the cane.

"They are moving closer, John," Marin called from the edge of the cliff that faced directly out to sea. "We need to get going."

("What's a sac…sacrifice?" the little brother asked, sucking on ice from his nearly empty lemonade cup.

"Well, sacrifice is when you do something nice for someone, but you lose something when you do it. You know you're going to lose the…whatever it is, but you do it anyway," the big sister replied.

"Why?" the brother asked.

"Why? I guess because you care a lot about someone. Someone you love and you want them to be safe, or happy, or healthy," the sister replied.

"Okay. Let me know if you need me to do a sacrifice," the little brother declared, causing his big sister to smile as she continued.)

At Marin's insistence, she and John left the chapel grounds and began the short trek to the blowhole at the cove, across from Walker's Point. Along the way, they spent a great deal of time stepping away from the sidewalk into the sea grass or the rocks to check various landmarks, in hopes of getting the old pirate to follow them, if he were actually still around. Only a few tourists were out, since the storm seemed to be moving closer, even though the winds were not howling like they had been.

At the Spouting Rock, just a few minutes from the chapel, the two found one of the three benches unoccupied, so they sat for a few minutes and just listened to the late evening sounds of the ocean. A few lone sea birds sailed by and the incoming tide caused the spout to spew a little water from time to time. The storm was still holding just off the coast.

"I wonder why we didn't think to include this place in the landmarks?" John mused to himself.

"Not strong enough and it's more recent than the much older blowhole," a disembodied voice called from just below where John and Marin were sitting.

Shocked at hearing Caleb's voice out of the darkness by the edge of the short cliff, John controlled himself and simply continued talking to Marin, who also kept her cool and did not react to Caleb's surprise comments.

"I guess the force of the waves here is not as strong as at the blowhole," Marin answered. "Funny, that we haven't seen anyone we know along Ocean. Didn't you say, John, that you had friends along here somewhere?"

John, well aware that Marin was telling the hidden Caleb and the other men with him that they had not detected the old pirate, joined Marin's comments.

"My guess is that most of them have left town. Maybe headed south for the long weekend," John answered, letting the hidden men know he felt that the pirate had already left town.

The ghostly voice then quietly answered John.

"We're moving down to the blowing cave, folks. So, see you there soon. The water is getting quite strong, but these guys...strange, how they seem to know where all the dry areas are, even though I can barely see a thing," Caleb called quietly and then went silent.

"Let's go. He's not going to need that," Marin said, motioning to John to put the small bag of food for Caleb back in his coat pocket. "And, it's not dry land he's walking on. But, no need to tell him now."

After making a number of gestures to appear that they were sighting along several landmarks from the cane, John and Marin then hurried along to the Blowing Cave Park just a few minutes up the road. Arriving at the closer entrance to the rocks, they were both surprised that there were only a few people waiting for the high tide to see the blowhole in all its grandeur.

One older couple was sitting on the bench at the top of the park and only a few younger couples were stepping carefully about the lower rocks.

("Did they see the anchor?" the little brother asked, recalling their walk along the coastal road a few days earlier. "It's from a really, really, really big ship. Huh? A pirate ship?"

"Uncle said this tale happened before the anchor was there, so I don't think they saw it," the sister answered. "And, no, it's not from a pirate ship, silly.")

At the lapping of the incoming waves, a small spray burst forth from time to time from the blowhole, with increasing force each time.

"Well, it's now or never. Three bells should be sounding soon," Marin declared and then, winking at John, she grabbed his hand and the two of them rushed to the very edge of the short cliff at the bottom of the park.

"Now we do the dance," Marin whispered and, taking the cane, she pretended to look at the now faded words and began hopping up and down.

John, taking his cue from Marin, made all manner of motions to calm her down.

"Hey, don't be so noisy. Someone will want to know what's going on," John shouted, suddenly realizing the wind had picked up again and it was hard to hear himself speak.

"Right! Let's get ready," Marin called, holding up Caleb's drawing. "I think the storm is coming. We'll soon lose the moonlight, so watch your step."

Standing with their arms locked, John and Marin forced themselves to look out over the ocean, beyond Walker's Point, to the massive storm bearing down on them. They did not want to look back up to the road, or to either side, in fear that they would scare away the old pirate, if he had followed them.

For the briefest of moments, John wondered if he had been crazy to have listened to the strange girl and to have allowed his friend to hide in the dark with a group of oddball strangers in order to pounce on a an old man of dubious pirate heritage. Shaking his head to clear it of doubts, John suddenly caught a quick glimpse of a deeper shadow in the darkness, close to Marin's side.

Was it Caleb or one of the dark men, John wondered? Or, maybe, the old pirate after all?

Marin's hand suddenly squeezed John's arm, causing him to turn to her and see, just over her shoulder, the looming figure of the old pirate.

Only, the old pirate was no longer old, but appeared young.

A darkly tanned man in his late thirties was staring back at John, wearing the face, albeit younger, of the old man from the dock that day.

The man's face seemed to swell as he suddenly yelled.

"Aye, fools! You've led me to my reward. All these decades I've waited. It's mine! I say! It's mine! The old madman left it to me, he did. Forsook all, I have these long years, to find it. Now you've brought me to it," the old, yet oddly young pirate called over the howling wind as he grabbed the cane from Marin's hands.

"Back. Back, I say!" shouted the pirate as he twisted the top of the cane twice and drew out a long, slender sword, which he then held aloft as if to strike John and Marin if they didn't obey his rants.

John and Marin grudgingly complied and moved as far away as they could without falling into the churning waters below. Just behind them, at a distance of what seemed only a few yards, the raging storm had slipped across the Point and had paused just inside the cove.

"Why?" Marin called, her voice cutting through the wind. "You know what terrors will be unleashed. You'll have nowhere to hide!"

"Terrors are what you make of them, little lady," the pirate yelled back, his face twisted by blind madness. "I've endless days to wander this land. Long after you and your kind have destroyed each other."

"The rift. You knew of the rift?" Marin called, holding on to John, not for support, but to keep John from falling into the sea with the strong winds buffeting them.

Marin, as she talked, slipped off her scarf and, wrapping it around her right wrist, she motioned for John to do the same on his left.

"It's sea silk, John, stronger than steel. Hold tight," Marin called into John's ear so that only he could hear, and then pulled John away from the slippery edge.

Marin's strength, which she had demonstrated at the dock, again shocked John, almost as much as what he saw next.

Rising up behind the crazed pirate, while Marin kept the raving man's attention by screaming insults and curses at the old, yet young rogue, John saw the three dark men and his friend Caleb appear, riding, of all things, a column of what looked like seawater. Inside the column, under their feet, thousands of creatures seemed to be swimming in a blur, in a circle, somehow keeping the column of rising water stable.

"The fool, lovesick sailor told everything," the pirate yelled, swinging the sword with crazed menace. "Near the end, he kept calling me his savior. Wanted me to take the bloody thing from some wretched cliff along this shore, he did. Described the place in detail, he did. Wanted me to find it to only give it back. Hah! Give it back?"

After his last shouted taunts, something in Marin's face must have revealed to the pirate that he had struck a nerve, for he began to laugh, hysterically, as if he had accepted going mad himself.

"Yes, my sad little lady, he told me everything. I see the fear in your eyes! I know where your kind's home nest is! And, little lady, with the proof of the heart, once it's in my hands, and with young blood coursing through my old veins, and with your rotting remains to show the doubters, I'll convince an army of thieves to descend on the place and ransack it and all the branches leading out of it. From Acadia, all the way down here to the one below the river...just a crab's crawl from here, to those all along the coast far to the south at the old Charles Town! It will be as if the old days were never gone!" the pirate, quite mad, screamed at the young Marin, waving his sword as if he were battling foes of old in the blustery winds.

"You evil man! How can you and your thugs, your henchmen be so cruel?" Marin called, seeming to cower in front of the pirate.

John struggled to put himself between the deranged pirate and Marin, but both her iron grip and the howling winds conspired to root him to his spot at the very edge of the cliff. Failing moving, he tried to distract the pirate to ease some of Marin's obvious pain.

"You old fool. Just because your body is young, you think you can trust your thieving friends? They are probably already plundering the riches of the nest, as you call it. Laughing at your stupidity," John screamed, hoping his words would carry.

They did, for the pirate not only heard John, he flicked his sword at John's face, just missing him and then did a little jig of a dance as he yelled his reply.

"Stupid? Who are you to think me a fool? Why would I have told them yet? They know nothing! Nothing! They wait in town. And up the coast. They think the place is below the cliff walk in Newport, fools! No mortal but me knows the truth! The old mad sailor told only me! Only me! I've told no one! No one!" yelled the pirate, yellow sea foam flicking from his raving lips.

Suddenly, Marin released her hold on the scarf and John's arm, and, calmly, regally, with an air of absolute control, she stepped right up and put her face in the face of the pirate, who, shocked at the girl's boldness, stepped back, but then held his ground, his knuckles white from gripping his sword.

"No one? You are not that smart, old buzzard!" Marin bellowed, her voice colder than the pirate's steel that hovered over her head.

"No one! I'm not a fool, little lady!" the pirate replied, then stepped back yet again, realizing the wind had suddenly died down and that he no longer needed to shout.

Not only had the wind died down, an eerie silence completely engulfed the little park. With the storm raging around them, their little spot was free of rain, wind, and any crashing waves, save the blowhole, which was shooting tall columns of spray into the air behind John and Marin.

Suddenly, a chilling sound penetrated the surrounding gloom.

Clang...clang...clang!

The peels of the far harbor buoy sounded three bells, as if the very hand of the Flying Dutchman had rung his ship's own ghostly bell.

"Three bells! Just as your clues demanded, in your twisted fairy tale to lure us here, old man! Thank you, you evil leech of a person, for saving us," Marin declared and then nodded to the tall man and the others who had been patiently waiting, silently, behind the pirate on the column of whirling water.

Seeing Marin's signal, the raving rogue spun around, his sword at the ready.

The pirate first gasped, then wailed in horror when he saw the four apparitions floating in front of him. Yet, young Marin's very elixir, that had renewed the pirate's aged blood, allowed him to jump backwards, away from the menacing column and the dark men. His leap took him beside Marin and John, where he used his sword to stab at his bewildering foe, the slim girl.

"Trickery becomes you, young lass. You would make a fine partner to any pirate of the old Spanish Main," the pirate yelled and, using a feint with his sword to distract Marin and John, kicked

Marin's legs out from under her.

"Go back to your mother's grave, little wench!" the pirate raved as Marin slipped over the side of the cliff.

John, thinking quickly when he had seen that the pirate was actually trying to push Marin over the edge, had wrapped the scarf around Marin's arm, just as she had slipped over the side of the cliff.

"Ha, ha, ha! Back to the watery grave! Where your kind have sent so many of my sad brethren, young miss...back...to...what?" the pirate stammered as he tried to comprehend what he was seeing before him.

John, using strength he did not know he had, had pulled Marin quickly back up and had steadied her on the cliff. He then turned back to the crazed pirate to stand between Marin and the evil man.

"Not this night, old man!" John yelled and, leaping at the pirate, wrestled the sword away from him and then tossed it to the side.

The old pirate, the shock of failure finally crawling up his face into his bloodshot eyes, could only mumble and whimper, while Marin stepped to face her foe one last time. Behind the pirate, the sound of the whirling column became louder and louder, causing the old pirate to turn and again stare in renewed horror at the fate that awaited him.

Marin and John steadied each other as the pirate's shoulders slumped nearly to his waist, while his long arms dragged on the wet stone. He wailed as the three dark men slowly reached out, together, and drew him towards them. The pirate's struggles, although intense, were fruitless, as the dark men placed the writhing prisoner in the center of the column while the three chanted and Caleb repeated the chant as best he could.

The old pirate, weighted down by barnacle encrusted, semi-invisible chains he and his kind had forged over the millennia with their evil ways, turned slowly back to face Marin, as he helplessly, feebly reached for his lost sword.

Marin's face was like stone as she watched justice unfold before her. John, awed by the spectacle of the swirling column, watched with pity as the old pirate was slowly engulfed.

Moaning and exhausted, the pirate dropped to his knees and spoke his last coherent words to the young girl with the dazzling hazel-green eyes, now as green as the deepest ocean.

"He wasn't mad, was he? He knew I'd lead you here. He knew the evil of men would drive me to trap you, to get at the heart," the pirate called from the living cage of the water column.

"Yes, he truly loved her," Marin called, keeping any sympathy she might feel for the old pirate out of her voice. "He knew he would never be able to return and, in his delirium, he revealed her home. Our home. Our heart. He allowed the evil of men to glimpse a doorway to our world. Yet, his mind cleared, near the end, and he knew he needed to drive you to us."

"He must…he must have loved her very much, young miss," the pirate called as the column began to sink into the sea.

"Yes, you old fool, of course he did," Marin called to the dark shapes as they slipped beneath the waves. "Of course he loved her."

As the living wall containing the evil that was the old pirate slipped into the violent sea, John stepped to the far edge and, looking down into the gaping hole where the column was disappearing, he called out to his friend.

"Caleb! Are you…?" John shouted, his voice echoing off the rocks in the eerie silence after the column had descended.

"John, no worries. It's wondrous, it is! I'll tell you all…later, John," Caleb called from somewhere in the watery pit, then the pit closed.

"Caleb!" John called, becoming frantic that his friend would drown.

"John, calm yourself, your friend will join us shortly," Marin said, placing her hand, cold from the night, on John's arm to steady him and herself. "He's just got to see our friends off, first."

Standing on the cliff, John and Marin waited, watching the storm abruptly recede across Walker's Point and then back out to sea, until the storm was no more.

John turned away from the fading storm and, after glancing down into the waters below, he pulled his eyes away from the cliff's edge and stared at the strange girl, seeing her, he realized, for the first time.

"Your home is the heart you sought…," John stated, rather than asking a question of Marin.

Marin simply stood, looking out to the quickly calming ocean. She kept her eyes downcast, waiting for what she knew her brief friend would ask. She didn't have to wait long.

"The landmarks, do any of the others really matter?" John finally asked, his mind accepting that the strange girl's goal all along had been to trap the one man who knew how to attack her home, her people's heart.

"Whatever to you mean, John?" Marin asked, her voice low and with forced coyness, as she raised her eyes to meet John's.

"Is there even a necklace?" John bluntly asked, turning to stare into the deep, absorbing eyes of the strange girl from some strange land.

"Why do you...?" Marin began, but then smiled and nodded, realizing John had rightly concluded that the necklace was the lure, the bait.

"Yes, John, and it may never be recovered. We've had those clues for years and none of our most brilliant counselors have been able to recover it," Marin replied, lowering her eyes again, not wanting to face the eyes of the young man she felt she had tricked.

John didn't reply, but just kept staring at the puzzle of a strange girl.

"Are you angry?" Marin then asked, suddenly lifting her head even higher and boldly staring back at John's questioning eyes.

"Angry? No. A little miffed at being deceived," John replied, trying to make his voice sound gruff, but was unsuccessful, as he could not bring himself to be angry with the strange summer girl from...from somewhere far out of town.

"Please don't be. I truly did not want to put you and your friend in danger. But, our heart was at risk. Our home. He was the only one, other than that sad, misguided sailor, who knew. We had to find him, and he had to show his true colors in order for the counselors to apprehend him," Marin answered, gently slipping her scarf back onto her shoulders.

"So, I suppose...now it's curtains for the evil pirate?" John asked, even though he wasn't sure he wanted to know what happened to wicked betrayers of Marin's people.

"What? No! We might be simple folk, but we are not barbarians. No, we will not extinguish his flame. He will, however, have plenty of time to think about the multiple errors of his ways," Marin replied and then turned John to face the blowhole. "Listen."

Suddenly, Caleb appeared on the rocks below them, with the three dark men standing in what looked like the water to John.

"Hey? Give me a hand, will you, John? It's a bit steep," Caleb called.

John slipped down to the lower rocks and, reaching out, grabbed his friend's oddly dry arm and helped him scramble up the rocks to where Marin was standing. Below, the three dark men nodded to Marin and, in the blink of an eye, vanished into the churning surf.

"Caleb, are you okay?" John asked, sincerely concerned that his friend had been party to something very wrong happening to the pirate. "What happened down there?"

"John, until my hair is old and white, I can only tell you that it was safe. We didn't, you know, do away with the old cad. He's in a prison, of sorts. Will be for, from what I could tell from the chants, for eternity, or until the world ends, whichever comes first," Caleb replied and then turned John back to the blowhole, just as Marin had done. "Listen."

For a few moments, nothing happened.

Then, as the high tide mark approached, and the receded storm waters rushed back, while the waves crashed into the ancient cave at ever increasing rates, the broad column of sea spray grew taller and longer, and, oddly, louder.

Quite a bit louder.

"Aiyeeeeee! Arggghhhhh!" a muffled, distant, tragic voice seemed to scream as the tower of seawater spewed to the heavens.

Each time the column of jet spray erupted, the haunting voice called out for mercy, from deep, deep within the very rock of the cliffs, beside the cheerful little park at the Blowing Cave of Kennebunkport.

Both John and Caleb looked at each other and shared a brief shudder at the sound, then shut their minds off to the image of the old pirate forever trapped in a dungeon beneath the cliffs. The two friends, the local and the summer teen, then turned to the strange girl from far away and both motioned to the exit at the top of the rocks.

"What now? Do you disappear, too?" John asked Marin as the three climbed out of the rocks, leaving the blowhole and the cries of the entrapped pirate fading into the sounds of the sea behind them.

"Well, I still have a necklace to find, so maybe I'll stay through the summer?" Marin quipped as Caleb winked over her head at John.

"That's something we can work with. And, the cane?" John asked, watching Caleb trying to return the sword to its hidden scabbard.

"The museum? This village deserves its memories. An object like the old pirate's cane, which was the young, lost sailor's before him, can help to nurture those memories," Marin said as the three stepped onto the sidewalk.

After retrieving their bikes and John's pack from the inn, the group decided to walk the bikes back to town and allow the day's events to sink in as they took in the much calmer coast along the ocean side drive.

With suddenly clear skies allowing an eerily bright moon to show the way, the three momentary adventurers, one a Maine blueberry-blood local and two long-term summer residents from very different worlds, headed back to the quiet, blissfully unaware of the evening's dark events, little village by the peaceful Kennebunk River, which runs happily down to the sea.

While the last words of the tale faded into the evening wind, the big sister allowed herself a dramatic pause as she finished the story, which had gone a little longer than she had originally planned. So long, that her little brother had finished not only his lemonade, but his mother's as well, and was greedily eyeing his big sister's untouched drink. When she paused, he looked up and smiled, so she closed out the story.

Lowering her voice, the big sister leaned over the table, causing her little brother to lean in to hear her mysterious words.

"So, to this very day, if you are at the Blowing Cave waterspout on just the right day, with just the right moon, and at just the right time of high tide...three bells...you can still hear the cries of old Bellamy, or whatever the name of the old pirate was, calling out from the depths of his ocean dungeon, hoping someone will hear his pleas, but never being answered. Ever!" the big sister declared as she watched the wonder of the tale sparkle in her little brother's wide eyes.

"Whoa...maybe we can go hear it? And they, you know...they might be right here?" the little brother whispered, his eyes darting from table to table. "Wait! Did they ever find the necklace treasure?"

"That's another story," the big sister quipped, smiling at her little brother's evident belief in the tale.

Just as the big sister finished, she saw her father carrying all their sandwiches and fries as he returned to their table. The tray was a little unbalanced, so it almost fell when the father stopped beside his family. Fortunately, the big sister reached out in a flash and, using one hand, grabbed the edge of the tray and guided it to the tabletop.

"Wow. Thanks. Almost lost it there," the father exclaimed. "Good thing you're such a strong girl, right?"

The father then sorted out the various items as he continued.

"Madylan, Greyson, have you guys been bored waiting for so long?" the father asked as he handed out the piping hot sandwiches, the hotdog, and the fries.

"Bored? Not at all!" Greyson, the little brother, quickly replied, dumping ketchup on his hotdog as he stuffed a fry into his mouth. "Sis told me a story about a mean old pirate, with a sword, and a secret mermaid looking for a lost...lost something, right here in this town! And a yelling blowhole, like the one we saw...and...and a big storm...and...and a hero summer boy, just like me!"

"Really?" the father replied, looking at his smiling daughter and wondering what sort of tale she might have been spinning for the last hour or so.

"It was just a simple summer story, Dad. About some folks trying to keep their home safe and everybody happy," Madylan, the big sister, replied as she munched on a French fry.

"No, Dad. It was about pirates, and ships, and lost jewels, they never found them, and merfish...hmm, no, merfolk," Greyson argued, then lowered his voice, looking around at the other diners at the cheerful, outdoor spot above the river and a mile or so west of the sea. "And, Dad, they could be around us...eating, right now!"

Seeing his sister's untouched drink, Greyson grabbed it to wash down his fries, but then made a face.

"It's warm! I forgot you don't like ice," Greyson said, then looked up from his fries to stare at his sister, his eyes growing wider. "Strong? Doesn't like ice...?"

The father smiled and, seeing that his thirsty son had already consumed two of the lemonades from the empties in front of him, he waved his son to follow him to the restroom at the back. As they walked away, getting closer and closer to the edge of the riverbank, the little brother, looking back at his sister with widening eyes, spoke up.

"Don't worry, Dad. Sis told me the old pirate is trapped in a sea dungeon. We'll be safe," Greyson, the little adventurer said, still eyeing his big sister with growing suspicion. "Dad? Did you know the mer-people don't like ice? And are strong?"

The father nodded absently at his son's comments, but was more intent on getting to the bathrooms before another parent got there first.

Back at the table, the mother was finally drawn away from her phone by the bite of a particularly aggressive mosquito. Slapping the bug, she then reached into her bag and took out a small can of repellent and sprayed herself. She then called the little boy back and sprayed his arms, legs and ears. He smiled and then turned to hurry back to his father.

"Dear, do you want me to spray you or do it yourself?" the mother asked the big sister.

"No thanks, Mom. You know they never bite me," Madylan answered, her voice a little loud as she watched a shocked expression suddenly appear on her little brother's face when their father led him around the corner.

The mother gave her daughter a puzzled look, dropped the spray back into her purse, and picked up her own sandwich, full belly fried clams, smiled, and dug in. At the corner of the building, the little brother was tugging at his father's shirt and pointing back toward the picnic table as he stammered out his sudden alarm.

"What...? Dad! She's strong! Doesn't like ice! No mosquito bites...? No, it can't be...maybe? She's...? She's...one of them!" Greyson called, his panicking voice fading as he and his father disappeared behind the building.

Smiling to herself, while silently thanking her uncle for telling her the merfolk tale, which she had embellished with a few additional elements for the benefit of her little brother, young Madylan of the coastal Maine summer locals took her first bite out of her own clam shack treasure, sipped a bit of amazing lemonade, winked at her mother, and began to hum a sea shanty she had heard, somewhere, years before.

Such are the wondrous, magical evenings of the summer residents in charmed, Maine coastal villages, nestled along cheerful rivers, like the quiet Kennebunk, that meander down to the welcoming, for now, sea.

5

AN EASTER TALE OF VIRGINIA

"I wanna play!" the little brother howled from his car seat, causing his big sister to roll her eyes at him, which made him howl even more.

"Honey, we've only been driving for a little while," the mom replied from the front passenger seat. "You can play with your figures. Dear, help your brother open the toy box."

As the big sister helped her whining little brother open the improvised toy chest for the car, made from a repurposed school lunch box, she began humming a tune that she was learning on the piano, one that her aunt had played with her during her aunt's visit to New York some months earlier. The big sister had been practicing so that she would be able to show her aunt how much she had progressed.

"No singing!" the little brother whined, his high pitch squeals causing the driver, the dad, to flinch once in a while.

"Silly, if I don't practice, then I can't play with Auntie on Easter eve. And, if I don't play, then the Easter Bunny won't hear us and be lured to the house by the pretty music and, since she'd love the music, she'll decide that there must be amazing kids in that house for Easter, even though there are no kids there during the other times. She'll then hear the music and decide to leave so many treats in our baskets that we'll barely be able to eat them all…before Dad steals all our candy."

The little brother had stopped his whining at the first mention of the Easter Bunny, for, even though he was still a toddler, the little fellow was well aware of the many treats associated with his aunt and uncle from Virginia and was more recently made aware of the fabulous yummies that the Easter Bunny carried around to all the good children at Easter.

"Singing okay," the little brother then sniffed. "I wanna see the Easter Bunny, too."

The big sister looked over at her little brother, strapped into his cramped safety seat, and had a brief moment of sympathy for her little 'bother-brother' as she sometimes called him. Scrunching her brow, she wondered to herself how she could keep him entertained for the remaining hour or so until Virginia. After a moment, a thought came to her and she spoke up in a cheerful voice.

"Okay. Tell you what, since you are being nice and said I could sing, I'll tell you a fun story about Easter at Auntie and Uncle's house," the big sister answered. "You probably won't remember the story, but maybe some parts of it will come back to you when you hear it. It's not all that long, but it will help the time in the car go by faster. Okay?"

At her little brother's sniffling nod, the big sister helped him with a tissue to wipe his runny nose and then helped him find a couple of his dinosaur toys in the toy box. One toy was a dark green T-rex, or maybe a raptor, and the other a triceratops, which always caused her to worry that her little brother would poke himself with the toy's hard plastic horns. Once the little brother was settled and absentmindedly playing with the two small beasts, the big sister cleared her throat like she had heard her uncle do a hundred times and began the story.

"Not too long ago, maybe two years ago, we were driving down this very road on our way to Virginia. We missed last year, well, because of the Covid virus. I was sad, for missing Easter, my garden, and making cookies with Auntie," the girl continued, using her hands to mimic driving. "But, Uncle had us do a Facetime Easter egg hunt. Some of the eggs were in my garden. We found a lot of them in the bushes, along the wall where the chipmunks live, and even high up in a couple of the little trees where the birds live."

Pretending to search imaginary spots around the car seat for eggs, the big sister let out little exclamations of joy, causing the little brother to watch intensely for the eggs to materialize.

"Eggs?" the little brother asked after no eggs appeared from the seat.

"In your head, remember?" the big sister replied. "Like we talked about. You imagine them being there."

With that sensible explanation, the little brother grinned and pretended to pick up an egg, open it, and eat the imaginary candy he found inside.

"Right. There were so many eggs, but we're not there yet in the story," the sister said and leaned back in her seat.

"So, let's begin, as Uncle would say, somewhere near the beginning, with you, me, Mom and Dad, and Auntie and Uncle. Oh, and Alex oppa via Facetime later on Easter. And California and New Jersey Grandpas and Grandmas, too," the big sister added.

"Far, far south of New York, down the long, winding road of the interstate, that's the road where Dad drives really fast, is the mythical land of Virginia, outside of Washington, D.C., that's the country's capital. In that wondrous land are many, many houses, but only one Auntie and Uncle house. That's where our story unfolds, like I said, about two years ago and a dream away. If you listen closely, you can almost hear the cardinals and the mockingbirds singing, telling the robins and the little chickadees that Easter is almost there."

The big sister then smiled at her little brother, who had stopped whining and had relaxed in his car seat. She then began the story, hoping she could capture her brother's attention for the remainder of the drive.

"Yep, just sit back, little man, and you will hear the birds, too. Yes? Who knows what adventures await, as Uncle always says? Yes, who knows...?" the big sister said with a hint of mystery in her voice as she wove her tale of Easter in, to her little brother, faraway Virginia.

The drive that year was calm and, since the dad drove most of the way, the time flew by. The little family from Manhattan only stopped once for snacks, near the Delaware-Maryland border somewhere, and had French fries and soft ice cream, while the dad had a huge Americano coffee and the mom had a small one.

Since the small family of four had made great time, they arrived in

Virginia in time for lunch. The Auntie was such a great cook that they knew there would be a lot of yummy things for lunch. And, yes, the big sister would make cookies after, with the aunt. She and her aunt usually made Easter cookies shaped like eggs, bunnies, and fat carrots that rarely looked much like carrots.

The sister and little brother didn't know it then, but one of the little brother's favorite dinosaur toys had fallen out of the car when he had climbed out of his seat. It had bounced across the driveway and had landed in the hyacinth patch near the garage door. Since the toy was mostly green, it matched the green parts of the plants, so no one had noticed it as they had unloaded the car. The little brother had other dinosaurs, so he hadn't notice it was missing, and probably had thought it had fallen in the back seat somewhere. So, no one gave it a thought because they were so excited to be visiting the happy household in Virginia.

Before everyone sat down to eat lunch, and right after all the hugs all around, the big sister asked Uncle to take her out to her garden. They went out and she saw there were all sorts of new flowers and a few from before that had not died. She had purple flowers, yellow daisies, orange flowers, and a patch of daffodils, which had mostly already blossomed and gone by. The little volunteer butterfly bush had a few purple flowers, but no butterflies yet.

("Madylan, why are they 'big sister' and 'little brother' and not our names?" the little brother suddenly asked, interrupting his sister.

"Oh, well, I suppose they should be," Madylan answered. "But, you can use any names when telling stories, Uncle said, so I just called them sister and brother. Would you be happier if we used our names, Greyson?"

"Yes!" Greyson exclaimed.

"Okay. But, remember, when you tell this story to your friends someday, you can use their names, or any names. I use my code names for some stories, but we'll go ahead and use our names today," Madylan answered, settling back into her seat.)

After their short tour of Madylan's garden, with the weathered, metal 'M' hanging on the butterfly trellis, Uncle took Madylan around the larger back garden to see the other plants. Greyson, munching on a treat Auntie had given him, joined them from the sunroom. The

Dad had also stepped out and had found a patio chair to sit in the sun while Madylan followed Uncle, with Greyson following them around the yard.

At the back of the yard, the lemon tree had just started to produce blossoms, which greatly excited Madylan, because she had gotten two lemons, the first lemons, in the mail from Uncle in the previous fall. She was also excited to see the volunteer tomato plants and the volunteer orange cosmos at the back of the yard where more of the sun hit. Her garden didn't show any volunteer cosmos yet, but it didn't get as much sun as the back of the garden.

Near the fence, the red roses were just peeking out of their buds.

Wait, what was happening at the front of the house while everyone was in the back?

There! Just to the left of the garage, something moved in the neatly trimmed grass. What was it?

It was small. Brown. No, brown with a splash of white on its belly and tail.

Belly and tail? What could it be?

As the little animal wriggled through the grass, the only thing someone could see, if they had been there and not in the back garden, were two brown bumps moving through the grass and then along the wide rows of daffodils near the hyacinth.

Those two brown and pink bumps looks suspiciously like furry ears, they did.

Yep. Bunny ears, creeping slowly through the flowers toward…toward the little dinosaur that Greyson had dropped.

The bunny, for the ears, the brown fur, the white on the belly and the tail, spoke to the critter being a bunny, stared at the odd creature in the hyacinth. Yes, definitely a bunny staring, or, maybe a squirrel if the ears had been shorter, the fur more grey, and the tail much, much longer.

The bunny, a young one, not much older than little Greyson, but not nearly as old as big sister Madylan, had never seen a dinosaur before, so he was a little bit afraid. Not as afraid if the dinosaur had been the huge red fox that lived in the forest on the way to the park and not as afraid if it had been one of the red-tailed hawks that circled high above in the sky at noon, when bunnies and others small creatures had to be careful and stay out of sight.

Getting close to the dinosaur, the bunny nudged it with his feet and then leapt back with a squeak when the dinosaur let out a roar. Well, more of a meow, since it was a small dinosaur after all.

"What was that?" Madylan asked, all the way in the back garden. "I thought I heard a rabbit squeak."

"Well, we are close to Easter, dear," Uncle replied, watching Greyson strain to hear whatever his big sister and idol might have heard. "Remember that video I sent last week of the large rabbit checking out our yard? She was probably scouting all the houses for the good kids. I'm not saying, mind you, that she was THE Easter Bunny, but probably just a helper, scouting out the neighborhood. Maybe she's sniffing around again?"

"Maybe," Madylan replied with a twinkle in her eye as she looked over at her brother and then refocused on the plants. "What's that over there? Oh, I remember, those are the azaleas that Mom just loves and will want lots of pictures in front of."

As the human tour of the back garden resumed, the little bunny in the front had beefed up his courage enough to step back to the dinosaur to nudge the toy again.

"Hey, that tickles!" the dinosaur suddenly squeaked, since his voice was quite high for a dinosaur.

"Oh, sir. I'm so sorry!" replied the timid little bunny, who started to shiver, thinking he had offended the odd little animal sitting sideways in the pink hyacinths.

Struggling to free himself from being trapped between the tall, green leaves and the overly fragrant flowers of the hyacinth, the little dinosaur realized he needed help.

"Could I get a push, mate?" the dinosaur asked, using a word odd to the bunny's ear.

"What's a push-mate, sir? Is that like a cart of some kind?" the shivering little bunny asked.

"A cart? No, I don't think so, fella," the dinosaur replied. "I just need a little shove. To get me feet on the right side of me body, right?"

A little confused by the critter's odd speech and even odder green color, the bunny moved closer and, using one of his padded front paws, he meekly poked at the little dinosaur.

"A little harder, mate. No need to be timid. I'm made of Grade-A petroleum products. Why, they make aeroplanes out of stuff like me," the dinosaur declared, grinning with his toothy smile, which suddenly made the bunny shiver even more, which then caused the bunny to whack the dinosaur with a lot more force, knocking the little toy out of the flowers and into the grass, after rolling over the shredded mulch.

"That's the ticket! Finally, I can get on my feet again," the dinosaur called from the grass.

Yet, even though the dinosaur had been freed, he was so small that he was hidden in the trimmed grass, out of sight of everyone, to include the bunny. The bunny, already nearly traumatized by running into a new animal on his usually uneventful morning rounds, became even more confused when he lost track of where the odd little critter had gotten off to.

"Sir, I'm sorry, but I think you are a ghost, now. I can no longer see you. I'm sorry if I caused you to be a ghost. I didn't know my front paws were that strong, sir," the bunny called, looking all around and then up in the sky.

"Down here, big fella. In the weeds, I am," the dinosaur replied, trying to walk through the stiff grass that was like a jungle to a small toy of his tiny stature. "Hard going, though."

The bunny, finally realizing the odd critter was just lost in the grass, wobbled back from the flowers and, using his twitching nose, finally found the little toy.

"There you are, sir," the bunny called in glee, standing on his hind legs to look down upon the dinosaur.

"Fella, I'm certainly glad you came along. Who knows how long I might have been stuck in that flower jungle?" the dinosaur called to the now tall rabbit. "Is this where you live?"

"Live? Here? Oh, no sir. I live in a den. Over by the Great Tree Stump, far across the many yards and wide streets there," the bunny replied. "I'm just here to check on the...well, you know."

The dinosaur shook his head, well, as much as a plastic toy could shake its head, and answered.

"No, I don't know. Don't really follow you, fella," the dinosaur replied.

"You know. For the top bunny. For her," the bunny replied, his face twitching at the odd creature's comment. "Well, this year she's a her. Some years a he. Some years I'm not sure. But, always in charge. I was sent here to scout for...for the children!"

Beyond the side fence in the back garden, Madylan and Greyson, who had been inspecting the pink and white phlox by the frog pond, looked up and spoke at the same time.

"Did you hear…?"

"Hear that…?"

Uncle looked at both of the children and shook his head.

"Hear what?" Uncle asked, as he looked around the pond for a frog that might be hiding that he could show his goddaughter and her brother.

"Sounded like my name," Madylan said, turning slowly back to the pond.

"No! Was Greyson!" Greyson declared, quite adamant that someone had called him.

"Maybe your mom needs you?" Uncle replied, but then saw that the sunroom door was shut, so there'd be no way to hear the mom or the aunt call from inside the kitchen where the two were catching up.

"Funny, huh?" Madylan said, then began pointing out things to Greyson, to include the 'reading frog' statue that had been reclining inside the colorful phlox for as long as she could remember.

Back at the front near the garage, the bunny had buried his head in the grass and had flattened his body to the point that only his white tail poked up.

The dinosaur, who had to duck when the bunny threw himself to the ground after uttering the word 'children,' brushed off the dirt from his short arms and waddled over to the bunny's face, where just the bunny's left eye was visible and wide open, as if waiting for something terrible to happen.

"Hey, fella, what's with all the drama queen antics?" the dinosaur asked. "Don't you like kids?"

"Shush! Don't say it so loud! They will hear you," the bunny cried, closing his left eye as well and burying his face farther in the grass.

"Fella, I'm no doc, but the kids are way behind this mountain of a house and are in no way going to hear anything you say or I roar," the dinosaur replied, poking the bunny in the left ear for emphasis. "Get up, you're going to have this tall grass all over your face."

Slowly, with a great deal of caution, the bunny lifted his head, then his front paws and then his body, all while looking around cautiously, ready to bury his head again if the children appeared at the gate, only a few yards away.

Seeing that no children emerged, the bunny relaxed a bit and then looked down at his new friend.

"It's not the sound, or the volume, sir. It's the Easter winds, sir," the bunny replied.

"Easter winds?" the dinosaur asked,

"Yes. You see, this time of year, as we scouts...well, even we junior scouts, third class, have to be very careful about saying...well, any word that might carry our voices to the ears of the...well, those who believe in the Easter Bunny and all that she brings, what she represents. You see, they are so young, these little humans, that's okay to say, I was told by the scouts, second class level, that they can hear their names called by the rolls of honor as the day draws nearer. We have to be very careful so that they don't see us scouting around."

"Why? What's to see, fella?" the dinosaur asked as he sat back and picked bits of dirt out of his claws.

"Well, nothing. If they accidentally see us before the day before the day. We look just like local bunnies before then. Those are the rules. But, if the...the little humans sneak around and intentionally look for us, even a junior scout third class like me, and, heaven forbid, actually see us on the day or the day just before, then its disaster," the bunny replied, his nose twitching even more nervously than before.

"What disaster?" the dinosaur asked, using a tuft of fur from the bunny's left hind foot to polish his claws after getting all the dirt out.

"Why, they would not have Easter, sir! It's the rule. They must be surprised, sir. If they are not surprised, then their Easter is given to the next kids on the list," the bunny said. "Haven't you ever wondered why some years the baskets are normal, but other years they are overflowing, to the point that we have to use paper and string to hold everything in? Those baskets are so fat, for good children, because some bad...some not very nice little humans decided to sneak a peek at one of us doing our duty."

"Well, I guess this neighborhood is through, then, fella," the dinosaur replied, pointing to a pair of adults walking along the far side of the street.

The bunny, initially afraid that the adults were there, quickly calmed down and answered the dinosaur, who was using the bunny's left hind foot as a perch to see over the grass.

"Silly, sir. Those are adults. They see us all the time. They think we are just the neighborhood rabbits, hopping about eating their flowers and the young bits in the gardens, they do," the bunny chuckled, but warily watched the adults to ensure they didn't suddenly produce a dog that would chase the bunny back to the forest.

Back in the back garden, Madylan had led Greyson over to the small arbor leading to the far edge of the side yard and to the huge, to Greyson, statue of the potbellied little Buddha, which Uncle called an Immortal, but, since Auntie called it a Buddha, that's what Madylan called the grey stone statue that stood guard at the second gate.

"It's okay, you can rub its belly for good luck," Madylan said, then whispered. "Wish for a lot of Easter eggs."

Suddenly, back in the front by the garage, the bunny shook so hard that the dinosaur tumbled off the bunny's foot and fell back into the grass and dirt. Sitting up, the dinosaur looked in disgust at his newly dirtied claws, sighed, and, renewed cleaning them using a small bit of cut grass, for the house giants had obviously cut the grass a couple of days earlier, no doubt to look good for the visitors.

"Earthquake?" the dinosaur asked, his voice dripping with sarcasm.

"What? Oh, no sir. A wish, sir," the bunny replied. "I've only heard a few, since I'm only...."

"...junior scout, third class. Yeah, we know," the dinosaur interrupted.

"Well, it is rare for us to hear them, sir. The little...the female human little one, sir. She just did a very kind thing and wished for her little...the other one that is her sibling, to have a lot of eggs. What a sweet thing to say," the bunny replied, his eyes starting to brim with tears of happiness.

"Whoa, fella. Don't start losing it now. I need your help," the dinosaur said, walking up and poking the bunny in the belly.

"My help? How, sir?" the bunny asked, choking back his almost tears.

"You see that huge carriage just there?" the dinosaur asked, back on the bunny's foot for a perch, while pointing at the New York car. "That's my home. Well, one of my homes with the boy. We have a house, too. And several aeroplanes. Another huge carriage. And, a lot of smaller houses, but those smaller ones have servants that bring food to your room. It's a pretty sweet life for me and my mates, so I need to get back in there. Wouldn't want to be left behind, no offense, here in the sticks."

The bunny then studied the huge carriage, which, to a small bunny, was a massive family car. White, with a little propeller symbol on the front that was far too small to carry the car anywhere, the bunny thought. The car filled half the sky above the bunny and the dinosaur.

"Get you back in that, sir? I would not be able to even get you to the top of one of those black wheels, sir, much less through one of those huge side gates," the bunny finally said, shaking his head as he looked over the doors of the SUV.

"Hmm. Well, that's unfortunate," the dinosaur said and then, signaling he was going to climb higher to get a better look at the carriage, clawed his way up the bunny's back to sit on the bunny's left shoulder.

"Yep, that's a big carriage. I see your point, fella," the dinosaur replied. "So, what do we do?"

For a long time, the bunny stood, his little eyes swaying back and forth, always on the lookout for the fox or the hawk, and any dogs from the area, and thought about the dinosaur's predicament, that's where someone has a bit of trouble that they have a hard time getting out of. At the same time, the dinosaur sat on the bunny's shoulder and mulled, thought carefully, over ways to get back in the car.

After a few minutes, neither the bunny nor the dinosaur had been able to think of a way to get back into the car. There were a lot of 'almost ways' to get back in, like climbing the small maple tree by the driveway, but the limbs didn't hang over the car. Another way that the dinosaur thought of was to run with all his might up a ramp and jump into the car. But, there was nothing to use as a ramp and the door would, of course, have to be open.

Finally, the bunny asked the obvious question.

"Sir, do you really need to be back in that huge carriage, or do you just need to be back with your...with the little human you call your...well, you know," the bunny asked, trying to avoid saying anything that might attract the child to the scout. "Back to the little human that has that scribble on your bottom."

"That? That's my little man's initial. Since I'm a toy, I can't read it, but it's supposed to be his name's first letter. Tickled when his big sister put it there," the dinosaur quipped, shoving his bottom into the air to see the small letter 'G' inked there.

For a long minute, the dinosaur stared at the initial and thought about his little boy, the boy's bossy, but kind big sister, and the rest of the family and, if the dinosaur had not been plastic, a small tear would have appeared in his eye. Just as the dinosaur let out a huge sigh, something the bunny had said finally sank into the dinosaur's very small brain.

"You know, for a rabbit, you are quite clever," the dinosaur suddenly declared, and snapped his claws. "That's what I need to do. Get back to my little man. He'll take me back in the carriage and away we'll go back home, right!"

For the next few minutes, the bunny and the dinosaur talked in hushed tones about ways to get back to the little boy.

First off, the bunny nixed any attempt to get the dinosaur into the big house, as the bunny, junior Easter scout, third class, was forbidden to enter homes, except on the morning of Easter to help the boss to leave treats in baskets. The bunny, as he had already told the dinosaur, also was not allowed to be seen by the humans, especially the little ones, so grabbing the dinosaur and hopping up to the boy or his family was out of the question.

So, the two then thought of places they might find outside where the little boy would see the dinosaur and pick him up and put the dinosaur back with the boy's other toys.

While the bunny and the dinosaur were scheming on places in the yard where the boy might spot the dinosaur, back in the house, where the boy and his big sister had gone after a full tour of the garden, the little boy began to sniffle and mumble as he rummaged through his toy box, sitting open in the comfy family room of his favorite auntie, and, oh yes, his uncle.

"Not here...?" Greyson sniffled as he finished searching his box.

"What's missing dear?" the mom asked from the kitchen, where she was having tea with Auntie.

"Ferocious...my dinosaur, is not here. He's lost?" the little boy called in a voice so plaintive, that his big sister hopped down from the kitchen table chair where she had been sitting with her mom and favorite auntie and joined her brother.

"Are you sure?" Madylan asked, poking around in the toys, for she knew which one was called 'Ferocious,' because she had named the toy for her brother.

"Wait, maybe it's in the car?" Madylan suggested and dashed off to find her dad and the keys.

Once she had the keys, Madylan was joined by her uncle and the two of them went to the driveway to check the backseat. After searching for a few minutes, they had to give up, admitting that the little toy was missing. What they both did not know was that the little dinosaur was only a few feet away, but hidden behind the daffodils where the bunny had hopped to when the two humans had appeared at the door. The bunny was also holding the dinosaur's mouth closed so that he couldn't call out, even though little girls and old uncles wouldn't be able to hear the toy's tiny voice.

"Hush, sir, or the humans will spot me and then it's curtains for Easter in this house," the bunny whispered to the struggling toy.

As the two watched, the little girl and the old uncle closed the carriage door, which the dinosaur thought he could have reached if the bunny had run up to the door just before it had closed.

"Be still, sir, here comes the little...the small human," the bunny said, his voice stressed, so very high pitched, to the point that several nearby birds flew away in fear at the odd sounds.

"Can we pick some?" Madylan asked of her uncle.

"Yes, of course. Let's go get your little flower basket first, though," the uncle suggested and, opening the garage door using the keypad to the far side, he led the girl into the cavernous garage to fetch the girl's basket, her gardening gloves that he kept on a hook next to her auntie's gloves, and a pair of shears to clip the flowers.

"Quick, we have to run," the bunny whispered to the dinosaur, who was still struggling to call out. "They will catch us for sure if we stay in the daffodils and hyacinths."

With that, the bunny bounded along through the young peonies lining the side yard to the gate, where the tall fig tree was just beginning to show leaves. At the gate, where the uncle of the house had recently removed the rabbit barriers at the bottom of the gate, so that the gate could be opened while the children were visiting, the bunny shoved the dinosaur under the gate's wooden planks. The bunny himself was able to just barely squeeze under the gate in the nick of time.

"What was that?" Madylan called out as she reappeared at the flowers with her pink garden gloves and small flower basket.

Fortunately, for Madylan and her little brother, she had only seen a bit of the bunny's left rear paw as it disappeared under the wooden gate. Since it was such a small part of the bunny, and the girl didn't know it was a bunny's foot, only a few pieces of candy would be deducted from her basket, the bunny thought as he dragged the protesting dinosaur away from the gate and to the small garden at the corner of the house, under the butterfly bushes, just beyond the small peony plants, to hide behind the little girl's garden flowers.

Panting heavily, the bunny finally dropped the dinosaur, who plopped into a stand of lavender and red miniature carnations.

"Ouch, these things have pointy leaves," the dinosaur grumbled, trying to wade out of the carnations. "Where are we now?"

The dinosaur was a little disoriented from the escape under the gate, because he hadn't been able to see well and, because he as a tiny toy, a few feet in human distance were leagues for the small dinosaur. As he looked across the back lawn, it looked like a massive, entire country in his eyes.

"We are in the back garden, specifically, that's the little g—, that little human's garden," the bunny replied, watching every which way for danger, from the humans, the hawks, and foxes that might be out during the day, and new dogs that the owners might have brought in recently, and generally anything that moved in the back garden.

"Wait, fella, how can this be my man's big sister's garden? She lives with us up in New York, not down here. These plants would not look so good," the dinosaur asked as he finally cleared the carnations and sat down beside a clump of yellow daisies, where he took a small bite out of a petal and rubbed his belly.

"Oh, the report on this house, from headquarters, where we keep reports on all houses that have children visiting for Easter, which is very common among these humans, but very, very confusing for us Easter scouts…where was I? Right, the garden," the bunny replied. "The uncle. Simple. All year, even though the little human and her brother only visit two or three times at the most, the old uncle carefully tends this little garden as if the little one might pop in any day. He takes care of all of it, with help from a gardener for some things, but the old uncle alone keeps this little garden in top shape. That's her initial there, hanging on the clematis trellis."

Munching on another daisy petal, the little dinosaur looked around the rest of the back garden, then scratched his head with his right claws.

"Fella, why would your headquarters keep such detailed records on the gardening habits of these big humans? Seems like a lot of paperwork for nothing," the dinosaur replied, scanning the far rock wall for signs of places where he could sit and then be seen by the little boy.

"Eggs, silly," the bunny replied, looking at the dinosaur as if the dinosaur had dropped in from another planet.

"Huh, eggs?" the dinosaur replied, looking up at the bunny with a squint.

"Easter eggs. If a garden is well maintained, trimmed, planted with nice flowers, a few that might be treats for us, and cared for throughout the years, it makes our jobs so, so much easier," the bunny replied, shaking his head at the dinosaur's evident ignorance. "Messy, overgrown gardens are a terror, where eggs can be lost for years. Nothing sadder than an Easter egg that hasn't been found. Tragic are the few that are never found, doomed to loll about in the different seasons, freezing, boiling, coughing, and the lot, all because of a messy garden and the little ones were unable to find it."

The bunny, moved by the mental image of a lost and forlorn Easter egg, looked like he was about to cry, so the dinosaur changed the subject.

"Right. Well, this looks like a well-kept garden, so there are probably no lost eggs here. Let's focus on finding me a spot where the little man can find me and get me back to my other toy friends," the dinosaur suggested, tugging at the bunny's right front paw for attention.

Sniffing back tears, the bunny nodded.

For a number of minutes, the two then tossed around ideas on where to place the dinosaur so that the little boy could easily find him.

"Uncle, can I pick a few from my garden, too?" Madylan then called from just on the other side of the gate, sending the bunny into a frenzy of activity.

Grabbing the dinosaur by his tail, the bunny hopped ever so fast across the widest part of the yard, jumped up on the low, stone wall, and dashed into the wide leaves of a group of purple hostas near a lone lemon tree near the tall back wall of the garden. Shivering from fright, the bunny then dragged the dinosaur deep into the darkness below a thick bunch of large leaves.

Suddenly, the bunny jumped, because he felt something else small and furry under his back paws. Thinking a fox was lurking in the hostas, the bunny almost ran out into the open, which would have exposed him to the little girl who had just opened the gate at that very moment.

Steeling his nerves, the bunny, holding his duty to Easter as more important than being eaten by a fox, turned to peer into the scary darkness behind him.

"Hey, big bottom buddy, who do you think you are sitting on me?" a squeaky, yet very authoritative voice called from the darkness. "This is my stash. Go somewhere else...wait, don't I know you?"

The voice's owner then stepped into a bit of dappled light falling through the leaves and peered up at the shivering bunny.

A small, brown, somewhat pudgy from springtime gorging on garden bulbs, wall-dwelling chipmunk was the owner of the commanding voice.

"Well! I'll be a mole rat's uncle! It's fifth class Easter boy himself. What's that? Some new toy for the holidays?" the little chipmunk asked, chuckling the entire time while he inspected the dinosaur.

"Chip? Is that you?" the bunny asked, inching closer to sniff the striped little fellow in front of him.

"The same, old bean!" Chip answered, slapping his thigh with his right paw, more like a hand, and chuckling. "Thought you were supposed to just scout around, not invade other people's stashes. Who's the little greenie?"

The dinosaur, not much smaller than the new arrival, stood up on his hind legs and tried to make himself look bigger.

"I'm my little man's toy, dark stranger Chip," the dinosaur replied, eyeing the little chipmunk suspiciously.

"A toy? And proud of it, you are? Well, scout of the sixth level, you certainly have interesting friends," Chip replied and turned back to a pile of flowers he had been sorting under the hosta leaves before he had been interrupted.

"Chip, he's a lost toy," the bunny said quietly, causing the little chipmunk to freeze in his tracks and then turn back.

"A lost...and you brought him here? Here? Into my garden?" Chip, obviously angry, yelled and then began to circle the dinosaur, sniffing and poking at the toy.

"Well, no question. We have to get rid of it," Chip said. "I know, I'll fool Harry the raven into fetching it."

"Wait, Chip. The toy's human is inside the big house. So, we're just going to put him somewhere the little human can find him," the bunny replied, reaching out to stop the chipmunk's circling. "No need to go to drastic measures involving unpredictable birds of prey."

"Harry, not the hawks. I'm not a barbarian. Harry will just bounce the little greenie around and chuck him over the back wall," Chip grumbled, then stopped circling and plopped himself down on a large clump of mulch.

For a moment, Chip was silent, looking from the dinosaur to the wide yard and back again to the dinosaur and the bunny. Finally, he spoke up.

"The table? The stone patio, near the flower pots?" Chip suggested, hoping to waste no time in getting rid of the green nuisance.

"Hush! I hear them!" the bunny suddenly hissed and spun around to peek out between the hosta leaves at the approaching old uncle and the little one.

"Uncle, are there any lemons yet, on the tree?" Madylan asked as she hopped up onto the slope above the low garden wall and, avoiding the hostas, skipped over to the lemon tree.

"There might be some small ones. Look at the blossoms and, if you see a little green baby lemon, then it might grow into a big one if everything works out," the uncle replied, then stepped in front of the hosta when he noticed some brown fur.

"He's keeping the little one from accidently seeing us," Chip called from his perch on top of the mulch. "Probably doesn't want her to be afraid when we run out."

"Run out? Why would you run out when the humans are right there?" the bunny whispered, holding onto the dinosaur's mouth again so that he couldn't call out.

"Why run? What a foolish question," Chip replied. "We always run when the humans are near. I mean, that's what we do!"

Chip then wriggled his long tail, hunched up his back and almost darted out of the hosta to head for his burrow. Almost, because the bunny, while holding onto the struggling dinosaur, stomped on Chip's tail and held him fast to the mulch until the little one and the old uncle had gone back to her little garden to pick a few more flowers.

Once the humans were on the other side of the yard, Chip relaxed his wound up muscles and turned back to the bunny.

"Okay, forth class, where do we stick your friend?" Chip asked, smoothing out the wrinkles in his tail fur.

"Hey, why are you guys deciding for me?" the dinosaur asked. "Maybe I'll just run over there myself and the big sister will find me."

Before the bunny could stop him, the dinosaur stepped out of the hosta leaves and, slowly, because he was a plastic dinosaur, after all, and tiny, with tiny legs and, also since he was plastic, very stiff legs, waddled a few human inches, which was a huge distance for his tiny body and then stopped, out of breath. Yet, it was not the short walk that took his breath, it was the shear distance from the small slope at the far back of the yard to the little girl's garden that took the dinosaur's breath away. Because the bunny had been so fast, the dinosaur had not realized how far they had come.

"That will take me a week, to cross alone," the dinosaur said under his breath, once he got his wind back. "I need the bunny and his kooky friend."

Turning back, the dinosaur could see the bunny's eyes blended into the leaves of the hostas. The chipmunk was standing out in the open, stock still.

"Hey, you're not afraid of the humans?" the dinosaur asked of Chip.

"They can't see me," Chip whispered out of the side of his mouth. "Humans can never see us if we just stand dead still, old bean."

"Okay, how do we get over to that table? That was actually a good suggestion," the dinosaur asked as he waddled back to the bunny.

"Have to wait until they have gone back into the big house," the bunny declared and then began to nibble on the corner of one of the hosta leaves.

"Hey, Mr. Chip, why were you so upset that I'm a lost toy?" the dinosaur asked as the chipmunk returned to the pile of flowers and started arranging them again.

"Lost toys have been the doom of many a well-made burrow and den. Not to mention birds' nests, rock wall hideaways, and the like," Chip replied in a grumpy voice. "The big ones, the big humans, will tear a garden apart, even a well maintained garden, to quiet the wails and cries of their little ones who've lost a beloved toy."

Chip then stopped his rearranging, which was something he and his kind always did with food before they took it home to a nest deep in a burrow. Chip's own home, with his wife and four little ones, was deep under the garden border wall, near the frog pond, about half the length of the back garden from where they were. A long way to haul food, without the humans, the foxes, the hawks, and even the owls, if they were awake early, catching him.

Nodding, the dinosaur signaled he understood and then joined the bunny in nibbling on a hosta leaf. But, the leaf did not agree with the dinosaur, so he spit it out and, using a small twig like a toothpick, dug a couple of bits of the leaf out of his teeth.

After what seemed like hours of waiting and watching, the bunny finally thumped his left rear leg in a sign of happiness when he saw the little one and the old uncle return to the house by way of the sunroom door.

"They're finally gone," the bunny declared and poked his head out of the hostas. "I think we can get to the patio now, and drop you where the little ones can see you."

Turning back to Chip, the bunny nearly squealed in terror at the sight of the chipmunk's bloated face.

"Good gracious!" the bunny yelled as he tumbled out of the hostas. "What has happened to you?"

"Habe do gut fud hum," Chip mumbled through the massive wad of flowers, stems, and seeds stuffed into his cheeks.

"Hey, fella, I think your little friend said he needs to get food home," the dinosaur called from under a hosta leaf as he emerged and waddled to the edge of the garden wall, then whistled.

"Whew! How do we get down from here?" the dinosaur asked, his head swaying from side to side, looking for some simple way to walk from the wall to the lawn.

"We jump," the bunny answered, and, picking up the dinosaur by his left hind foot, the bunny jumped off the wall.

"Aiyee!" screamed the dinosaur, his eyes bugging out from, for him, the long fall to the lawn.

Thump!

Back up on the wall, Chip was mumbling through his packed cheeks again, but the bunny just shrugged, not understanding anything.

"Your mate says he has to drop off lunch at home first, then he'll join us near that table, on the wide stone terrace," the dinosaur answered, shaking his head as he gingerly poked at his body to ensure he had not suffered any broken bones from the bunny's leap.

"Right, let's move on," the bunny said, his voice cautious. "We are very exposed here, in the open lawn. The windows there are to the kitchen. Luckily, the little humans are too short to see out of them. If the adults see us, we'll just look like a local rabbit out for a nibble."

To make the journey across the wide lawn easier and much faster, the bunny motioned to the dinosaur to climb on the bunny's shoulder again. Once the dinosaur was there and holding on for dear life, the bunny looked all around and up in the air, and began taking short hops, with his nose close to the ground to reduce his silhouette, his body's outline, as they moved across the dangerous ground of the open lawn.

Passing from the protection of an overhanging wild cherry shrub, the bunny began to look mostly up at the sky as he wriggled more than hopped toward the patio, what the dinosaur called the stone terrace. Every time a small bird flitted to the feeder just above, the bunny would freeze in place until he had identified the bird as a harmless song bird and not one of the scary hawks, or the annoying, bossy crows. Crows, and their big cousins the ravens, liked to pick on the bunny scouts, no doubt jealous of the little humans getting so many yummy snacks and shiny toys, so the bunny was always on the lookout for the pranksters of the air.

When the two were only a few feet, human feet, from the patio, the dinosaur almost fell off the bunny's shoulder when the bunny abruptly halted and fell into a patch of clover nestled in the grass.

"Clover!" the bunny cooed and rolled over in the lush patch, almost crushing the dinosaur.

Then the bunny reached out to grab a paw full, but jerked his paw back and knocked himself in the head.

"No. I'm on official duty. Must not eat the…must not smell…must not roll in…clover!" the bunny said to himself and then rolled over again in the patch, just as the dinosaur jumped clear.

"Fella, what's happened to the scout third class you're supposed to be? Something about you frolicking in the clover doesn't look like an official act," the dinosaur called, trying to get the bunny's attention, but with little success.

After tugging at the bunny's ears, the dinosaur then had an idea. Grabbing a few sprigs of the dark green clover, he pulled with all his might and managed to break several free. He then stepped to the bunny's nose, which was hovering over a delicious looking spot. The bunny, with his mouth open and drool dripping down into the clover, all the while kept telling himself not to eat, smell or roll in the clover.

"Here, fella! Here's some tasty morsels for ya!" the dinosaur yelled and then waved the freshly plucked clover under the bunny's nose, causing the bunny to abandon the patch and follow the dinosaur to the patio.

"Must…not…eat…clover!" the bunny repeated each time his mouth hovered over the plucked clover, its green clover juice dripping on the grass as they walked.

Finally, once the two had reached the edge of the paving stones at the patio, the dinosaur, using all of his strength, threw the sprigs of clover over his and the bunny's heads to land far up on the tall planter, out of the bunny's reach.

Shaking his head, the bunny looked around like someone who had been asleep and, looking down at the dinosaur, he spoke quietly, almost guiltily.

"I…I didn't eat any, did I?" the bunny asked, his ears drooping in shame.

"Well, not really. I figured from all your mumbling that eating clover on duty as a third class junior scout might get you busted down to a fourth or fifth class baby scout," the dinosaur replied, wiping his hands on the grass, mainly in fear of the bunny smelling the clover and taking a chomp of one of the dinosaur's claws. "Must be your kryptonite, right?"

"Kryptonite?" the bunny asked, his voice finally clear and back to normal.

"Your worst weakness. It's a term my little man uses with his action figures," the dinosaur replied.

"Oh. But yes. Very. Clover's so hard to find in these manicured, suburban lawns, that, when we do find it, we call all of our friends and have a feast. To stumble on one while alone is heaven. But, we eat too much of it that it makes us slow and sleepy, which is dangerous during Easter season, since we are so busy, so the bunny patrol HQ ruled years ago that we are not allowed to eat it from one week before and one week after Easter," the bunny replied, his eyes straying back to the luscious patch only a few feet away. "And, it tends to grab all of our attention, so many a colleague has been…well, let's just say it's very unlucky for a bunny to have his or her attention diverted when out in the middle of a wide yard like that. But, we're here now at the stone terrace, so let's look around for a place for you to sit and wait to be discovered."

Just as the bunny and the dinosaur stepped onto the edge of the circular patio, the screech from the screen door sent the bunny under the large wooden planter that the uncle and aunt used for growing vegetables off the ground, so animals like bunnies could not reach them. There the bunny froze and held the dinosaur's mouth as the two watched the little human step onto the patio with the uncle.

"Ferocious! Where are you, boy? Ferocious!" Greyson called and called, walking around the garden, looking at the wall, under bushes, and behind flowers.

As the little human moved around the garden, the bunny would shift his position, dragging the kicking and mumbling dinosaur with him. Once or twice, the bunny felt they would be discovered, but, each time, the uncle would inadvertently block the boy's view.

Finally, looking sad and lost, Greyson asked the uncle to pick him up. After he had done so, the uncle walked back to the door, where Madylan was just stepping out.

"No luck, huh?" Madylan asked her little brother, who just answered by giving her the saddest and slowest headshake she had ever seen.

As her little brother was carried into the house by their uncle, Madylan stepped over the edge of the patio and scanned all around the garden. She then pushed one of the patio chairs to the edge and, sitting, stared straight at the pond's gurgling waterfall for several minutes, just thinking.

As the little human sat in the huge chair, the bunny began to shake, almost uncontrollably. With a child so close, he was certain she'd eventually see him. The dinosaur, alarmed by the bunny's heavy breathing and continued shaking, tried to calm his new friend by patting the bunny's long ears.

"Easter Bunny?" Madylan suddenly called, looking out over the pond to the sky through the trees.

"Oh no, she knows I'm here!" the bunny blurted out and tensed up, ready to hop like mad toward the gate and escape. "If she sees us, she and the other little human will have no Easter and I will have failed!"

Suddenly, Madylan stood up and, walking right by the bunny's hiding place under the large planter, she walked slowly over to her garden, stopping at the yellow lilies to sniff them. She then walked over to the garden wall and, stepping up the slope just above, leaned over the grouping of hosta plants and called out to them.

"Miss Easter Bunny? Uncle told me you sometimes like to eat the bottom leaves of the hostas. He also sent us a video last year of one of you running across the front yard, so you might be in there. I know I might sound crazy, but there's no one here to listen, except maybe you," Madylan said quietly, as if she were talking to a friend and not a hosta plant.

Stepping to another large hosta, one with striped leaves, the big sister spoke again, her voice low, but loud enough for the bunny to hear her back at the patio.

"My little brother, even though he can be a bother, is a good kid. He's lost a special toy, one that means a lot to him. I helped him name it. Its name is 'Ferocious,' but he's a sweet little dinosaur," Madylan said, her lyrical voice causing even the birds to pause and listen.

Turning to yet another bush, one with a tall, lavender clematis climbing a trellis just behind, Madylan continued her monologue. Her voice was so clear that the bunny and the dinosaur easily heard every word.

"If you are here, Miss...or Mister Easter Bunny, I just wanted to ask you a favor. Maybe, since you bring many small things for us every year and even more when we visit Uncle and Auntie...I was wondering...that maybe you might have a way to find my little brother's lost dinosaur? Since you move around everywhere, and bring treats in the night, and hide eggs all over the town, even the world in the morning, I think you might bump into the little dinosaur. If you do, or your friends do, could you put it in my little brother's basket? I know it's a lot to ask you to deviate from...to change your Easter routine for something so small, but it would make my brother so happy. He's quite sad now. Not a fake sad like he can be sometimes, but truly sad," Madylan called quietly as she continued to look from hosta to hosta clump.

"So you don't lose time if you find the dinosaur, you can...you can skip my basket, Miss Easter Bunny," Madylan finally said, her voice choking up a bit. "I've always loved Easter. The treats and toys are always amazing. Yet, being here with Auntie and Uncle are Easter treats enough, if only my little brother were happy. So, would you please consider this, Mister Easter Bunny, or Miss, whichever it is? Thank you and, Happy Easter!"

Holding back her tears, because she knew she'd be questioned if anyone saw her cry, Madylan held her head up high, took a couple of deep breaths of the flower scented garden air, and marched back into the house, taking a long look at the happy garden where she had hunted eggs since she was little, before her little brother had even arrived, and then with him in more recent years.

Stepping into the sunroom, Madylan paused at the glass table with Auntie's Easter decorations. It was the table where she had discovered her basket for so many Easter mornings and where, when Greyson had only been a little over one-year-old, she had first shown him the wonder of Easter morning. Reaching out her hand, she briefly touched the spot where her basket had always appeared, picturing those earlier Easters and telling herself to not be disappointed and to show no sadness if she had an empty basket the next morning. For, if her basket were empty, then the Easter Bunny had heard her, had found the dinosaur, and it would be in her little brother's basket.

"Dear, can you help with the cookies now?" Auntie called to Madylan from the kitchen.

"Oh, yes, Auntie, I'd love to help with cookies! Cookies!" Madylan answered, and putting on her most cheerful face, which was easy for her whenever she baked anything with Auntie, or did anything with Auntie, she skipped bravely into the kitchen.

"Hey!" the dinosaur called to the bunny. "You're drowning me here!"

As Madylan had spoken her soft and eloquent plea for the return of her brother's lost toy, the bunny had gotten quite emotional. Once the courageous little girl had stepped into the sunroom, the floodgates of bunny tears let go, drenching the dinosaur and creating a wide puddle around their planter hiding place.

"I can't...can't...can't help...help it," the bunny wailed, heedless of whether he could be heard or not. "That was...so...so beautiful. I think I'll just perish!"

As the bunny continued to cry his little eyes out, the dinosaur decided he'd solve everything, to include saving Easter for his little man's big sister, by walking over to the entrance to the sunroom and finding a spot there where the humans could easily find him.

Patting the bunny on the back, the dinosaur bid his momentary companion goodbye.

"Pluck up, fella. She's a fine little lady, that big sister, she is," the dinosaur said as he wiped the water off his face from the bunny's tears. "And, you've no need to cry. She will get all her treats and toys, and will find dozens of eggs in the garden, tomorrow, she will. No problem, once they've found me and taken me inside to my little man."

Whiskers quivering, the bunny finally slowed his crying and wiped his runny nose with his left paw, which held a small, neatly folded handkerchief. Nodding to the dinosaur, the bunny extended his front right paw and shook the dinosaur's right set of front claws.

"Good luck, my friend. I'm so happy you will be back with your little human, that the other one will have her Easter, and you will be back where you belong," the bunny said.

At that moment, before the dinosaur could say his last goodbye, the chipmunk appeared near the closest table leg.

"Did I miss anything?" Chip asked, his face normal, no longer distended by all the food that had been in his cheeks.

Chip's question caused the bunny to remember the big sister's words, so the bunny began to bawl again like a baby, thoroughly confusing the chipmunk. However, once the dinosaur had taken the time to explain to Chip why the bunny was crying, Chip also got a bit choked up by the little human big sister's willingness to sacrifice for her little brother.

Trying to console both the bunny and the chipmunk, the dinosaur did not notice the shadows growing longer and the wind picking up. Late afternoon, nearly evening, was fast approaching.

"Well, what are we going to do?" Chip asked, finally controlling his own emotions and helping the bunny to calm down.

"We must get our new friend to that doorway, so they can see him before the sun goes down. And, I must return to the local HQ to file my reports on my area, so that the little ones in this zone will have Easter tomorrow," the bunny replied, wiping the final tears from his eyes. "I'm already late and haven't sent word, so I hope my colleagues are not worried."

Just as the bunny and Chip agreed to help the dinosaur to get to the doorway, all the way across the open patio, a loud screeching sound froze them both in their tracks, under the tall planter. The dinosaur, however, had already started to cross the great stone terrace, with slow going because of all the deep joints that he had to navigate with tiny dinosaur legs.

Screech! Screech!

Frozen, but alarmed that their new friend was out in the middle of the patio, or great stone terrace, both the bunny and the chipmunk began to yell for the dinosaur to stop moving, or, if he could, to jump under one of the chairs not too far away.

"Hey! Don't move! He'll see you!" yelled the bunny.

"Or jump under that chair!" yelled Chip, as he nervously eyed the sky above.

Screeeeeech!

The dinosaur, thinking that his two new friends simply wanted him to find a better place than by the door, just waved at them and kept heading to the sunroom door. The loud sound from somewhere overhead did attract the dinosaur's attention, but, since he was a toy and an inside toy at that, he had no idea where that sound was coming from. Besides, to the little indoor toy, the front garden and the back garden had already presented so many different and weird sounds that he just shrugged it off as one more mystery of the great outdoors.

"He's not listening!" the bunny cried, and stepped forward, causing Chip to reach out to his friend and hold the bunny's fluffy white tail.

"You can't go out there. You'll be snapped up in less than a breath!" Chip cried to his friend, pulling with all his might at the bunny's tail.

Screech!

Suddenly, a huge shadow blocked the rays of the setting sun, causing even the dinosaur to look up. Unfortunately, all he saw was a wide, kite-looking thing growing bigger and bigger. He smiled, because he remembered how much fun his little human had had with a kite the year before, and paused to watch it fly about the sky.

Just as the dinosaur looked up, Madylan stepped to the back door, her hands covered in flour, from making cookies. She shouted over her shoulder to her uncle.

"Uncle, I hear the hawk! I think it's back!" Madylan called and, shading her eyes, she looked up into the sky for the hawk, but she was looking the wrong way.

At the same time that Madylan called out to her uncle, a huge, majestic bird, a red-tailed hawk, swooped down and snatched the dinosaur from the patio in a split second, and, with one flap of its huge wings, flew back up into the sky and over the trees and out of sight.

The sound of the hawk swooping down caused Madylan to turn, so she did see the hawk flying away, with something in its talons, but that something was too small for her to see with the sun in her eyes. After a minute, she turned back to the kitchen, calling out in excitement to her uncle that she had seen the hawk, but only just a bit.

Back at the planter, both the bunny and Chip were devastated.

The bunny had nearly fainted when the massive hawk had grabbed the little dinosaur. Chip, even though he had stopped the bunny from running out to save the dinosaur, where the bunny would no doubt have become the target, given that bunnies are plumper and tastier that plastic toys to the hawk, he, Chip, had made a last minute dash out from under the planter and had made it to the chair when the hawk had grabbed the dinosaur. So, after watching the hawk disappear over the tall trees, mostly pines and a few tall ash trees, Chip slowly walked back to the distraught, very upset, bunny.

For a long time, as the sun began to disappear behind the neighbor's house, the two friends just sat, both silent, alone in their thoughts for the little toy. For, both the bunny and the chipmunk had lost friends and family to the mighty hunters of the sky, and never, ever, did those who were snatched ever return. Even the few legends of those who had escaped were rare, with Chip having heard one story from his great-grandfather, also called Chip, from the Chippewa Nation, as all of Chip's male ancestors were called, since the Chippewa people had given the European settlers the name for chipmunks. In that old story, the hawk had flown too close to a tall spruce tree and the chipmunk had been able to grab a branch and pull herself free and return home some weeks later after a harrowing adventure in the wild forest along the wide Potomac River.

Finally, the bunny coughed and Chip looked up at his sad friend.

"Well, I…I have to get back to HQ and file my report, Chip. Are you okay, old friend?" the bunny asked, trying to keep his whiskers and lips from quivering.

"I'll walk with you to the gate, old buddy. Sad about your new friend. Can't understand how that bird got so close before we knew he was there, though," Chip replied, resting his front paw on the bunny's shoulder as they headed across the lawn to the gate.

Once at the gate, Chip said his goodbyes and that he'd see the bunny the next morning when the bunny would be doing his official rounds, helping the Easter Bunny deliver treats and hide eggs.

"Going to be a cold night," the bunny answered. "So there will be a chill in the morning, with dew on the grass and on the rocks where we hide the eggs."

"You know, old bean, you said the boy and the big sister called your new friend by a fierce name. What was it?" Chip asked, pausing his dash back along the wall to his burrow.

"She...and the little one, called him 'Ferocious,' which doesn't seem to suit him, but I only knew him...I've only known him a short while," the bunny answered, blinking through a couple of late tears.

"Ferocious," Chip repeated. "Strong name. You know, with a name like that, there just might be a chance he...well, you know."

Without answering, the bunny nodded, patted his friend the garden chipmunk known as Chip for many, many generations, and ducked back under the gate to head back to headquarters to report.

Chip watched his friend disappear under the gate and then, reverting to his cautious, always alert chipmunk stance, he sniffed the air, listened to the various sounds, and noticed the wind chimes had increased their racket with the setting sun. He then dashed off in a flash so quickly that he was a blur all the way back to his burrow, where he dived in to be home safe with his wife and kids, two boys, both named, of course, Chip and two girls, named, of course, Chipsy.

Back in the human house, the family had gathered for dinner, with Madylan trying her best to cheer up her little brother by acting especially goofy, to include planning to show him how to make Play-Doh hair for Uncle, who was a little challenged in the real hair department. Once everyone was at dinner, she whispered an additional prayer that her little brother's favorite dinosaur would appear on Easter morning, just like the magic Uncle and Auntie brought when visiting New York.

Out in the gathering night, far away from the cozy home, the little lost toy dinosaur known as Ferocious was thinking hard about his unfortunate situation stuck in the huge talons of a massive hawk as it flew back to wherever hawks took the things they snatched up off of patios. Realizing he'd never find his way back to the patio if the beast dropped him by accident, he gripped the bird's talons with all his might, just in case. Looking down, the houses, trees, roads, and strange, huge buildings streamed by as the hawk flew home.

Ferocious, which was not really his name, which was, for a toy, simply 'dinosaur,' decided at that moment, flying through the sky to an unknown fate, that he'd use the name his little human had given him, out of respect for the little human and, in particular, for the big sister who was willing to sacrifice so much to get Ferocious back for her brother.

"Junior, what have you got there?" a booming voice suddenly called out of the evening air from somewhere over the hawk.

"Dad! Hi. It's my last catch of the day. I'm headed home to show you and Mom," the excited young hawk replied, surprising Ferocious that he had been snatched by a kid.

"Kind of a funny looking thing, isn't it?" the father hawk asked, flying lower where he could see Ferocious, the tiny plastic dinosaur, hanging onto the younger hawk's talon. "And, your grip is a bit off, son. That...whatever that is...seems to be holding on for dear life. Where did you find...I'm sorry, but it's the ugliest little critter I think I've ever seen! Where in the world did you find it?"

"Back at the big house with the feeding lure, where the song birds gather. The one with the chipmunks that we can never catch because they use that stone wall for hiding," the young hawk replied, holding out his right claw with the dinosaur in his talons. "I was actually flying home and saw some brown fur, but, when I swooped down, my talons caught this...you know, I'm not sure what it is either. And, you are right Dad. It's mighty ugly. Funny color, too."

The father hawk flew in a little closer to examine the catch and, just as he was about to tap the toy with his wingtip, Ferocious decided he'd had enough of their mean spirited banter.

"Hey, you big lug! Who do you think you are calling someone ugly? Does your dear mother know you use such words? Huh?" Ferocious called in the strongest voice he could muster to be heard over the rushing wind and the flapping of the massive wings.

"Ho, ho! Junior, we have a talker here," the father hawk laughed and poked at the toy. "Must be a mighty warrior to not fear us, the hunters from the sky."

"Fear you? More like pity you and this young one who can't tell a meal from a plaything," Ferocious yelled back.

For a moment, the father hawk fell silent, circling around his son as the two flew toward their nest, high up in a tall, tall pine not too far away at that point. He studied the odd morsel his son had caught, evidently by accident. As he examined the toy, the father's other thoughts were with his other two children, a slightly older brother to the one holding the toy and, more importantly, a twin sister to Junior who took every opportunity to make fun of her clumsy twin brother.

"Junior, you say you were aiming at a bit of brown fur?" the father hawk asked quietly.

"Yes, Dad. Odd, isn't it, that this green thing is what I picked up?" the young hawk replied, a sheepish look creeping into his face.

"Hey, I'm not a 'green thing,' you two big bullies," Ferocious yelled, waving his free claws at the bigger of the two huge birds. "I'm my little human man's favorite toy!"

Suddenly, the father hawk reared up and, pointing to the nearest tree, still some distance from home, he motioned to the younger hawk to land on a set of branches at the top of the tree. The young hawk, who always obeyed his parents whenever they were out flying, because of all the hazards they might encounter, immediately slowed down and landed softly in the tall pine, with his father landing just beside and above him.

Breathing deeply, the father hawk leaned over to stare into the little dinosaur's eyes and then let out a deep sigh.

"A toy? A human toy?" the father hawk repeated a few times as he shook his powerful head slowly back and forth.

The young hawk, well aware that, when his father became quietly thoughtful, that it was best for young hawks to keep silent.

"Do you...is there a mark? A mark of the humans, odd critter?" the father then asked.

Wriggling around so that the father hawk could see his bottom, Ferocious showed the huge bird the fading 'G' that his little man's big sister, the one called 'Madylan,' had drawn there long ago. Seeing the mark, the father hawk leaned in closer and, using his own, monster-sized talon, tried to see if the mark was real or something temporary that the odd creature had just placed there to fool them.

No, it was real, the father hawk finally admitted to himself.

"Please talon that...that toy to me," the father hawk demanded.

"But...Dad! I want to show Mom. And...and sis! I want to show sis what I can do!" the young hawk replied in protest, but did, indeed, quickly talon-ed over, which is how hawks say 'hand over,' the tiny green toy. "Besides, how was I to know it was a human toy?"

The father hawk took the little dinosaur in his huge talons, which were so large that Ferocious disappeared inside the bird's huge right foot, staring out from behind the closed talons like he was in a cage.

"Get on home, son. And, don't say anything to your mother. Just tell her I'll be a few minutes late," the father hawk said as he stretched out his huge wings.

"Father! It's nearly dark. Are you sure you want to fly back...?" the young hawk began, but was silenced by a look from his father.

Waiting for his son to fly away, the older hawk delayed his own departure until he saw his boy land at their nest far away, though the hawk watched easily since hawks have very superior eyesight. He watched as the boy's mother embraced him and imagined her scolding him for coming home so late. The father bird also saw in his mind's eye the sudden look of concern on his wife's face when their son told her that the father would be a little late. The father hawk also knew that, once the sister and big brother had fallen asleep, soon, that the younger hawk would tell his mother the whole story. So, the father hawk figured he had just enough time to return the toy and get back home before his wife began fretting.

As the huge bird took off from the tall pine, Ferocious was very curious about what was happening, but, no matter how loud he tried to yell, he couldn't make himself heard over the roar of the wind and the flapping of the great wings. The father was far bigger, stronger and faster than the young hawk, so there was no chance that the little dinosaur would be heard, so he settled down and watched the world below stream by, in reverse.

Reverse?

Ferocious suddenly realized the older hawk was retracing the flight path that the young hawk had just taken. Was the older hawk taking him back to the house? Or, was he just toying with the dinosaur and would gobble him up in the blink of an eye?

Ferocious got his answer in a flash, that's how fast the older hawk was.

Slowing down, the father hawk coasted over the big house's back garden and then spiraled down over the circular patio until he had landed at the top of the large umbrella sticking out of the middle of the patio table. Fortunately, for Ferocious, the umbrella had been folded up by the uncle for the night, to avoid getting fouled by the higher winds. After settling, the father hawk held out his right claw and, gently placed the toy on a fold in the umbrella fabric, where Ferocious was able to grab hold with his own tiny claws, avoiding a long fall to the table or, worse, all the way to the stone terrace below.

Just as the hawk stretched out his mighty wings, his sharp eyes watching the night sky for other dangers, even for large hawks, usually safely in their nests by that time, he heard a loud squeaking near his feet. Looking down, he saw that the little toy was saying something.

"Why? Why, big fella, did you bring me back? Thank you, by the way," Ferocious called, trying not to look down.

"Toy you are, odd creature and toy you will always be," the father hawk replied, his eyes turning back up to the sky as he continued. "These humans are an odd lot. They love animals so much that they make copies of them for their little ones to play with. But, if a toy is taken by one of the real animals, the humans can become angry and will search high and low for it. I've seen entire gardens upended, with homes of many creatures destroyed, in the hunt for a lost toy. The shrill wails of the small humans disrupt our own calls, confusing us and causing all manner of accidents. So, toy you must remain, odd creature, and return to your humans. This large landing where they take food from the great firebox, just there, is an ideal spot for them to find you in the morning. No need to worry. You are too large, even as small as you are, for the night bats to carry you away and I will pass the word to the owls that you are toy and not morsel, so they will not snatch you up. A few of the young ones might come by to look at you, but they are very obedient and will not eat you. My son is still young, but knows the rules about toys. He simply made a bad call. We are not crows or magpies to rob the humans of their toys and shiny objects. We are the masters of the sky hunt, and must maintain our position and dignity. We must maintain the order and the balance of things. So, toy you remain. Farewell, odd little one."

With that, the large hawk, a good deal wiser than Ferocious had originally thought, flew off into the night, the only sound of his parting a loud whoosh that rattled the tall mulberry tree as he ascended.

Hanging onto the fold in the green fabric, Ferocious looked around for an easy way to crawl down, probably backwards, to the bottom of the folded umbrella, which was not too far away from the glass tabletop. Finding a long furrow between two folds, he began to do just that, feeling his way in the dim light of early nightfall. Since he was so tiny, the journey to the bottom of the fold took what felt like hours to the little dinosaur toy. But, he finally did get to the bottom, or, at least, almost to the bottom before he heard the first chirping croak, right by his left ear.

Chirp…croak…chirp!

Forcing himself to be very still, Ferocious slowly turned his head to see what or who was making such a racket.

Eyes!

Huge, black and silver eyes stared back at the startled little dinosaur and caused him to almost lose his grip on the fabric.

"Chirp…croak…what? I say, bud, this is my spot," the eyes said to the little toy, the words tumbling out of the creature's dark pit of a mouth like a stream of marbles, all garbled up.

"Well, fella, I beg your pardon, but I'm not sticking around. I'm just trying to get to the great stone terrace below," Ferocious replied, squinting to see what was talking to him through the dark.

Suddenly, a piece of the fabric moved and, reaching out with its long, skinny legs and impossibly long, skinny fingers on an impossibly elongated hand or paw, a large tree frog suddenly appeared just inches from Ferocious' surprised face. Shuddering when the thin fingers found Ferocious' shoulder, the little toy gritted his teeth for whatever terror was about to happen.

"The stone terrace? Oh, you mean the patio. Danger at night, bud. Much danger. If the rats, they are so dirty they smell just like the dirt, so you can't tell when they are near, except for their constant snickering at some odd, inside joke they always seem to be telling themselves," the tree frog croaked to the toy. "If they don't get you, the big leaf slugs will slime you, trying to figure out if you are a plant. And, worse, the night flying owls can snatch you up without a sound, they can. Of course, the foxes and the raccoons might take a fancy to you, but you're a little small for them to bother."

Ferocious, regaining his composure, shook his head at the last comment and found his voice, which was a little squeaky after his momentary fright.

"No worries, fella. The big hawk said he'd tell the owls to lay off me," Ferocious replied.

"So, you're why the sky hunter landed on my night lodging?" the tree frog replied, his huge eyes bugging out to look up at the darkening sky. "Guess I can now let my friends know he wasn't looking for us. Chirp…chirp…croak-chirp!"

Suddenly, all around the table, the garden, and especially near the pond, a loud chorus of tree frogs began their nightly calls, once they had heard the all clear from the sentry tree frog. The sentry was the one who was elected each night to find a high spot to watch for and warn about night predators, like the owls and the bats and some other, unnamed birds. A hawk landing that late had been very unusual, so everyone in the local frog king's domain, which was two houses wide on each side of the big house on all sides, had gone silent when the bird had landed.

"Sorry to interrupt, fella, but, if the stone terrace…patio is too dangerous, what am I to do before the morning? I have to be down there where my little man or his big sister can find me," Ferocious yelled over the deafening din of the hundreds of chirp-croaking tree frogs.

"Sleep in the bottom fold, bud. No one can see you or find you there. Then you wake up and hop down to the table. Take care, for in the morning there are other dangers. That's when those goof-ball squirrels return, digging into everything looking for nuts they buried and can't find again. Truly annoying, they are, but, what can you do? They're squirrels," the tree frog said with a shrug.

The frog then turned back to where he had been hiding and, with a flick of his rear legs, which were also grotesquely long and thin, but muscular, literally flew to the top of the umbrella where Ferocious saw him fade into a small fold near where the hawk had landed earlier.

Slowly, then, the little toy dinosaur, having decided the wild, outdoor animals had better judgment than a toy, wriggled down to the fold at the bottom of the fabric, finding that it was snug, out of the wind, and warm. He then decided to settle in for a long night in the jungle of a suburban back garden.

Turning, Ferocious looked longingly at the big house, with the lights shining through the windows and the shadows of the family enjoying their time together. He wondered how his little man was getting on, but didn't worry too much because his little man had a lot of other toys to play with and make him happy, and a loving big sister and two amazing giants he called Mom and Dad. The aunt and uncle, whom the toy dinosaur had seen a number of times in New York, were also kind and would take very good care of his little man.

So, covering his tiny ears to keep out the now pounding din from the tree frogs and other creatures of the night that he had no idea what they were, Ferocious snuggled farther into the fabric fold and went to sleep. Well, he tried to go to sleep, at least. But, the din of the frogs kept up most of the night, so the poor little toy dinosaur barely was able to grab a few minutes of sleep the entire night.

Tweet-too-wheet!

Chi-chi-chi!

"Bird songs?" Ferocious said to himself, deep down in the darkness of his fabric fold. "Wait, that means it's...yes, morning!"

Struggling to unwind himself out of the umbrella fold, Ferocious climbed up a bit and saw that the sun was still hiding behind the other neighbor's trees, but was up enough to spread dappled light all around the dew covered garden. Mercifully, the tree frogs had quieted down before the dawn, so the toy had had a little more sleep than he thought he would, but his head was still groggy and not very clear.

Taking in a deep breath of the chilled morning air, Ferocious tried to peer into the big house through the windows to see if anyone was awake. He didn't see anyone, but he did see a light suddenly come on in the kitchen window and then in the sunroom.

"They're coming!" Ferocious said to himself. "I must get down now, or never."

Dropping farther down the fabric until he was hanging a few inches, human inches, so about two body lengths for the toy, over the dew covered, glass tabletop, the brave little dinosaur steeled himself to jump.

Plop!

Whish!

Thunk!

Ferocious had taken a deep breath and had let go of the fabric, falling to the wet, slippery tabletop where he had slid on impact and had shot over the edge, landing, fortunately, on the grassy side of the table and not the hard paving stone of the patio side.

"Oooo…!" Ferocious said to himself as he rubbed his bottom, but was happy he had landed on the wet grass and not the hard stone.

Standing, the lost toy looked back up at the top of the table and, sighing, knew he'd never be able to climb back up there. So, he turned to look around the patio and, after scanning all the best spots to be found, he decided to stick to his original plan and get to the doorway where they would have to see him as soon as they stepped outside to hunt for eggs.

"Wait," Ferocious said to himself. "Where is that bunny, junior scout third class? Did I miss him? If this is Easter morning, I'd guess he'd should have been here by now?"

Straining to see over the grass, the tiny toy looked for any evidence of Easter baskets or other signs that the bunny had already made his rounds. Unable to really see anything, the dinosaur began to slowly wade through the grass, which was slow going since the ground was also wet and a bit muddy, causing him to sink a few times as he approached the firmer surface of the great stone terrace, or patio as the tree frog and others had called it.

Suddenly, the screech of the screen door of the sunroom scattered the few birds who had been at the feeder.

Out from the sunroom stepped the uncle.

"He's too far away and the table is blocking his view," Ferocious grumbled to himself, so he just sat at the edge of the patio and watched the odd antics of the big human.

Walking around the back garden, the uncle appeared to be searching for something, or a number of things. He first went straight to the big sister's little patch of flowers, 'Madylan's Garden,' and poked around in the flowers. He then carefully followed the curving line of the low garden wall, poking and lifting as if looking for something. By the time he had finished the entire wall search, all the way over to the far side of the garden near the tall, overhanging trellis by the white lilac bush, the uncle was muttering to himself.

"Nothing yet. I don't understand. They'll be up soon. Guess I'll have to get out the backups," the uncle mumbled to himself as he quickly returned to the house, slamming shut the series of doors.

Puzzled at the odd antics of the uncle, Ferocious started his long waddle across the patio, which, in his estimate, would take him several hours. Remember, he's a tiny dinosaur with plastic legs, which don't bend very well and especially not well after sleeping in a fold of fabric, outside, on a cold night.

"Duck!" a loud voice shouted, out of the blue, in Ferocious' left ear, causing the toy to turn instead of ducking.

"Chip! It's you…!" Ferocious started to shout, but Chip grabbed the toy's mouth and dragged him under the table and then under a chair that was shoved under the table, forcing the toy to hold very still.

Above, no higher than the top of the holly tree, a mob of noisy crows was harassing the songbirds down at the feeder. Taking turns, the crows would swoop down and startle the sweet singing birds, scattering them all around. The crow pranks continued for several minutes until Ferocious thought he'd be stuck under the chair with Chip all morning.

Finally, the crows seemed to become bored and, one by one, flew off to harass something one had seen across the road. Away the mob flew, cawing the whole way and generally making a nuisance of themselves as they went.

"Close, old bean," Chip finally said, releasing Ferocious and wiping the dew from his very wet fur. "They would have made short work of you, yes. Saw then dismember a small dog toy once. Horrible to watch. The little pooch was devastated. A cute black and white little thing, visiting with the boy who used to live next door, but who comes back time to time. Parents are the two big humans who live there. They patched him up, but he was never quite right after that."

"Chip! I'm so glad to see you! Could you drag me over to the door? It's going to take me ages on these little legs of mine," Ferocious pleaded.

"Wait. Wait!' Chip responded. "First, you have to tell me what happened. How in this world did you escape from the clutches of that hunter hawk? I saw you with my own eyes. We both saw you! Oh, no. We have to tell junior scout fifth class…."

"Third class," Ferocious corrected Chip.

"…third class, and let him know you are back. With all your arms and legs," Chip finished and, grabbing Ferocious, dragged him, not to the doorway, but to the garden wall, only a few feet away.

"Hey, 'Wrong Way Corrigan,' the door is over there!" Ferocious yelled, using a phrase he had heard the uncle use in the past.

Ignoring the little toy's pleas, Chip pulled the little dinosaur up to the top of the wall and, holding the toy up so he wouldn't hit the stones as he ran, Chip scooted along the top of the low garden wall until he was all the way around to the far side where the bunny and Ferocious had squeezed under the fence the day before. Once at that end of the wall, Chip hopped down and, pulling the protesting toy behind him, found a hiding place under the yellow lilies in Madylan's Garden, just under the large, metal 'M' that the uncle had hung there when the big sister had been younger than her little brother's current age.

"Really, all the way back? It's going to take me a month to get through all that grass!" Ferocious mumbled to Chip, who kept shushing the toy.

Finally, Ferocious gave up his grumbling and, plopping himself down, watched two yellow butterflies flit about the big sister's flowers while he waited for whatever Chip was waiting for.

After what seemed only a few minutes, Chip's ears perked up.

"He's coming!" Chip whispered and stilled himself, causing Ferocious to do the same.

First, a pair of brown and pink fuzzy bumps appeared under the gate where the grass had been depressed from other journeys. Then, a round head appeared, facing down, and then a chubby body, which, for a brief moment, seemed to get stuck and then popped through, one of the paws holding a small bag, dragging those enormous bunny hind legs with it.

"Junior Scout!" Ferocious cried out, causing the bunny to immediately freeze in place, his twitching whiskers guiding his darting eyes to the unexpected source of the outcry.

"Little dinosaur? It that...no, that can't be you! It's your...your ghost! Argh! What have I done! Now you've come back to haunt me! You're so right to do so. It's all my fault! If I had just taken you to that door...so what if I had let the big s—, the little human see me...?" the bunny wailed, dropping his small sack and then falling to the ground to roll about wailing for the ghost to do its worse to the unworthy bunny.

Chip, having seen enough of the dramatics of his friend, dashed over and, grabbing the bunny by the shoulder, shook him something fierce, causing the bunny to actually wail even louder.

"Oh, my word! Chip! The hawk got you, too! But, I saw you go home, my friend. Oh, your poor children. Your dear wife! What have

I done...?" the bunny cried and began to bang his head on the ground.

Ferocious, recovering from his shock at the bunny's antics, joined Chip and, with both of them grabbing the bunny's waving paws, they pulled him to his feet and stood him in front of them, waiting for him to come to his senses, which he did after he had gotten his breath back.

"Not...ghosts?" the bunny asked, a wry look coming onto his relieved face. "But, how...?"

Suddenly, another bunny popped out from under the gate. A bigger, more muscular bunny with a no-nonsense look and a huge belt that held all manner of devices, so was quite scary looking.

"Junior Scout Third Class, what is the delay?" the tough bunny barked, eyeing Chip and Ferocious with suspicion.

"Delay? Oh, no delay. Local auxiliary, sir...ma'am. Scout Sergeant, ma'am, sir!" the bunny replied, snapping to attention and grabbing his small sack. "They're part of this garden and know the best spots, sir...ma'am."

Leaning over Chip and Ferocious, the tough sergeant sniffed them and, seeming to be satisfied, she clicked her heels and turned away. Just before she dived back under the gate, she barked an order to the Junior Scout.

"See that you are quicker with this. You're already two houses behind everyone else for sleeping in, Junior Scout! The boss will be by soon and all best be in order!" the tough bunny barked and then disappeared.

"Yes sir, ma'am!" the bunny called, saluting the retreating rear of the tough bunny.

"Right, we can talk later. I'm so late I might be busted back to Under-Junior Scout Fourth Class if I don't speed things up. Hop up, little one, back on my shoulder and you can talk as we work," the bunny said, and then, once the toy was aboard, hopped over to the wall.

For the next ten frantic minutes, the bunny hid Easter eggs all along the wall, running back to place a few in the big sister's garden. At first, Ferocious couldn't understand how his little humans would be able to find such tiny, tiny eggs that came out of the bunny's small sack. But, after a few had been placed, Ferocious looked back and saw that they popped out into much larger eggs a few seconds after being placed.

"So, that's how you carry so much, so far?" Ferocious mused.

"Yep, old bean. His HQ gets help from you-know-who, up north. Pixie dust or some such, which allows him to stuff all manner of things in that bag," Chip called, running along beside them, keeping a lookout for danger and for the humans.

"Wait here!" the bunny suddenly demanded, dropping the toy off his shoulder near the reading frog statue at the pond, and bounded toward the sunroom at such a rate that Ferocious called after him.

"Hey, you're going too fast! You're going to hit your...," Ferocious began, but was dumbstruck when the bunny didn't bash his head, but disappeared, just a bunny tail's breadth to the right of the closed door.

"What? How...?" the little toy stuttered.

"Timing. You see that little mark near the base of the wood framing the door?" Chip asked, pointing at what looked like a dark smudge to Ferocious. "Easter door. Only works on Easter and only for the Easter Bunny and his helpers."

"About that. If bunny there is the scout, when does the...?" Ferocious began and then fell silent, his jaw dropping almost to his belly, for the largest bunny rabbit he had ever seen suddenly appeared from near the gate.

Accompanied by a squad of tough bunnies, led by the sergeant they had seen earlier, the tall, almost regal bunny, the Easter Bunny of the Middle Atlantic region, strode across the lawn, almost floating in the eyes of Chip and Ferocious, both of whom remained silent and only nodded when the Easter Bunny saw them and smiled down at them.

Arriving at the door, four of the tough bunnies stood on either side of the spot where the scout had disappeared and, all together, as a team, they reached into the wood where the smudge was, and, pulling with muscles taut and faces grimacing at the effort, opened the special doorway so the Easter Bunny simply stepped inside. The four tough bunnies held their positions for about seven breaths and then the boss reappeared, nodded at Chip and Ferocious and, joined by her entire squad, floated over to the next house on her long, long list.

Just as the Easter Bunny disappeared around the other side of the house, the junior scout popped out of the smudge and, shaking himself free, stood up and let out a long sigh.

"Just in the nick of time! I just saw the big s——, the big one run into the kitchen," the bunny called over his shoulder as he took off for the far wall, on the way to the next house. "Let's get back to the wall so they won't see us."

"But, wait!" Ferocious tried to call out, but Chip had already grabbed him and was running across the lawn to the far wall, following the bounding bunny.

"Hey, don't you have to be at that house before the boss gets there?" Chip called to the bunny once they had gotten to the far wall.

"No kids in that one and I did the next one already," the scout bunny replied. "So, I've got about a minute. What do we do with our friend?"

"Hey, rocket scientists! I was trying to tell you to just leave me at the door! Where they will see me! Way over here, how in the world are they going to see me?" Ferocious grumbled to Chip and the scout bunny, both of whom had silly looks on their faces, realizing what they had done.

Chip and the scout bunny shrugged. Chip then hopped down from the wall, put Ferocious back on the bunny's shoulder and they all prepared to dash back to the door, but then froze at what they saw and heard.

"Let's go now!" Madylan called from the sunroom door, her face glowing, but with a subdued hint of sadness. "I think I see one already!"

Madylan's happy face revealed she had received her treat-filled basket, but the note of sadness, which she quickly erased when her little brother joined her in his bare feet, came from her realizing the Easter Bunny had not heard her prayer for her little brother's toy. Grabbing her brother's shoulders, she turned him back to the doorway and helped him wiggled into his shoes.

"Quick, back on the wall, behind the old apple tree," the scout bunny said, helping Chip drag the toy back over the wall.

"Hey, Scout, what's the worry. They have their treats and candy. The eggs are all hidden. What does it matter if they see us?" Ferocious asked, frustrated by being bounced around.

"Oh, sir. The little ones' memories will be wiped. Not today. Not even tomorrow. But, soon, very soon," the scout bunny replied, his voice very serious. "If, on Easter day, they see the boss or one of us scouts, even us junior ones, then they will soon lose the wonderful memories of this Easter morning. Of the egg hunt. Of making cookies with their aunt. Of the funny stories their uncle tells them. And, as the years pass, they will drift away from Easter much faster than if they were allowed to fully enjoy the memories. You see, Ferocious, it's just like a favorite toy. The memories are what the little ones hold onto as they age and grow into the big people. Without those memories of the wonders of Easter, or whatever they celebrate, only a dark and empty space will remain, clouding their ability to bring back those loving memories from their yesterdays."

Nodding, Ferocious relaxed and sitting down, slipped on one of the stones and fell into a crevice in the rocks. Chip, being smaller than the bunny, dove in after the toy and, backing out, dragged the little dinosaur back to the old apple tree.

"Hey, what's that on your feet?" Chip asked after he deposited Ferocious by the tree.

"Not sure. It felt cold when my foot hit it. Odd. Looks like a pink turtle shell," Ferocious replied, tapping the rounded thing with his claws.

"Dare I hope?" the scout bunny blurted out, leaning over to inspect the odd turtle shell, sniffing and poking.

"Chip, quick. You're small enough. Is there more?" the scout bunny shouted so loud the two children on the other side of the garden heard the squeaking, but then went back to hunting eggs. "Go! Go now!"

Diving back into the crevice, Chip rummaged around in the dark, finding something that crinkled to the touch. He grabbed it and pitched it out of the hole. When it landed at the toy's feet, the scout bunny inspected it. A candy wrapper. The candy long gone, probably from ants.

"Eureka!" Chip called from deep within the crevice, and then scrambled back out, pulling the other side of the odd shell behind him.

"What's that?" Ferocious asked, looking at the oddly spiraled, white cone shaped thing.

"That, sir, is your salvation!" Chip called, a huge grin on his face as he winked at his friend the scout bunny. "I think he'll fit nicely."

"Right. Let's do it quickly, they are already at the dogwood!" the scout bunny yelled, but wasted no time and, with Chip's help, shoved the two pieces over Ferocious, one over his head and one over his bottom.

"Wrong way around!" Chip called, looking back over his shoulder at the approaching children, the little boy running in front of the big sister.

To his horror, Chip also saw the parents and the aunt and uncle walking straight toward their hiding spot.

Struggling to shove the toy dinosaur into the two pieces, the scout bunny didn't dare look around to see if the little humans had spotted him. He finally managed to jam the toy into the two shells and, praying that the latch still worked, slammed it shut. Giving it a quick kick, he knocked the thing back to the crevice, with Ferocious inside, mumbling to himself.

Fortunately, Chip caught it just as it was about to fall back down into the dark hole. He then shoved a few twigs under it, so the thing was only half hidden by the wall. He then turned and grabbed the scout bunny's tail as his friend took a huge chance and leapt behind the lilac tree and froze in place, not even letting his whiskers wiggle.

For a long minute, the two friends, the scout bunny and the garden chipmunk, held their breaths as the two children approached the spot where the toy rested in the precarious cradle over the deep crevice.

"What's that!" Greyson called to his sister, spotting a shiny gold object near one of two bronze crane statues, a number of feet beyond where Ferocious was half hidden.

"Oh. It's the special...let's look!" Madylan answered and, stepping almost directly over the toy dinosaur's spot, she helped her little brother over to the shiny gold object.

"Look, Greyson, a golden egg...wait, there are two. A small one and a big one," Madylan laughed and then handed the smaller one that had a large 'G' printed on it to her brother and dropped the one with the 'M' into her basket.

Smiling, Madylan knew there would be special toys in the large eggs, so she helped her brother back down from the wall and watched him run to their parents to show them his prize.

As she stepped back across the wall to the lawn, Madylan turned and looked hard at the lilac bush. She wasn't sure why she looked, but, after seeing nothing of interest and no more eggs, she turned and fully stepped off the wall, narrowly missing the crevice.

"Uncle. Here's another hole," Madylan called, remembering a couple of years before when her uncle had repaired a section of the wall when he felt the crevices and holes were too large and might catch the shoes or hands of his little goddaughter and her brother.

Standing by the spot, Madylan took her golden egg and shook it a bit, listening to the items rattle around inside.

At the same time, the scout bunny was itching to run to his next assignment, but wanted to ensure the family had found the toy before he continued on with his official duties.

"Old bean, you be careful," Chip whispered in his friend's ear and slapping his friend's rump to spur him on, Chip dashed out into the open, chattering away like...well, like a chipmunk, drawing the big sister's eyes away from the scout bunny, who bounded along the side of the house and then froze at the second gate and waited a few seconds to watch his friend and to see if the girl discovered the toy.

"Uncle, look!" Madylan called, pointing at the chattering little chipmunk perched by the old apple tree. "He's mad about something."

"Maybe we are close to his house. They live in these walls, you know. That's why I have to be careful when I fix it, so that I don't destroy his or her house," the uncle replied when he arrived beside the big sister. "Like that hole you found, maybe it's part of the little guy's tunnel. Wait, what's that? Did you two miss one?"

Madylan, certain she had found all the eggs with her brother, leaned over and, to her astonishment, saw that there was another egg halfway down the hole she had just pointed out to her uncle. The egg was covered by some twigs and leaves, so had been hard to see. Reaching in, she almost picked it up, but stopped herself, pulling her hand back.

Staring at the egg, Madylan realized she had seen the style a few years earlier. It was part of a set she had collected before her brother had even been born. Faded, the pink bottom was still visible and the curling top, that was supposed to look like ice cream, while a bit beat up, still had the right shape.

"A lost egg, Uncle," Madylan said in hushed tones. "From when I was little."

"Yes, dear, I think you are right," the uncle replied, just catching a glimpse of brown fur near the second gate. "Do you want to pick it up? I can if you think it's too dirty. Wonder what's in it?"

"No. I mean, yes. Greyson!" Madylan called to her brother. "We missed one."

Running back to his big sister, the little brother's grin was huge when he saw the egg in the hole near the wall. His smile grew even larger when he realized just how much his big sister loved him to let him find the final egg.

"Pick it?" Greyson asked as he peered into the crevice and let his hand hover over the egg. "Dirty?"

"It's okay, I don't mind. I'll pick it up and open it for you, okay?" Madylan asked.

"Okay," Greyson replied, beaming at his amazing sister.

At the gate, the scout bunny had wriggled halfway under, with only his head and flattened ears peeking out as the big sister reached in and pulled the egg out of the crevice.

Smiling, the scout bunny finally disappeared under the gate, content that the lost little dinosaur toy had been found. He then hurried to his next assignment, which only had one child, so would be faster to prepare. Just before departing, he had waved at his friend Chip, who had waved back as the chipmunk had dashed away as soon as the big sister had touched the egg.

"Chipmunk!" Greyson squealed with glee as the small striped back of the fleeing chipmunk seemed to prance all the way to the back of the forsythia bushes and disappear.

"Okay, the last egg," Madylan declared after her brother turned back. "Let's see what's in it."

Slowly twisting the egg over her brother's outstretched palms, Madylan opened the small plastic ice cream egg and out plopped the treat.

"Not candy? Not a truck?" Greyson asked, peering down at the small, green toy.

For a long moment, the young boy had a puzzled face, his furrowed brow an echo of his father's similar look when puzzled. Then, slowly, as Madylan looked on, Greyson's face began to show recognition, then excitement, and then sheer joy as he realized what had fallen out of the faded old Easter egg.

"My dinosaur...? Yay! My Ferocious! In the Easter egg!" Greyson yelled for all to hear. "Dad! Mom! Auntie! Look Auntie, my lost dinosaur. Uncle, I was looking and looking and he was hiding in this little egg the whole time! It's magic!"

Hugging the tiny green dinosaur to his chest, Greyson then grabbed his big sister, Madylan, the greatest Easter egg finder, ever, in his adoring eyes, and hugged her as well, happy as any kid on a bright Easter morning.

"That's amazing, Greyson. Just like your magic dresser where things appear," Madylan said as she led her brother back to the house and breakfast, all the while looking suspiciously at her uncle, suspecting the old softy had had something to do with the old egg and the lost dinosaur.

"Who wants pancakes?" Auntie called from the sunroom door. "Specially made for Easter morning? Madylan, can you help me?"

"Oh, yes, Auntie, I'd love to," Madylan answered, pausing to watch her uncle raise the large patio umbrella.

"Hey, little guy, time to find a tree," the uncle suddenly said to something on the umbrella fabric.

Picking up one of the potted plants, a bushy red flower, the uncle coaxed a small, grey-green tree frog off the umbrella and onto the flower and then sat the flower on the wall near the pond, all in one fluid motion.

"You know, Uncle, isn't it pretty amazing, the magical things that happen in your garden on Easter?" Madylan asked, smiling up at her uncle when he had turned back.

"What? Oh, the dinosaur? I thought you did that," the uncle replied, scratching the back of his head.

Shrugging her broad shoulders while shaking her head, Madylan took her uncle's hand—yes, his hands were always dry and scratchy, and led him back into the house for breakfast, as she realized that her uncle was telling the truth. Something else had put her little brother's toy in that egg, she decided, but didn't think about it too hard.

As she stepped back into the sunroom and heard the cheerful sounds of her little brother playing with his now found favorite little dinosaur, Madylan, the big sister with the even bigger heart, smiled at her full basket and that of her little brother's. She even smiled at the small baskets for her parents and her aunt and uncle. She then whispered a gentle thank you to the Easter bunny, the scout bunnies, the chipmunk for making her look at the wall, and all the garden creatures for helping return the toy. Somehow, deep down, she knew they had managed to save the little dinosaur. Crossing into the kitchen, she silently thanked all the creatures for answering her prayers and for bringing a big, Easter smile back to her favorite little 'bother brother.'

"Dear, I think Greyson's asleep. You can stop your story now," Madylan's mom called quietly from the front seat, bringing the big sister storyteller back to the present.

"Oh, I know. He fell asleep when the frogs appeared in the story, so he doesn't know how it ends. I'll tell him later," Madylan replied and put her own head back to snooze for the remainder of the drive.

After what seemed like only a few minutes, Madylan awoke and saw that they were turning into their aunt and uncle's street. Leaning forward and craning her neck, she caught her first sight of the house at the end of the lane and had to choke back happy tears, seeing the wonderful place where she had so many fond memories.

"We're here! We're here!" Madylan suddenly called, waking Greyson from his nap as the large BMW SUV rolled into the driveway. "Mom, I want to see my garden first thing! Well, second thing, after seeing Auntie and Uncle."

Madylan was out of the car in a flash, hugging her aunt and uncle.

After his dad had released the child seat belts, Greyson hopped down and ran to hug Auntie, one of his favorite aunties. Madylan, seeing that a bunch of toys and snacks had fallen from her brother's child seat, ran back and helped her dad put the items back in the car. Uncle joined them to help carry the bags inside.

"What about this, Madylan," Uncle asked, picking up a small green dinosaur from the driveway. "Does it stay in the car?"

Madylan, a wide grin forming on her face, gently took the toy from her uncle and, holding her finger up to her lips to silence him, she tiptoed over to the flower patch full of daffodils, hyacinths, and not quite ready tulips. Waving her uncle over, she dropped the little toy into one of the large, pink hyacinth blossoms, where it fell between the blossoms and the tall green leaves. She then took her sandaled foot and rubbed it across the freshly mowed lawn beside the garage, just to the left, as if thinking of what to say to her uncle.

"Uncle, later, when we are looking at my garden, just the two of us, I have a...I have a funny story to tell you," Madylan said, almost whispering. "And, do you think the Easter Bunny, and her junior scout, third class, would mind some minor human help this weekend…?"

"Help?" the uncle mused, wondering what his precocious goddaughter was up to. "Madylan, I think the whole Easter array of critters would love some help from a clever big sister and an old uncle this weekend. Let's first go join your Auntie and start making some memories."

"Thank you, Uncle," Madylan replied and, taking her uncle's hand, quickly led him away from the flower patch.

Madylan forced herself to not look back, just in case, just in the smallest, slimmest case that a scout bunny, just like the one Uncle had sent a video of munching by that very flower patch, was hopping up to the tiny dinosaur and wriggling its nose at the funny little green thing in the flowers. A funny little green thing with a small, handwritten 'G' on its bottom.

"Yes, Uncle, let's do help the Easter creatures…critters this weekend. I think this will be a weekend for wondrous memories, old ones and a few new ones," Madylan quipped.

Just before she stepped through the front door, on the first day of an all too short Easter visit to her godparents' embracing Virginia home, Madylan whispered a thank you so quietly that only she could hear. Yet, she also hoped her happy words would float out into the cheerful gardens where maybe, just maybe, they might be heard by a little junior scout bunny tucked out of sight, somewhere beyond the hyacinth, only a few hops away from a big sister's vivid imagination.

6

THE DRAGON MEDAL, A KOREA TALE

The old, glass fronted china cabinet, with its collection of curios from across the globe, was tucked away in the side gallery of the landing of Madylan's aunt and uncle's Northern Virginia home, and had always been in the periphery of Madylan's vision her entire life. During visits to her godparents' home, a long car ride from New York's Manhattan Island, she'd glance at the mysterious items through the beveled glass, wonder for a moment about this or that, and then continue on to the large playroom at the end of the upstairs hall. Yet, for some unknown reason, one spring visit, not too long ago, she stopped, fully, for the first time by the tall cabinet, her eyes drawn to a small, circular piece of bronze metal hung over the top of a board full of colorful bits of ribbons and shiny metal shapes. The round piece of metal seemed almost out of place in the cabinet of half-forgotten family mementoes. To her young eyes, the little disc seemed to be pulsating, signaling it wanted to get out of the stuffy cabinet and see the world.

"Do you want to see it?" a familiar voice asked, interrupting Madylan's musing on what the disc might be and why she had noticed it.

"Oh, Uncle, I didn't see you," Madylan responded, jumping a bit at being pulled out of her trance while staring at the bit of metal.

"It's okay. I can take it out," her uncle replied and, gently pulling open the glass door, which protested for a moment with a low squeak, he reached in and retrieved the disc, which was attached to a short ribbon of mostly green with a wide blue stripe.

Once she could see the ribbon clearly, Madylan noted that it also had white stripes and yellow stripes running on either side of the wider blue stripe. Her uncle carefully placed the small item in her upturned palm. Turning the small disc over in her hands, she studied both sides, recognizing the map on the back, overlaid with two crossed swords. The other side, which had writing, so she assumed it was the front, was a little harder to figure out. She could read the text, but the image in the center was a little puzzling.

"It's hard to tell...? Maybe an animal? Looks like it has scales. A big fish?" Madylan guessed as her uncle looked on.

"Well, here's a hint," her uncle offered. "What is your Lunar New Year animal? From your birthday? Do you remember?"

Scrunching up her nose, Madylan held the disc up closer to her right eye.

Slowly, like an unfolding morning flower, recognition dawned on the youthful face.

"A dragon! Maybe a water dragon?" Madylan whispered in hushed tones.

"Yes. A dragon. A symbol for...?"

Flipping the disc over, the girl pointed to the map.

"Korea, where I'm from...well, where my family is from," Madylan replied. "Well, not you, Uncle. I know your family comes from South Carolina."

The uncle nodded.

"What is this for? Why do you have this?"

"It's a medal. It's like the ones you see there that look like a bunch of multicolored ribbons. Those are other medals, for other awards or actions. They represent medals like the one in your hand, but they are easier to wear on a uniform than a bunch of clanging metal, unless it's a special occasion. The one you're holding is a military honor given to those who have served in the defense of South Korea. I was assigned there, years ago, long before I had even met your aunt in Washington. Years after I left Korea, the president, President Bush, approved an award for those who have served in defense of Korea, since the war. And those who still serve, even today."

Madylan turned her wide, dark eyes back to the medal and, with the utmost care, moved to return the disc to the top of her uncle's awards plaque.

"Is that the president who lives in Kennebunkport?"

"Well, one of them, yes. Remember from your class that there have been two presidents named Bush, father and son. This medal was awarded to the military by the son."

Madylan reached up to return the medal to its spot on the shelf.

"Wait, you can hold it for a bit, if you'd like."

A huge grin spread across the young girl's face as she withdrew her hands from the cabinet. Her uncle closed the door.

"Can you tell me about the medal and when you were in Korea?" Madylan asked, nearly whispering as the two walked down the hall to the cavernous playroom at the end of the house, over the garage. "And maybe the other medals on the...what do you call that board?"

"It's a career montage, shadow box, put together by a great friend, Greg Lassila," the uncle replied. "He was Air Force as well."

Arriving in the large playroom, Madylan sat down and barely squeezed herself into the decades old Little Tykes table that she had used since she was a toddler. The table had been a favorite of her older cousin decades earlier, so she enjoyed the family connection. She placed the medal on the smooth plastic surface, which still held two worn stickers that her older cousin Alex, her aunt and uncle's son, had put there over thirty years before.

A number of other items from her cousin's childhood were scattered about the room. Brio train sets from three decades before, brought out for her little brother to play with, were resting in boxes for the next day. Playmobil people were packed sideways in another box. Lego bricks were in yet another box. A small bag of marbles rested on the Lego box. A stack of old board games cluttered one of the glass tables her aunt's mother had brought with her when she had moved from California to live there for several years before deciding on getting her own apartment close by.

In fact, the grandmother had left a number of pieces of furniture in the large room. There were mother-of-pearl inlaid black lacquer cabinets from old Korea in one corner, two massive, comfy leather chairs along the wall that wouldn't fit into her new place, a nearly unused exercise bike that was gathering dust at the other wall, and a large, mirrored vanity, also from old Korea, near the door. Finally, a wide, multi-panel, art-filled screen was hiding stacks of boxes of other possessions rarely used.

"Was Korea old and dark when you were there, like in the old photos Grandpa shows us?" Madylan asked, twirling the small medal's ribbon on her finger, which then slipped as she turned, falling to the carpeted floor.

"Here, let's pin the medal to your sweater. Do you think you can do it?" the uncle suggested, sitting back as his niece pinned the medal on her sweater and then placed her hand over the small disc, beaming up at him. "And, no, not dark at all, unless visiting those caves on Jeju Island counts. Korea, when I was there, was a bright, cheerful place, focused on the future, even though the war, which hasn't really ended even today, was still fresh in people's minds."

As the niece tapped gently on the medal, the uncle collected his thoughts on how to explain some of his Korea experiences to one so young, without boring her to tears and, of course, without going into the scarier aspects of the Korean conflict.

"Now, if you sit back, close your mind to this room and open it to travel to faraway Korea, I'll try to transport you to your ancestral lands with a few insights from my military time in Korea and visits over the years."

Closing her eyes, but only briefly, Madylan smiled with a look of anticipation, and then extracted herself from the nearly too small child's table. Near the ornate screen, a pair of her aunt's well-loved house slippers attracted her eye, so she quietly put them on, glad for the added warmth in the drafty playroom. She then plopped herself down on the cushy leather chair just opposite her uncle, pushed aside a huge Hello Kitty, grabbed one of the even softer side pillows, and draped herself across the chair, her hand still over the small medal. Her other hand dangled the Mardi Gras beads hanging from the Hello Kitty, which had been from a visit by her uncle and Alex years and years before, she had been told, to a popular Murrells Inlet restaurant in South Carolina.

Since her uncle had been known to put her aunt to sleep with his long, detailed, historically heavy stories, Madylan fought back an anticipated yawn, although brought on more by the long drive from New York City that morning than by her uncle's melodious voice.

"Ready? Okay, sit comfortably in the chair, maybe lean on the big Hello Kitty, and let your mind drift among the clouds and then the stars to glide across the lands and oceans to Korea," her uncle said, his voice carrying his little niece far away from the house.

As she listened to her uncle's mellow voice, Madylan slowly sank deeper into the large chair and, blinking the sleep from her eyes, she strained to hear his voice, which seemed to come from far away. So far away, that she felt as if she were listening through a long tunnel.

Against the far wall, the old painted screen, inlaid with semi-precious stones, seemed to swirl as the uncle's voice became fainter and fainter, talking of the old days in Korea. He spoke of the cold of the winters, the stunning beauty of spring, the cheerfulness of the farmers near his base, called Osan, the little orphanage at Songtan that his unit supported, and the high fashion, fast pace, and complex society of Seoul, the capital and where her grandparents had been born.

Long ago.

Long, long ago, Madylan mused to herself as her eyelids fought with her mind to close and snatch a bit of sleep. Uncle would not notice, she thought, if she let herself snooze for just a second, while he talked on about his first encounter with that land far, far away.

A calming quiet descended on the young girl's mind as she finally let the heavy eyelids win.

Long ago.

Far, far away.

Clang!

Suddenly, a sharp sound startled Madylan out of her slumber. Looking around, she didn't see anything out of order, but did notice that her uncle had apparently drifted off to sleep while he had been telling his tale in the big comfy chair.

Smiling, Madylan leaned back and let her eyes drift around the room, her right hand tapping on the small medal, while she listened to the distant voices of her mother and her aunt downstairs in the family room, with the occasional outcry of her boisterous little brother. Her dad had gone out to see a friend's car, she remembered.

Finally, Madylan ceased her tapping and snuggled into the chair, her gaze resting on the old screen, with its forest and village scenes, steep mountains, oddly dressed people, and many birds and animals. She had always wondered how the artist had made the screen, in that it was painted, had stone or gem inlay, and was made from different colored cloth.

Snuggling even deeper into the cushy chair, she smiled at the sound of her tapping on the medal, feeling warm inside and happy resting in the protective cocoon of her aunt and uncle's home.

Tapping?

What tapping?

Madylan shook her head and looked down at the little medal hanging on her sweater. She then looked down at her hands resting on her lap.

Resting on her lap…?

Slowly raising her eyes, Madylan looked around the room, trying to find the source of the tapping, which certainly was not from her fingernails.

Tap…tip…ting!

The screen?

Staring hard at the old painted screen, Madylan leaned in her chair until she almost fell out, then cautiously stood, wondering for a moment if she should wake her uncle. But, since he looked so peaceful, she decided to investigate herself. If she found a mouse or other creature, then she'd wake her uncle in a flash.

Slipping her feet back into the house shoes, Madylan tiptoed over to the screen, cocked her head and listened.

Tap…tap…tap, tap, tap…tap, tup, tap, tup, tap!

Tip…tap…tap…ting!

Astonished at what sounded all the world like the little melody that she, Madylan, had just been tapping, she leaned so close to the screen that she held out her right hand to steady herself on the screen's heavy wooden frame. Leaning farther in, she strained to hear the tapping again, but suddenly felt herself falling, the tapping sound receding into the distance.

Falling?

Catching her breath, Madylan grabbed at the air around her as she slipped and fell into the screen, fearing she would tear it and ruin it.

Falling!

Grasping at the screen's frame, Madylan finally found a good handhold and, laughing nervously at herself and her clumsiness, she pulled herself up and stepped away from the tall, majestic pine tree she had been holding onto.

Pine tree?

Slowly, Madylan let her gaze travel up the side of the towering pine tree, to stare at the top and the other tops of trees around it.

A forest?

Madylan jumped back, thinking she had bumped her head and was acting dizzy, but only crashed into another tree, an old oak, twisted and dark, seeming to lean down with its tangled branches to snatch her up for a morning meal.

Morning?

But, it's nighttime, Madylan said to herself, finally looking around for her sleeping uncle to wake him and figure out what was happening.

No uncle. Only a jumble of large stones and rocks where he and his chair should have been.

Far away, up a long hillside, Madylan could just make out the top of a large house behind a high wall. Smaller houses, or rather huts, were scattered around the larger house. Yet, try as she might, she saw no people, or even animals anywhere near the house.

Okay, Madylan said to herself, think, think!

A dream?

Yes, that's it, I'm asleep and this is a dream brought on by the long drive and the cookies Auntie and I made, Madylan reasoned with herself.

So, thinking she might find answers at the big house far up the hill, Madylan turned to make the long trek to the only civilized thing she could see, with her mind on how to wake up, get back to normal and away from the steep forest world around her.

"Brave, you are, little sister, to face those who may remain at the manor," a voice, low and guttural, but matronly and kind, suddenly pulled Madylan from her brief reflection. "But, I fear you will only find sorrow behind those old walls."

Looking around, Madylan let out a small gasp. Not only was she no longer sitting across from her uncle and was lost in some dark forest, but she also was facing the oldest woman she had ever seen. The woman, somehow, seemed familiar, even though Madylan had never seen her before. She was dressed in clothes from old photos her grandfather had shown her. Clothes that also appeared in some of the old Korean postage stamps her grandfather had given her to add to her stamp collection.

Just like the clothes in the old screen, Madylan realized, stepping backwards, away from the ancient woman.

Yet, even with her momentary surprise, Madylan was not afraid of the old woman, and felt she must be part of her dream. Yes, a dream brought on by the long drive from New York and the lack of sleep the night before at the excitement of visiting her aunt and uncle. So, without fanfare, she mutely nodded at the old woman and then involuntarily reached for and found the little medal her uncle had let her wear. At least that's still real, Madylan thought, feeling some level of comfort in the familiar in such a strange place.

"Well, we haven't much time, have we, little one?" the old woman said, pointing toward a long, tunnel-like trail that headed off into a vast range of grey and green mountains, with long shadows from an early morning sun carving deep valleys across the far landscape.

Madylan looked from the old woman to the far house on the hill, her young eyes asking the obvious question as to why she shouldn't run away to that house. The old woman followed Madylan's gaze, then slowly sighed and spoke in a sad, distant voice.

"The house will survive. It has for many, many centuries. The clan may even survive, in some form. Such is the fate of those who attract the attention of the unjust and greedy. Shall we go?"

With that, the old woman turned away from the rocky trail that led up the hill and started down the same trail in the opposite direction, down the hill, or, more accurately, the mountain.

"Dear, little sister, I know you must be confused. Many are during these troubled times," the old woman called from just beyond the first tall pine tree. "My sedan chair rests some lengths up the hill, where my servants were escorted away by soldiers. So, now I walk. Do not fear this path, but respect those also about. I spy strength in you and in your odd little talisman hanging near your neck. Clutch it when you feel unease, and follow me."

Unsure as to what the old woman meant by most of what she had said, Madylan fully understood that going up to the apparently abandoned house would be a waste of time and maybe dangerous. So, trusting the old woman for some unknown reason, Madylan nodded and, taking one last look around, committing the small clearing and the faraway old house to memory, she stepped to the open trail and stopped, looking out at the scene before her.

Far below, for the little spot looked out over a high slope of heavily forested mountain, a stream or river crawled along like a winding snake among the distant valleys. Along the near end of the visible section of the waterway, Madylan could see a number of old farm houses and a few grand houses, but only a few. No city or village was visible.

As she caught up with the long strides of the old woman, who was wielding a tall walking stick on the uneven, but clear trail through the woodland, Madylan had the growing feeling that dozens of tiny eyes were watching her from behind the wide trunks of the old trees, from the branches above, and even from the small underbrush and dark spaces scattered about the forest floor. Yet, every time she jerked her head one way or the other to try to catch a glimpse of the owners of those phantom eyes, she'd simply be staring at an empty space between trees, or a dark nook among the underbrush.

Shaking off the thought of little creatures scurrying about, Madylan simply followed the old woman for a number of minutes, wondering where they might be going. As she followed, she realized that the day was getting warmer, so the season was the same as at her aunt and uncle's house, mid-spring. The forest was also becoming lighter, no doubt from the sun moving higher in the sky. However, she was not able to determine their direction from the sun because the tree canopy overhead was too dense.

Suddenly, Madylan came to an abrupt halt when the old lady held up her hand like a policemen and uttered a curt, shushing noise.

"Shish!"

As the two stood frozen to a spot just a few yards from a second trail that crossed the one they were on, Madylan saw a group of small people, maybe four or five, paused in the middle of the crossing of the two paths. One of the small people, a rough looking fellow with a mashed up face, shouted something unintelligible at the old woman.

The old woman then shouted back in the same language, her voice quite menacing, which caused the little people, who were all about half the old woman's height, to stagger back a bit. However, the spokesman, who was the largest, and, to Madylan, the ugliest of the group, with matted, unruly hair over a face that looked like something her little brother would make out of Play-Doh, stepped forward, dragging what appeared to be a large baseball bat, but fatter than a bat.

The ugly little man again shouted at the old woman, who then stepped closer to the little man, loudly talking over his words until he finally stopped talking.

"Speak in the new tongue, old fool, for she only knows her own, but can ken some of ours, I think," the old woman said, in English,

Madylan assumed, since the old woman's words were clear.

"Who is she to command understanding?" the squat little man grunted, leaning in to stare at Madylan, all the while scratching at his side, which she noticed was covered in what looked like dirty sacks from a grocery store, but made out of cloth.

Madylan also suddenly realized why the old woman had not questioned Madylan's clothes. The little people were wearing loose fitting, cotton, or other light fabric, pajama-looking outfits, not too different from her own, light colored cotton slacks and blouse, which was covered loosely by her sweater. While she had slippers, the shouting man had sandals. The others seemed to be barefoot.

"Little sister, she is our champion!" declared the old woman, stepping to the side so that the group of little people could see the little girl more clearly.

Two of the smaller people, who might have been girls or women, from their fuller clothes and from the fact that their faces were not as hideous as the larger one who had spoken, giggled at the sight of Madylan, who was about their size. Both of them carried large bunches of greens or weeds, tied up with string or vines.

"Champion? Why, grandmother of the far dwelling, do you bring us such a weak and skinny champion? Have all your sons gone off to the wars? Have your servants all fled to the coast with the others? Have you gone soft as age creeps up on you...?" the ugly little man barked, his language choppy and, at times, nearly incoherent to Madylan's ears.

"You know you can't question the choice of champion, old oaf that you are. You can only accept or decline. Accept and have at her. Decline and let us go our way!" the old woman suddenly bellowed at the little man, causing him to wrinkle his already heavily wrinkled brow.

The little man then looked from the old grandmother to Madylan and back again, as if trying to understand what his next move should be. He then rubbed the back of his tangled hair, puffed out his chest, and growled at his new opponent.

"Stand, then skinny champion, and meet your fate," the little man growled at the surprised girl, throwing down his fat bat. "I'll even lose my club, for even a...what is it called...? Yes, even a forest dwelling house goblin can have fits of fairness."

The little man then flexed his back and arms, revealing massive muscles, scarred from what must have been many battles. Stamping his feet, which seemed to look like one large foot to Madylan's blinking eyes, the little man then planted himself squarely in the center of the crossroads, while the others, two girls and one undetermined companion, moved to the sides, their eyes wide with anticipation, staring at Madylan.

"Uh, excuse me, madam, but, what is happening?" Madylan finally asked of the old woman, who had stepped farther off the path to a fallen tree trunk and had sat down, her billowing dress draping itself over the impromptu seat.

"Little sister, we must continue along that path, which will take us out of the forest to…well, to our first stop. Of course, this could be our first and last stop, depending on how well you do as champion," the old woman replied and then gestured to the little man to get on with whatever was happening.

Madylan was about to protest such bizarre behavior when the old woman, her face hidden from the squat little man, winked at Madylan and motioned to the medal hanging from her sweater, causing Madylan to reach up and touch it.

Suddenly, a flash of inspiration welled up inside Madylan and she immediately understood what she must do. Turning back to her odd opponent, she flexed her ankles, shifted her weight, and waited.

"Champion, you will not pass!" the little man then shouted in broken language, stomping his feet, or one big foot, as he spoke.

Madylan, fully aware that she had to fight or wrestle or do something with the ugly little man, looked again at the old woman for any signs of help.

"Stay, dear. Stay on the path, young one," the old woman called, her long dress and shoulder-wrap billowing in a strong breeze that had just stirred up. "Your strength lies in staying the course."

Madylan then looked back at the little man, letting a tiny crack of a smile cross her lips when she again thought about the man's face looking like a blob of poorly shaped molding clay. She also had, at first, held her breath, thinking such a bedraggled figure would smell horrible, but quickly noticed the little man smelled of the very forest, as if just after a summer rain.

"Laughter? Are you so confident that you laugh at the danger you are in?" the little man called, slamming his large, claw-like hands together as he spoke, scaring off a brace of birds that had just

189

alighted in the branches overhead.

Suddenly, an array of familiar voices in Madylan's head whispered calming advice to her. Her older cousins' voices at first, with Alex telling her she could do anything she put her mind to and introducing her to such wonders as diverse as the Museum of Natural History and her first musical instruments. Zany cousin Lee repeating 'balance and counter-balance' over and over, when they would roughhouse during his visits from the Pacific Northwest Coast. Her other cousins' words of sound advice floated in and out. She then heard her Dad's commanding voice giving her life lessons to survive the often-unpredictable streets of New York, while her Mom's calming voice steadied her stance. Then a blur of teachers' and friends' words of advice and encouragement filtered into her mind as well. Even her mother's father's strong voice was whispering encouragement in her ear.

Setting her jaw like she did with a math problem or a brain teaser puzzle from Uncle, Madylan then stared straight at the little man, her eyes boring into his. She quickly decided that no little forest goblin, if that was what he was, was going to keep her from wherever the old woman was guiding her. It was her dream, after all.

Stepping forward, while steeling herself for the little man's first lunge, Madylan turned her body slightly, waiting. Waiting.

The shock at his small opponent still lingered on the ugly little man's smashed face, then gave way to a grin that surprised Madylan, who suddenly felt the little man was trying to hold back laughter. Shaking her head, she then resolved not to let the little man distract her with tricks.

Circling to the right, slowly, the little man did seem to be holding back laughter, no doubt at having to prove himself against such a small and, to him, puny opponent. He finally stopped and, winking at Madylan to throw her off, he bellowed out his challenge.

"Attack!" the little man yelled as he threw himself at Madylan, his red-rimmed eyes burning with the desire to squash her like a bug in his path, but with his mouth hiding a wide grin at the same time.

For less than the blink of an eye, Madylan held her ground, unmoving, until she felt the hot, sour breath of the ugly little man on her cheek. Then she moved.

Like a warrior ballerina, Madylan stepped to her left, turned and, as the little man lunged at where she had been, she threw both her arms at the right side of his back, thumping him with all the force of her own twisting body. To her shock, her quick move sent the little man into the dirt and leaves of the path, causing him to fall over and roll, almost like a lumpy ball, several body lengths along the forest floor, scaring off a couple of scrawny squirrels that had paused to watch the show.

Standing her ground, her breath heaving, Madylan watched as the little man came to a sitting halt, shook his head, with leaves, sticks, and dirt flying about. She ignored the swelling pain in the palms of her hands from thumping the rock hard back of the little man.

Slowly, with some difficulty, and after a couple of comical, failed attempts, the muscular little man finally rose and turned back to Madylan. As he did so, one of the little girl people gathered up his fat bat and, passing Madylan, walked over to the ugly little man and handed him the bat.

Madylan's face took on a look of alarm, as she knew she could not combat the little man if he used the enormous club.

A club, Madylan scolded herself. It's not a fat bat, but some evil forest dweller's club for bashing dreaming children.

Looking back to the old woman, Madylan hoped her guide would say something about the unfairness of the club, or come to her rescue.

Nope. The old woman seemed to be studying a long piece of yellowed paper, which had strings hanging from the top.

Turning back to the hideous little man, Madylan again steeled herself as she also tried to figure out how to avoid the gigantic club.

Her tough opponent leaned on the massive club and stared hard at Madylan. He then hefted the club over his right shoulder and took a step forward.

Madylan tensed up, every muscle ready to fight or, if necessary, run. She carefully watched the ugly little man's eyes, just like her father had taught her. Oddly, the man's eyes then shifted away from her, almost dismissively, and he then spoke, a hint of humor hidden in his gruff voice.

"Old grandmother of the far dwelling, we concede the prowess of your small champion. You may pass," the little man abruptly said, with halting formality, even bowing low several times to the old woman, but not to Madylan.

The old woman looked up from the paper, and then stashed it in the folds of her many-layered dress. Standing, she nodded a small acknowledgement bow to the little man and then waved Madylan over.

The little man then barked something at his undetermined companion, who reached into a tattered pocket and then tossed something flat and silvery at Madylan, who was quick enough to catch the object.

A small spoon.

Puzzled, Madylan looked up at the old woman, who simply motioned for the girl to put it in a pocket, which she did. Then, as they continued on the path, Madylan kept looking back at the small group of little people until they had melted into the darkness of the forest.

Glancing up at the old woman, Madylan spoke up, once she felt they were far away from the ugly little man.

"What was that all about? Is this their forest? What's with the spoon? And is he really, what did he say, a goblin? And, he seemed to be laughing inside, instead of trying to scare me or hurt me," Madylan mused, stealing glances back along the trail.

The old woman glanced down at Madylan and, in a voice tinged with deep sadness that shocked the little girl, replied.

"Many are the jovial house goblins…as good a name as any, I suppose…who no longer have houses to haunt and create mischief, little sister. Yes, he prefers a good laugh over a sound thrashing. Yet, the constant wars have broken so many of the old homes that these few we encountered, and we may see more, wander the forests in search of worthy opponents, in order to give meaning to lives that, without their masters' homes, are slowly fading away, young one. You have given him, and his small family, a few more months by your heroic, and, yes, to the little troll, amusing actions. The spoon, a symbol of plenty in a land of dire wants, is his way of recognizing you as worthy. Keep it, as it may have use."

Confused, but not wanting to sadden the old woman further, Madylan remained quiet as the two odd companions stepped lightly along the forest path. A path, our little adventurer noticed, which was angled downward, possibly taking the two off the side of the mountain to the valley and the river below.

Once in a while, as the two passed large rocks or even huge boulders that rested beside the trail, scruffy, wild looking house cats would appear sitting on the tops of the rocks, their usually yellow eyes following the two hikers down the path. Usually yellow, in that at one huge, grey boulder, a blue-eyed Siamese stood guard, watching the two pass, and tossing the little girl a quick purr before it disappeared behind the rocks.

After some minutes, Madylan decided to try getting more information from her curious companion.

"Grandmother," Madylan called, using the honorific her parents had taught her for older women. "Grandmother, could you please tell me where we are going? And, why? And, aren't you curious about where I came from?"

The old woman turned her head back briefly to gaze at the girl, but continued walking as she spoke.

"Where we are going, our strange little sister wants to know," the old woman repeated, seeming to talk to the birds above in the tree branches, rather than to her questioner.

Just as the woman appeared to take a long breath to supply an answer, Madylan was startled by a loud bang coming from just beyond the next jumble of rocks. The old woman, instead of stopping, waved Madylan forward and sped up the pace, disappearing behind the pile of rocks before Madylan could reach her.

Bang! Clang! Bang!

Madylan stopped, wondering if she should run the other way, away from the loud sound. But, she reasoned, she only knew the old woman in the dream, so decided to step gingerly toward the rocks and peek around them to see what was what. At the rocks, she paused, placed her hands on the cold stone and leaned around, looking for the old woman and whatever was making the loud noise.

A wagon?

Looking more closely, Madylan saw that the wagon, low slung, with a tattered, rounded, tent-like top covering the front half, had a hard looking old man standing at the back, where he was slamming a large hammer onto a big chunk of what must have been metal, from the sound it made. The old man was wearing dark, heavy clothes, maybe made from thick leather, with flat metal bits around his cuffs and his shins. On his head, he wore what looked like a dirty rag.

Bang! Clang!

Without the muffling effect of the rocks, Madylan heard the full force of the old man's hammer blows on the makeshift anvil. Off to the side of the wagon, which looked as if it might fall apart at any moment, the old woman was cooing to the oldest horse Madylan had ever seen, even in movies.

Stepping into view, the young girl stood for a moment, with no one paying any attention to her.

"Hello? Excuse me?" Madylan called to the old woman. "Remember me?"

"Isn't he just divine?" the old woman called back, stroking the rather tangled, windswept mane of the ancient horse. "Come, dear, say hello."

Crossing the small clearing, Madylan kept one eye on the old man, banging away at the anvil, as she approached the old woman and the moth-eaten old horse.

"He's...he's quite tall," Madylan finally replied, at a loss as to how to describe the old horse.

"Yes, little one, that he is," the old woman answered, then stepped away from the horse, who looked at the newcomer with interest.

"You can stroke his nose. He loves that," the old woman called as she interrupted the old man's work by stepping in front of his hammer.

The old man paused, with his eyes, which had been a bit glassy from the repetitive motion of hammering, slowly clearing, and leaned in to look at the old woman. Leaned down would be more accurate, for the man seemed to be twice as tall as the old woman, even though he had seemed the same height when Madylan had first peeked around the corner of the rocks.

Nudge.

Madylan jumped, and then chuckled at herself for being skittish around the old horse, who was nudging her shoulder with his nose. Smiling, she then patted the old beast on the small white star in the middle of his drooping head and stroked his mane, even though she had to stand on tiptoes to do so.

"Have to finish, old woman," the old man finally said, in a voice so deep that Madylan thought she had imagined that he had spoken.

"Finish you will my good blacksmith. We are only passing. I saw your noble steed and wanted to pay my respects," the old woman answered, her voice more formal than it had been with the ugly little warrior, but still somewhat aloof.

"That you've done, mother. So, be off with you now, and take that…," the old blacksmith replied and then paused mid-sentence, dropped his huge hammer on a makeshift table, more a tree stump, and took one long stride that put him beside the little girl.

Towering over Madylan, who was now no taller than the knees of the horse, the tall old man leaned down and roughly plucked the medal from her sweater, which looked more like a dark colored blouse at the moment.

"Ah! It is good. Good. It is from beyond the sea, this is. Just what I need. Yes, just what I need," the old man mumbled to himself while he ignored the little girl's protests as he stepped back to his anvil and picked up his massive hammer.

Shocked at how quickly the rude blacksmith had grabbed her uncle's medal and a little confused at how the horse had become as large as the old man was tall, Madylan hesitated just long enough for the old man to raise his hammer.

"Stop!" Madylan yelled as she ran between the old man and the anvil, although she was so short compared to him and his wagon, she wondered for a moment if he would even see her, or hear her.

"Who is this bug to command me?" the old man asked, not of Madylan, but of the old woman, who had moved to the side and was sitting on a barrel leaning against a tree stump, reading another long sheet of paper, a darker color this time.

"What?" the old woman asked, looking up from her paper in a slightly befuddled way. "Oh, the little sister? She's my traveling companion."

"Move aside, little one. I must finish," the old man roared at Madylan, his breath almost as hot as the fire she had just seen at his side.

Fire?

Madylan stared in disbelief at what she saw as a large, orange to red to blue-black column of flame that danced about the man's side, without anything under it. Just as she was cringing from the old man's roar, he thrust her uncle's medal at the licking flames, his massive left hand encased in a thick leather glove, blackened from years too close to fire.

"Eeeee! Take it away! Take it away! It burns! It burns!" a thin, high-pitched voice called out, almost in agony.

Blinking, Madylan watched in amazement as the flame leaned away from the medal, turning almost a blue white color where the old man's hand held out her uncle's medal. She then leaned one way, and then the other to see the person behind the flame who had cried out.

No one was there.

Gruffly, the old man thrust the medal several more times at the cringing flame, which moaned in agony each time, turning an even whiter blue.

Finally, the old man withdrew the medal and the column of fire slowly regained its color, but still leaned away from the old man like an orange tabby cat avoiding water.

"What witchery be this, old mother?" the old blacksmith called, holding up the medal to peer at it more closely.

"Came with the little one, I'm afraid, old father," the old woman replied as she tucked her paper in her dress and stepped away from the barrel and the tree stump.

"Please give it back. It's my uncle's medal!" Madylan demanded in the most grownup voice she could muster. "He...he trusted me with it."

"Well, you should take better care, little bug," the old man laughed, then leaned far down. "What is this witchery that scares my flame?"

"Witchery? No, it's for protecting the country," Madylan replied, feeling the sheer heat of the old smithy's leather gloved hand close to her face.

"Protecting? Humph! Must not be very good at it. Hasn't worked very well, has it?" the old man grumbled as he dropped the small medal into Madylan's outstretched right hand, and turned away.

Suddenly, from deep within a place that she did not know she had, a deep anger at the old man's dismissive words welled up inside Madylan and she jumped in front of the turning old man. Her anger was so palatable that even the flames skittered sideways, away from the scary little girl, and hid behind the towering blacksmith.

"Hey! Sir! You can't say that about my uncle and the...the countless others who have protected the country. They are better than you! You...you smelly old blacksmith!" Madylan roared in a firm, suddenly commanding voice.

Shocked at the disrespectful tone and forceful words that she had just shouted, Madylan stepped back, but then stood, defiant, waiting for the old man to crash his massive hammer down on her head.

Nothing.

Looking up, Madylan saw the old man and the old woman talking, both looking the same size, which was beginning to annoy Madylan, the size changing thing. After a moment, the two stopped their whispering and the old woman waved at Madylan to join her on the trail.

The old blacksmith, resting his hammer on the tree stump, stepped over to the old horse, which seemed younger the closer the old man got to the beast, and busied himself setting up the horse's feedbag. The flames were nowhere to be seen.

Puzzled at the normality of the scene, and the sudden absence of the flames, Madylan slowly turned back to the trail, barely hearing the words the old man spoke in his low, almost canyon echo voice.

"Good you challenged me on the small disc, little bug. This test of loyalty to family is my gift," the old man's words seemed to say as they drifted after Madylan while she hurried through the narrowing forest trail to catch up to the old woman, who seemed to have greatly increased the pace.

Glancing back one last time before the forest swallowed up the old man, his horse, and the wagon, Madylan was shocked to briefly see, not the worn out wagon, ancient horse, and old man she had just seen, but a young man, a youthful, prancing horse, and a brightly painted, shiny new wagon fading into the trees.

"What...?" Madylan said to herself as she turned back and picked up her pace, almost running to catch up to the old woman.

Once she had caught up with her companion, Madylan moved a little in front of her and gave the old woman a questioning look.

"The great foundries have all but been destroyed, little one," the old woman replied to Madylan's unspoken question. "His kind have forged temple bells from Mount Baekdu at the top of heaven, to Samgaksan along the backbone, all the way to Mount Hallasan in the southern sea. He and his brothers and, yes, a few sisters, have wrought the very foundations of the old empire. Few are they now. Wandering the deep forest, followed by their homeless flames, forever doomed to repair the castoffs of the oppressors."

The old woman then fell silent, a deep sadness engulfing her and even draping over Madylan's shoulders, broad for a little girl, but still those of a little girl, causing Madylan's stomach to make a flip.

"You've given him and his ilk a brief, but sorely needed view into the old days. He thanks you for that, but could not tell you himself, of course, for he and his ilk are of the old ways, when little girls were invisible to such," the old woman continued, her voice far away. "Let's walk quietly, now, for a while. There are others wandering these woods who might not be as understanding."

Nodding, Madylan moved a little closer to the old woman and kept her small stride in step with her taller companion, resolving to bring up her questions later.

Far down the tunnel-like forest trail, Madylan could see the bright light of a wider opening, a large clearing or maybe a river crossing. She pulled her sweater around her shoulders, seeing that it was her sweater again and not the dark purple blouse from before. As she walked, she also pinned the medal to the inside of her collar, at the left, so that it rested beside her heart, underneath her sweater and blouse, and over her light undershirt. She felt it was safer from other potential thieves if out of sight.

As the two moved through the forest, Madylan was finally able to look around at the trees, which were impossibly tall, taller even than the oldest ones in Central Park. Birds flew above and in between, but she could never quite see what they were. Small animals rustled about in the underbrush, sometimes scurrying away, unseen, when the two approached. Once in a while, a dark, shrouded side path would snake away into the darker trees, causing her to walk even closer to the old woman, lest Madylan become disoriented and disappear down one of those rabbit holes. Somewhere, not too far away, she could hear water rushing over rocks, just as she had heard at the falls on the Potomac the year before. It was a soothing sound, almost musical, that kept her and the odd old woman company as they made their way through the shadows of the old forest.

"The cottage. Just there."

The old woman's brusque words snapped Madylan out of her river water induced daze. Looking toward the now large opening that appeared just beyond the shelter of the massive forest trees, she saw the object of the old woman's words.

A small, rustic cottage.

Almost like in a storybook, Madylan thought, as she stopped beside the halted old woman. Old. Very old, that cottage in the wide clearing, she guessed from the droopy timber framing, cracked, mud-colored stone sides, and thatched roof.

Thatched roof?

When had she ever seen a real thatched roof, Madylan wondered, outside of the pictures Uncle had sent from trips to England? She then looked over the rest of the little cottage or farmhouse.

The house rested on a slight rise in the land, with what looked like a smaller stall or outbuilding just to the left, or south. South because, now that they were at the edge of the forest, Madylan could see enough sun and shadows to know directions.

West. They were heading west, at least at that moment, Madylan realized, and filed it away in the back of her mind.

Circling the cottage, a low wall of dark grey stone of varying sizes protected the cottage's garden, just visible beyond the wooden slats of the ash colored gate. From the stone chimney at the right side, or north, a thin trail of white smoke rose lazily, then bent almost ninety degrees and blew apart toward the river. A sturdy fence, quite high, made from stout logs, ran from the wall all the way to the forest and disappeared there. The fence was so strong and so high that Madylan imagined some huge beast must be kept behind the massive fence. Along the top of the fence, near the house, several jet-black birds, crows, she thought, sat without moving, watching her and the old grandmother approach.

The trail the two were using led right up to the house and seemed to pass under a long, slanting overhang on the right side, the side closer to the unseen river. A large shelf of grey stone, scorched black in places by some long ago fire, bordered the trail for about a quarter of a mile, so that the trail under the overhang was the only way to pass the cottage that Madylan could see.

"Dare we approach?" the old woman mumbled to herself, her head swinging one way then the other, and even looking back along the way the two had just come.

Stepping out of the shadows of the forest, the old woman seemed to shrink in size and looked like a normal adult to Madylan, who had given up trying to figure out why things seemed to change sizes. The old woman then picked up some sandy dirt from the trail and let it fall out of her fingers. The sand blew only a few inches as it fell, and in the same direction as the smoke from the chimney.

"Too late. She will have already smelled our scents," the old woman said, clear disappointment in her voice.

As if to answer her, the oddly wide front door of the little cottage flew open and the roundest, plumpest little cook that Madylan had ever seen stepped, or rather wobbled out of the doorway, getting stuck briefly, but forcing her bulk through as she waved at the two with what looked like a large wooden spoon or spatula, calling to them, her voice smooth and syrupy.

"Welcome! Welcome!"

The plump lady seemed to be overjoyed at the surprise company and, after wiping something gooey on her broad apron, more of a full housecoat that fit over a dark red dress underneath, she waved with both hands.

"Welcome. I say, welcome, dear ones."

Waddling to the gate, the plump lady struggled to open it, but was obviously far too wide to pass through the narrow gate, so stood back and beckoned to the two new arrivals.

"Welcome!"

"Is that all she knows how to say?" Madylan finally whispered to the old woman, who hushed her immediately.

"Heed my words, little princess. Say little to this round one. Say so little as to count your words, dear. No more than seven, three times, can you speak to this one. Heed me. No more."

With that, the old woman put on the fakest smile Madylan had ever seen, and replied.

"Yolisa, Mistress Chef, how are you this fine morning?" the old woman called in a cautiously cheerful voice, while stepping in front of the little girl, shielding Madylan from the squinting, almost pig-like eyes of the rotund woman.

"Oh, it's you, lady of the far great manor. And, a friend...?" the round chef cooed, her syrupy sweet voice revealing a tinge of what Madylan could only call hunger.

"Just passing, dearie. Just passing. No need to disturb you," the old woman replied, her voice betraying a sense of concern.

"Passing? Oh, but you can only pass through the trail here, dear. The hill route has been closed many, many moons after the bridge over the gorge was dismantled for the iron," the plump chef replied, tapping her spoon on the top of the wall.

"We travel light, Mistress Chef. Very light. We carry few supplies," the old woman answered, still rooted to her spot just beyond the trees, with Madylan directly behind. "Only a bit of rice flower and some dried...."

"Tsk, tsk," the old chef replied, her slit-like lips seeming to writhe more like two competing snakes than a cheerful old housewife's smile. "We have plenty to share. You've no need to worry about the usual toll. Not at all."

Then, for a long moment, the rotund little chef seemed to study the old woman as hard as the old woman seemed to be studying the chef. Finally, the syrupy voice spoke again, addressing the little girl.

"Sweetie, don't you want to come in and eat something?"

Madylan looked to her companion for some sort of signal, but the old woman continued to stare at the plump little chef, so Madylan had to think of an answer herself.

"Well, grandmother, I am a little hungry...?" Madylan replied, addressing her question more to her companion, and remembering to count her words.

Seven words.

"Yes, little one, I think we can pause for a quick bite," the old woman quickly replied, drawing a small bundle out of one of her dress's many folds. "Here, you can use this to make up some rice cakes and, add a little water from this jug, and we'll have a great little snack."

"Oh, kind lady, you do not need to worry yourself, we have plenty of rice cakes, and greens, and...meats...," the plump chef responded, her sharp, pencil thin tongue sliding back and forth between her quivering lips on the word 'meats.'

Quivering?

Madylan took a small, involuntary step sideways toward the old woman, while wondering why the chubby little chef seemed to be so excited to have guests. Something in the back of her mind was telling Madylan to be careful with the outwardly cheerful chef.

As if to confirm her fears, the old woman leaned over and whispered so that only Madylan could hear.

"Caution, little sister, with our overly friendly host, for all is not as it seems," the old woman said quietly. "Only let what you create pass your mouth, little one. Fight the urge to take whatever sweets or savory morsels this one will supply. Only by your own hand made, do you consume."

With those words of caution hanging in the air, the old woman waved Madylan to continue on the path to the small, outdoor kitchen area at the side of the house where the trail led.

Mumbling to herself, the plump chef waddled along on her side of the low wall to meet the two travelers under the slanted roof, where several of the gaunt crows from the sturdy fence had silently flown to without Madylan or the old grandmother seeing them do so.

Once all three were under the broad roof, Madylan saw that the small gate in the wall there was also too narrow for the chef to pass through. So, the chef stood at the end of a long, sturdy, well-worn table that extended over the wall and into the outdoor kitchen area where the two travelers stood. All standard items where there, and a few that were quite foreign to Madylan's eyes, so she filed them away for another time. What she did recognize were the pots she'd need to make the rice cake soup or stew.

A toasty, low fire was burning in the long, old-fashioned oven, with several iron pots sitting in depressions in the top of the oven or stove. The chef stuck her wooden spoon into the largest of the pots, which was right at the wall and within reach, and stirred a murky soup or stew. Madylan leaned over the smallest pot, which was closest to her and saw that it was empty. The old woman, using a cloth she extracted from somewhere in a fold in her dress, wiped the inside and outside of the pot very carefully before she poured a little water into it for the rice cakes.

Abruptly, the portly chef ladled out a large portion of steaming, but not yet done rice cakes from the middle pot, which the chef could reach from behind the wall, and flipped them expertly onto the board where Madylan was setting up.

Frowning at the old chef, Madylan, as she began to form her rice cakes, wondered how she was going to ensure she only ate her own rice cakes if the chubby old chef was going to mix the two batches together. Suddenly, a thought came to her.

Quietly, without either the plump chef or the old woman seeing her, Madylan slipped her uncle's medal into the palm of her right hand, dragon seal side facing out. As she shaped her small rice cakes, she was able to secretly press the image of the dragon into each of the cakes she prepared. Not perfect images, of course, but enough to mark the rice cakes she needed to eat, versus the ones of the old chef's that the old woman had warned against eating. She whispered a silent apology to the former president and her uncle for using the medal in such a way, but mentally assured them that it would clean up easily.

Near the end of the preparation, the plump little chef dropped her wooden spoon, and, being unable to bend over to retrieve it, she had to step back into the kitchen to fetch a new one. Through the open door, which, when opened, released a vast, green-yellow plume of acrid smoke, both Madylan and the old woman were given a glimpse of a pile of shoes and sandals beside the woman's door. Not an unusual sight in Korea where everyone removed his or her shoes as a sign of respect and for hygiene, but the large stack of footwear, spreading from the door far into the darker interior of the old chef's small house, spoke to dozens or more individuals inside a house that might have held three or four if they were all a lot skinnier than their rotund host.

"Here we are," the old chef chirped as she returned, kicking the kitchen door closed with her own chunky foot spilling out of her protesting sandal. "Almost ready."

Without asking for Madylan's help, the old chef then tried to sweep up both bunches of rice cakes to drop them into the large stew pot. Madylan, however, suspicious of the chef, was just a hair quicker, and scooped up her rice cakes herself and dropped them into the small pot the old grandmother had been tending.

"Our water's hot…!" Madylan began, but then stopped herself, trying to remember how many words she had left.

Seven, now three. Ten from twenty-one. Only eleven words remaining, Madylan mentally tallied.

Madylan kept silent as the boiling water did its work. All the while, the heavy breathing of the chef as she stirred the large pot of stew sounded less like a person and more like the distant trains she would hear on trips to Queens, outside of Manhattan.

Again, once the small rice cakes had finished cooking, Madylan was much quicker than the old chef, scooping the small morsels out of the pot and into the three bowls lined up on the table, one large one from the chef and two smaller ones that the old woman had produced from somewhere in her folds of clothing.

Reaching into the stew pot, the chef busied herself fishing out small bits of gristle-bound meat, which she dropped into her bowl first. She then moved to sneak some of the meat into the smaller bowls.

"A snake!" Madylan called out, pointing with her ladle at an imaginary visitor to the small house as she watched the chef's ladle hover close, too close, to the small bowls.

Two more words, nine remaining.

"A snake? Where? Oh dear, oh dear," the plump little chef called out in real fear as she dropped the ladle back into the large pot, surprising Madylan, but to a knowing nod from the old woman.

Madylan's ruse, a small fib, caused the old chef to not only halt her attempt to add to Madylan's dish, but also caused the heavyset woman to focus on climbing onto a rickety stool to escape the supposed snake. The frightened chef even dropped the additional meat she had been hiding behind her back and it fell to the hardened dirt of the outdoor kitchen, attracting a couple of scrawny, sickly looking cats who had been hiding in the shadows.

Pouncing on the meat, the slightly larger of the two cats gobbled up a couple of huge mouthfuls, preventing the smaller cat from having a chance at it. So, the smaller cat simply hissed at the quicker cat and plopped down to wait for any other scraps that the larger, evidently meaner cat might miss.

At that moment, the old woman took the confusion of the chef to call out, pointing towards the far end of the trail, where it passed from view beyond the cottage.

"Dearie Chef, I think the little monster has made a slithering line for the pasture," the old woman said, holding her hand over her eyes to reinforce the small fib. "A path that we must take as well, leaving your kind hospitality."

The chef, suspicion crossing her round face, gingerly stepped from the stool, using the long spoon to knock the gorging cat away as she stepped very close to the wall by Madylan. Reaching out with one of her sausage-like arms, the old chef stroked Madylan's dark hair and purred a deep response.

"Dear lady, how can you be so cruel to take such an excellent helper away from me, a poor, lonely old mistress with only the animals and a passing beggar to befriend?" the rotund chef asked in a voice so syrupy that Madylan thought she might drown and so stepped away from the woman's attentive and clawing hands.

"What say you, young one? Would you like to stay a little longer and…and prepare more succulent dishes with this old mistress chef?" the old grandmother asked as she wrapped up the rice cakes Madylan had made, even though they were still hot.

Nine words, Madylan reminded herself.

"Kind grandmother…"

Seven words left.

"...we must move on."

Only three left, Madylan mouthed silently, but then felt her head swimming, almost as if she might faint. Shaking her head to clear it, she stepped even farther away from the chef, who seemed to have grown double her size in Madylan's suddenly blurred vision.

Why was the plump old chef leaning toward her with such a look of anticipation on her massive, jiggling face, drool oozing from the side of her thin mouth, Madylan wondered through a growing haze?

"Farewell!" Madylan called, her voice slurred and choppy.

Two left over, Madylan wondered to herself? She then stumbled toward the old grandmother, who took Madylan's right hand to steady the girl and lead her back to the path.

"Argh!" the plump chef grunted, flinging herself toward the wall and the two travelers.

Yet, the old woman had anticipated the chef's move, and, after grabbing Madylan's shoulder in addition to her hand, the aged companion took a long stride to the path beyond the overhang of the slanted roof, calling back to the angry chef.

"Dearie, our fee true sits there upon your wretched toll booth. Enjoy!" the old grandmother called and pointed with her free hand at one lone rice cake from the group that Madylan had formed. "Our toll is paid."

"Argh!" the chef yelled after them, her face flushed beet red from all the futile efforts. "Please dwell a little longer upon your inevitable return. I'll be more prepared for...for clever guests next time."

Madylan watched as the old chef took her obvious frustration out on the now limp and, Madylan gulped, lifeless body of the larger cat by first hitting it again with the spoon, then picking it up and flinging the sad little beast into the large cook pot boiling on the stove.

Grabbing her stomach so as to not retch at the sight, Madylan was calmed a bit by seeing the smaller cat running away from the old chef as fast as its scrawny little legs could carry it, away into the far forest.

As she and the old grandmother hurried up the trail, Madylan, her head slowly clearing, took a quick look back and saw the old chef banging about on the house side of the wall. The crows, which seemed to shift to look more like little people, were walking to the edge of the slanted roof and dropping out of sight behind the cook stove where Madylan and her companion had just been standing.

Shuddering, Madylan turned away, not wanting to see what other creepy things might appear at that spooky cottage by the winding path.

Once the cottage had disappeared around a small hill, and after the two travelers had put some distance behind them, Madylan commented to the old woman that she was still very hungry and wanted to eat her rice cakes.

"I'm sorry, little one, but the old witch dropped her own into the bowl, so we don't know which are safe to eat," the old woman replied as she unwrapped the bowls and prepared to dump them out.

"Wait!" Madylan blurted out, and gently took the bowls from the old woman, and, using a stick from a nearby bush, speared one of the rice cakes and held it up for the old woman to see.

"Why are you...? Oh, those marks? Your...talisman...?" the old woman asked, her face breaking into a wide grin at the little girl's nodding, and beaming, silent response.

While faint, the distinct impression of the dragon medal lined one side of the rice cakes that Madylan had made.

After removing the rice cakes the old chef had dumped into the bowl, the old woman insisted on burying those, concerned that some poor forest animal would suffer the same fate as the doomed cat. She then rinsed Madylan's marked cakes with a little water.

"Let's sit there, dear," the old woman suggested, pointing at a series of rocks piled by the trail, almost like a low wall, where the two settled for a few minutes.

Even lukewarm, the rice cakes seemed utterly delicious to a very hungry Madylan. Some added bits of meat, which the old woman had assured Madylan were simply bits of tofu, rounded out the small meal with relish.

"Grandmother, is that what I should call you?" Madylan asked, after swallowing the last of her rice cakes and tofu. "We haven't had the time to be properly introduced. And, I'm not really...I don't know why...well, what are we doing wandering down this skinny little road?"

The old woman didn't answer for a moment, but looked up and down the road, as if she were looking for other travelers. Yet, other than a few animals, that could have been goats or sheep, in the far distance, and a few birds flitting about, nothing stirred from either direction on the trail. Far below, beyond the edge of the clearing or small valley they were currently in, the river peeked out between a couple of tree covered hills. Beyond, the mountains that had seemed to be far away, now appeared quite close.

"The old land is crying, dear. If you hold your hand to this stone, or lean against that old oak just there, or wade through the slower rivers, before they crash down the mountain on their way to the western sea, you can feel the sadness of our ancestors...your ancestors, little one. That sadness has called you here, we think. Called you for a task. For some action. What, alas, we do not know. Yet, we must believe that you will know when the time is right, dear little sister," the old woman replied cryptically.

Madylan thought about the odd answer for a bit, then continued her line of questioning.

"Do you think that little ugly...that little man was really, like, really a goblin, like he said?"

"Who are we to question what someone believes, dear one?"

"And that blacksmith? What was with his changing how tall he was, and the horse, too? And, what did he mean about a gift of loyalty?"

"Size and the appearance of things can be very confusing. His, I think, was a test to see if you would protect your talisman. Protect your uncle's trust."

"Talisman? You've said that before."

"Your uncle's medal, dear. I'm sure you've wondered why it has been so convenient, especially with our brief encounter with the gorging witch in the cottage of no return."

"What...? Witch? I thought that was just a word...? Wait! The shoes!"

"Yes, dear. The shoes of countless lost souls who were too weak to escape the ravenous clutch of that...that nightmare from a long ago past. A past that seems to be creeping back into the land. Laying waste to the good and promoting the more sinister."

"Wait...a...minute...," Madylan replied, her jaw hanging open in disbelief. "She wanted to eat...eat us? Like the old witch with the candied gingerbread house in Hansel and Gretel?"

The old woman slowly nodded as she replied.

"I know not your Hansel and Gretel, young one, but I hope they were as clever as you and escaped such a fate."

"Yes, they did escape. But, then, why did we stop there? We could have gone back or walked around. Or run by really fast?"

"Ah, were it so simple, little one. I've lived a long, long time, little sister, and have come to accept that there are crossroads that we can only pass using our own wits and good hearts. So...," the old woman replied and lowered her eyelids, waiting for Madylan to realize what the old woman was telling her.

"Oh. I...these are crossroads where I have to make the right decision," Madylan finally replied, awareness dawning on her young face. "But, wait. You mean...if I had chosen the wrong way to handle them, like used more words than you said, I might...might not be here now?"

"Little sister, this trail follows a path laid down for you long ago, no doubt by ancestors much wiser than I. We do not know if your path ends at Hanyang, the revered and ancient seat of power of our fair but troubled land, beyond those mountains there. Maybe your destiny lies there. Or beyond? But, I know your path will be difficult, with obstacles and, maybe, some help as well."

The old woman then fell silent, which was good for Madylan as she was trying to wrap her young brain around the complicated dream she seemed to be in. She decided she would hold off on more questions about her uncle's medal until later.

For a few quiet moments, the two companions shared a growing bond as they pondered the trail before them, with unknown obstacles on the way to...? What had the old woman called it?

Hanyang, ancient city of kings for the troubled land.

"Grandmother," Madylan asked as the two stood up from their rocky seats and resumed walking down the mountain trail. "Is that the proper name to call you?"

"Little sister, or maybe I should call you little princess? Your parents must be very good parents. You have been nothing but polite, even when you bested the little dokkaebi wrestler and challenged the wandering blacksmith. Even the chubby witch was surprised at your graciousness. You call me grandmother, which gives me a warm, almost forgotten feeling, lo' these many, many years. I'd like you to continue to call me this, for it warms an old heart," the old woman replied, staring straight ahead and avoiding letting Madylan see her tearing eyes.

For the next half-hour or so, the two followed the direction of the shortening shadows down the winding trail, passing a few more clearings, with obviously empty and abandoned cottages and farms. To the north, or their right, the river rushed down, much faster than their walking pace, but over rocks and around sharp bends, making the fantasy of an easy boat ride beyond consideration. Maybe lower down, where the river slowed down at the flatlands, they might find transport, Madylan thought, her legs beginning to ache a bit.

Suddenly, the trail left a clump of forest and made a sharp turn at the edge of a high cliff, not far from a thin waterfall, formed by a small tributary of the larger river. Beyond the sharp bend in the trail, Madylan was both surprised and awed by the sights before her.

An ornate, if weathered, old, very old, building was clinging to the side of the mountain, a large part of the structure seeming to float out beyond the edge of the trail and hang in mid-air. Her mouth agape, Madylan remained speechless as she followed the grandmother along the path that would take them by the ornate building.

As they approached, another dwelling came into view on the left, more a cave than a building, with a rough entrance of sorts driven into the face of the mountain. Most of the second structure was buried within the mountain, giving the building a more rustic and, to Madylan's eyes, a more woodland or forest-like appearance. She expected small animals to prance out of the entrance, rather than people.

Both structures were a great deal larger than the cottages they had seen, but not anywhere near the size of the Manhattan skyscrapers that Madylan had grown up with.

The old woman suddenly spoke, looking back at her little companion with cautious eyes.

"Tread softly, little one. It's not quite noon, so the members to our right will still be in their hours of silence. The more down-to-earth dwellers on the left might be away, given that the entrance to their cavern appears to be closed. We may be able to slip past without disturbing the brothers and sisters," the grandmother whispered to Madylan.

Lowering her head, thinking that doing so would make her steps quieter, Madylan crept along behind her companion, but couldn't take her eyes off the more ornate building, dazzled by some of the designs on the walls and the multiple roofs that glistened gold and silver in the late morning sun. Blinking, she would swear later that the colors, the little creatures lining the edges of the roofs, and the sparkling designs were all singing and swirling, drawing her to the edge of the trail, dangerously close. Just when she thought she'd step over and touch the swirling images of colorful little men and women dancing and swaying to music that she had never heard, but knew she knew it in her heart, a hand grasped her shoulder and pulled her back, causing her to look down at the sheer cliff and gulp.

"Thanks…oh! What?" Madylan managed to say when she saw that the hand that had pulled her from the trail's edge was not attached to the grandmother, but to a square little bald man in a brownish yellow robe.

Just then the old woman turned and rushed back, calling as she approached.

"Brother, thank you. My companion is new to these mountain paths. We will no longer trouble you as we go on our way."

As the old woman wrapped her arm around Madylan's shoulders, the little man let his hand drop, but he did not move. His immobility seemed to freeze the old woman in place as well, for she simply stood, waiting for the little man to bid them pass.

Silence.

For a long, long moment, the little man, whom Madylan finally saw was really quite old, but had a very youthful look about him, simply stared at the little girl. Finally, he waved his right arm and the sound of a loud gong or bell resonated from the ornate building and bounced all around the trail, flowing around the three and then dropping off to be lost in the rustle of the trees far below.

Noon.

Madylan felt the old woman, the grandmother, tense up at the sound of the loud, but oddly soothing bell.

"She saw the ancestors, this little one did, dear lady of the far manor," the little man said, slowly, choosing his sparse words carefully, as if he did not want to waste even one syllable.

The old woman visibly flinched at the little man's comment. She then stepped away from Madylan and bowed to the little man, causing Madylan to do the same.

"Yes, she is from old stock, brother of the mountain tigers. I have a request," the old woman asked, her head still bowed, which was beginning to worry Madylan, who also continued to bow.

"You may speak this request," the little man said and then waved the two travelers to stand straight.

"Thank you for your benevolence, brother," the old woman replied, her voice very deferential to the man. "I would ask that you allow me to accompany her. She is not...she is from far away and is unfamiliar with our ways."

"She is a daughter of the old ones, is she not?" the man bluntly asked, leaning in to look into Madylan's eyes.

"Yes. Yes, but she...her people have been away. Far away, so I feel I need to be with her, and ask that your gracious brotherhood grant me this small request," the old woman answered, with an uncertainty in her voice that was worrying Madylan even further.

For a number of stretched out seconds, the little man did not reply, but waved his left arm and a trio of youthful acolytes appeared at a door in the side of the ornate building, not far from where the travelers were standing. He then said something unintelligible, to Madylan's ears, and the three young men, dressed in similar, but darker robes, scurried out and stood around the old woman. The little man then nodded and the three youths escorted the old woman into the building. The old grandmother did not look back.

"Young miss, please follow me," the little man said to Madylan and then, with a flourish of his arms, which made his robes seem to fly in a swirl around him, he stepped to the doorway and was gone.

Madylan, suddenly alone on the trail, a mountain behind her and a long drop to the valley beside her, wondered why the little man didn't think she would just run away, which, of course, she would not do because the odd little group of youths had captured, yes, that was the best word, captured her companion. She would never abandon the old woman, so Madylan took a deep breath and, trying not to look at the beckoning little creatures lining the roof ridges of the building, she prepared to duck into the doorway, still wondering why those little creatures seemed to all be leaning over and looking at her while they pointed and chattered among themselves high up on those steep roofs.

Abruptly, before Madylan could step through the elaborate entrance, she felt yet another hand on her shoulder. Looking down, she momentarily flinched, because the hand looked like a cross between a tree branch with no leaves and a far too thin bear's paw.

"Wait, little sister, before you cross that threshold of the new order," a voice, musical and enchanting, sang softly in Madylan's ear. "Step back from the edge, dear sister and let us speak for a moment.

Yes? Just a moment…?"

Checking her stride, Madylan turned and, looking into the eyes of what might have been a caveman in an old movie, or maybe a witchdoctor if the person staring at her were from a different land, she let out a little gasp.

"Little sister, fear not. We but look as the wind and the woodlands," the person (Madylan thought it might be a woman) responded, a wide grin spreading over her face (yes, definitely a woman, Madylan decided).

Suddenly, the doorway behind her erupted in quite a commotion as the old grandmother, the little bald man, and even the three acolytes all piled out of it and arrayed themselves beside Madylan.

"Stand down, old troublemaker," the little man called in a disdainful, elite voice to the wild looking woman. "The girl is no use to you. She is of the new ways, but kens the ancestors, so will follow our path, given the right instruction."

The old grandmother then stepped to Madylan's side, reaching out to hold the child's arm.

"Dear wanderer of the mountains and valleys of old, she is only a child, with some heavy weight, as yet unknown, thrust upon her. Allow us to pass," the old grandmother said quickly, almost in a pleading voice, as if she were looking to the wild woman as an ally to help pull Madylan away from the little man and the acolytes.

Madylan, for her part, was finally starting to understand. From what she gathered, the little man wanted to spirit her, and the grandmother, away to the temple or palace hanging over the cliff's edge and teach Madylan some sort of something, she was not sure what. The wild woman seemed to just want to talk, and she seemed to be the lesser threat to progress along the trail, given how the old grandmother had spoken.

For a few tense minutes, all parties were silent, with the wild woman swaying back and forth in her fantastical costume of multicolored silks, with small bells that tinkled when she moved, long streamers flowing from her wide sleeves, and a hat or head piece that seemed to change shape as she swayed. Behind the wild woman, Madylan finally saw several other young women, in colorful, but less complicated attire, holding burning sticks, maybe incense, and standing by the dark, deeply black opening to the cave house just on the other side of the trail.

"Great shaman of the mountain bear, I speak to your heart when I tell you true that the little sister is far from home, but is on a journey to her fate and must be allowed to pass without delay," the grandmother asked, her voice strong and commanding, her hands poised at her side as if she were preparing to fight both the little man's men and the wild woman.

Sensing she needed to make some sort of statement, Madylan searched her mind for something that might help and, then, a light sparking in the back of her head, she spoke up, trying to keep her small voice strong.

"At the party after my little brother's christening and at the one after his Dol, my uncle, who is my godfather, talked of how the world had many ways of thinking about life and the paths we take and even what happens after...after life is over. He told me of the old beliefs in my grandparents' lands, and of the even older beliefs, long before the land had a name. I am of the old, and I am of the new. I bow to both of you, but I alone choose my way."

Madylan then did a low bow, first to the wild woman of the ancient rites, and then to the little bald man brother of only a dozen or so centuries of presence in her motherland. She then reached out to the grandmother's hand and continued, keeping her voice steady.

"Grandmother here has been kind and full of guidance during this journey. I stand with her wishes," Madylan declared, trying, and succeeding in making her voice sound older than the young child she was.

After Madylan had fallen silent, for the blink of an eye, the wild woman looked as if she might simply grab Madylan and drag her to the cavern house. At the same time, the little man and the acolytes were circling around behind Madylan, no doubt with similar intent.

Just when Madylan thought there would be a big fight over who got to drag the little girl into whichever structure, the clear sound of horses on the trot could be heard from up the trail where the two companions had just come from.

Turning, the entire little group was treated to the sight of a small group of smartly clad warriors riding huge horses, which were also clad in heavy leathers, bronze plates, and silk streamers. The riders were bearing down on the two buildings, straight for the group standing in the middle of the trail.

Violently checking their horses, so that they would not trample

Madylan, the grandmother, and the various parties trying to entice the child, the five or six warriors stopped only a few feet away, the horses snorting and prancing in place, as if they wanted to continue, regardless of the people blocking the trail.

"Good people, are you looking to find your competing paradises sooner than later?" called a young man, tall and handsome in his uniform, from the lead horse. "Standing about on the king's road is a certain way to hurry up that meeting."

While the young man's voice was strong and authoritative, no doubt used to his soldiers and servants following his orders without question, the twinkling humor just behind his eyes relaxed Madylan and she finally started breathing again, but continued to hold the grandmother's hand.

As the young, maybe officer, Madylan thought, waited for a reply, the various parties reacted to his group's sudden arrival very differently.

The little man of the ornate temple bowed and waved two of the acolytes back into the sanctuary of the building. He then turned to face the young soldier, doing a half bow of greeting.

The wild woman, at least in Madylan's eyes, seemed to suddenly look younger as she swept her hands across the face of the lead horse, causing the animal to stop prancing and lean down to nuzzle the wild woman's hands. The three young women did not retreat, but actually stepped closer, their clothing more appealing that it had been just moments before. Each of the youthful women seemed to focus on different soldiers, sharing embracing smiles with the somewhat dumbstruck young men.

The grandmother, squeezing Madylan's hand in a gesture that said 'trust me,' was the first to reply to the young officer's challenge.

"We are two travelers, on the way to the seat of power, by way of the great river, kind sir, leader of the king's yeomen," the grandmother replied, using surprisingly formal speech with the officer. "These good people were simply helping us find our way along the trail."

The young soldier, after pulling his horse away from the far too attentive wild woman, nodded to the grandmother and, his eyes taking in the entire scene, waved over an older soldier, one with a tough, battle-scarred face and a very scary look, Madylan thought to herself.

"Captain, do you think the horses need to walk for a few miles, to give them a rest?" the young soldier asked.

"Sir, yes, I think you are wise to walk them. We are far ahead of time and these good people would probably enjoy the company," the older soldier answered, at the same time waving back the younger soldiers who were edging their horses closer to the three young women.

Sensing it was not wise to question the young leader and his tough looking captain, the little man from the ornate temple again bowed low and finally spoke.

"Safe journeys young one," the little man mumbled, seeming to address the young leader, then waved at the remaining acolyte, who scurried forward and thrust a small brass object at Madylan, who, looking surprised, took it, discovering it was a small bell, shaped like an upside down cup.

Then, with a curt nod to the grandmother and none to Madylan, the little man from the ornate building scurried back into the doorway, with the acolyte pulling it shut behind him.

The wild woman, on the other hand, was not as willing to walk away and sidled up to the tough, older soldier, cooing her words like a morning dove to its mate.

"Captain, you and your men, and even your esteemed leader here, all must be exhausted from the long ride. Yes, I know the garrison moved beyond the forest of persimmon trees several weeks ago. Please, rest your tired bodies for a brief moment, eat your fill, and have a little rice wine," the wild woman cooed, her voice nearly mesmerizing all those around her.

Even Madylan felt herself being drawn to the wild woman and her followers, who were all suddenly holding all manner of delicious dishes, steaming pots, and bottles of what looked like wine to her young eyes.

"Be off, shaman, we are wise to your tricks," the old soldier hissed at the wild woman, who stepped back in mock shock and threw her hands in the air.

"Hold your hurtful blows, good leader of the central kingdom, for ill fortune will follow any who cause harm to the Clan of the Bear in the Mountain!"

With that admonition, the wild woman spun around, her clothes returning to the rougher, more nature laden look as before, and stepped over to face Madylan, causing the grandmother to pull Madylan to her side.

"What trickery does this little one employ, dear lady of the far manor, that she can summon soldiers to rescue…to escort her safely through these dark woods, during this bleak time of brothers warring with brothers?" the wild woman asked, her voice oozing from a deep well inside her, conjuring up images of snakes and spiders preparing to leap from her woodland clothes.

Suddenly, Madylan's small medal slipped from behind a fold in her clothing, catching the eye of her inquisitor, who leaned in for a closer look.

"Ah! She carries a talisman. From afar, this bit of…what is it? Bronze from the south? No, bronze from across the sea," the wild woman chanted as she let her right hand caress the small bit of metal.

Suddenly, the wild woman reached up and plucked a small, dry branch from a dead limb of an old oak that grew on the temple side of the trail. Stripping a few twigs off the branch, she then mumbled some incoherent words and handed the stick to Madylan.

At the grandmother's nodding, Madylan took the stick from the wild woman, yet the shaman did not release the stick, but uttered several more incoherent words while the two both held the stick.

Visions!

For the blink of an eye that the two held the stick, the ancient wild woman and the young girl from a faraway modern city became one.

Madylan felt herself flying through the forest, witnessing countless events, people, foods, the very earth beneath her feet, and endless experiences she barely understood. Above all, she suddenly felt at peace in the strange land of her ancestors, even if she didn't fully understand what she was seeing. Her mind flew to the snow-covered mountains in the far, frigid north, then down to the pristine, idyllic beaches on the shores of Jeju Island, and then back to the woodland trail. Looking down, she finally saw herself and the little group at the edge of the road and felt herself dropping back into the group, from far up the mountain.

The wild woman then released her grip on the branch and smiled, allowing Madylan to stagger back into the grandmother's arms. The old woman gently placed the small branch in Madylan's pocket with the spoon from the little ogre.

The wild woman then looked to the grandmother and bowed low, walking backwards toward her cave house as she spoke.

"Travel with your charge's eyes as your own, old one. And, beware, escort, of what you cannot control. Pass by here on your return, if your manor still stands after your kingdom's betrayal, and you will be welcome, with or without the little one from afar," the wild woman said as she disappeared into the cave house, its massive, oak and iron doors slowly closing behind her, seeming to absorb all the sounds of the forest.

"Beware!"

The shaman's last word echoed all around the trail and then floated down to the far river as those remaining on the trail stood silently until the sounds of that very river and those sounds of the forest returned to normal.

For those moments, no one spoke. But then, once the world seemed to be back in order, the young leader climbed down from his horse and his men followed. Only the old soldier remained on his mount, evidently to see better beyond the far bend in the trail as it continued between the two structures.

"Grandmother, may I speak to your young charge?" the youthful leader asked, bowing slightly.

"Of course," the grandmother replied, nudging Madylan to bow to the officer.

"Little one, what is this magical talisman that has caused our almost hostess to retreat back into her lair?" the young officer asked, his voice betraying a note of humor.

"Sir, yes," Madylan responded, making a small bow to the handsome young officer. "My uncle's medal, sir. For defending my country...my grandparents' country, long ago, he said."

The young officer nodded as Madylan spoke, his brow furrowed as if in deep thought, but occasionally looking at the grandmother with more of a disbelieving twinkle in his eyes.

"Defending the motherland, and her huddled mob, the most noble of duties of the noblesse oblige," the young officer replied. "Interesting, this talisman from afar. I wonder...just how far?"

Madylan, detecting the young soldier's hint of veiled mockery, felt she needed to defend herself, but was waved down by the grandmother.

"Sir, if you let us walk a short way in your shadow, we will be quiet as mice sleeping by a warm cupboard. You will soon forget we are with you," the old grandmother stated, her arms still around Madylan.

"Captain, let's move on," the young leader then called to the tough soldier, nodding to the old grandmother and giving little Madylan a shortened bow.

As the little troop moved away from the buildings, Madylan positioned herself so that the horses blocked her view of the two structures, both sitting by the trail waiting for another pilgrim to pass by and engage in banter until one or the other led the poor pilgrim away.

Shuddering, but just a bit, from the odd and thankfully brief encounter, Madylan took some chewy, dried meat from one of the younger soldiers, after the grandmother had okayed it, of course. Relishing the salty but smooth flavor, she walked along trying to understand what the soldiers were saying, but, unless they spoke directly to her, Madylan found it hard to understand anything that they said.

For several miles, or what felt like endless miles to Madylan's youthful legs, the little troop walked in mostly silence, save for a report once in a while from the captain who had remained mounted and would ride forward for a look and then ride back to report to the leader on what lie ahead.

As they walked, Madylan quietly whispered to the old grandmother, outlining as best as a young girl unfamiliar with the surroundings could, the brief, but dizzying flight through the land's culture and people when the wild woman had given Madylan the oak branch. After listening carefully, the grandmother assured Madylan that the flight was not harmful and had been the shaman's gift for the little girl. The gift of ancient knowledge, even if Madylan didn't know what to do with it.

"So, each of these people we meet will give us some sort of gift?" Madylan then asked. "Wait. Not all, right? The little bald man did not give us anything...oh, wait, the bell. But, the scary old chef wanted us, rather than wanted to give us anything."

"Best to wait, dear, and see what the road brings," the old grandmother replied, waving Madylan to silence when one of the soldiers looked back at the two.

As the little troop moved along the trail, Madylan noticed that small bands of ragged looking ruffians who had been visible on the trail far below, would be nowhere to be seen by the time the troop passed the spots where the gangs had been. She felt, rather than saw, the random groups staring out of the cover of the woods or the high rocks, waiting for the armed group to pass, so that they could descend once again to the trail and accost the few travelers who might be brave enough to wander about unprotected.

During the hour or more that the soldiers accompanied the old woman and her strange young companion, the young leader had been chatting with the two from time to time, with special interest as to which families the two belonged to, from which he could no doubt deduce their loyalties. While he was aware of the old woman's respected clan, he was puzzled by the young girl's strange explanation of living far over the sea, but coming from one of the eastern clans, according to the names of her mother and father. But, with more pressing issues on his mind, the young gentleman warrior no doubt filed away his puzzlement for later.

At one point, the young leader asked of the grandmother if the girl had a cloak or some sort of coat to ward off the cold of the coming evening. He also wondered aloud about where the two would pass the night on the road and seemed to be satisfied when the old woman assured him that she had sent a messenger ahead to procure rooms at the river inn not too far down the road. However, he insisted that one of his men loan the girl a jacket, which the grandmother was able to quickly trim down to better fit the slim girl.

During a short rest by the roadside, two of the soldiers had a brief archery practice, using a large mound of rotting hay as a target. Seeing that Madylan was curious, the young leader gave them permission to show her their equipment and even offered her a chance to shoot one of the hefty bows. As suspected, the bow was far too strong for the young girl to pull, so one of the soldiers, the one who had volunteered one of his coats, produced a much easier to pull practice bow. She was not only able to pull the bow, she also hit the target six times out of seven tries. Impressed, the young leader presented Madylan with the practice bow and a number of arrows, which she hung in a bundle from her back with a long cord. However, he had instructed his men to remove the valuable and scarce steel arrowheads, since a young girl would not need such for leisure archery practice. One of the soldiers then fashioned small lead tips, for the arrows to remain balanced.

After another hour together, the captain rode up to the walking soldiers and their young leader and let the group know that it was time to remount the horses and move with haste to a far mountain pass. The small troop's assignment was to guard the narrow pass to prevent the enemy from advancing into a valley that would allow the enemy easier access to the king's stronghold.

At a wide, multi-trail and roads crossroads, deserted except for a few escaped chickens who seemed to think the horses were from their home farm and so attached themselves to follow the horses, the young leader ordered the captain to order the men back on their horses and to prepare to gallop off. The young man then turned to the two companions.

"Grandmother of the far manor, little sister of the far lands, we must ride on, now," the young officer began, obvious worry on his face. "Our less friendly path carries us over the mountain of the turtles, away from your path to the river. And, yes, I know warmth and happiness of your grand home from my visits as a youth, back in quieter times."

The old grandmother bowed at the leader's kind words, her eyes answering him with gratitude.

"Little sister, your path is intriguing. In another life, I'd follow to simply observe your adventures. Alas, our lives are called to duty to our leaders, our family's honor, and our men's trust, little sister. So, I part hoping that the good grandmother here carries you through to the capital, or beyond," the young leader said, with sweeping formality to Madylan, causing her to blush a bit at his grand words.

"And, if the gods will it and our little sister's talisman is strong, you'll be back at that hearth again some day, dear grandmother. Let's hope well before these troubled years have grown this little one into your contemporary," the young soldier called as he led his small troop away from the narrow river valley and toward the dark and forbidding mountains.

Both Madylan and the old grandmother called their thanks for the troops' protection, their hopes for safe travel, and their wishes that they meet again. The young soldier echoed the two companions' call for meeting again and then disappeared into an even darker tunnel of trees on the road to the mountains.

Standing in the broad crossroads, Madylan wondered what the various signposts said, given that they were written in the old language that she could not read.

"Wait, is that a...?" Madylan asked, stepping closer to one of the signs pointing to where she thought the river must lie. "It's a picture of a river, and a small boat, yes?"

"Yes, little sister. Makes it easier for the vast, uneducated populace to find their way on these roads. Literacy it still, sadly, elusive for many."

Puzzled that grownups might not be able to read, Madylan turned toward the trail to the river, which seemed to run parallel with a long, rock ridge toward an even rougher jumble of stony outcrops, where the river trail disappeared into those less than welcoming rocks.

"The river is through those...those rocky hills, grandmother?"

"It does appear so, dear. I've only come this way once, when I wasn't much older than you, but we rode sedan chairs in those days, so I remember little. From what the young leader told me, we must take care not to be confused when we enter those trails that pass through the rocks. The path is marked, with strikes on the stones where turns are needed. But, he suggested an old trick from our youth, his more recent, of dropping small pebbles as we walk in case we need to backtrack to find our way out."

Taking the river trail, Madylan began to collect small pebbles of dark stone, given that the grandmother had said the trail would be of lighter, crushed rock, so the darker pebbles would be easier to spot. By the time the two had reached the entrance to the rocky path, Madylan had a couple of dozen small pebbles weighing down her various pockets.

"Take care not to drop them too close together dear. Maybe a dozen paces, and particularly when we take one side of a fork or another," the grandmother said as she pulled her jacket around her and suggested Madylan do the same with the small jacket the soldiers had given her to fend off the coming chill of the evening.

Caw! Ca-caw!

Several large crows, or maybe ravens, flew away and circled overhead as they scolded the two companions for disturbing the dark eaters of souls, as some old timer might call them. The grandmother mumbled a small prayer and Madylan held tightly to her medal as they left the fussy, sinister birds, and plunged ahead into the maze of rocks and jumbles of large boulders that formed the trail that wove its way to the river's edge. The grandmother remembered that the trail eventually paralleled the river, when they would, hopefully, break out of the labyrinth of rock canyons and confusing dead ends.

As they walked, Madylan dropped one of the shiny black stones from her pocket about every twenty paces or so. Whenever they took a fork, she'd drop a couple extra.

Every now and then, the grandmother would suddenly stop and hold up her hand for Madylan to stop, who would. One time, after a particularly difficult stretch of rocky trail, Madylan thought she heard additional steps somewhere behind them. Or, maybe in front?

"Grandmother, do you hear other footsteps?" Madylan whispered as her companion peered around a large outcropping of grey, white-streaked stone. "Wait. They've stopped."

"Mayhap, little sister, we have unknown and unwanted companions. From the echoes, though, it's hard to tell who is following whom."

When no additional footsteps were heard, the grandmother motioned to her small companion and the two walked along closer together, watching not only the trail forward and behind, but also looking up at the tops of the rocks and the few trees that grew in the stony soil along the path.

Caw! Caw!

Looking around, Madylan did not see the crows, so was not surprised when the grandmother leaned over and whispered in her ear.

"Not all calling birds fly, dear. Stay close."

After less than a minute, Madylan fully understood what the old woman had meant when the two travelers passed through a narrow gap between two tall piles of rocks and came face to face with a band of youths, most not much older than Madylan.

The grandmother pushed Madylan behind her and spoke slowly to the ragtag group of rough looking children gathered in a small clearing between two high walls of stone. Far up the left wall, a skinny young boy sat in a bent over tree, watching, not the new arrivals to the clearing, but up and down the trail from above.

"Good day, fellow travelers," the grandmother called, using a more polite term than Madylan thought the rough youths warranted. "We hope we do not inconvenience you when you step aside to let us pass."

One small group of children, sitting around a cold fire to the side, had been in the middle of an old folk song, singing quietly amongst themselves to no doubt pass the time. One of the little ones sitting in the singing group, a girl, cradled a small boy in her arms and was cooing to the child, as one would do with a little brother. Upon seeing the appearance of the elegant old woman and the strange youth, the others in the singing group nudged the girl, who then looked up with the most expressive, doleful eyes, and began to sing an even older folk song.

The pensive child's voice seemed to circle the little clearing, flowing off the grey stone and caressing the scrawny trees above. The song was so old the meaning of the words had been long forgotten. Such little singing troupes, usually older in years, but apprentices could be quite young, would often sing the old tune at taverns or fairs for food money or, in the larger cities, for the pockets of the music men who cared for the usually orphaned children. The song, as sung by the slip of a girl, was so compelling, so tragic, that the old grandmother and even Madylan, who had no idea what the words meant, were mesmerized and felt themselves nearly crying by the time the little waif, the little angel of the woodland, finally fell silent. The angel girl then looked at them with passionate eyes and turned back to coo at her little brother.

"Free to you good travelers. We usually demand a high fee for one of her folk songs, but our little golden voice chose to freely bless you with song, so we'll not press for any coins," a large youth, the only one with any fat at all on his bones, called from a fallen tree near the middle of the clearing.

Chuckling, the youth, who must have been the leader of the little band, because he had the least torn clothing, the most jewelry, odd though it was, and, yes, upon closer examination, seemed the best fed of the skinny bunch, waved his hand as if to calm his little tribe.

"No need to pass, old woman," the leader then answered the request for passage, using a less than flattering term for the grandmother. "We've no need to move over. You can happily join our little band. We're heading south, to the far sea."

"Yes. Yes. To the sea. We do. Yes!" called a small child, dirty and with wild hair, who seemed to scurry about in all directions, his, or maybe her, head swinging violently side to side. "Join the sea, we do. Yes!"

The leader youth reached out and shoved the confused child, who fell to the side, curling himself, or herself, up into a filthy ball of rags and bones. A large boy, a head or more taller than the rest, stepped away from the singing group and over to comfort the shaking child, his eyes never leaving the young bully.

Madylan, horrified at what she considered very hurtful brutality, stepped forward to take the scruffy leader to task when the old grandmother spoke first.

"May we be assistance with your friend there? I have some experience in these matters, young sir," the grandmother asked.

"Yes! We will help the boy!" Madylan declared, stepping close to the young bully, deciding there were some fights she had to fight herself, especially when she saw the wretched state of all the children.

"How dare you push that child? You have fat on your bones, you...you!" Madylan continued, her face flushed. "I'll bet you have hidden food these little ones could eat!"

"Get away, little bug, before someone steps on you!" the young bully yelled back at Madylan, but his hands betrayed him by covering his right pocket.

Thinking quickly, before the grandmother could stop her, Madylan grabbed at the bully's pocket, spilling a large bundle of rice cakes and strips of dried meat onto the ground.

A hushed silence fell over the little clearing, as all the hungry children stared at the bounty. Even the singing children fell silent, but not before they all sang one word together.

"Food!"

The single word rang out from the little singers, their harmonic, if weak voices bouncing off the stone and trees, causing even the watcher waifs in the forests above them to peer over the edges with wide, frantic eyes.

"I was saving it, for you!" the young bully called, as he tried to shove the food back into his pocket. "Once we make the deep forest, I'll give it out."

"Let them help the touched one," the large boy called, standing over the curled up youth.

The young bully mumbled some weak objections, while several of the other children argued with the leader. After a very heated exchange, the leader reluctantly nodded and the old grandmother approached the whimpering ball of rags.

"What is his name?" the grandmother asked.

"Mother, no one knows," a waif of a girl, with huge eyes and twigs for arms and legs, replied in a voice laced with heavy despair. "He sort of found us as we passed the western hills, below the beacon peak where the foreign soldiers...where much destruction has happened, grandmother. A lot of the farms...they were burned or abandoned, mother. Even the animals are gone."

"Looted, all," whispered the large boy who had argued to let the grandmother help the babbling child.

Taking the shaking child's thin hand in hers, the grandmother pushed the stringy hair out of the boy's eyes, felt his pulse on his skinny neck, and tried to get him to open his mouth so she could see in.

Calling Madylan away from the young bully, the grandmother motioned for her to take out the remainder of the rice cakes and tofu. When she did so, the other children audibly gasped at seeing even more meager food. One child even emitted a low whimper at the sight. Several others stepped closer to the bully, eyeing his fat right pocket.

Madylan then helped the grandmother feed a few bites to the boy, who seemed to not understand that it was food and let the first rice cake sit in his mouth until the larger boy, who had spoken for him, stepped over and manually worked the thin child's jaw, which finally elicited chewing on the skinny boy's part.

As the boy slowly chewed the food, his cloudy eyes cleared for a moment and he looked up at his two angels, the old grandmother and the odd young girl, who wore a small talisman at her collar. Seeing the talisman, the child uttered a heart-rending plea.

"Oh, dragon of my father's father's father's dreams, fly to the flaming mountain to save my village, all!" the boy cried and then, smiling up at Madylan, continued to chew the meager food.

Madylan, tucking the small medal back under her coat, was then able to feed the boy several more of the small rice cakes and a bit of tofu, stopping only when the grandmother signaled.

"That will do, dear. Not too much, or he'll lose it," the grandmother said softly, as she took the bowl from Madylan and handed it to the large boy.

"Give him the rest in two sittings. One tonight and one in the morning," the grandmother said as she poured some sort of oil over the remaining food. "This should bring him back. Remember, twice, not all at once."

Seeing how the other children stared hungrily at the small bowl of meager fare, the grandmother reached out and touched the large boy's arm, her eyes telling the boy that to deny the skinny child any of the remaining food would fatally condemn the weak child.

The large boy's jaw set and he bowed low to the grandmother. Tearing a rag from his already torn shirt, he carefully wrapped the bowl and shoved it into one of his trouser folds. He then stared down all those around him, to include the bully leader, and tapped a long scabbard, nearly concealed by his clothing, hanging from the side of his waist, tucked in a pouch with oddly clean paint brushes.

"Grandmother, thank you for your kindness. I will attend to the boy," the larger child then said, turning back to the old woman. "I am Jeo—…no, Kwan is enough. Please be safe on your long road."

The large boy then moved between the grandmother, with Madylan at her side, and the bully leader and stood firmly, both feet planted, forming a clear barrier to allow the two accidental visitors in their temporary lair to depart.

"Hey, we were going to have them go with us…?" the bully leader called as the grandmother, wasting no time, pulled Madylan behind her toward the far end of the small clearing in the rocks.

As the two waited for the ragged children to step away from the trail to let them pass, the little singing girl stepped close to Madylan, and, pointing with her free hand, as her other held her little brother, she indicated she wanted Madylan to touch the little boy with the medal. Looking up at the grandmother for guidance, the old woman whispered so that only Madylan could hear.

"Theirs is a hard life, little sister," the grandmother said quietly. "Big sister there has no doubt been going hungry to ensure her little brother eats. She thinks, as many simple, but kind folk do, that your little talisman will bring good luck to the boy. She's not asking for herself, but for the little child."

Nodding, Madylan smiled at the girl and let the little singer lift her brother's tiny hand to touch the medal at Madylan's collar. Madylan noticed that, other than being thin, the small boy was smiling and seemed happy, his eyes always following his sister's pale face. Seeing the child so close, she felt a lump in her throat at missing her own little brother, so she resolved to remember the dream so she could tell him of her adventures one day.

Once the child had touched the medal and smiled with a small giggle, the little girl, her face beaming her thanks to the odd youth with the strange talisman, made a slight bow to Madylan and then turned away. However, Madylan reached out and motioned for the girl to also touch the medal. The girl shook her head, but Madylan gently took the girl's free hand and, pulling the medal off her collar, rested the medal in the girl's hand.

Darkness!

Madylan suddenly felt she had fallen into a pitch-black tunnel, or a hole, far, far away from anything warm or loving, and was being pressed by jagged stones of abject despair. Hunger, cold, dark corners, and unknown paths danced through her mind. But, after a few seconds, music floating around her head, like cheerful fireflies in the misty night, seemed to temporarily ease the heavy sense of hopelessness. Disoriented, Madylan called out to the grandmother, but heard no response.

Unable to tell which way was up or down, or what to do next, Madylan simply stood, trying to will herself out of the darkness, focusing on the tiny pinpoints of light from the music. She suddenly remembered the medal and the little girl and, pulling at her hand, Madylan felt herself slowly, slowly extract her hand from that of the little singer, and a renewed brightness flew in from all around.

Light!

Back in the clearing, Madylan was surprised to see that the little singer's tragic eyes had somehow gained a renewed sense of hope. Madylan then realized that some of the little girl's pain had been left in the darkness that Madylan had just seen.

"Thank you, eonni, for showing me and my brother that there is still light. Briefly, you were me, and, I you," the little girl said, so quietly that Madylan was not sure the girl had even spoken.

After calling Madylan by the term for a beloved older sister or girlfriend, the golden voice singer then stepped back to her circle of little friends, who all surrounded her and the little boy with comforting embraces. The young singer whispered how she had been uplifted by visions of light and plenty when she had touched the strange girl's talisman.

Madylan then immediately understood that the frail girl had seen something of Madylan's full and healthy life, while Madylan had seen the girl's tragic young years and how the gift of music had been the child's salvation.

Kwan, the large boy who had appointed himself the protector of the shivering boy, patted the singing girl on the shoulder and then spoke, his voice strong, resolute.

"Grandmother, a healer for these sad times, and the little sister, a child of the old ones, are not for us," Kwan declared, stepping closer to the leader. "They must go their own road. We will make for the old fat chef's hut, the one that tinkerer told us about. He said she would feed us for a small fee. We will share what you have now with the little ones first."

"Fee? What coins do we have?" the leader growled back, but reluctantly reached into his pocket, took out the bundle of hidden food, and gave it to the waif of a girl to distribute.

"We can give her the silver you took from that old house," Kwan replied, stepping closer to the bully.

Hearing the heated words, the grandmother paused at the far opening and turned back to call over to the arguing boys.

"Young sirs, avoid the old fat chef. The tinkerer is one of her henchmen. He sends such as you to a dismal fate. Take the high road around her, through the forest. There you will find game and I saw a few of the farms, while deserted, still had edibles in the fields and maybe in the storage sheds. Beyond those fields, there are army camps, mostly of good men. You may find a few coins and food there for your singing. The gods know those boys need such to uplift their spirits during these times. Safe travels."

After hearing the grim news about the old chef from the kind grandmother and the possible good news about food and places to make a little money, even the gruff leader was thankful and so offered a bit of advice of his own.

"Grandmother, thank you for your concern. I'm ashamed that I thought to have my strong ones fall upon you and the little sister to rob you. Thank you for what you did with our crazy...with our weak brother," the bully called, his head hung low as he spoke. "When you make the river, keep going for a few leagues. Avoid the old boatmen. All the honest ones have gone to the coast, or to the city. Only the thieves and broken ones remain. Yet, there is a younger one. Oddly tall, and only an apprentice, but a true boatman who waits for his master to return, though the kind old man who took him under wing has probably perished in the east, as have so many others. Again, kind grandmother and tough little sister, look for the ungainly tall youth, almost a fish out of water, he is."

With that, the boy turned away and walked over to check on the skinny boy who had stopped shaking and babbling and was sitting up, looking almost normal, except for the rags and bones.

The grandmother waved, as did Madylan, and the two disappeared into what they hoped was a short path to the river.

As the two put hurried distance between themselves and the little lost tribe of minstrel singers, they heard the little voice that the bully leader had called 'golden' began to lead the entire troupe in another popular ballad, one with more hope and light than the earlier song. The encouraging words, clear and resonant, helped spur the two travelers on their way.

After only a few minutes, the two companions emerged onto a narrow cart path that ran along beside the swift river. On the opposite shore, a large village lay in ruins, deserted. A bridge, once a mighty stone edifice, had been reduced to two piles of rubble on each bank. Weeds had already started to flourish in the rubble, which told the grandmother that the village and the bridges had fallen some months before.

"We must step with care, little sister. There is little cover along the river and we must be cautious when we see others, especially the boatmen as the young boy told us," the grandmother whispered to Madylan as the two walked along under the cover of the few trees that sat back some yards from the cart path.

After about half a league, a roguish looking fellow with dark streaks in his white hair called to them from a shiny, well-maintained boat which was moored to an old stone pier a few feet out in the rushing water.

"A fair price to cross, grandmother?" the old man called, waving at the grandmother, but staring at young Madylan.

"Thank you, no, kind sir, for we have already arranged for transport down river," the grandmother called back, hurrying by quickly, nearly dragging Madylan with her.

Several other older boatmen called after them from floating platforms just a few yards out in the river, but the grandmother ignored those and kept moving, keeping Madylan in front of her.

Stepping around a bend in the river, only another half-league on, the two were suddenly greeted by a fallen tree blocking both the cart path and the area they were walking on by the trees.

Looking ahead, the grandmother gasped at the wide landscape of tree stumps and piles of smoldering trees, stretching all the way to the base of the mountains.

"What is this, grandmother?" Madylan asked. "Has a forest fire happened here?"

"No dear. This has been done by the hand of man. Why, I know not. But, we must take care to avoid the beasts that would do this to our lovely forests," the grandmother replied as the two continued on, walking more cautiously.

After some minutes, the two heard a faint chopping sound, which increased in volume as they proceeded.

Suddenly, not thirty paces in front of them, a large, straight pine tree shook and then crashed to the ground, falling away from the river.

A minute later, a team of sturdy, but tired workhorses stepped from the forest dragging the tall tree in a harness. The horses, without a master, dragged the tree to one of the smoldering piles and stood waiting. Another minute passed and a tall woodsman, his broad shoulders bearing both a long saw and a broad axe, stepped from the trees and joined the horses. There he gently placed his tools on the ground and unhitched the tree from the horses, freeing it to roll to the smoldering embers, where the tree suddenly caught fire, given that the sap in the pine tree was like oil, so the flames grabbed at it quickly.

The woodsman then turned the horses to a small patch of tall grass and left them to feed, while he walked back to the stand of trees, which held only a dozen or so remaining trees.

Behind the woodsman, as far as the eye could see up the mountainside, only small, young trees still stood in a sea of tree stumps and smoldering piles.

Suddenly, the woodsman stopped and turned to stare at the two travelers. For a moment, he looked as if he might speak, but then shook his head and stepped out of sight into the stand of trees.

The grandmother called after the woodsman.

"Sir, woodsman of the river dales, we are asking to pass before you fell another majestic giant, possibly on our heads," the grandmother called to the woodsman somewhere hidden in the stand of trees.

For a long breath, the woodsman did not answer. Finally, he stepped from the trees holding the massive, double headed axe and spoke, his voice booming around the narrow valley like cannon shot.

"Do not judge me, old mother. Yes, I can see disapproval in your eyes and in the way you and the little one stand in shock at my deed," the woodsman called, his eyes defiant.

"Good sir, I will not deny we are truly shocked. But, I know your heart is pure. You are killing this vast forest to save the people to the west, yes?" the grandmother called, her voice sympathetic and soothing, finally understanding. "The small trees remaining will grow up to replenish this ravaged land one day. Yes?"

Madylan looked up at the grandmother, wondering how chopping down hundreds of trees would protect anybody.

The tall woodsman, his face a mix of emotions, bowed low to the old grandmother and, stepping onto the path, he leaned his massive axe against a wide stump, kicked a log next to the stump and sat. He then pulled a round bag from his side. From the bag, the woodsman extracted a narrow water gourd and several wooden cups. He also pulled out a lump of cheese and a half-eaten loaf of hard bread.

"Join me? The tea is cold, but made this morning," the woodsman called, dragging a second short log up to the impromptu table, the stump, to serve as a bench.

The grandmother nodded and led Madylan over to the log, where the two sat and waited as the woodsman poured tea from the gourd.

"Sir, I do not understand as well as the good grandmother," Madylan said after thanking the woodsman for the drink. "Why is it that you shave the trees from this mountainside?"

"No bridge can span the river, no engine of war can be lashed together by the enemy, if no trees are there to use," the woodsman said, his deep, yet clear eyes seeming to pierce Madylan's heart with his pensive words. "Many are these giants planted with the hands of my grandfather's father. Yet, their spirits stand with me as I do this work."

The woodsman then leaned in close to Madylan and peered at her clothes, particularly the coat the soldiers had fashioned for her.

"My brother rides with a young lord of those colors, little miss. How is it that you wear them, a girl?" the woodsman asked. "And carry a bow from the training academy?"

After her surprise faded, Madylan and the grandmother related how the small troop of soldiers had helped them along the road. However, when it came to where the soldiers had departed to, the grandmother would not say, so Madylan also did not reveal what direction they went.

"So, even though he is my brother, you will keep from me his whereabouts?" boomed the woodsman, standing up and reaching for his axe in a menacing way. "Who are you to keep secrets in my lands?"

"A spy!" Madylan shouted and also stood, her face defiant as she stepped toward the woodsman. "You could be a spy who only says one of the young soldiers is your brother. We will not betray their trust!"

Madylan, standing her full height, which was barely high enough to see over the log the tall woodsman had been sitting on, stepped in front of the grandmother in order to protect her older companion. The girl then reached for her little medal, grabbed it, and whispered a prayer that the woodsman would miss with the huge axe.

Towering over her, the woodsman at first glared at the brave young girl, then, slowly, very slowly, a long chuckle rolled up out of his chest and then burst out in a hearty laugh.

Infuriated at being laughed at, Madylan dashed toward the woodsman with the wild thought that she'd push the human mountain into the river.

"Wait, little sister. I'm not laughing at you, brave little warrior. I'm laughing at my sad attempts to scare you into talking," the woodsman said, his words kind and full of warmth, stopping Madylan in her tracks. "You've protected my brother from me, who could be a spy, as you said. So, I honor you, brave little warrior and your escort for being suspicious of those you meet on the road. Thank you."

The woodsman then bowed low, his great bulk's shadow passing over the stump and the two travelers like an eclipse.

"We thank you in return for your understanding, kind woodsman," the grandmother said as Madylan stepped back, her brow furrowed at the woodsman's comments.

"Yes, sir, we thank you," Madylan repeated, a little color rushing into her face once she realized how bold and a little foolish she had been in challenging the tall woodsman.

Suddenly, the woodsman returned the pouch and the empty cups to his bag and, taking up his axe, bid farewell and safe travels to the two travelers and prepared to cut down another tall tree.

"Sir, wait. Can you tell us if there is a young boatman nearby? One who is honest and will take our trade without robbing us?" the grandmother asked as she gathered her things.

"The boatmen are nearly all thieves and scoundrels these many months, grandmother. Yet, yes, I have heard of an odd, gangly youth who meanders about, taking on fares as he waits his master's return. Sad, as his master will never return. Few do from the east," the woodsman replied and then pointed downriver toward a double peaked mountain.

"This side of the old beacon peak, there is what was once a fishing village. Nothing but a few huts now. The boy lingers there, as it was his master's village. Say nothing to the other boatmen as you approach. Nothing at all and the boy will find you," the woodsman said and then, pausing, he turned to the grazing horses and whistled.

The horses, hearing the whistle, lifted their heads and trotted over to the woodsman, their harnesses clinking as they walked. Once they had stopped by the woodsman and eyed the two strangers, the woodsman opened a bag hanging from the lead horse and extracted a small wooden box. He looked it over carefully and then turned back to Madylan, leaning down to hand her the small box.

"For the coming cold night, I'm guessing you two do not have a fire starter. Please take this one, as my small thanks for protecting my brother," the woodsman said.

The woodsman then opened the small wooden box to show the two its simple contents. The small, flat box held a small chunk of flint, a piece of steel fastened to a short wooden handle, and some very dry strips of old cloth, mixed with fragrant wood shavings.

"You do know how to make a fire, dear lady?" the woodsman then said to the grandmother as he closed up the box and handed it to Madylan.

"Yes. When I was young, my mother let me play in the kitchen with the cook, where I learned many useful things. I will show the little sister how to use it. Thank you, young man," the grandmother replied.

"Oh, sir, I'm so sorry that you miss your brother," Madylan then said, but still did not say which way the brother and the troops had gone as she tucked the small fire making box into her coat.

"One brother to protect the sea. One brother to protect the court.

One brother to ride into battle. Their older brother to give them time to do so," the woodsman replied, his voice neither boastful nor sad, just stating a simple fact.

"Thank you, kind sir," Madylan answered and bowed low to the woodsman, who bowed in return and then moved away with the horses back to the small stand of trees.

"Be safe, little warrior. I can work in peace, knowing my brother and the patrol are safely on their way to Hawk's Pass in the mountain of the turtles to hold it against the enemy's force, until the king's messengers can tell the armies in the west from whence those forces attack. Not from this valley, we know, as there are no trees for building bridges or war machines. Be safe!" the woodsman called as he faded into the trees.

"Grandmother, he knew all along where the soldiers were going!" Madylan exclaimed as the two started down the cart path toward the far fishing village.

"Yes, dear. It stands to reason that such a man, from such a loyal family that is giving all to save the kingdom, would know his brother's movements. Better to protect the small troop by seeming confused," the grandmother replied.

For the next hour, as the shadows lengthened and the sky shifted from blue-grey to more grey, the two companions followed the riverside cart path, ignoring the calls from the tough looking boatmen they encountered. On the path itself, they only passed a few families of old grandmothers, young wives and small children. No men, but for one or two very old grandfathers.

At a brief stop, the grandmother showed Madylan how the fire starter worked. Once Madylan had managed to light some twigs, the grandmother gathered the coals and stuffed them into a strange tube that had a cap with small holes in it. The grandmother told Madylan that, since night was not far off, the small fire stick was a good way to have some embers ready to more easily start a cook fire, or light a lantern, if they came upon one in an abandoned house.

After another few minutes, the two travelers approached a sorry cluster of broken down huts that clung like clumps of matted mud to the side of the river, leaning so far over that they all appeared ready to fall into the river at the slightest breeze.

"The village?" Madylan asked, with doubt in her voice, but the grandmother kept silent as they walked.

Just at the edge of the dismal huts, gathered at a makeshift pier, more a few old logs strapped together, several boatmen were laughing and drinking as they played some sort of game of chance on the deck of the largest boat. The men saw the two coming and, from the way they eyed the grandmother and her clothes, seemed to agree to end the game and collect up their monies. Each gambler returned to his respective boat and all began to cajole the two travelers to use their services. However, remembering what the woodsman had said, both the grandmother and the girl kept silent and walked along without looking any of the calling boatmen in the eye.

Once past the boatmen, Madylan was tempted to looked back, mainly to see if any of the rough looking men might be following, when another voice called out from the darkness of an alley by several of the decrepit huts.

"Best to continue on, little lady. Any sign of weakness or interest and our ruffian friends will pounce," the voice advised.

Stepping into view, the owner of the voice proved to be a tall, thin, quite gangly youth who seemed to be uncomfortable on land, as his long legs seemed to wobble as he walked. The youth smiled at the two travelers and, pointing forward, walked along the path to a long, slim boat moored at the end of the string of broken down huts.

The boat, however, was in pristine condition. Well built, polished and, from what the grandmother could see, also well provisioned, given all the strife in the land.

"Are you in need of transport down the river? As you probably know, grandmother, the trail turns into the dark mountains just a hundred yards on, so the river is the only way to reach the beacon peak village and beyond. All the way to Hanyang, we can carry you. For a fair price," the youth called as he busied himself on the boat.

"We?" the grandmother asked.

For an answer, a large dog suddenly jumped up on the makeshift dock and sniffing the air, looked at the grandmother and Madylan and gave a short yelp of approval.

"Yes, good boatman, we do have need of your services," the grandmother replied.

As the lanky boy busied himself with preparing the boat for departure, he and the grandmother bantered a price back and forth until a reasonable fee was agreed upon. Half before they departed and the other half once at Hanyang, if they wanted to go that far.

Madylan sat with the large dog, who seemed to take to the girl immediately by placing its shaggy head in her lap.

"We go," the tall youth suddenly declared and the boat slid silently into the flowing water.

For some time, the three, four with the dog, floated down the river without incident, passing only a few barge boats laden with meager crops from the few farms that were still operating. The barges were headed to the capital, according to the boatman.

Madylan spent most of the time on the boat scratching the dog's neck and watching the countryside slowly roll by, while she wondered where her dream might take her next. As she pondered, she reached up and touched her uncle's medal, which caused the dog to suddenly bark and the boatman, who was at the tiller, to turn and look over at the strange young girl in the soldier's coat, carrying a bow that looked too large for her.

"Traveling to the war, little miss? If so, it's farther east. Although, if you wait a few days, it will probably be in our valley," the youthful boatman called. "Your talisman will probably not be much help, though, as I think the spirits have taken a holiday around here."

"Young man, you should never give up hope," the grandmother replied.

"Ah, good grandmother, and you, young miss, hope is always there. But, so is the world, which is bleak, you agree?" the boy replied, his words far older than his apparent years.

Nodding, the grandmother used her silence to agree with the boy. Madylan nodded as well, tucking the medal back into her collar as she answered.

"No, I don't think we are going to the war, boatman," Madylan replied. "Our journey seems to be taking us to the capital, where I know not what awaits us there."

"Maybe your water spirits, just there, can answer you?" the lanky boy suddenly quipped, pointing forward, causing both Madylan and the grandmother to turn.

Several boat lengths down the river a small waterfall, fed by a tributary to the wider river, dropped from a high cliff into a wide semicircle carved into the rocky sides of the river over the millennia. When the falling water hit the calmer water of the river, a swirling whirlpool appeared, seeming to dance just like in the old legends about water dragons or the young ones, the imugi, or wingless snakes of other legends. Birds, forest animals, sea creatures, and all manner of strange images also danced about the flowing water.

Laughing at the cheerful sight, welcome after the tragedy of the lost children and the sadness of the lone woodsman, Madylan felt a sense of wonderment watching the light play tricks with the various images that emerged from the swirling water as sprays of mist.

"Boatman, should you not get so close to that spiraling water?" the grandmother suddenly asked, with Madylan noting rising concern in her companion's voice the closer they got to the waterfall.

"Boatman?" the grandmother repeated.

However, the boatman was ignoring the old woman and was steering the slender craft straight for the churning water, his eyes watching the edges, as if anticipating something.

"Little sister, we must jump!" the grandmother suddenly called, reaching over to grab Madylan's arm, but was stopped by the dog who stood between the grandmother and the girl.

"Fear not, dear grandmother," the boatman shouted over the din from the falling water as they got dangerously close to the whirlpool. "A pure heart will pass unscathed."

Madylan, quickly assessing the dangers that suddenly confronted her and the grandmother, realized there was no time to escape the boat and, since they were already on the edge of the whirlpool, any attempt to jump in the churning water would probably be disastrous. So, she stood and turning to the boatman, shouted with all her might to be heard over the roar of the falling water mixed with the groaning whirlpool.

"You were supposed to be kind! The woodsman and the singing children sent us to you!" Madylan yelled at the top of her lungs. "And...and we carry the dragon talisman!"

Holding up her uncle's medal, since she couldn't think of anything else to convince the boatman, Madylan leaned over so far that she almost fell in the water. She was quick enough to catch herself, though, and only dragged her hand, the one holding her uncle's medal, through the raging water before leaning back into the boat.

Suddenly, as Madylan removed her hand from the water, an eerie silence blanketed the boat and the river around them.

Looking up, Madylan saw that the waterfall had frozen, almost as ice, but was still flowing water that had simply stopped. All around the boat, the whirlpool had disappeared and a clear, mirror-like surface held the boat steady, almost as if the boat had been stuck in a frozen river.

Looking over at the grandmother for answers, Madylan saw that the old woman was leaning back, almost lying down, looking up at something behind Madylan, something moving as the grandmother's eyes followed the something as it approached the boat from behind Madylan.

Slowly turning, Madylan looked for whatever the grandmother was seeing, but only saw the bright greens and blues of the nearby hillsides.

Bright blues, a puzzled Madylan asked herself?

And wet. Very wet. Yet, there was no rain, so how could the hillside be sparkling green and blue and silver, from no rain, Madylan wondered?

Silver? Sparkling?

Suddenly, Madylan stopped trying to see the hillside and, instead, lifted her eyes and craned her neck to see what was at the top of the undulating, twisting hill of glimmering colors that seemed to be rising, not from the riverbank, but from the glassy water itself.

Tall. Very tall, Madylan realized as her eyes traveled up the rippling chest of the massive hill and finally spied the top, far above them.

A head?

A pointy head?

With large, what were those called, Madylan wondered? Her mind tried to understand the ridge of spiky leaves or thorns sticking out of the beast's head and back.

The beast?

"Who asks for passage, this dark and murky day, boatman?" a ferociously loud voice called from the head, its green and purple eyes staring down at the boat and its tiny occupants.

"A fair grandmother and her strange charge from distant lands, old one," the boatman called in a sing-song fashion, in words that seemed to float above his head, rather than come out of his mouth, Madylan realized.

"The little one carries your mark, old one," the boatman's words added to the floating message above his head.

Madylan, oddly unfrightened by the huge beast that had emerged from the water, was more concerned for the old grandmother, who seemed to be whispering enchantments and hiding her eyes from the beast. Resolving to protect the old woman who had protected her during the journey, Madylan raised her hands and waved at the beast to attract its attention.

"Hello? Over here! I carry the talisman, not the dear old grandmother, kind…uh…kind…?" Madylan called, but was then lost for a word to use to address the beast, for the only word that had come to mind seemed beyond fantastic.

Dragon!

The glistening beast then leaned far down, almost to the small mast of the boat and stared at the strange girl out of the side of one huge eye.

"Speak, young morsel, for I am tired and not happy to have been awakened before my time," the beast said, its words seeming to come from inside Madylan's head, rather than from the mouth of the beast.

"We travel…the kind grandmother and I, to the capital," Madylan replied.

"Why?" the beast asked.

"Why? Well…we're not exactly sure, old one," Madylan answered, using the title she had seen floating in the words above the boatman's head.

"You are a peculiar little one," the beast replied, switching sides of its head to look down at Madylan with its other eye. "And, your speech is all wrong. And your clothes, except for the coat of my devotees, are all wrong. Why do you wear my soldiers' colors, little strange one?"

"They made it for me, to protect me from the cold nights, old one," Madylan replied, her hand involuntarily gripping her uncle's medal.

"Few of us remain, little strange one, for those such as you to disturb our slumber. If you don't know why you are traveling to the capital, then why should we let you pass? Why should we not feed you to the young ones, like my kin the boatman, so they can grow stronger and, someday, earn their wings?" the beast asked, seeming far more rational than Madylan thought such a beast should be.

"The boatman?" the old grandmother repeated, finally finding her tongue.

"Guilty!" the boatman quipped and flashed a long, silvery tail from beneath his loose fitting clothes.

Madylan, thinking quickly, boldly faced the huge beast's massive eye and spoke.

"For the lost children, old one. And for the old blacksmith that labors in the woods. And for the woodsman! The man who fells the trees to save his brothers. And, yes, even for the boatman here and for you!" Madylan declared, suddenly standing in the slim boat, holding her uncle's medal up to the beast. "Just as my uncle and my father's fathers did one day, I must be here to help those people. The soldiers. The priest and the wild woman, the one who gave me this branch."

Madylan pulled the branch out of her pack and waved it at the beast, who leaned down for a sniff at the small stick.

"Yes, the shaman of the mountain bear, I know her well. She has sent me many a welcome dinner guest," the beast replied, then looked over at the grandmother.

"But, what is this old woman? Of the ancient ways, I can see, but is riddled with doubt and remorse? What of her?" the beast asked, the fading light glinting off the beast's enormous teeth.

"She guides me in your world, old one. In this...whatever this is," Madylan replied, trying to step around the dog to stand with the grandmother.

The dog complied, and Madylan rushed to the old woman's side.

For several long, deep breaths, the beast remained silent. Then, just as suddenly as it had risen out of the water, the beast began to sink back beneath the mirrored surface, its words again seeming to come from inside Madylan's head.

"You are too soon, little strange one. You were to be another. Your path will be cut short, ere you reach the king's seat. Too soon, little strange one, for you to march into the capital. A task you will do, or fail. But, return you must, to restore the balance, until another day. Another day, little strange one, when we can speak freely in your world. Do the task, or fail. Do not delay. On your way, little brother, carry these to where they need to go, but protect yourself, for so few of you remain. I go."

Suddenly, the beast was gone and the waterfall began to flow once more and the whirlpool, instead of being a churning, boat-destroying storm, was simply a small ripple on the surface of the flowing river.

Without further comment, the boatman set off, while Madylan and the old grandmother watched him with wariness, given that the beast had called him brother and that the tall, lanky boy sported a long, silvery tail that was gripping the railing as the boatman steered.

After the boat had rounded a wide bend in the river, not far from the waterfall, the boatman let out a long whistle, which caused his two companions, plus the dog, to look up at the mountain scene before them.

Almost as a wide picture painted on a broad canvas, the vastness of the scene took Madylan's breath away.

To their left, far in the distance, the troops that had helped them were stationed on a cramped ledge along a wide mountain road. To their far right, a mass of troops was snaking their way up the side of another far hill, seeming to be on the way to the mountain path protected by the small group of soldiers. Almost in the middle of the scene, a fight of some sort was happening far up on the mountain where two sharp peaks were close together.

"What's happening up there? At the two peaks?" Madylan asked, straining to see.

"Sadly, although it's far away, it appears the enemy is trying to gain control of the signal beacon. If they can, they can stop any messages from getting through to the capital, so the king will not know what direction the enemy is coming from and will have to divide his forces to protect all the ways, thereby weakening his forces," the boatman answered, his voice heavy.

"What of that small group protecting that narrow pass up on the side of the mountain?" Madylan then asked, her heart in her throat when she thought of the kind young leader and his men being caught in that narrow pass by thousands of troops crawling over the hills.

"They will hold, for a time, little strange one. For a time," the boatman replied. "But, with such a key signal beacon lost, no one will know to come to their aid, until all is lost."

"Wait! The guardian could swim...could fly up the mountain and clobber the enemy soldiers and save our friends!" Madylan suddenly declared. "Let's go back and ask him...please? Ask him?"

Madylan's plea seemed to stir an old, painful memory in the young boatman, who paused shifting the rudder to lean back and stare at the scene in the far mountains. Letting out a long sigh, which caused the dog to emit a low whimper of sympathy and then curl up at the boatman's feet, the young guardian-in-training answered the strange young girl in a voice that seemed to come from a much more ancient heart.

"Alas, dear little sister, the days when man could summon a guardian have long passed. Few are the old ones any longer. We know of only a handful, and few young ones like me," the boatman replied, his eyes seeming to glow like yellow embers. "No, we can only observe and serve, such as the two of you, on the fringes, little sister. The soldiers, whichever side is victorious, and the kings and their people, will soon forget us. We will then fade into the tapestries of shadowed history that are thought of as mere legends, little sister from the far lands."

Madylan, deeply saddened by the young boatman's almost poetic lament, was on the verge of tears when the old grandmother reached out and tapped her shoulder.

"He's telling you, dear one, to remember the guardian and the young ones, like him, when you return to...well, when you return, little princess," the grandmother said softly, helping Madylan to fight off the tears and turn back to address the boatman.

"I will never forget, good sir...boatman, sir. I will tell everyone of your kindnesses to me and to grandmother here," Madylan declared, her voice strong and focused. "I will tell everyone. I will tell your tale to my little brother, who will tell his friends. Your story...your lives will not die. Tell the guardian that he...and you...will live on far, far beyond this battle."

The boatman slowly nodded to the strange young girl, and then, with obviously heavy heart, slowed his small craft and turned it toward the shore.

"I'm sorry, grandmother, little sister, I can carry you no farther. Those enemy troops would take my master's boat if I were to go near them, so I must return to my village and wait for him. Until I have captured my own orb, I happily serve my kind master. I'm happy to take you back to the village with me," the boatman said as he guided the boat to a small outcrop. "Your fee, of course, I will return."

"No. We must go on. And, yes, you must protect your master's craft and the old one's home. Thank you, but the fee is yours, and, when you can, thank the guardian for us," the grandmother replied.

"Yes, kind boatman, thank you," Madylan added, rubbing the dog's ears. "Please do tell the...the guardian that I think I understand his words. I think I will return. I just don't know when. Tell him...please tell him I'll bring my little brother one day. My brother would just love to meet the…the guardian…and you."

The boatman smiled at Madylan's words and then nodded to a well-trod path, indicating the road the two should take. He also gave them a few provisions, mostly food, but also some cloth and twine to build a shelter if they found themselves far from a farm or village once night had settled in. The bundle was not heavy as the cloth was made from very light, but strong old sails.

After saying their goodbyes to the boatman, the grandmother and Madylan began the arduous trek through the rough landscape, following the marked cart path that pointed toward the capital as it wound its way along. As they walked, the grandmother explained what the boatman had meant by capturing an orb.

"Long ago, our people believed that the young dragons, in order to grow wings to take flight, or to swim in the seas, had to catch a falling star, or an orb, as part of their rites of passage, little sister," the grandmother explained. "While I don't quite know what to think of our talking guardian and the silver-tailed boatman, I also know not to rudely question something that I simply do not understand. I also think your telling the young boatman that you would bring your little brother to meet the guardian speaks volumes to such ancient…such traditional spirits, little sister. However, let's put them behind us, to consider another day, for we now must simply make it over these mountains."

Madylan nodded and realized she had seen similar themes in her own books and television shows, so concluded that many of those stories had their origins in much older beliefs. She filed those thoughts for later and tried to walk a little faster, since her older companion was outpacing her by several yards.

"The light is failing," the grandmother called back to the trailing Madylan, whose shorter legs were quite tired, even with the break they had had on the boat.

"Do we need to stop somewhere for the night?" Madylan called in return, but was answered by a different voice.

"Stopping? Not advisable before the crossroads of the battling tigers, young one," a high-pitched voice called from somewhere in front of the two.

Fearing yet another encounter with sinister strangers, the old woman waited for Madylan to catch up and then called out.

"Who calls from the shadows like a snake from a cave?" the

defiant old grandmother demanded. "Show yourself!"

Slowly, as if crawling along, the sounds of feet scraping on the rough path grew louder and louder until the two travelers were greeted by an old man sitting atop...what?

A tortoise. An immense tortoise.

"Kind grandmother, please do not be cross. We old folks must work together," the old man replied, yet was looking down at a sort of lap desk where he was writing as he talked, while the huge, brown and grey tortoise the man rode slowly crawled along, not even looking at Madylan and the grandmother.

"Royal scribe...," the grandmother began, but was cut off by the little man's raised hand.

"No longer, I'm afraid. Banished for writing a true history, I have been. To the south, to exile on the fair isle of Jeju, I am sent. Not by swift horse, or fast boat, but by the slowest means his highness's scheming uncle could send me and still tell the king that I was safely on my way to exile," the little man rambled, still scribbling on his papers on the small desk.

"What are you writing?" Madylan asked, causing the little man to pause and raise his head. "A diary? I keep a journal, but not every day."

"What's this? A little girl who is not afraid to speak to the court's...to an old scribe? And, a girl who can write? What manner of child are you, that you speak strange words and wear the coat of soldiers, little one?" the scribe asked, peering at Madylan from under his high hat.

"Just a child on her way to the capital, scribe, sir," Madylan answered, bowing slightly, distracted by the odd sight of the tortoise.

"Fine. Fine. The king's court can always use a few new hands, even as the war rages around us, the affairs of state must proceed," the little man replied, then flicked a discarded brush with worn hairs at the little girl.

"Here, take this old brush and practice your writing. Yes, I know of young girls who learn to write in secret, so not too surprised. Keep up your learning," the scribe mumbled as he studied something he had just written. "But, the bridge at the end of this road is down. The only way now is over the mountain."

The grandmother allowed herself a short sigh and then spoke.

"When did the bridge fall, sir?" the grandmother asked.

"Three nights, maybe four. My steed is not very fast, so I lose track of time," the scribe replied. "Our loyal men destroyed it, so the enemy must trek around the mountain of the hawks to the mountain of the turtles. Fortunately, my noble transport floats quite well, so we crossed without incident."

Madylan and the grandmother shared a shocked look, both understanding why the huge army they had seen was moving toward the narrow mountain pass where their helpful soldiers were encamped. Turning back to the scribbling scribe, Madylan then spoke.

"Sir, what is it you write so furiously?" Madylan asked as the lumbering tortoise with its busy passenger slowly passed her and the grandmother.

"Write? Why, I'm writing the definitive, final history of this war, little one," the scribe replied, his voice annoyed.

"How, sir? With war as yet undecided? How is it you can write the definitive history already?" Madylan replied, puzzled, but smiling at the tortoise's peaceful face.

"Why, little stranger child, history is always decided by those who write it, regardless of what actually happens," the scribe quipped and, waving absently, slowly disappeared down the trail, the scraping of the tortoise's feet eventually melding into the sounds of the trail, the forest, and the river.

"Which way?" Madylan finally asked after the sounds of the tortoise had faded away completely. "Or, do we rest somewhere since night is soon to fall?"

"On that subject, I think our scribe was correct. Best not to tempt fate by wandering around between armies. Better to keep going and find shelter on the other side of the mountain, away from the troops," the grandmother answered, checking the sky for how much longer they would have even a little light.

"Let's go back to the side trail. I'm sure that's the trail over the mountain, little sister," the grandmother continued. "Save your strength and let's travel in silence. Also, to ensure we are not discovered before we want to be."

So, after spending a few minutes backtracking, the two found the mountain road and began the long trek up and over one of the many mountains that surrounded the far capital. Fortunately, the mountain was not overly high, which caused Madylan to whisper hopes that her aching legs would have a short journey.

After about thirty minutes of hard climbing, with the sun touching the tops of the hills far to the west, the grandmother called for a brief rest and sat down upon a wide boulder, surprising two country cats who had been catching the last rays of sun nearby.

After the cats had sniffed the air of the two intruders and had determined that no treats were forthcoming, the two mountain residents sauntered off to less crowded boulders farther up the trail.

As Madylan watched the two cats wander off, she felt a twinge of homesickness for her own two cats, and her family, so she smiled when she saw the cats happily spread themselves out on another boulder quite a ways up the mountain. Watching the two, her eyes drifted up and to the right, where she saw movement between the far trees and rocks of the upper trail.

"Grandmother, what do you think that might...?" Madylan began, but the grandmother cut her short by grabbing her arm and dragging her off the boulder and into the cover of several pines beside the trail.

"Soldiers!" the grandmother whispered and put her hand to her mouth to show Madylan to be silent.

For a few minutes, the two huddled under the pines and watched as a group of soldiers, who were too far away to determine allegiance, trekked up the far trail toward the very top of the mountain's twin peaks. After some time, with the light beginning to cast long, thin shadows around the two travelers, the soldiers stopped at a clearing and seemed to be forming up into lines.

"They are the enemy, little sister. See that banner?" the grandmother whispered.

"What are they looking at? I don't see a fort or even the rest of the trail," Madylan asked.

"I'm not sure. There's no real bridge crossing there, or even a major trail. In fact, they left the main trail to get up that high. I don't know. The only way to get down is to come back the way they came, maybe from the eastern trail," the grandmother replied, her voice a little louder, once she realized the troops were too far away to hear her.

"Maybe they are going to spy on our friends from up there? With binoculars?" Madylan suggested.

"With what? Oh, wait! The beacon! The second peak, where we

can just see that tip. That's one of the beacons the kingdom uses to send messages…warnings of troop movements. They are…they are going to try to capture the beacon!" the grandmother cried, her despair thickening her voice and causing her to stumble to a low limb to lean against. "Lost! All is lost, for our protectors, the young lord and his troops, our king's fair city, our very land!"

The grandmother then seemed to sink into the darkness of the stand of trees, her breath coming heavily, alarming Madylan.

Looking back to the troops above, Madylan mentally calculated how long it would take her and the grandmother to go back down the mountain, find the correct trail in the dark and then race to the young leader and the small group of troops to warn them that the enemy was closer than they knew. Shaking her head, she accepted the blunt reality that she and the grandmother would never be able to get there before morning, even if they could find their way around the mountain trails in the dark. Jamming her hands into her coat, she kicked hard at a small pebble, which bounced off the boulder they had just been sitting on, causing a brief spark, visible in the failing light of early evening.

Startled by the tiny flash of orange from the spark, Madylan froze for a moment and then frantically dug into her small pouch and extracted the little wooden box, the fire starter, that the woodsman had given her.

"Grandmother. Do you know how to read the signals? From the beacons? And what that beacon up there is supposed to send on to the capital?" Madylan asked, her little jaw set steel-hard.

"The signals? Well, they change, to confuse the enemy, but any signal from that beacon would repeat what is seen from the farther beacon. It would warn the city, and our friends guarding the narrow Hawk's Pass that the enemy was on the way, and from what direction," the grandmother replied, straightening her shawl and regaining her usually calm composure.

"Then, let's go, grandmother. We can light the beacon!" Madylan declared as she gathered her small pouch and began to run up the trail.

"Little sister! Are you mad, girl?" the grandmother called, momentarily stunned at the little girl's burst of energy.

The grandmother then quickly gathered herself and her things and took off on a dignified trot in pursuit of the speedy little girl.

After about thirty minutes of running, Madylan slowed her pace and, finding a set of three boulders, looking the world like the three bears from Goldilocks, she crouched down behind the papa bear and peered at the trail ahead while she waited for the grandmother to catch up.

After only a minute or so, the grandmother, breathing heavily, joined Madylan and crouched down beside the child.

"Can you see the soldiers better now, grandmother?" Madylan whispered.

"Sadly, yes dear. Not our friends. And, the light will fade to darkness soon, so I am unsure as to what you and I can do before...wait! Look there!" the grandmother replied, her face shocked as she pointed with her outstretched hand.

Above them, the enemy troops had evidently already vanquished whatever small force had been guarding the beacon towers, because the enemy troops were chopping away at a narrow rope bridge that was the only way to access the beacon itself, just across a deep gorge between the two peaks. As the two watched, the little bridge's right side fell limp and the lines dangled in the air. Then the left side was attacked with the axes, and with a grunt of triumph, the troops stood back and watched as the little bridge twisted, fell, and crashed into the opposite side of the gorge with a loud thud.

"So close, yet so far," the grandmother lamented, watching the narrow rope bridge's wooden cross slats crash to the rocky gorge below, leaving only remnants of the ropes flapping in the wind on the opposite side. "All is lost."

Just after the little bridge had fallen, Madylan and the grandmother saw, far to the east, the double fires of another signal beacon burning brightly.

"The signal comes. But will not be answered," the grandmother sighed, finding a small rock to sit on, her face showing her exhaustion.

Madylan, still reeling from the sight of the bridge being destroyed, held back her own anger as she watched the troops turn and head back down the other side of the trail, eventually disappearing from view. She stood in silent shock, watching the shreds of rope slap against the opposite side of the gorge, the wind acting like a spoon stirring a pot of noodles. She also watched a large batch of last season's leaves, caught up by the bridge when it had fallen, dance and swirl all around the ropes, but, being lighter, the leaves spiraled up, landing along the ridge and a low stone wall just below the massive pile of fuel lying in one of several signal pyre stone columns.

The leaves seemed to mesmerize Madylan and, as she watched, she wished she had the freedom of the leaves. If she were as light as those leaves, she could easily float over to the pyre and, using the fire starter from the woodsman, light the pyre to signal the kingdom.

"Dear, we need to go back. The wind is too dangerous here for someone so small, so near the edge," the grandmother said and glumly turned away from the gorge to head down the darkened trail.

Sighing, Madylan nodded, taking one last look at the destroyed bridge, the flapping ropes, and the leaves as the setting sun flashed a few dying, yet brilliant rays across the wall and the signal pyres, where even more leaves were dancing in the wind, almost mocking the young girl in their playfulness.

"Playfulness?" Madylan suddenly mumbled, a distant, wild thought creeping into her disappointed mind.

"What's that, dear?" the grandmother asked, pausing at the beginning of the stone steps leading back down the trail.

"Playfulness, grandmother! That's the answer. Look at the leaves!" Madylan shouted and, dropping to the ground, emptied her pockets of all the gifts she had been given along the trail.

"Dear, I know you must be very disappointed, but now is not the time for play," the grandmother replied, reaching out to help the little girl pick up her things.

"Grandmother, what did the starving boy say? 'Dragon, fly to the flaming peak and save my village' were his words! And, the...the guardian said we would do a task...or fail. This must be that task!" Madylan declared, sorting the various objects. "We have the twine, we have the small fire starter, we have the long, narrow sticks in the arrows, we have the sail cloth, and, if you don't mind, we have the silk cloth in your shawl, Grandmother, if the cloth the boatman gave us is not enough."

Gathering up all her items, Madylan rushed up the final few yards to the small clearing by the destroyed bridge. There, she spread the items out across a cleared area and began sorting the items. Behind her, the grandmother, obviously worried that her strange companion had become rattled by all the events of the day, finally appeared and moved to embrace Madylan.

"Dear, we must depart the mountain before those troops return. We're exposed up here," the grandmother said quietly, leaning over the busy youth.

Puzzled by Madylan's frantic activity, the old grandmother stepped back and looked at the shape her little companion had laid out on the rock using the long arrows, which Madylan was quickly tying together to form a sort of stretched diamond. As the old grandmother watched, the girl finished tying a number of the arrows together, and then spread out the sailcloth underneath. Only when the frantically working child had placed the cloth under the narrower bottom of the frame she had just made, did the grandmother finally understand why the little girl was madly working.

"A kite...?" the grandmother asked, then looked over at the signal pyre. "Maybe...maybe. It just might work. I thought maybe you were going to try the jwibulnori, the fire game to rid the fields of rats at the Lunar New Year. But, I think the distance is too far to throw the swinging fireboxes. Yes, a kite just might work. There are two fires from the far beacons, so we'll have to light two fires as well."

"Oh, a tail! What to use? The cloth was just enough, so maybe...?" Madylan asked of the old grandmother.

Pulling off her silk shawl, which had been a family heirloom for countless decades, the old grandmother did not hesitate to hand it over to Madylan. Once the silk tail was tied in place, the old grandmother reached into the folds of her robes and brought out the last of the water and the rice flour.

"This should hold long enough, dear," the grandmother said as she mixed just a little water into the rice flour. "It dries very quickly, and will reinforce where you've laced the cloth to the cross pieces."

Carefully, very carefully, Madylan used the brush the scribe had given her to apply the sticky rice flour glue to the cloth's edges along the kite's frame.

As the grandmother watched, and then helped fasten the cloth edges, she suddenly had a horrible thought when she saw that Madylan had tied small loops to the center crosspiece of the kite.

"Little princess! You don't think you're going to fly on the kite over to that signal pyre, do you?" the grandmother cried, alarmed at the ominous turn of events.

"Grandmother, I don't think the kite will hold you," Madylan quipped as she finished applying the glue.

"No. I thought you wanted to fly a small tin of fire. I can't let you...," the grandmother began, but was silenced by a look from the determined little girl.

"We had no earthly idea why I was along for this trek through the woods, down the river, up the mountain, did we? Now we do," Madylan said in her matter-of-fact voice.

Controlling her own voice, which was shaky, the old grandmother replied, choosing her words very carefully.

"Dear, even if this works and the glue holds, the twine doesn't break, you don't drop the fire starter, and the wind takes you to the other side safely and doesn't bash you into a thousand pieces on the rocks...how, dear, do you...do you return?"

Pausing in her preparations, Madylan looked back over her shoulder at the looming signal towers, which suddenly looked miles away, even though they were only a few dozen feet. Turning back to the grandmother, the lady who had been her protector, her mentor, and her friend, the little girl reached out and took the old woman's warm hand and spoke, her voice seeming to come from far away.

"Grandmother, you have been such a wonderful friend over this odd journey. I am...as you well know, I am not of this place. Yet, I came from this place, through my grandparents, and their many generations of grandparents before them. Somewhere in that long line, there must have been a young girl who was needed for an important task. Maybe she was not able to do it. Maybe something happened before she could finish. Maybe a bridge broke on that long ago young girl. I must be here, in this dream or in this other world, to mend that break, to help that unknown girl from my grandparents' past. I think all I need to do is get to the other side and light the fire. Maybe I can use those ropes on the other side and tie them together to throw over to you and you can pull me back. Or, maybe I can climb down the ropes and meet you at the bottom. Maybe I will just wait until the soldiers come to rescue us as they did before. After all, they will see the lighted signal."

The grandmother then pulled Madylan up and gave the brave young girl a tremendous hug, finally acknowledging there was no other way to warn the thousands of souls in the city and the gallant troops who had befriended them.

With both of the companions fighting off tears, they resumed preparations.

Once the kite was ready, with hopes that the glue was dry enough, Madylan stooped down to test the arm loops. Standing, she quipped to the grandmother in an attempt to lighten the seriousness of the moment, especially since she had never been fond of heights.

"Well, Dad always bugged me to try parasailing on our trips to Turks and Caicos. Now I guess I'm going to have to try it," Madylan said in the cheeriest voice she could muster.

"How are you going to carry the fire starter, little one?" the grandmother asked, trying to keep her own voice upbeat. "If it gets hit or smashes on the rocks, it could ignite and burn up the sailcloth and silk in the kite in an instant."

"The bell, Grandmother. I'll turn the bell upside down. It's small and doesn't weigh much," Madylan replied as she carefully placed the fire starter box in the bell, then put them in her coat's front inner pocket and used some twine to tie the coat tightly around her.

"Wait. Take the fire stick. Just in case you have a problem with the fire starter. The embers are weak, but may work," the grandmother said, carefully hanging the small fire stick from Madylan's side.

"Once we pick up the kite, the wind is going to immediately catch it, so you will have to be quick on your feet," the grandmother warned as she wrapped the strong silk twine around her waist and then grabbed the old pine tree for support.

"Right. Grandmother, could you do one thing for me. In case I do get stuck over there?" Madylan asked, avoiding saying anything more dangerous that might happen.

"Anything, little princess."

Madylan then unpinned the little dragon medal from her sweater and, pressing it to her heart one last time, she handed it to the amazing woman who had become a third grandmother to her.

"Would you, when you can, return this to where you found me in the forest? I don't know why, but I think that's where it might go back to Uncle, who, I think, is either hundreds of years away napping, or taking a nap right now. I don't want his medal to fall into…to not get back to him," Madylan asked, her eyes holding back the tears she felt coming.

"Dear, I think your uncle would want you to carry it, for luck. He'd want you to take it with you."

"Yes, I thought that, too. But, I'd feel bad if something happened to it."

"Wait," the grandmother then said and picked up the flat stone that held the remaining paste of the rice flour.

Taking the medal from Madylan's outstretched hand, the grandmother pressed one side and then the other into the rice flour paste, and then handed the medal back to the little girl.

"There. I will have the blacksmith craft another medal, if needed, and return it to the forest by the rocks that look like a chair," the grandmother declared.

Smiling, Madylan pinned the medal back to the inside of her collar, knowing it would be safest there, and then squatted down to slip her arms into the loops on the kite.

Slowly, with the evening winds pushing her around, Madylan managed to stay on her feet as she walked to the cliff's edge and forced herself to look only up and not down. Smiling back at the kindly grandmother gripping the old pine tree while she held the twine around her waist, Madylan nodded and called back.

"Thank you, Grandmother, for showing me the old days and old ways. My grandparents and my uncle tell me that many things have remained over the years, and I hope I can return one day. Take care!"

With that, the brave little girl from Manhattan, by way of an improbable dream, while visiting her favorite auntie and uncle in Virginia, leapt off that tall, Korean mountain somewhere east of Hanyang, old Seoul, and, with her hastily made kite suddenly catching the wind, was jerked skyward so quickly she had her breath knocked out of her. Yet, she recovered in the blink of an eye and focused on bending her body ever so slightly to better catch the wind and to try to guide the shaky kite to the walls of the signal towers.

Back at the tree, the old grandmother was slowly letting the twine feed out, to keep the kite line taut and as straight as she could, letting the little pilot guide the fragile sky ship.

Suddenly, over the sound of the wind rushing through the gorge, the grandmother heard the voices of the troops that the two had avoided earlier. The voices were so loud and increasing in volume that the grandmother realized that the troops were returning.

Letting the twine out a little faster, the grandmother hunched down so that the troops would not see her. She didn't think they would see the kite, because it was almost at the other side, although it dipped down once or twice.

Madylan, getting closer and closer to the other side, held the loops as steadily as she could. Looking straight ahead and telling herself over and over to not look down, she tilted her body to move the kite toward the towers.

Each time she felt she could reach out and grab the wall, the kite caught another gust of wind and pulled Madylan's hand back. She felt the grandmother loosen and then tighten the twine, so that the kite didn't just fall out of the sky, but it also made it nearly impossible for Madylan to use her hands to grab the wall.

After several attempts, Madylan suddenly realized, with a sinking feeling in her stomach, that she'd have to take one of her arms out of the kite loops if she had any hope of grabbing the wall. Unfortunately, she well knew that, as soon as she took her arm out, the kite would flip and maybe even rip apart, so she only had one chance.

As she was pushed by the wind a little farther away from the ridge and the wall, Madylan twisted her body just enough to force the kite back to the wall for her one try at grabbing it.

"Here goes!" Madylan yelled at the top of her lungs, to build up courage to spur her to quickly to pull her arm free of the kite.

Bam!

Into the wall Madylan crashed, but she was just able to grab the top of the wall with her now free hand. Holding the bell steady against her body, she dragged herself over the wall, with the remnants of the kite flapping wildly in the wind.

On the other side of the gorge, the grandmother was holding onto the twine, so that she could maybe use it again by having Madylan tie the twine to the broken bridge ropes and then the grandmother could pull Madylan back over.

Yet, fate had other plans, as the enemy troops suddenly appeared at the top of the trail. They had not yet seen the little girl on the other side, since the soldiers were so focused on the old woman, whom they were obviously shocked to see.

Madylan had seen the tops of the enemy troops' heads just as she had dropped to the far side, so she reached back over and jerked the kite over the wall as well, so that the troops would not see it and start firing arrows in her direction. She kept her head low and said a little prayer for the grandmother.

Afraid the troops would figure out why she was holding the twine, the grandmother quickly tied it off at the base of the tree and then turned to face the enemy, using her height and her billowing robes to block their view of the little girl struggling to cross the wall.

Letting out a silent sigh of relief when she saw the twine go limp, and, glancing to the side, she saw that Madylan had made it over the wall and had removed the remnants of the kite, the grandmother then made a slight bow to the troops and spoke defiantly.

"Little bugs of the bloody silver, why do you disturb my evening stroll!" the grandmother demanded, using the old, highest level tongue, while waving her walking stick to give her more height.

Pushing past the troops, the grandmother started down the trail, hoping to lure the troops to follow her. It worked.

The enemy troops, initially frightened by the tall, dark apparition of the old woman, turned and, arguing amongst themselves as to what to do with an old woman who was so rude, followed her down.

Peeking over the wall, Madylan had watched the grandmother's convincing performance, so let out a little sigh of relief that her companion was safe.

At the bottom of the short section of trail, the troops, still unsure as to what to make of a crazy old woman, but fearing that she might, just might be a witch, decided to send her on her way with a warning. They did and the old woman faded away down the steep trail, while the troops continued on their journey back to the enemy lines by the main trail.

Far back up the mountain, on the other side of the deep gorge, little Madylan was shivering from the cold of the wind and the mind-blowing ride on the kite across the chasm. She had seen the grandmother lead the troops away and had even blown a kiss to the old woman just before she had started down the steps, which she hoped the grandmother had seen.

Sitting lower against the wall, Madylan was better protected from the wind, so she gently took the fire starter out of the protective bell and, carefully, set the bell upright.

Smiling, Madylan then took a bit of twine and tied the bell to a small, twisted pine growing beside the wall. She then took her little spoon and tapped the bell several times, playing the tune she had tapped on her uncle's medal in the big playroom. The sound of the bell, which was crisp and clear, was amplified by its hanging over the gorge, so it sounded like a much grander temple bell sending prayers skywards.

Down on the trail, the old grandmother smiled from the hiding place she had ducked into to wait for the troops to be far away before she could rush back up the mountain to help the brave little girl back across the gorge somehow. The little sister, her little princess, was okay, the grandmother realized when hearing the bell, and, for a moment, she allowed herself to take a calmer breath.

The troops, for their part, once they heard the spooky sounds of a bell where they knew there was no bell, were convinced that the old woman was a witch and hurried so quickly down the trail that they stumbled over one another trying to be the first down the mountain.

After waiting for what she felt was enough time for the troops to be far away and the grandmother to be somewhere safe, Madylan crawled up to the first signal pyre, trying to stay low to avoid the wind and to protect the fire starter. The bell, probably due to the high winds, Madylan thought, continued to sound every few seconds, its amplified voice echoing like a tiger in the mountain's gorge.

At the first signal pyre, Madylan took a bit of the dry hay stuffed under the huge logs stacked far higher than she was tall and, using the fire starter, carefully, very carefully, set the hay alight, its warm glow bringing a smile to the little girl.

Once the clump of hay was burning, Madylan grabbed another and, lighting the second clump from the first, she jammed the second burning clump back under the logs of the pyre and the hay burst into flames. She did the same thing in five spots around the entire first signal pyre, which began to burn brighter and brighter and hotter and hotter.

Crawling over to the second tower, Madylan was startled to see that the stacks of wood were soaking wet. No doubt the enemy troops had watered down the wood in case someone managed to get by them to the beacons. Distraught, she then crawled to another tower. It, too, had been drenched with water. Somehow, probably laziness had played a role, the first pyre she had managed to light had not been doused with water.

Looking around, Madylan searched for anything else that might burn that she could throw onto the slightly drier top of one of the wet piles, so that two beacons would shine down to the city.

Nothing. Not even dead tree limbs, since those had already been used to build the pyres.

Frustrated, Madylan struck her fist on the stone and called out.

"Why? All this way? All these crazy things and, because of a little water, we have failed? Why?" Madylan called into the night.

For a moment, the little girl from New York felt on the brink of utter defeat, but, true to her character and that of her ancestors, she refused to give up.

Then, in a flash, an idea came to her.

The kite!

Throwing caution to the wind, Madylan stood, making herself visible to anyone looking up to the mountain. She then ran back to the wall and, grabbing the kite and pulling it loose from the twine, she rushed back to the tower. She scrambled up the least wet pile and jammed the kite into the top. Seeing that the kite was such meager fuel for the massive pyre, she then pulled off the heavy coat the soldiers had given her and, with a moment of hesitation to lock the design in her mind, she added it to the top of the pyre. She then took out the dry branch the shaman had given her and, clutching her uncle's dragon medal, mumbled to herself as she used the fire starter to light the stick.

"Old shaman woman, if you really do have any powers, now would be a good time to show them off!" Madylan then yelled as she thrust the flaming branch at the kite.

Whoosh!

A massive fireball flew up from the crumpled kite and wadded up coat, causing Madylan to stagger back, almost dropping the fire starter. She then realized the little stick was shooting out a long flame, so she threw it into the growing fire, where the stick seemed to grow into a massive log, causing her to rub her eyes in disbelief.

The flame from the shaman's stick then flared up, showing Madylan many of the scenes that had flashed through her head when the shaman had given the little outsider the small branch. Blurry and quickly fading, Madylan felt she was watching a parade of history on fast forward.

As the flames from the kite, the coat, and the shaman's stick were starting to die down, several of the pyre's logs began to smolder. Then, just as the arrows framing the kite were burning out, the large logs caught fire and even taller flames jumped up and out, eliminating the visions from the shaman's stick.

Suddenly, Madylan realized she needed to back away from the signal pyres before they were fully burning, so she retreated down the ridge, following the wall to a small, crude stone hut that offered protection from the fire and its heat.

Sitting in the hut, Madylan could just see the lights of the far city. A dark mountain rose up among the lights, which seemed to be near the center of the city. She tried to recall what her uncle had called the central peak in Seoul. South Mountain? No. Korean. Namsan? Yes, she realized, as she watched the darkened peak.

Suddenly, a faint light appeared at the top of the darkened mountain. Then, as the seconds crept by, the light became brighter and brighter and several more fires sprang up in a line.

"They've seen the signal!" Madylan yelled at the top of her lungs, waving her arms in triumph and pressing the small medal to her lips in thanks as she watched other signals spring up all around the city.

Yet, even in her triumph, Madylan was worried, because the heat from the signal beacon towers was becoming nearly unbearable. So she tucked the medal back into her sweater and crawled out of the hut. She then found a spot on the small ledge near the ruined bridge, as far from the fires that she could get without going over the edge of the cliff.

It was by that ruined bridge that Madylan realized the soldiers who would have ignited the signal fire were never meant to remain on the peak, but would have dashed across the bridge to escape the searing heat and repressive smoke of the fire.

Luckily, the wind was blowing away from Madylan toward the fire, so she was safe from having to breathe in all the smoke. But, the heat was beginning to frighten her.

At that moment, the grandmother reappeared at the top of the path. She dashed to her side of the ruined bridge when she saw Madylan crouched on the small ledge, the orange glow on the nearby heated stones telling the grandmother that the fire would soon be too much for the little girl.

Taking up a water pouch, left behind by the soldiers, the old grandmother tied a length of the twine to it and, swinging the pouch in a great circle, she released the twine and the pouch flew across the gorge to land just behind Madylan.

"Pour the water over you. On your clothes, your hair! Quickly!" the grandmother yelled.

As Madylan poured the water over herself, the grandmother reached down and pulled up the two longest lengths of rope dangling from her side of the bridge. She pulled at them and they remained strong, so she then tied the kite string to the ropes and again yelled at Madylan.

"Dear child, pull these ropes over to you and tie them to the ropes that hang there! Grab the kite and pull the twine! Pull the twine!" the grandmother called, not realizing that the kite had been sacrificed to light the second fire.

Madylan nodded and, found that the kite twine had, by some miracle, become tangled in the small pine where she had tied the little bell. She pulled at the twine and the ropes inched their way across the gorge. Once the ropes were on her side, she then pulled up two ropes from her side and using all her strength, tied the ends together with several knots. She then let go and the two ropes formed a rough bridge of sorts, one she should be able to crawl over, just like climbing bars at the Ancient Playground near the Met at home, she told herself.

Madylan waved at the old grandmother, who was beginning to look faded, so Madylan rubbed her eyes, wondering if the smoke was getting to her. The grandmother waved back, but became alarmed when she saw the little girl's clothes and hair begin to steam from the immense heat.

"Hurry little princess! Hurry! There is little time!" the grandmother yelled, then grabbed the ropes to steady them.

Slowly, with her gaze fixed on the grandmother and not on the long drop to the bottom of the gorge, Madylan shoved the fire starter into her pocket and, glancing at the little bell, she gave it a whispered good-bye and began to crawl over the thick ropes, making good progress. About halfway across, embers from the signal fires suddenly blew toward her and the ruined bridge, where a few alighted on the ropes. She was able to kick several off, watching the glowing spots disappear into the gorge. However, several managed to lodge into the rope behind her and the ropes began to slowly burn.

Hurrying, Madylan scooted across the gorge and, as the fire on the ropes began licking at her legs, the old grandmother leaned out and, with strength she had not known for years, scooped up the child and pulled her to safety, just as the fire severed the ropes and both ends fell to the sides of the cliff with a terrific slapping sound.

As the two stood beside one another, the old grandmother smiling down on the young warrior princess from far away, Madylan's eyes were becoming even foggier, more watery, to the point that she was having trouble seeing the old woman.

"Thank you, little princess. You have saved us. You have saved your grandparents. You have saved those starving children who will sing songs of your deeds one day. You have rescued our young leader and his soldiers. Aided the woodsman and his noble brothers. So much more! Thank you…!" the grandmother called, as if from farther and farther away.

The distant words of the old grandmother were mixing with the high winds, making the old woman's thanks hard to hear for Madylan, who leaned into the wind and reached out for the old grandmother to both give her a hug and to thank her companion for saving her from the very fire that had saved the kingdom.

"The woodsman's gift worked!" Madylan called against the winds, placing the small fire starter in her companion's shifting hands. "I had to burn the kite and the soldier's jacket, but it worked! Look to the next signal mountain, below, grandmother! Look!"

Madylan felt her voice growing hoarse trying to shout over the winds and through the thick smoke, so paused to listen to her companion.

"Yes, dearest young warrior, we all thank you and owe you," the fading grandmother called from somewhere that seemed far away to the squinting Madylan.

"No, sweet grandmother, thank you for saving me!" Madylan called into the shadows, trying to see the shape of the grandmother, but everything was getting darker, while a thin, grey film had descended, covering Madylan's eyes like an old blanket.

"Recall dear, the words of the guardian. Safe journeys, little princess," the old grandmother, a mere shadow at that point, called from a great distance to Madylan, who felt herself slipping.

Slipping?

"The fire? Did you see? On the far mountain at the center of the city?" Madylan called, pushing at the grey film covering her eyes and wondering why the sound of the little bell had faded into a sound of tapping.

"What's that, dear?" Madylan's uncle asked, looking over at his goddaughter, whom he had thought had been asleep. "A fire? I think we can have one in the living room fireplace. It is a little cold."

"Uncle?" Madylan called from the ruined bridge, trying to see her uncle through the smoke. "I can't...see. Can't see. The smoke, it's too thick."

Suddenly, the smoke peeled back from Madylan's eyes, the tapping faded away, and there stood her uncle, holding Auntie's grey shawl.

"I think the shawl fell over your face while you were snoozing," the uncle replied, his voice softer than usual, since Madylan was obviously very sleepy from the journey from New York. "Are you okay? You look a little...?"

"Strange?" Madylan asked, cautiously looking around to ensure she was actually in her uncle's house.

Wriggling out of the cushy chair, Madylan stepped over to the screen she could have sworn she had fallen into hours and hours before.

"Sorry that my story wasn't all that exciting and that it put you to sleep," the uncle said, watching his grandniece examine the old screen of his ninety-plus-year-old mother-in-law.

"No, no, Uncle. Your story did not put me to sleep. I think this screen did," Madylan cryptically replied. "Where...where did you say it came from?"

"That's your auntie's mother's screen. I'm told it's quite old. Came with her from Korea long ago. Right after the war. Tells some story from history, she said, after a famous artist, Jeong, maybe? Why do you think it put you to sleep?" the uncle asked, but Madylan barely heard the question because of what she saw in the screen.

In the far right bottom corner of the old, old screen, the tiny figure of a blacksmith was holding up a small, disc shaped object, showing it to a tall, older woman, who was smiling. Leaning down to squint at the blacksmith, the old woman, and the object, Madylan suddenly let out a little gasp.

"What...?" Madylan said more to herself than her to uncle. "How did your medal get in there?"

Staring back at Madylan, from across the ages, was the miniature, but distinct face of the dragon on her uncle's medal, crafted by the mighty hammer of the old blacksmith, using the rice flour cast the old woman had made when a visiting young stranger had tried to give the dragon medal to the kind grandmother.

Farther along the screen, Madylan saw a troupe of cheerful child singers at what looked like a palace setting, with food overflowing. A narrow river flowed beside the palace and a thin young boatman was ferrying a tall, stately soldier and several other soldiers to a distant shore where tall trees soared to the skies. Other scenes stretched on, far wider in scope than the paneled screen had panels.

Stunned, Madylan stood quietly for a moment, with her uncle standing next to her wondering why his little niece was suddenly so interested in the old screen. She reached up to her collar and pulled out the little dragon medal and, holding it, reached out with her other hand and touched the living screen of her long ago ancestors. Flashes of her dream flew through her mind before she withdrew her hand.

"Dear, what's that hanging from your side? A whistle of some sort?" the uncle asked, puzzled that he had not noticed the toy earlier.

Madylan reached down and her hand found the grandmother's fire stick, stone cold and nearly ashen grey from years of neglect. Pulling her hand back, her eyes widened as she then reached in her pocket and froze when she felt the small spoon that she had used just minutes ago in her dream to ring the small bell. At the bottom of her pocket, she felt the cold, smooth roundness of the old river pebbles.

With the small hairs on the back of her neck standing up, Madylan slowly withdrew her hand from her pocket and, giving her uncle an astonished eye shrug, she turned, slowly, very slowly, back to the ornate screen.

Madylan leaned to the side to look up at the entirety of the ancient, elaborate screen, with its many images that she had never really noticed before, but felt she knew intimately now. After a minute or two, she took a long breath, reached out again and touched the image of a tall mountain with a waiting signal pyre, with a slim dragon flying off, far above the peak. A lone painter, at his easel, watched the scene from the far corner.

At that moment, Madylan's little brother burst into the room, his eyes droopy with sleep, to say goodnight, while the father called from the bedroom. Before the small child could speak, she ran over to him, threw her arms around him, and gave him the longest hug she had ever given anyone, including her bestie best friend.

"Goodnight, brave bug stalker. I'm so glad you are my little brother!" Madylan cooed, wiping a small tear from the corner of her eye.

The little brother was very tired, but not so tired that he didn't puff out his chest at the rare compliment. Earlier in the evening, he had been the great bug stalker and whacker, showing no fear and 'protecting' his big sister and his aunt from some overly friendly stinkbugs. Smiling, he then mumbled his goodnights and wandered back down the hall to the bedroom.

After composing herself, Madylan turned back to the screen and bowed her head once, ever so slightly, to the old woman and all the other characters arrayed before her. She then stepped away and turned to face the puzzled look of her uncle.

Taking a deep breath, the little lady from Manhattan, who knew in her heart of hearts that she had briefly, just briefly, stepped into her own family's history, quietly informed her uncle that they would switch roles, and that she would be the one who related a tale.

"Uncle Charles, once upon a time...? No, wait! Now! Now, upon a time...!" Madylan began, running her dream...her...whatever it was, through her head. "Your niece has a story to tell you, for a change. This may take a while. Let's sit."

With the ancient screen watching over her, young Madylan found her chair and, sitting upright, nodded to her uncle as he leaned forward from his own chair, with keen interest in his searching eyes to hear her tale. She took a long, even deeper breath, collected her thoughts, and, slowly, with care to recall the details as they had happened, began her fantastic tale of faraway adventure in old Korea, where she hoped she would walk those mysterious paths again one day, soon.

EPILOGUE

A calm, quiet blanket of warm thoughts, from the day's adventures, the amazing meal the mother had prepared, and the wide range of stories, slowly enveloped the comfy apartment nestled on the tree-lined street just off Park Avenue, causing Madylan's eyes to valiantly try to fight off the coming sleep. Hair wet from her nightly shower she had taken between the Easter and the Dragon Medal tales, her head bobbled in the final minutes of her uncle's final story. She suddenly snapped her head up and looked around as if surprised to find herself in the living room, tucked into the middle of the couch with her uncle on one side and her sleeping aunt on the other. Her aunt, who had worn herself out taking her favorite niece and goddaughter around New York during the day, looked gracefully peaceful to the young girl, who smiled, then spoke quietly to her uncle.

"Maybe one more?" Madylan yawned, trying, as she always did, to prolong her special day with her aunt and uncle.

"Dear, I think your uncle is tired. And, they have a long drive tomorrow," Madylan's mother called from the study.

"Do you have anymore, for next time?" Madylan then asked her uncle, hoping to drag out her departure to sleep.

"More? I should think so," the uncle replied, with his kind eyes signaling that the young girl should listen to her mother. "Not tonight, of course."

"You know, some of your stories are when I was little. Do you miss the younger me, Uncle?" Madylan asked through sleepy yawns.

"Miss those days of bench talks and doughnut hunting? Of

course, I do. Miss your making me a colorful toupee out of Play-Doh? Miss the long chats during our walks at dinner when you were too small to sit still while it took forever for the grownups to finish? Of course. But, the 'now' you and the 'future' you are just as interesting, just as inspiring to us, to your parents, your friends and relatives, and to your little brother," the uncle replied, giving his niece a wide smile.

"Why do you tell stories?" Madylan then asked, climbing down from the couch to check on her small window garden, mostly of herbs she had brought back from her trips to Virginia.

"Why? I suppose it's in my blood, dear," the uncle replied, his eyes taking on a faraway look. "My father was a storyteller. He was a newspaperman, but also wrote articles, poetry. Even up until he passed away, he could recite poetry from his grade school days. Amazing memory. My older brother, who you know died far too young, John Henry was his name, he could whip up outlandish tales with little preparation. He was a keen debater in school. Even went to Washington for a national debate, his last year in high school. My younger brother tells stories through his music and song. He's the one who cooks those amazing chicken wings Alex talks about still. My sister is an accomplished poet, with a string of books, articles, poems...the works. So, yes, it's in the blood. I've always written stories. I've always told stories. I'm really good with ghost stories, but you and your brother are still too young for those, so we'll wait a few years."

"You tell them because you want us to remember the old days?' Madylan asked as she absently scratched the neck of her youngest cat that had hopped up on the window shelf.

"Yes, the stories help me capture memories, of a place, of friends, of family, of special events. Sometimes the stories have lessons in them and sometimes they are just silly tales to make someone laugh. The pandemic has taught us all to laugh more and to cherish the good memories, and face, with a level head, the bad," the uncle offered, then held up his phone and waved it at his niece.

"I know it's hard for you, your little brother, and your friends to believe, but these phones were not everywhere when I was young. In fact, even your cousin Alex didn't have one until he was eleven. And that was because of 9/11. No, we used to have to tell stories, especially on long drives, to be entertained. My older son, Ian, the one who grew up with his mother in New England, used to have to listen to me make up all manner of tales. From his home up there, down to D.C. was nine hours. Then, another eight hours to drive to my parents in South Carolina. Later, Alex and I would travel south and I'd dream up stories based on the names of villages, or rivers, or even interesting stores as we drove those long hours. Eventually, Gameboys took away a lot of that story time. But, later, Alex's cousins, Zachary and Jeremy, they were kind enough to let me tell them wild tales when we'd get stuck on the parking lots that Los Angeles seems to think are highways. As I told you earlier, I used to do a little kid's parody called 'Clueless Blue' that made Jeremy laugh for hours. That was a long time ago."

Madylan nodded and then returned to the couch to check on her aunt.

"She's still out," Madylan whispered, a content, wide smile on her tired face.

"Nooooooo!"

Madylan's sleepy reflection on the day was abruptly shattered by the sudden arrival of her little brother, who was whining that he did not want to go to sleep. He then claimed he would, but only if Auntie put him to bed because he 'loved Auntie.'

Rolling her eyes at her little brother's fast developing ability to poke the right buttons to get adults to do his bidding, Madylan wondered if she were teaching him too well, too soon. Fortunately, her uncle always had an answer to momentary crises and, winking at Madylan, called her whimpering little brother over to him.

"Greyson, come here, let me show you something," the uncle said to Madylan's little brother who, already in his pj's, had a hopeful look that his uncle would help him escape going to bed.

Pouting, the child climbed onto the couch with his uncle, and then let his sleepy eyes follow his uncle's pointing arm to look out the window and up at the sky at an elusive few stars just visible through the trees.

"Just up there, in the sky, you see those lights?"

"Stars, because the street lights are down there," the practically minded four-year-old replied.

"Yes. And, you know what? When you and your sister look up at those little lights, guess who else is looking at them at the same time?"

"Dad and Mommy?"

"Well, yes. But, also your auntie and me. Your grandparents. Your cousins. Your friends and your teachers. But, yes, especially Auntie and me. Every time we look up at those stars, and the moon when it's out, we think about how you two are looking at the same moon and stars, and that makes us happy knowing you are warm and safe. That's the same thing I told my sons, years ago when they were your age and I had to be away."

The little brother sat very quietly for a moment, his big sister gazing over with both love and a little trepidation that he might start bawling again. Yet, the boy unexpectedly leaned over, gave his uncle a short hug, hopped down, and hugged his sleepy aunt who stirred awake and gave the child a warm hug. He then ran over to his dad, who picked him up.

"Say good night, Greyson," the dad coaxed.

"Goodnight!" the little brother chirped, then leaned into his father's chest as they walked back to the bedroom.

"I remember you used to say that to us when we had to leave Virginia," Madylan commented, very quietly so as to not raise the renewed ire of her little brother. "It used to make me happy-sad."

"And now?" the uncle asked.

"Happy. With just a tad of sad," Madylan replied, with a wink to her sleepy aunt and a nod to her uncle.

For the next few minutes, everyone remaining in the room, Madylan, her aunt, and her uncle, kept very quiet, not wanting to disturb the little brother's trip to sleepy land.

Madylan then stepped over to the side and ran her slim fingers over the silent keys of her piano keyboard, smiling at the duet she and her aunt had played after dinner. The aunt, suddenly awake, watched her darling niece at the piano, but quickly lost her battle with sleep, again, and let her eyes close, just for a moment. The uncle, after checking the weather on his phone, had excused himself to the bathroom, but had, instead, made stealthy stops in both his niece and nephew's bedrooms.

In the nephew's room, empty as the boy was falling asleep in his parent's room, the uncle tucked a small Hot Wheels car into a nook on a shelf, not wanting to put something with corners under the young boy's pillow. In the niece's room, as he had done since she was a baby, he slipped a couple of small items into different hiding places.

On a shelf in her closet, he placed a packet of Pokémon cards, her current craze, and then hid a squishy, Siamese cat plush animal under her pillow.

Pausing, the uncle smiled at memories of the 'old days' when the much younger Madylan had marveled at finding Shopkins or Hello Kitty or small, backpack dangler plush toys under her pillow after visits from her aunt and uncle. One day, when the girl had been the same age as her little brother, her mom had texted the aunt and uncle the next day after one of the visits when only the uncle had stopped by for a few hours. The texts had been priceless.

"Mom, I think I have a magic pillow.

Why dear?

Things just appear there. Like magic.

Really?

Yes, every time Aunt Elena and Uncle Charles visit. Even, when he visited alone, you know. Things appear there after Uncle visits.

Oh?

You know, mom. I think Uncle Charles brings the magic."

Chuckling to himself at his then wee niece's keen observation skills, and for her putting up with his continuing to do the 'magic' even long after the bright girl had figured it out, the uncle quietly backed out of her room and returned to the living room, giving the mom a nod and a grin at her playfully suspicious look.

Back in the living room, the uncle returned to the spot where he had been telling stories to the little ones and nodded at Madylan's silencing finger, which was pointed at her Auntie. She then grabbed a sweater, one that her aunt had taken off earlier, and then lovingly draped it over her aunt without disturbing her.

Listening for the telltale signs of little brother prowling about, Madylan was relieved to hear only the light tapping of her mother's hands across the laptop's keyboard in the study. Blissfully asleep, Madylan concluded, given that her dad had also disappeared, exhausted as well, to carry her little brother off to the sandman.

Turning back to her uncle, Madylan saw that he, too, seemed tired, and, somehow, older than the silly fellow who had let her craft new hair for him out of multi-colored Play-Doh only a few hours earlier. Taking a long breath, the young child spoke up in a soft voice to her uncle.

"I think Auntie is tired from doing so much today. Maybe we

should only do a half Madylan Day next time?" Madylan asked, almost rhetorically, as she patted her aunt's arm.

"Oh, she's not tired, dear. She is wonderfully happy. That's a happy face, not a tired face. I think she's just resting up so she'll be even more energetic for the trip home tomorrow," the uncle replied.

"Are you sure you can't stay another day?" Madylan asked, her voice drifting away, her own sandman trying to draw the little one to sleep.

The uncle looked down at the child, thinking for a moment before answering.

"Well, you know it's a long drive back to our house, but we'll be back. And, soon, now that the epidemic is manageable, dear. Besides, we have to bring up the...the boxes for...well, for the good kids, that is," the uncle replied, looking away from his niece when he saw her realize he was talking about Christmas gifts. "And you know you can come down anytime. With the family or even by yourself one day."

"By myself?" Madylan yawned, covering her mouth with the back of her right hand, as not even the thought of the never-ending stream of gifts from her overindulgent aunt and uncle could scare off sleep.

"Of course. We'll call it Camp Virginia...no, better, Camp Mitchell," the uncle declared.

"By myself?" Madylan repeated, not sure she had heard correctly through her sleep clogged ears.

"Sure. We'll buy you a ticket. Your parents drop you off and hand you over to the flight attendants. They keep an eye on you. Then they hand you over to us in Washington," the uncle quipped, his eyes smiling at a comic angle.

"By myself? What if I end up in Europe, or somewhere I don't speak the language?" the tired niece quipped back, putting on what she hoped was a confused face.

"Now who is being silly, silly? Of course we'll come collect you," the uncle answered, poking his sleepy niece in the side for effect. "We would never let you travel alone. Well, at least not until you are in your teens, right?"

Madylan slowly nodded, a new light growing in the back of her eyes at the prospect of spending a week at her aunt and uncle's house in far, garden-like Virginia.

"Uncle, do you really have more stories?" Madylan then asked, flipping her little plush toy acquired during her day out with her aunt and uncle.

"Well, there's always the never-ending tale of the wandering Madylan hat," the uncle replied, referring to the well-worn school ball-cap his niece had given him years before.

"Mom is so glad you are wearing the new one this visit. But, I like the original one you sent pictures of from Italy and Maine and Florida and other places," Madylan whispered.

"And, there's the tale of the turtle king of Central Park, the story of the fairies of Lower Manhattan, the haunted café we used to go to when you were little, and, well, many more," the uncle continued.

"Where do you get the ideas?" Madylan asked, stifling a yawn.

"Everywhere. For instance, you know that little glass tiger we brought back for you from our last trip to Murano, in Venice? The one that the glassblower artist had to fix his foot? Well, her shop was hit hard by the storms that flooded the Venice lagoon. She was so proud of her shop, because it's hard for a woman to open a shop there. Well, we could dream up a tale of how the glass animals she makes come to life and help her repair her shop. Like the shoemaker and the elves," the uncle replied.

"The shoemaker and the elves? Oh, yes. I know that one," Madylan answered.

"You can do the same. Like you do when you are making up adventures during your Madylan days with Auntie and me. That's where most of the 'not very' evil princess story came from. You could have easily written that yourself," the uncle said, shifting his position on the couch. "School comes first, of course, but think about something you'd like to make into a story next time we visit and we'll write it together. We could even write a younger story for Greyson and you could read it to him, until he can read for himself."

Smiling at the idea of creating a story with her uncle, Madylan slowly nodded. She then leaned back on the cushions and waited for the inevitable visit from her mother, now that the quiet sound of keys tapping had subsided.

Sure enough, not a minute after the conversation had died down, Madylan's mother poked her head around the French doors.

"Honey, say goodnight. They have to get back to the hotel and pack for the drive back tomorrow, sweetie."

Looking at the young girl suddenly fighting back involuntary tears pushing at the corners of her tired eyes, the uncle leaned over and spoke quietly.

"Tell you what. We'll come by in the morning and walk you to school, if that's okay with Mom?"

"Certainly, she'd love that. So, say goodnight and let's get you to sleep."

Gently rocking her aunt awake, Madylan gave her a long hug, and then turned and gave her uncle a warm hug, but a bit shorter than with her aunt.

"Good night, sweetie, I hope you enjoyed the day," the aunt mumbled through sleepy eyes.

"Magical, Auntie. Just magical," Madylan responded as she padded, backwards, to her room down the corridor, but then paused to watch as her aunt and uncle prepared to depart. "Simply, magical, Uncle. I can't wait to tell all my friends at school tomorrow."

As the aunt and uncle collected their things, the two of them straightened up the toy-strewn living room, noting that most of the scattered cars and trucks were, of course, the little brother's. A couple of wandering origami animals were also rounded up and added to the group Madylan had created in between piano and play, and during the uncle's storytelling.

The uncle checked his sweater pocket for the small purple origami flower his niece had given him earlier in the evening and decided he'd put it with the pipe cleaner flower she had given him at her little brother's Dol and first birthday celebration several years before, for, of course, uncles always held onto such treasures.

"Are you guys okay?" the mom asked, returning to the front of the apartment where the aunt and uncle were putting on jackets and shoes.

"We're fine. We might take a little walk, but just a short one," the uncle replied. "The rain has stopped."

"Oh, where?"

"Near the hotel. Not for very long."

"Are you sure you want to wake up so early? To take her to school?" the mom then asked, sincere concern in her voice.

"He lives for that," the aunt replied, playfully rolling her eyes at her husband. "I love it, too. It's fun. And, if you are free, we could bring back yummy breakfast bagels."

"That would be great."

After a few more minutes of goodbyes, the aunt and uncle hugged their niece again and then her mother goodbye. They paused when the dad appeared, telling them that the little brother was conked out.

After a few minutes explaining the next morning to the dad, the aunt and uncle again gave and received hugs all around and quietly left the apartment. They rode the elevator down to the lobby in silence, said goodnight to the well-respected doorman, and walked out into the night.

"Taxi?" the aunt asked.

"Yes. Easier if we go to Lex," the uncle replied, turning the two to point downhill.

"Okay."

Walking down the block, hand in hand, the aunt suddenly spoke up.

"You know she knows you hide things."

The uncle smiled as he replied with no hesitation.

"Doesn't matter. Even if the magic of her former four-year-old self is not as magical for her older, middle school self. I like to think at least a wee bit remains. Besides, the magic is always there, for me. And, she gets a kick out of Greyson discovering the surprises. She's growing into an amazing big sister. And, she wants to write a story together, next time we are up."

"Yes, if she remembers," the aunt replied, chuckling at the uncle's never-ending optimism when it came to his goddaughter and her little brother.

"Oh, she remembers, that one. She remembers," the uncle replied, glancing back at the building the two had just left.

Smiling, the two tired, but happy godparents then picked up the pace to head down the block and engage in the ancient New York City ritual known as the 'dance of the taxi cabs.' Both were warmed inside against the damp night from the busy, but uplifting couple of days with their darling goddaughter Madylan, her growing little brother Greyson, and their amazing parents, Andy and Jina.

Back in the now quiet apartment, as her parents prepared for bed, young Madylan tucked the surprise her uncle had left back into its hiding spot for another day. She then stepped to her tall windows and looked down to the tree-lined street, in what she knew was a fruitless attempt to see her aunt and uncle, since the trees and the angle blocked the view of the sidewalk. Yet, she let her eyes, heavy from fighting the coming sleep, follow the line of trees as far as she could, silently wishing her godparents a safe trip back to the hotel, and, after she was to see them all too briefly on her walk to school in the morning, a safe journey back home.

Turning away from the window, Madylan, the (not very) evil princess of the Upper East Side and early discoverer of the magical underground streets of the city, fluffed up her pillow and put her iPad on her massive pile of plush animals. The big sister narrator of pizza horror stories, mermaid and pirate adventures in Maine, and magical Easters in Virginia then quietly tumbled into bed, wondering if she'd ever look at the little dragon medal in the old curio cabinet the same, the next time she visited her aunt and uncle.

Just before her head hit the pillow, Madylan let her eyes drift to her cluttered bulletin board over her equally cluttered desk. There she spied a warmly familiar small card, pinned near the right bottom corner, which granted her multiple 'Madylan Days,' with variations authorized, which her aunt and uncle had been sending her since she was little.

Inwardly smiling at the experiences of her special day, for which she was always grateful, even with the happy-sad feelings at the end, young Madylan finally let the persistent sandman close her eyes. Her weekend adventures and her uncle's stories melded into her dreams as she slipped off to sleep, happily ensconced in the protective embrace of her loving home, nestled in a quiet Manhattan neighborhood in the busiest city in the world, with endless stories to discover there, and beyond, during her next amazing adventures.

#

Madylan of Manhattan

Will Return.

ABOUT THE AUTHOR

A writer of both novels and short stories, Charles Mitchell is a retired U.S. Air Force intelligence officer and national security consultant, and has lived, worked, and traveled throughout the U.S. and the globe, to include having lived in South Korea and Crete, Greece. A native of South Carolina, he now calls the Washington, D.C. metro area home. Attuned to the many fables and legends of his southern roots, he enriches his writing with tradition, myth, folklore, and superstition from many peoples and cultures. He holds a Bachelor of Arts in History, University of Maryland Global Campus, and a Masters of Science of Strategic Intelligence, U.S. National Intelligence University, Washington, DC.

Other works:
- Hues of Seoul: Mystery and Suspense in Today's Korea (2021)
- The God Song: An Artificial Intelligence Awakening Over Appalachia Way (2019, updated 2023)
- Dark Sings a Distant Herald: A Christmas Story on Holding Back the British Twilight (C. Talmadge Mitchell) (2014)
- Beach Time: Tales from Several Shores (2005)
- Hues of Tokyo: Tales of Today's Japan (2003)

www.ingramcontent.com/pod-product-compliance
Lightning Source LLC
Chambersburg PA
CBHW020304200626
46814CB00006BA/2071